PENGUIN BOOKS

Broken Heart

Broken Heart

TIM WEAVER

PENGUIN BOOKS

PENGUIN BOOKS

UK | USA | Canada | Ireland | Australia
India | New Zealand | South Africa

Penguin Books is part of the Penguin Random House group of companies
whose addresses can be found at global.penguinrandomhouse.com.

First published 2016
003

Copyright © Tim Weaver, 2016

The moral right of the author has been asserted

Set in 12.5/14.75 pt Garamond MT Std
Typeset by Jouve (UK), Milton Keynes
Printed in Great Britain by Clays Ltd, St Ives plc

A CIP catalogue record for this book is available from the British Library

ISBN: 978–1–405–91782–7

www.greenpenguin.co.uk

MIX
Paper from
responsible sources
FSC® C018179

Penguin Random House is committed to a
sustainable future for our business, our readers
and our planet. This book is made from Forest
Stewardship Council® certified paper.

For Lucy

00:00:01

The camera pulls into focus.

    Retired detective Ray Callson is seated in a chair in a nondescript office with pale walls and little in the way of furniture. There are blinds at the window, but they're ajar, the skyscrapers of downtown Los Angeles reduced to a petrol-blue fuzz in the background. Callson takes the microphone that he's handed. Off camera, a small, stilted voice says, 'Just clip it to your shirt.'

    Callson does as he's asked, then straightens himself, smoothing down his grey hair, which is parted arrow-straight at the side. He is in his early sixties, but still handsome. He's clean-shaven except for a moustache, and has bright green eyes, each one painted with a single blob of yellow — a reflection of the light attachment that's sitting close to the camera. As he waits, he clears his throat a couple of times and checks his watch.

    'Are you ready?'

    'Sure,' Callson responds.

    A hum as the camera starts to roll.

    'Can you begin by introducing yourself?'

    Callson clears his throat again and says, 'My name's Raymond J. Callson. I was an officer with the Los Angeles Police Department for thirty-two years.'

    'What sort of work did you do there?'

    'I spent most of that time working homicides.'

    'Did you enjoy it?'

I

'Enjoy?' He shrugs. 'I don't know if that's the right word.'

'Why not?'

'I'm not sure you go into police work, especially homicide cases, thinking you're going to enjoy it. I mean, you're dealing with people who have been raped, stabbed, shot . . . Does that sound like it's enjoyable to you?'

There's no response from behind the camera.

Callson shrugs again. 'You do what you have to do.'

'Did you ever want to be anything else?'

'What do you mean?'

'Did you ever want to do another job?'

Callson takes a long breath, as if he's asked himself the same question many times over and is still searching for the answer. 'Sure. There were times when you'd wonder, "What if?" My old man used to work for the county doing maintenance. There were days when I'd duck under that crime scene tape, see what one human being was capable of doing to another, and think, "What the hell am I doing this for? I'd be better off mowing the grass in MacArthur Park."' He smiles but it's humourless. 'Actually, there were a lot of days when I thought that.'

'But you never did.'

'Never did what?'

'You never ended up mowing the grass in MacArthur Park.'

'No,' he says, 'I just kept turning up to those crime scenes.'

'How many homicides do you estimate you worked?'

'In thirty-two years?' Callson blows out a jet of air. 'I don't know. Couldn't tell you. A thousand, two thousand – literally no idea. I'd probably just have to go with "a lot". LA was, is, a pretty violent place sometimes.'

'Are there any cases that have stuck with you?'

Callson seems to hear the question, but doesn't reply.

'Mr Callson?'

Again, he's silent.

'Mr Callson, are there any cases that have stuck with you?'

Very slowly, he starts to nod, his eyes on an empty space beyond the camera. 'Yeah,' he says. 'Yeah, I can think of one case right off the top of my head.'

PART ONE

I

The Queen of Hearts was a three-storey pub halfway along Seymour Place, south of Marylebone Tube station. The pub was finished in the same glazed terracotta tiles used on Underground stations all over the city, and the inside was marginally cooler than outside – but not by much. The weather had been sweltering for weeks, baking the veins and arteries of the city – all its buildings, all its pavements, rinsing every window with light – until finally, here at the end of August, it felt like there was no escape from it: inside the pub an air-conditioning unit was working overtime, extra fans were stationed on a long bar, and neither made any difference at all.

A waiter showed me to a table at the back, set for two, overlooking a well-kept residential garden, where I ordered a beer, grabbed my laptop from my bag and logged into the Wi-Fi. I'd only got as far as opening the browser when my phone suddenly burst into life. I expected it to be the woman I was having lunch with, Melanie Craw. Most of the time, if she was late – which she rarely was – and she called me after the time at which we'd agreed to meet, it was to tell me something had come up and she wouldn't be able to make it. But it wasn't Craw. It wasn't any of the other names I had logged in my address book. Even more bizarrely, it wasn't actually a UK number at all.

It was a call from the US.

My contact details were all over my website, and three

years ago a case had taken me to Nevada, so I'd established contacts in and around Las Vegas, even if I rarely spoke to them. But it wasn't a 702 area code, so it wasn't Vegas, and when I pulled my laptop towards me and put in a search for the number's 952 prefix, I found out it was a chunk of land in Minnesota, to the south-east of Minneapolis. Who did I know in Minneapolis?

Curious, I pushed Answer.

'David Raker.'

'Oh, Mr Raker.' A female voice. She sounded surprised that I'd answered. 'My name's Wendy Fisher. I hope I'm not disturbing you.'

Wendy Fisher. I cast my mind back through conversations I'd had over the past few weeks, trying to remember if her name had come up anywhere. I felt sure it hadn't. I didn't know her; I didn't know anyone in her part of the US.

'I'm real sorry for calling you out of the blue like this,' she said, 'but I was, uh . . . I was wondering if you could spare a few minutes of your time.' As if reading my thoughts, she then added, 'We've never spoken before. You don't know me.'

'Okay. What is it you think I can do for you, Wendy?'

'I, uh . . . I need . . . I was hoping . . .'

Straight away, I realized that the hesitation in her voice had nothing to do with surprise at me answering her call. The staccato nature of her sentences, the way they caught in her mouth: it was distress, it was helplessness. I'd heard those same emotions before, on repeat, in every missing person's case I'd ever taken on.

'Has someone gone missing?'

'Yes,' she said, and stopped for a moment. 'My sister, Lynda. She's been gone since last October. I don't know what to do . . . I don't know what else to do.'

As soon as she mentioned her sister's name, her voice had started to fray. I gave her a moment, my eyes returning to the laptop, to the map of Minnesota.

'I see you're calling from the Midwest.'

'That's correct,' she said, taking a moment more to recover her poise. 'I'm in a place called Lakeville. It's about twenty-five miles south of Minneapolis.'

'Minneapolis is a long way from London, Wendy.'

'I know,' she said. 'I know it is.'

'That makes it hard to help you – if that's what you're calling about.'

Words caught in her throat, and then she simply said, 'Oh.'

'I know the States a little – I've lived and worked on the coasts – so maybe it would be different if you were in New York or Washington or LA. But Minneapolis – I don't know your area at all. You'd be better off with someone local.'

'My sister lives in England.'

I took that in. 'Okay.'

'Lynda has been in Europe most of her adult life.' She was finding her rhythm now, her confidence. 'I found your name on the Internet, and I googled you, and I read about some of the cases you've worked. Some of the people you've found. I saw a story about you on CNN, on Fox News. I saw what happened to you when you came out to Las Vegas. I saw something else about you on the BBC, about a case you worked on last year. I thought, "This is the man that can help find Lyn."'

I didn't say anything.

'Will you help me find her, Mr Raker?'

'David.'

'David,' she said quietly. 'I feel so far away from what's happening there. I don't know what else to do. The police, they've got nowhere with her case. Maybe for them it's just a number on a file, or some paperwork in a cabinet, but for me it's everything. No one's heard from her since last October, and I just . . . I miss her so much.' A pregnant pause, a sniff. 'I've got savings. I can pay you. Please help me.'

I looked towards the windows of the pub, where the sun beat through the glass. This was always the worst part: hearing the desperation in their voices, the way it forged a path through to money. I'll pay you whatever it takes. I'll give you all I've got.

Just find them.

What they never knew, or maybe didn't choose to find out, was that it was about more than that for me. I needed to pay the bills, just like everyone else, but I needed the cases for other, less obvious reasons as well. After I buried my wife six years ago, the cases became how I grieved for her. The missing became a lifeline.

Now they were my oxygen.

Yet I still felt a minor hesitation in taking Wendy Fisher's call, felt more than that as I considered the possible repercussions of accepting work from her. She was thousands of miles away, and so much of missing persons cases was about sitting down with people, about watching the subtleties of their expressions as they reacted to questions. Skype could never relay the delicacy of emotion, grief, pain.

'Mr Raker?'

I tuned back in. 'Yeah, I'm here.'

'Will you help me?' she asked.

'I don't know yet, Wendy.'

She remained silent, clearly knocked off balance.

'You said your sister's name is Lynda.'

'Yes,' she said softly, still a little bruised. 'With a *y*.'

'And her surname?'

'Korin. Lynda Korin.'

'And she lived here in the UK?'

'Yes. She's been over there since 1984. Before that, she was in Spain. She moved to Europe in the mid seventies and loved it so much that she decided to stay.'

'So how old is she now?'

'Sixty-two – almost sixty-three. Her birthday is next month – 13 September.'

'Okay. And she disappeared when?'

'Tuesday 28 October.'

Today was 26 August, so she'd been gone almost ten months.

'Where was she last seen?' I asked.

'Have you ever heard of Stoke Point?'

'No, I haven't.'

'I've never been there, obviously, but I've done a lot of research. I've seen pictures of it. It's some kind of beauty spot in the south-west of England. I think it's in Somerset, on the coast there, a few miles north of . . . uh . . .' She paused, and I heard papers being leafed through. 'Hold on a second. Uh . . . Weston-super-Mare.'

'Okay. I know Weston.'

'The police found Lynda's car there.'

'She'd abandoned it?'

'That's what it looked like. Her car was locked. Her purse and her cellphone were in the glove compartment. But her keys were in scrub nearby.'

'She'd thrown the keys clear of the car?'

'That's right. I don't know why.'

I didn't answer, unwilling to speculate in front of her – but one potential reason came to me right off the bat: *Korin wasn't the one who threw them away.*

'Did anyone see her on the day she disappeared?'

'No,' Wendy replied.

'There were no witnesses?'

'None.'

'What about security footage?'

'Nothing.'

'They didn't have cameras there?'

'They had *a* camera.'

'But it didn't pick her up?'

A momentary pause. 'That's the weird part.'

'What do you mean?'

'There's only one way in and out of that place.'

'Okay.'

'A security camera at the entrance showed her going in through the main gate – but Lyn never came back out again. She never exited. Not on foot, not in her car, not in anybody else's. Dead or alive, there's never been any trace of her. It's like the minute she passed through the gate to that place, she basically ceased to exist.'

2

All of a sudden, I became aware that I'd opened a new document on my laptop, doing it automatically, instinctively, creating it despite all the impracticalities of Wendy Fisher being in another time zone. I'd made notes as well: Lynda Korin's age, the date she went missing, the circumstances of her disappearance.

It was like she basically ceased to exist.

'No one's ever found any trace of Lynda?' I asked.

'No,' Wendy said. 'Nothing.'

'Who reported her missing?'

'I did. I filed a report on 2 November, after going five days without hearing from her, but your people over there never found the car till the tenth.'

'Who did you file the report with?'

'With Avon and Somerset Police. I stayed up all night so that I would be able to catch them as soon as they got in that morning. The name of the man I spoke to, the officer, was Stewart Wolstenholme. After that, the case got passed to someone else – a Detective Constable Raymond White. He was a bit better at his job than the other guy, Wolstenholme – a bit more senior, I guess, or more experienced, or whatever. But he couldn't find her either. And now she's just . . .' Her voice died away.

Forgotten. Lost.

'When was the last time you spoke to DC White?'

'Two, three months ago maybe. He called me and said

there was nothing new to report but that they were still looking for her. I'm not sure that was true.'

'What makes you say that?'

'I think it was empty talk. I had to leave about five messages before he even called me back. *I* was chasing *him*. He's always been very polite, but I could tell it was a low priority for him. You could just hear it in his voice.' She slowed to a halt, her words prickled with tears. 'I know they're busy. I know they have other cases. But this has been ten months of hell for me.'

Softly, I asked, 'Was Lynda in any sort of trouble?'

'No. Nothing like that. Financially, everything was up together. She has this house on the Mendips, but it doesn't have a mortgage on it any more. I've been there a few times. It's really beautiful. It overlooks this huge lake, lots of countryside. She has a good pension, she was still working a couple of days a week, looking after the accounts for some local businesses . . . Lyn was doing fine. She was happy.'

'Is that what she said?'

'What do you mean?'

'Did she tell you she was happy?'

'We texted each other every day. We spoke on Skype a few times a week. I never got the sense she was worried or upset about anything – and, if she was, I genuinely believe she'd have said something. Or I would have been able to tell.'

Maybe, I thought. *Or maybe not.*

'The place she disappeared from,' I said.

'Stoke Point.'

'Right. What do you know about it?'

I started googling it myself.

'Know about it?' she said, sucking air through her teeth. 'I'm no expert, I'm afraid. I've only seen satellite maps. Pictures. I can tell you what I've found out.'

'That's fine.'

'Well, it looks isolated. The parking lot is at the end of a two-mile coastal road – it's a dead end, so that's the only road back out – and then the peninsula is on the other side of the parking lot and sticks out into the sea for . . . I guess . . . half a mile or so. I don't believe it's a . . . you know, a place for . . . suicides.'

The last word weighed heavy.

'I've read that the peninsula is only about fifteen feet above sea level, and on both sides there's another ten to fifteen feet of rocks, boulders and shingle before you even get to the water's edge.' She stopped, breathed out, the idea of what her sister may have been doing out there, the anguish of it, like glue in her throat. 'My point,' she said faintly, 'is that if someone did want to make a jump from the edge of the peninsula, the drop would only break a few bones – if that.'

'It doesn't sound like you thought Lynda was suicidal.'

'No. No way.'

'You said there was one security camera, at the entrance?'

'That's what I was told, yeah.'

'There definitely weren't any others?'

'I asked DC White that, and he told me that there weren't. He said the only camera was at the entrance. He emailed me some shots from the video: it's definitely Lyn entering the lot. It's her car. It's her in the front seat. It's Lyn.'

'But there's nothing after that?'

'No, nothing. She just vanishes.'

'She couldn't have exited anywhere else?'

'I don't think so. From what DC White has told me, and what I've managed to find myself online, the entrance to the Stoke Point parking lot is on the other side of a stone bridge that connects the peninsula to the main coastal road. Even if she exited on foot, she still would have had to come back the same way she went in. She'd have been caught on camera, crossing the bridge, as she left.'

'What about once she got on to the peninsula? No one saw her getting into a boat the day she disappeared, or wading into the water to get to one?'

'Like I said, there were no witnesses.'

'So someone could have picked her up in a boat?'

'From what I read, I think it's unlikely. I don't know for sure, but anyone picking her up in a boat was taking a risk. According to the time code on the shots of the video, Lyn entered the parking lot at about nine in the morning. DC White told me that the tide would have been almost out at that time. He said, in that part of the world, all that's left then is mud that's like quicksand.'

She was right: due to its tidal range, great swathes of the Bristol Channel became mudflats at low tide. It not only made it an impossibility that someone could have guided a boat in, but it made it treacherous on foot too.

So where did Lynda Korin go?

'Did DC White send you any other information?'

'Some photographs. I've got a few emails from him.'

'That's it?'

She let out a long breath. 'That's it. All I know about Stoke Point is what I've read and what I've been told. I wish I knew more. I wish I could see it for myself. But leaving my husband, my kids, my grandkids, telling them I'll be gone for I don't know how long – I can't do it. I love my sister dearly, but I can't leave my family behind for months on end, pretending to be a detective . . .' She made a short, desperate noise, a sound that spoke of her heartache clearer than any words could. 'The reality is, I wouldn't know where to start. I'm not a cop. I work as a nurse, for goodness' sake. It's why I decided to call you.'

I looked up from my laptop, and at the doors of the pub, backed by bright sunlight, I saw Melanie Craw.

'I will give you everything I have,' Wendy said, 'every dollar, every cent. I don't own much, I'm not worth much, but I will do it for Lyn. I will pour my heart and soul into helping you in whatever way I can, David. Please help me find her.'

I thought about it. But not for long.

'Have you got a scanner there, Wendy?'

She seemed momentarily thrown by the question.

'A computer scanner? Yeah, I've got one of those.'

'This is what I need you to do, then. Scan in anything physical you've collated that's directly related to Lynda's disappearance, and email that over to me, along with the stuff DC White sent you. I'll take a look at it all, and then call you back later on.'

'Oh, thank you,' she said, 'thank you so much.'

I heard her voice trip even before she'd finished her sentence, and by the time she went to say *thank you* again, there was no sound from her but her tears.

3

'I know,' Melanie Craw said as she got to the table. 'I'm hideously late.'

I got up and kissed her on the cheek. She was slim and understated, her blonde, shoulder-length hair tied up, her dark grey trouser-suit pristine. She looked sharp and formidable. It was exactly what she needed to be in the industry she was in, where any hint of weakness was pounced upon.

'I've only got an hour,' she said, waving one of the waiters over. 'I've got a meeting at Paddington Green station, and I still have to swot up.'

Craw had spent almost half of her forty-five years working at the Met, and was currently a DCI in the Central command, which meant she was in charge of about fifty detectives, officers and support staff, all working murders. It was the job that had first brought us into contact with one another and, in the beginning, she – like many of the people she worked with – had viewed me with a deep and pervading suspicion.

Gradually, though, things had changed between the two of us, particularly after her father had gone missing. Desperate for answers, and out of options, she reluctantly asked me to find out what had happened to him, and in the aftermath I think she caught a glimpse of the person I was. She saw what my cases meant to me, how consumed I became by them. Those were often the qualities that had driven a wedge between me and other people – but with Craw it had done the opposite. Yet I still couldn't say for certain whether we were in an official relationship or not. I liked her a lot. I found her attractive, interesting, challenging, but it always felt like she was hovering on the cusp of commitment, never willing to make the final leap. Her need to protect her reputation at the Met, staving off whatever vultures were currently circling, and my willingness to take risks, to skirt the very edges of the law in a way that she loathed, cast long shadows. In my most cynical moments, her reluctance to fully acknowledge what we were doing looked a little like an escape plan – if things went badly for me, she could just turn around and leave, her reputation intact, her job unaffected.

'So what have you been up to this morning?' she asked.

'Not a whole lot.'

'I didn't realize self-employment was so relaxed.'

I smiled, sinking half of my beer. 'I just got off the phone to a woman in Minneapolis. She asked me to try and find her sister.'

Craw looked at me. 'As in Minneapolis, *America*?'

'Relax,' I said. 'Her sister lives over here.'

'Good. Last thing you need is a US tour. So what happened to her?'

I shrugged. 'She drove down to some beauty spot out on the Somerset coast, abandoned her car and then vanished off the face of the earth.'

'Are you going to take the case?'

'Yes.'

She eyed me for a moment. What would once have been a blank, unreadable expression was more lucid now that I'd got to know her better. As unlikely as it seemed, this was a look of concern.

'You're in the same line of work as I am,' I reminded her.

'Except I'm not coming out of my cases looking like I've spent six months in a war zone.' She paused, fingers drifting to the chain at her neck. She'd seen the scars on my body and, just as clearly, she'd come to know the scars that didn't show. 'Just keep in mind that, ten months ago, you were diagnosed with PTSD.'

'*Mild* PTSD.'

'A mild amputation is still an amputation.'

'I'm fine,' I said to her.

'You were supposed to see a psychologist.'

'I don't *need* to see a psychologist. I had one blackout, and one brief panic attack. That's it. I'm sleeping well.' I gestured to us. 'Things are good. I'm happy.'

'Don't try and grease me up, Raker.'

That made us both smile.

I finished my beer, but by the time I was done, she was still watching me, the same look on her face. 'You've got a daughter to think about,' she said. 'You've got Olivia to think about too.'

My daughter, Annabel, was twenty-six, and Olivia was her eleven-year-old sister. Biologically, Olivia wasn't mine, but – as both her parents were gone and Annabel was all she had left – I looked out for her in the same way. They were in Spain with some of Annabel's friends for the last week of the school holidays.

'I'm fine, Craw.'

'Look, I'm not going to sit here going over old ground with you. But when things are going well, of *course* you're sleeping better and you're feeling good. That's just how life works. It's when it all goes to shit that you stop sleeping and you can't think about anything else.' She paused as one of the bar staff brought a salad and a mineral water over for her, and a sandwich for me. Once we were alone again, she continued: 'I know what you're going to say. "How am I supposed to know, when I take on a case, which one is going to turn out well, and which one isn't?" You can't. But when you get to the stage where there's a knife to your throat, *that's* when you know.' She shrugged, spearing some chicken. Craw wouldn't ever ask me to give up my work, but her argument against it was always the same: at the Met, she was confined by rules, by procedures and structure; in my work, there were no rules. I had no one to stop me – and no one to prevent me from tumbling over the precipice.

'Just promise me you'll go to your doctor's appointment on Friday morning,' she said, and when I didn't respond, she looked up at me. 'Okay?'

I nodded, but in truth, I'd forgotten all about it.

'Don't end up like Colm Healy, Raker.'

This was something else she often reminded me of. Healy had been a man we'd both known, and had both worked with: a brilliant ex-cop, reduced to a shell by bad choices and deep wounds. Ten months ago, I'd been forced into a search for him and the case had overwhelmed me. I'd suffered a panic attack for the first time in my life, I'd blacked out, I'd spent a month unable to sleep more than a few hours. I became obsessed with finding Healy because it felt like I was the only person he had left. Eventually, I did find answers, but in the months since, Craw had started to believe that the hunt for him was a scratch I couldn't itch; a case that continued to haunt me and affect my judgement.

'The search for Healy made you sick,' Craw said. 'You did all you could for him. You don't want to get like that again.'

I continued nodding, letting her know I was taking on board what she was saying. But this time I chose not to say anything for a very different reason: Craw could read me as well as anyone – and I didn't want her to catch me in a lie.

I'd gone past the point where I could tell her what I'd really found at the end of my search for Healy. Too much time had passed now. My deceit had gone on too long. I wanted to tell her, often thought about what it would be like, whether it was likely she would forgive me, and, in the end, I always reached the same conclusion: she wouldn't. It would be too much to forgive.

So I said nothing.

And in an old fisherman's cottage on the south Devon coast, left to me by my parents – inside the rooms they'd once lived in – a man's life went on, his existence undiscovered by anyone else except the few people he passed every day in the village. The man called himself Bryan Kennedy now. That was the name on his bank account, on his driver's licence and in the pages of his passport.

But he and I knew the truth.

4

I left the Queen of Hearts and headed west along Marylebone Road. The day had become so hot, even in the shade, that while I could see a breeze disturb the trees that skirted the pavements, there was no hint of it against my skin.

As I walked, I made a couple of quick calls.

The first was to an old contact of mine, Ewan Tasker, who I'd got to know during my newspaper days. Back then, he'd worked for the NCIS and its successor, SOCA – both precursors to the National Crime Agency – but these days he was semi-retired and doing consultation work. What started out as a marriage of convenience – he fed me stories he wanted out in the open; I tapped him up as a source – had long since turned into friendship.

He answered after a couple of rings.

'Raker! How's things?'

'Pretty good, Task. You?'

'Not bad. Still able to go to the toilet by myself.'

'Always a bonus. You okay to talk for a moment?'

'Sure. What sort of trouble are you in this time?'

I smiled. 'No trouble. Yet.'

'Yeah, well, don't make me come around there and force-feed you those pills. I may be old, but I reckon I could still hand out a damn good beating.'

'I reckon you're right,' I told him, and thought of the pills he was referring to. They were in an unopened white bottle at home – antidepressants I'd been prescribed before the

23

turn of the year, after the case with Healy had dragged me beyond my limits. As far as friends like Tasker were concerned, the pills had become a daily part of my life. But the truth was I'd never swallowed a single one of them. I hated the idea of not being in complete control of myself.

I manoeuvred us away from the subject.

'Task, I'm after a missing persons report from October last year – a Lynda Korin. That's Lynda with a *y*, K-O-R-I-N. She disappeared from somewhere called Stoke Point on 28 October.'

'Stoke?'

'Yeah. Usual spelling. It's in Somerset.'

'Okay. We expecting any nasty surprises?'

'You mean, does she have a record? I don't know. I don't think so.'

'I'll check anyway. You got her DOB there?'

'Yeah – 13 September 1952. One other thing: I'm also looking for some CCTV footage. It's from the camera at the same place. I'm interested in the day prior to Korin going missing, the day of her disappearance, and maybe the day after – *if* you can get it. There'll definitely be a reference to it on the system somewhere, but I don't know if the video is digital or physical. I'm hoping digital.'

'I'll take a look and give you a shout later.'

'Great. I appreciate it.'

I reached the entrance to Edgware Road station. Slick with sweat, and having sidestepped what felt like a million camera-phone-wielding tourists, I paused there for a moment, finding a second number. This was for another old contact I'd made in my days as a journalist: a hacker called Spike. We'd known each other for years, and although we'd never met in person, he was a useful contact to have. As long as you made your peace with the fact that he was breaking the law for you, email accounts, landline and mobile records, financial backgrounds and personal details were all within easy reach.

After Spike answered, I told him exactly what I was after.

'So, basically, everything I can grab on this Korin woman?' he asked.

'Phone records, emails, financials, anything.'

'Do you want to set some parameters?'

I thought about it.

'Korin disappeared on 28 October, so maybe play it safe and grab me the six months leading up to her disappearance – and then the ten months since.'

'You got it.'

'Thanks, Spike. How long do you reckon this will take?'

'For a man of my means?' Spike paused, the silence filled with the sound of a pen tapping a desk. 'I should probably have something for you tomorrow.'

I headed into the station.

5

The District-line platform at Edgware Road was busy, but I managed to find a space on a bench at the very end of it, beyond the reach of the sun. Next to me, a man in his sixties was talking to himself, or maybe to his shopping bags, so I pulled out some headphones and plugged them into my mobile. Once I'd drowned him out, I went to the browser and started seeing what kind of media coverage had greeted Lynda Korin's disappearance. It had no bearing on my decision to take the case – once I'd agreed to find someone, I didn't back out – but until I got the chance to talk to Wendy Fisher again, and to fill in some of the gaps, this would have to do.

In the end, though, there was little coverage in the national media, except for a brief story on the BBC website, which had been buried in the Bristol section of Local News. There were bigger stories in both the *Bristol Post* and the *Western Daily Press*, but neither offered much more than the bare bones, naming Korin, giving her age, her occupation as a part-time accountant, and then stating that she'd abandoned her car, a Ford Focus, at Stoke Point. Neither paper made any allusion to the most compelling aspect of the case – that she was seen entering, but never exiting, the car park – but that was probably more to do with the fact that, so soon after she vanished, the police would still have been in the process of procuring security footage, or at the very least going through it, so wouldn't themselves have been fully aware of the circumstances. It was hard to see the perplexity of her disappearance burning to dust so quickly otherwise.

I'd hoped to find a picture of her in the local newspaper stories, just to get a sense of what she looked like, but the web versions only carried generic, photo library shots of the peninsula, so I shifted my attention to social media instead. That proved to be another dead end. Her surname was unusual, at least in the UK, so it was pretty easy to see that she didn't have a Facebook page, a Twitter account or anything beyond that. I'd held on to the hope, as she'd still been working a couple of days a week, that she'd maintained a LinkedIn profile – a photograph perhaps, or a CV – but that was another blank.

I decided to head back to Google and widen the search. Instead of tagging *Lynda Korin* with terms like *Stoke Point* and *disappearance*, I just typed in her name and hit Return. It would mean getting a ton of hits for women with the same name, but that didn't matter.

The top hit was for a doctor in Tampa, the second was for a psychiatrist in Cleveland, and the third was the MD of a corporate training company in Munich.

It was the fourth that caught my eye.

Lynda Korin – IMDb
www.imdb.com/name/lk0091251
Lynda Korin, Actress: Ursula of the SS. **Lynda Korin** was born on September 13, 1952, in Lakeville, Minnesota. She is best known . . .

It's her.
It was the town she was born in, it was her date of birth.

Confused, I clicked on the link and followed it to an IMDb profile page. On the left, there was no professional photograph of her, only a cropped poster for a film called *Cemetery House*. Her name was at the bottom in tiny black letters and she was running towards the camera, screaming, while a vague, monster-shaped shadow lurched in her direction from the background. It was the only picture of her anywhere on the page. I'd never heard of the movie before, I'd never heard of *any* of the movies listed in her filmography, but the way she looked on the poster stopped me dead. She was absolutely stunning – pale skin, blonde-haired, blue-eyed.

A moment later, the train wheezed into the station. I waited for the doors to slide open, stepped inside, then switched my attention to Korin's biography.

Lynda Korin is an actress and former model, primarily known for her eponymous role in the cult Nazi exploitation movie **Ursula of the SS** (1977), as well as its sequels **Ursula: Queen Kommandant** (1978) and **Ursula: Butcher of El Grande** (1978). Famously, she married the director **Robert Hosterlitz** after meeting him on the set of the first *Ursula* in Madrid, which he was making under the alias Bob Hozer. She went on to appear in all eleven films Hosterlitz made in Spain between 1979 and 1984. After his retirement, the two of them moved to Somerset, UK, where Korin gave up acting to retrain in accountancy.

I felt completely thrown – and not just by Korin's former career as an actress in low-budget horror movies. I'd grown up watching films in an old art deco cinema along the coast from my parents' farm in south Devon; movies had become an obsession, a way of escaping the boredom of life in a one-street village, the routines of the farm, the solitude of being an only child. The cinema had a film noir evening once every couple of months, and one of the movies I remembered most vividly was *The Eyes of the Night*. It was a brilliant noir, startling and beautiful, perhaps one of history's best, and it won seven Oscars when it was released in 1953. Robert Hosterlitz, the man Lynda Korin had been married to, had written and directed it.

But then something had gone wrong for him. His career had gone south somehow. Before my wife, Derryn, had died, before they'd closed the Museum of the Moving Image on the South Bank, we'd been there to an exhibition on film noir and listened to a talk on *The Eyes of the Night* and on Robert Hosterlitz himself, and heard how his life had been turned upside down. It had gone so bad for him, he'd ended up leaving America entirely.

As the train started to move, and before my phone signal died inside the bowels of the Tube, I quickly tapped the link for Hosterlitz in Korin's biography in order to try and fill in the gaps in my memory.

Robert Hosterlitz was born in Dresden on February 15, 1925, but emigrated with his family (his father was German actor **Hans Hosterlitz**) to Los Angeles in 1933. His debut as a writer-director, aged just 24, came in the surprise commercial hit **My Evil Heart** (1949), but it was his fourth movie that should have propelled him to superstardom: his film noir **The Eyes of the Night** (1953) won seven Oscars, including Best Picture, Best Director (making Hosterlitz, at 28, the youngest ever recipient of the award) and Best Screenplay. Yet, in 1954, after being subpoenaed to appear before the House of Un-American Activities, accused of being a member of the US Communist Party, Hosterlitz chose to flee America. It was hoped that a much-publicized return to Hollywood to make the western **The Ghost of the Plains** (1967) would kick-start his career, but instead the film proved a commercial and critical disaster for Paramount. Hosterlitz never recovered. After reportedly suffering problems with both alcohol and drugs in the late 1960s and early 1970s, financial hardship forced him to spend the last decade of his life making cheap horror movies for the grindhouse producer **Pedro Silva** in Madrid. He died in 1988.

Wendy Fisher hadn't mentioned any of this – but then why would she? It had been twenty-seven years since Hosterlitz had died, which meant Korin had been a widow for over a quarter of a century, which in turn made her marriage an irrelevance. Or, at least, *probably* an irrelevance. Certainly, it was hard to see how it might connect. She was sixty-two, an accountant, living in a house on the edge of the Mendips, decades on from the life, and the husband, she'd once had.

I planned to catch up with Wendy on a video call later, so I'd ask her more about Korin's marriage then. I was also hoping that, by the time I got home, she would have emailed the material that DC White had sent through to her. She'd talked about pictures, some documents, any of which might be a useful starting point before Tasker and Spike got back to me.

As I thought about that, about Robert Hosterlitz, about echoes from the past, my eyes returned to the picture of Lynda Korin, a woman forgotten as an actress and forgotten by the police.

But not forgotten by her sister.

6

Once I got back to Ealing, I opened up the windows of my house, trying to get some air circulating, and then messaged Wendy to arrange a time for me to video-call her. While I waited for a response, I showered and changed, then took my laptop through to the back deck to continue building a picture of Lynda Korin. Wendy responded a few minutes later to tell me that she'd emailed over everything she could lay her hands on, and confirmed our Skype call for 8 p.m.

I headed straight to my inbox.

It turned out that everything she could lay her hands on mostly seemed to amount to photographs of Stoke Point. They were a mix of ones she'd sourced from the Internet herself, and shots that DC White had emailed to her when he'd taken a trip there on 11 November. Even at a quick glance, it was clear that his messages to Wendy were carefully stage-managed, a mix of well-intentioned reassurances, minor updates and rudimentary delay tactics.

For now, I ignored most of the stuff on Stoke Point because I planned to drive down there in the morning and take a look at it myself – but, in setting all that aside, it quickly became obvious how little else there was.

In the end, only one email really caught my eye. In it, I found a picture of Lynda Korin and Robert Hosterlitz. 'This was Lyn's husband, Bob,' Wendy wrote. 'He died in 1988.' It was a scan of a Polaroid, both sides of it, with a handwritten caption on the back: 'Madrid 1983: Bob and Lyn, by

Ronnie M'. I did a quick search through the rest of the emails for anyone with the name 'Ronnie M', but came up short. However, the 'Madrid 1983' reference made sense: according to what I'd read about Korin and Hosterlitz earlier, in 1983 Korin would still have been working with her husband on the low-budget horror movies in Spain.

I studied the picture.

Against a sun-bleached, whitewashed wall, Hosterlitz and Korin were side by side. Hosterlitz, fifty-eight at the time, was small and thin, a striped T-shirt clinging to his narrow frame, his hair white and untidy. He had an arm around Korin and was smiling, his skin browned by the sun, his face creased up in the light of the day. A thick blanket of stubble covered his chin and jawline, making him look older than he was, and as I studied him, it became hard to see the person the world had known him as, or the one I remembered. This didn't look like the man who had directed a film that had won seven Oscars, it looked like his ghost; an imitation. When I'd attended the exhibition at the MOMI all those years back, the film historian who had given the talk had shown us photos of Hosterlitz from the early 1950s – a younger, bigger, rounder version of the man, with a gold statuette, oiled hair, and expensive suits that bulged when buttoned. But that Robert Hosterlitz was long gone by the time the photo in Madrid had been taken. By this time, he'd been reduced to directing films with titles like *Axe Maniac* and *Savages of the Amazon*.

Lynda Korin was different. She was nearly thirty years younger than Hosterlitz, and as pale as milk, her eyes like pools of pure blue water, her blonde hair – permed in a 1980s style – framing her face and placing the accent on her high cheekbones. Even with her sitting down, it was clear how tall she was, her long legs crossed in front of her, and while the size of her breasts looked oddly out of place on her slender frame, straining against the dark vest she was wearing, it took nothing away from her. I wasn't exactly sure what I'd been expecting before I saw her in the movie poster on IMDb, but it wasn't what I saw there and it wasn't what I saw here, for a second time. She was so striking, such a stark contrast to the man she'd married – yet hers was a beauty that she was almost trying to disguise as she leaned into Hosterlitz and allowed herself to be protected by him. There seemed a shyness to her, a quietness and a reticence, her eyes darkened by the surrounding shadow, her smile just an upturned lip.

Something about that didn't make sense to me.

She'd been an actress and a model, comfortable in front of the camera, comfortable – judging by the types of films she'd made – taking her clothes off too. So, as I continued to look at this picture of her, this portrait of a past life, it made me wonder about Lynda Korin. It made me wonder about her reasons for driving out to the edge of the sea on 28 October; about the reason she'd never been seen again; whether she'd gone there out of choice or out of fear; and it made me wonder about whether the woman in the photograph, frozen within the confines of a yellowing, thirty-year-old scan of a Polaroid, had some sort of story to tell.

A story the world might get to hear, if she was alive.

Or get buried for ever, if she wasn't.

At just after seven, Ewan Tasker called me.

'This is going to be short and sweet,' he said once I'd picked up. 'I emailed Lynda Korin's missing persons report across to you, but footage of her – that's harder. I've had a look and there's some listed in evidence down in Bath, but it's a DVD. Apparently, the tech they use at Stoke Point is old, so there's no digital version – as in, the security system at that car park isn't uploading it in real time to a server somewhere. So the only way you're getting your hands on the footage – unless you're into breaking and entering – is if you know someone who works for the police down in Bath. That way they can rip the footage from the disc and send it to you. Or they can just mail you the DVD itself. You got someone you know down there?'

'Not at the moment.'

'Could be time to unleash your winning personality.'

I laughed. 'All right, old man. I appreciate it.'

I hung up, went to my email and found the message from Task. Attached to it was a digital version of Korin's missing persons report.

Right up front was a recent photograph of her. She looked remarkable, her sixty-two years like a number that didn't compute. There were age lines at the corners of her eyes, and her blonde hair had become seeded with grey along her parting and across the arc of her forehead. Otherwise, her sharp, attractive features made her look ten years younger than she was. But, as good as she looked, it wasn't her that caught my attention, it was the photograph itself. Although it was taken in a living room, presumably Korin's – she was perched on the arm of a sofa – it looked professional. The lighting was too perfect, she'd had her hair and make-up done, her pose wasn't natural. I made a note of it, wondering where the shot had come from, and moved on.

The first section of the file just confirmed a lot of what I already knew, starting with Wendy reporting her sister missing on Sunday 2 November. Wendy was five years younger than Lynda and still lived with her husband in Lakeville, a suburb south of Minneapolis, where Lynda was born in 1952, and later grew up.

Wendy had phoned Avon and Somerset Police in Bath after failing to hear from Korin, either via text or email, for five days. The timing fitted: five days earlier, on Tuesday 28 October, Korin had been caught on CCTV camera entering Stoke Point. In the report, Wendy called the lack of contact between them 'worrying' because 'Lyn and I were in touch many times a day, every day.'

The response from the police in Bath was slow. Wendy said she'd looked up police stations on the Internet, close to where Korin lived on the eastern edge of the Mendips, and Bath just happened to be the one she called first. Initially, she spoke to a uniformed constable called Stewart Wolstenholme.

From this point, however, there was a leap of nine days.

The next activity in the case was on Tuesday 11 November – the day *after* Korin's car had been found at Stoke Point. That meant, even if Wolstenholme had told Wendy Fisher he was going to look into things for her on 2 November, he'd done nothing. It wasn't until a National Trust employee – who checked on the car park at Stoke Point three times a week – reported Korin's car as likely having been abandoned that the case found its way to DC Raymond White's desk and something began to happen. White quickly began ticking boxes: he called Wendy to inform her that her sister's car had been found; he conducted a more extensive interview with her over the telephone; he organized for a DNA sample to be taken from Korin's toothbrush, and then cross-checked it with the Missing Persons Bureau to see if any of the unidentified bodies they had on file matched that of Lynda Korin. They didn't.

White had conducted a background audit on Korin, though neither a credit check nor her medical history held any real surprises: she had a steady income from the two days of accountancy work she was doing every week, she had a £15k-a-year pension, and at sixty-two she seemed well – a yearly check-up, just a few months before she went missing, had found her to be in excellent health.

I moved on and, again, picked up on the detail about how the vehicle had been left; how Korin's Ford Focus had been locked, her purse and mobile secured in the glove compartment, while her keys – for the car, for the house – were found in some scrub nearby. That rubbed at me, and it had clearly bugged White too. He'd made a couple of notes: 'Why throw the keys away? Why not leave them or take them with her?' I thought again about the idea of someone else – and not Korin – throwing them away, and then looked at the photos of the keys in situ. They were at the foot of a tree, in a copse. All the trees had been vandalized with graffiti.

As I searched White's paperwork, I got confirmation that he'd managed to secure the CCTV footage from 28 October, as well as footage from the day after Korin vanished, just to be sure she hadn't, for whatever reason, stayed over and tried to exit the next day. He'd also used the registration plates of the cars that came and went on 28 October to track down potential witnesses, talking to the vehicles' owners to see if they recalled seeing Korin at the peninsula the day she disappeared. All of them were frequent visitors to Stoke Point, which was good because it meant they knew the place and might have spotted something that didn't fit. But the frequency of their visits also meant that they struggled to be exact about the day they were there. In fact, while all the people interviewed remembered being at Stoke Point around the time of the disappearance, few could offer much else, and one man in his eighties argued he wasn't there at all on the twenty-eighth, despite being recorded on tape.

For now, in lieu of the actual footage from the day, I had to make do with printouts from the six seconds Korin had been caught on film. They were all rinsed-out colour stills from Stoke Point's solitary camera: caught at various stages of her approach was Lynda Korin, visible inside her Ford Focus. The last shot was the back end of the vehicle disappearing through the main gates.

I kept going and found the transcript of the interview that White had conducted with Wendy over the phone. It was long and detailed, but, while Wendy's answers were clear and concise, its length didn't disguise the lack of insight. Just one section leaped out at me, and more because of my personal interest in Robert Hosterlitz, the director.

WHITE: Lynda was married – is that correct?

FISHER: Yeah. To Robert. Bob. He died in 1988.

WHITE: What did he do?

FISHER: He was a film director. But not a famous one. Well, not by the end, anyway.

WHITE: That's, uh . . . Robert Hosterlitz, right?

FISHER: That's right.

WHITE: Anything in his life that may have come back to bite Lynda? I realize he's been dead a long time.

FISHER: I can't see what. They were very happy. Well, from what I saw of them.

WHITE: What do you mean?

FISHER: I just . . . Look, they were living in Europe. Lyn would fly out to see us once or twice a year, because she'd only have to pay for one ticket, whereas if you put me, my husband and my two kids on a plane it would

37

have cost us four times as much. We didn't have that sort of money back then.

WHITE: So are you saying you hardly knew Robert?

FISHER: She moved to Europe to model in 1971, she got married to him in 1978 after they'd only been dating six months, and then he died in 1988. We didn't see him enough to know him. We went out to Europe in '82, and they flew out to us once during the summer of '79, and then again for Christmas 1984, although that final time he wasn't around much.

WHITE: You only met him three times?

FISHER: Yeah. I *feel* like I knew him because – when she got married to him – I read up about him, about how he won all these Oscars in the early '50s. But, the truth is, I didn't know anything about him.

I returned my attention to Lynda Korin.

The search for her had been complicated by the fact that she seemed to live quite a solitary existence, which meant few really close friends, and so fewer people to notice she was gone. After searching her house and coming up short, White had decided to go door-to-door in the village and in others nearby.

As I turned the page, I saw that he'd included photographs from inside her house, but it was hard to get a sense of whether anything was awry – the rooms looked tidy and up together. Certainly, there was nothing in White's report to suggest he'd found anything at the house to raise an alarm, and his decision to go door-to-door seemed to be a fairly obvious reflection of that. After asking around in the villages, he went on to speak to people Korin had done accounts for. He'd even interviewed the women at a book club she went to on a Thursday morning.

Again, he came away with nothing.

Buried deep in the file were her mobile phone records and printouts from her email inbox. Her relatively dormant social life meant there was little in either landline or mobile calls to get excited about. Across the three months that White had got hold of – from 28 July to 28 October – he'd gone to the effort of attributing each number to a name, listing who Korin had contacted, or been contacted by. The issue wasn't really his level of care, more the lack of activity on the phone, something that was also true of her emails. My hope had to be that Spike's more extensive background search – and the fact that he was going back six months instead of White's three – might bring me something extra.

The most obvious person missing from the phone records was her sister, and that was down to the fact that the two of them used WhatsApp. White had gained access to Wendy's mobile and exported the history of WhatsApp conversations between them, but the news they shared was routine: what Wendy's kids – both in their thirties, one single, one married with children – were up to, or what fruit she was growing in her garden; messages from Korin about what books she was reading, her job, yoga classes. It was only at the end that something stopped me. The last ever message Korin sent to her sister.

> Love you so much, Wendy.
> You have always been the
> best sister anyone could
> have x

Given the fact that she'd driven to Stoke Point the next day and vanished off the face of the earth, the words felt especially prescient. There were all sorts of reasons to believe she *hadn't* committed suicide – the lack of a body being the major one – but there were, equally, major reasons to believe she might be dead: no activity on her mobile for the ten months she'd been missing; her purse and credit cards left in the car, and – according to bank statements that White had included later on in the file – no attempt to withdraw any money or apply for any other cards. As well as that, she'd had no contact with her sister at all, a woman she'd never failed to keep in touch with for the entire time she'd been in Europe.

I sat back, looking out at the garden. Beyond the birdsong and the faint sound of traffic, I could hear the thump of distant music. But most of it hardly registered with me. I was too busy trying to make sense of what I'd read so far: that a woman, without any clear motivation for doing so, had driven herself to an isolated beauty spot, left her purse and her mobile phone in the car, tossed her keys into some nearby scrub – and proceeded to vanish into nothing.

No cameras. No witnesses.

No trace of her anywhere.

7

The video call with Wendy Fisher began just after eight o'clock.

It was the first time I'd seen her in person and, as I took her in, I instantly saw echoes of her sister. They had the same cheekbones, the same eyes, the same mouth. Elsewhere, though, the differences were obvious. It wasn't just the fact that Wendy was brunette, her hair cut short, styled slightly boyishly around her ears and jaw, or that she was overweight, her upper arms thick beneath a cardigan, her belly gathered under an oversized T-shirt like the folds of a curtain. It wasn't her slightly old-fashioned glasses either, although all of those things added to the general picture. It was the way she carried herself, the sadness in her face, the way age and worry and sorrow clung to her, all of it evident even through the pixelated, jumpy quality of the video feed. She may have been five years younger than Lynda, but it was hard to believe it.

She was sitting in a living room, photos on a mantelpiece behind her, one side of her face painted brighter by daylight coming through an unseen window. The first thing she did was to apologize in case the connection played up, telling me they'd been having problems with it for a couple of months, but I told her not to worry and gently steered the conversation around to the weeks leading up to her sister's disappearance.

I asked, 'You never noticed anything out of the ordinary in

her messages during the last few weeks before she vanished? I've managed to get hold of Lynda's missing persons report, and have been through the messages myself – but maybe you got a sense from what she wrote that something was bothering her?'

'No,' she replied. 'I really didn't. Believe me, David, no one's looked back through our conversations more times than me. I spent the first month after she went missing poring over every message, trying to find some hidden meaning in them.'

I flicked back to notes I'd made earlier. 'The last message that Lynda sent you read, "Love you so much, Wendy. You have always been the best sister anyone could have." She sent you that the day before she vanished.'

'I know what you're going to say.'

'It sounds like a goodbye.'

'Right.' Wendy paused, a sigh crackling in the microphone of her laptop. 'I don't know,' she said finally, her voice flat, a little sombre now. 'I suppose, in retrospect, it *was* a goodbye. And maybe I should have seen it for what it was at the time – but it just never really occurred to me then.'

'What do you mean, "seen it for what it was"?'

'I don't know,' she said again, 'it's just that Lyn has never been terrific at showing her emotions. She's like Mom used to be. Mom was brought up on the plains of North Dakota, freezing her butt off all winter, hunting for food, peeing in a hole in the ground. She was loving in her own way, but she was tough. My dad, he was different. I was more like him. Lyn and I, we loved each other, we really did. But we just expressed it differently. I'd tell her I loved her and missed her all the time; she'd tell me how a book she was reading reminded her of the house we'd grown up in. That was how she expressed what she felt – these slightly abstract, throw-away comments. Don't get me wrong, she wasn't cold – far from it, actually; most of the time she was the life and soul of the party – it was just she was so rarely willing to let her guard down, even with me. If she felt she was being led somewhere she didn't want to go, she'd stop dead.'

The implication was that Korin was fun, she was good company, she was gregarious and open with her sister, and presumably others too – but only with regard to things she *wanted* to be open about. That wasn't particularly abnormal: a lot of people were like that, especially missing people, because when they went missing, they did so having buried secrets no one ever knew they were keeping.

'So what did you think when you received that message?' I asked.

'I was surprised, touched. You said you've got all the messages we sent to one another there, so you can see for yourself. She didn't send many like that. That's what I meant when I said I should have seen it for what it was. The second it came through, I should have thought, "This is weird. She never sends me messages like this." But I didn't. I read it and it made me feel happy, and that was enough.'

'Would you say Lynda had many good friends?'

Her image pixelated slightly as she said, 'She had friends, of course – lots of those. But *good* friends, people she'd open up to and share things with? I doubt she had many in England. In a weird way, I think she preferred it like that.'

'Why?'

'Lyn just wasn't built like that. She was always fine in her own company. She didn't need to be in a crowd to feel comfortable. Plus, it wasn't like she was a recluse or something. She went out, had dinner with acquaintances; when we

WhatsApped or Skyped, she'd tell me about a book club she went to, yoga classes — all sorts of things. It sounded to me like she had an active social life and she had plenty of people she knew, but I'd be surprised if any of them actually *knew* her.'

I thought of the file I'd been through, the evidence of a lack of good friendships, of people she'd shared her life with. Maybe it *was* a consequence of never quite being able to let herself go — or maybe it was more deliberate than that; something more premeditated. Maybe she didn't give anything away, not because she was incapable of doing so, but because she had a reason not to.

I changed tack. 'You said your sister's an accountant?'

'Correct.'

'But that's her second — actually, third — career, right? I found out this afternoon that she did some modelling — and some acting too.'

'Oh, sure. But that was way back.'

'In the seventies and eighties?'

'Well, the seventies and early eighties. She went to Europe in 1971 because she got offered some modelling jobs out there — and then she ended up staying. After that, she got into the movies — but not real well-known ones. They were, like . . .' She paused, grimaced slightly, clearly searching for a way to describe her sister's films in the most respectful way possible. 'They were kind of low budget. Horror movies, really. That was where she met Bob, her husband. He directed them all.'

'That's Robert Hosterlitz?'

'Right. Have you heard of him?'

'I have, yeah. She didn't take his name when they got married?'

'No. Korin is our family name. She'd built a modelling career with that surname, so it was just easier to keep it. Anyway, like I said, Bob was a director. Back in the fifties, he won a bunch of Oscars. In his day, he was a pretty big deal, but by the time we met him . . .' She stopped again; a sad smile. 'Well, he wasn't . . . Not any more.'

'Did you ever see any of Lynda's films?'

'One or two, but not many. They weren't really my thing. I supported her in what she did, because she was my sister, but I didn't necessarily like what she was doing – you know, taking her clothes off, pretending to have sex on camera, that sort of thing.'

I paused to check my notes. 'After Robert died, did Lynda ever have any other relationships?'

She shook her head. 'No.'

'None?'

'Not that I knew about.'

'Would she have told you if she had?'

'Yeah, I think so. I mean, why conceal it?'

I shrugged. 'Maybe she thought you wouldn't approve.'

Wendy smiled. 'Lynda's a big girl. I'd love to think that I hold that level of influence over her, but the reality is she's older than me, more independent than me, and wouldn't *not* do something just because I said that I didn't like it.'

'So, as far as you know, she's been single since 1988?'

'As far as I know. She may have been out on a few dates or whatever, but she's never had another relationship.'

I nodded. 'Okay. Why do you think she decided to stay in the UK?'

'What do you mean?'

'I mean, you're her only family, she's originally from the US, you said yourself she didn't really have any close friends, and that's certainly borne out in what I've seen and heard so far. So why not move back to the States with you?'

'She liked England.'

'You think that's all it came down to?'

'Have you seen the place she owns?'

'No, not yet.'

'It's right on the top of a hill with stunning views across this big lake, and it's where she made a home with Bob. She was devastated after he died – totally and utterly broken. I'd never seen her like that in my life, even after Mom and Dad went on. Maybe she just didn't want to sever her final connection with him.'

I chewed on that for a moment. It was clear her decade with Hosterlitz had cast a long shadow, even almost thirty years on. Korin loved him, missed him, perhaps never got over him. It was becoming easier to understand why she may have chosen to remain single.

'I'm going to let you go now, Wendy.'

'Oh, okay. Have you got all you need?'

'For now, yeah.'

'If you need anything else, absolutely anything else at all, please get in touch. My hours are all over the place this week, and at the hospital I tend to keep my cell on silent because the bosses don't like our phones going off on the wards – but I can sneak a look at texts or emails easily enough.'

'Okay, I'll do that. I do have one last question, though.'

'Sure.'

'I've just sent you a screenshot of a picture I found in the missing persons report. It's of Lynda.' I glanced to the left of the video window, where I had the picture open. 'It looks vaguely professional to me. Could you take a look at it?'

'Now?'

'If you can.'

She leaned closer to the laptop and started using her computer to access her email. While she did, I wrote up a couple of notes, trying to condense my thinking. I heard Wendy muttering to herself, her mouse clicking, and then – a few moments later – she said, 'Right, here we are,' and leaned back again.

'Have you got the picture there?'

She squinted slightly, her eyes magnified behind the lenses of the glasses, and then her face became a mishmash of tiny squares, the connection unable to follow her movements exactly. 'Yeah.' Her accent made it sound more like *yah*. She leaned in again. 'Oh, *this*. Yeah, I gave the police this one. She looks so beautiful.'

'Did you take it yourself?'

'Oh, no. No way. It was from that magazine she talked to.'

'Magazine?'

'Yeah, they took it for the article.'

'Which magazine is this?'

'Uh . . . *Cine*. *Cine* magazine.'

'The film magazine?'

'Right. That's right.'

'What did she do with them?'

'Um . . . it was an article about Bob, I think, like a celebration kind of thing, because it had been sixty-something years since he made that film that won all the Oscars. This journalist went to the house to talk to her. Uh . . . Colsky, I think.'

'That was the name of the journalist?'

'I think so, yeah.'

I wrote that down.

'When did the article come out?'

'I think it came out in, like, November last year. We don't get *Cine* in the US, so I'm not sure exactly. Lyn said she would send me a copy when it went on sale in England, though.' A brief pause, a flicker of pain, visible even over the poor connection. The magazine had never arrived, just like her sister had never arrived home from Stoke Point. 'Anyway,' she went on, her voice a little softer, 'I'm not sure when it came out, but I remember she did two interviews with this guy, Colsky. She did the first at the end of June last year, and the second . . . I don't know, maybe a week later.'

'Did she say it went all right?'

'Yeah. She said it was great fun.'

A couple of minutes later, after finishing the video call with Wendy and telling her I'd be back in touch soon, I found out that the journalist Korin had talked to was a guy called Marc Collinsky, rather than Colsky. He worked as a senior staff writer for *Cine*, the UK's biggest movie magazine. I found a profile picture of him on their website, an email address and a landline. I tried calling the landline, even though it was after 9.30 p.m., hoping he might be working publishing hours, and got lucky.

'*Cine*.'

'Is that Marc?'

'Speaking.'

'Marc, my name's David Raker. I'm a missing persons investigator. At the moment, I'm looking into the disappearance of Lynda Korin.'

A pause on the line. 'Disappearance?'

'You didn't know about that?'

'No. What happened to her?'

'She's been missing since last October. I know you did an

interview with her the summer before that. I'd like to discuss it with you if I can.' I thought about my schedule, and where best to fit him in. I needed to get down to Stoke Point as soon as possible because, without seeing it, walking it and getting a feel for it, I had no clear idea about the last place Lynda Korin had been seen. It also made sense, while I was down in Somerset, to take a look at her home on the Mendips too. That meant the whole of tomorrow was out.

'How about Friday?' I said.

'I won't be around then. I'm flying out to Berlin tomorrow evening.'

I was silent again, thinking about whether the *Cine* article mattered for now. It was hard to gauge without seeing it for myself, but from what Wendy had told me, the article was on Robert Hosterlitz and not Korin – Collinsky was just using Korin as a bridge back to her husband. That instantly made it less compelling.

'Okay,' I said. 'When are you back?'

'Next Tuesday.'

'Can we arrange something for . . .' But then I paused. I'd been absent-mindedly scrolling through the back issue section of the *Cine* website, and something had caught my eye.

'Actually, are you free tomorrow lunchtime, Marc?'

'Uh, I can be. I fly out at six.'

'How about I meet you outside your office at 1 p.m.?'

'Okay. Yeah, okay, then.'

I hung up, my eyes still fixed on the same part of the website. Beneath the cover of the issue that had featured the Lynda Korin interview, there was a link to the digital edition and confirmation of the date the physical copy had gone on sale.

23 October.

That was five days before Lynda Korin disappeared.

I stared at it, mulling it over. Maybe it didn't matter. Maybe it was just coincidence that she'd vanished so soon after her photograph had run in the magazine. Except the more I tried to support that argument, the less certain I became. Hundreds of thousands of copies of the Korin interview would have been out there on news-stands, in homes, lying around in waiting rooms and discarded on public transport. Korin, elegant and beautiful in her photograph, would have been seen by all sorts of people who'd never heard of her until then – and that worried me. It worried me because I had no way of knowing who those people might be. It worried me because five days after the world found out who she was, she was gone.

I clicked on the link for the issue and left the digital edition to download. After that, I headed straight to bed. I needed to grab some sleep while I could.

It was going to be an early start.

8

I left London at 4 a.m. and was skirting the northern fringes of Bristol at just gone 5.50. Ideally, I would have left later and stayed for the day, especially as I'd wanted to take a look at Lynda Korin's house too – but that wasn't going to be possible now. I needed to be back in Ealing for midday in order to meet up with Marc Collinsky at 1 p.m., so I'd just have to go to Korin's house tomorrow. It was annoying, but there was no way around it. I definitely needed to see Stoke Point before the case got any further, but I also needed to speak to Collinsky about the interview going out in *Cine* and Korin disappearing just five days later. If I didn't, I wouldn't get a chance to sit down with him until Tuesday.

As I came off the motorway east of Weston-super-Mare, the sky was still dark, and it stayed that way for a while. The crawl into the wetlands of north Somerset – big, flat, open country that eventually became the ragged edges of the coastline – seemed to take for ever in the blackness, but then ten minutes from Stoke Point the light finally broke at the horizon. As the peninsula emerged from the gloom, I could see it stretching into the Bristol Channel as if it were the arm of some huge, fallen giant; minutes later, I spotted paths on the headland weaving in and out of one another like braided hair, and the waterfall of rocks bordering it, all the way around. It made me realize the impossibility of Lynda Korin coming here to commit suicide. The peninsula was too flat, too low. She might have broken some bones making a jump, but she wouldn't have killed herself.

She didn't drown either. The tide was in now, but it hadn't been the day Korin had disappeared. If she'd been depressed enough, scared enough or brave enough to make her way on to the mudflats to try to end her life, she wouldn't have succeeded: the mud was certainly dangerous, but it would have consumed her to her knees, at worst to her waist. She'd have needed rescuing by the coastguard, but it was unlikely to have killed her – plus, she would have been seen by the lifeboat crew, by people watching from the headland. Instead, no one saw anything. There wasn't a single witness.

The entrance to the car park was small and unremarkable. It was carved out of a thick crescent of trees on the other side of the stone bridge that Wendy had described to me. In front of the entrance was a cabin with a National Trust logo and a board screwed to it, and a half-open gate. To my surprise, there was a man inside the cabin, partly obscured behind milky glass, and a bike leaning up against it.

I pulled up at the gate and looked around. Off to my left was the one and only security camera. It was attached to a metal pole – like a street light – and focused on the entrance. I thought of the CCTV stills of Lynda Korin, of her car entering through the gate. Where had she gone from here?

'Good morning.'

The man from the cabin was standing by my car now, a National Trust T-shirt on. He was in his early sixties, balding and bearded, with a maze of broken capillaries in his cheeks and a slight paunch. He had a smile on his face, but he made an obvious show of checking his watch and then looking at the car park beyond the trees, which was totally empty. I remembered from the police report that someone from the Trust came to check on the car park three days a week, and that a guy called Len Fordyce had reported Korin's car as having probably been abandoned. I looked for a name badge, but if he had one, it wasn't on his shirt.

'Morning,' I said.

'You're keen.'

I smiled. 'I hear it's going to be a nice day.'

'Thirty degrees,' the guy told me in a broad West Country accent. 'Anyway, make yourself at home. We close at sunset.'

He opened the gate the rest of the way, and I headed in and parked up.

A set of concrete steps – buried among oak trees thick with leaves – led from the far end of the car park, thirty feet down the slope of a bank, to the peninsula.

The tide was in, the mudflats obscured. As I got to the bottom of the steps, the light improving the whole time, I looked out at the Bristol Channel flanking me on both sides. The grey water was streaked with coils of brown silt, like snakes twisting beneath the surface, and the sea was being hacked at by the wind, churned up, rolled. The air was noticeably cooler here compared to the car park, even though, above the crest of Steep Holm – an island five miles offshore – the arc of the sun was now above the horizon, the sky an incredible prism of pink and orange and claret. As I started along the headland, in the direction of a Second World War pillbox on the left, a series of gusts ripped in, making it hard to maintain a straight line along the path. It made me wonder what this place had been like the morning Korin had come here. *Colder, the wind probably even worse.* It had been the end of October then.

The pillbox was just a shell: a circular concrete shelter half consumed by the long grass of the headland, with a window that looked out over the water. Its flat roof – slabs of moss-dotted concrete – sat unevenly on top, its walls yellowed by age, pockmarked and coarse. If I'd had any thoughts about it being part of Korin's escape plan – or someone else's escape plan for Korin – I soon let it go. Once, this had been the last line of defence between Hitler and the shores of Britain; now it was just a decaying ring of stone that kids used for hide-and-seek.

I continued my way along the path. The further I went, the harder it got to hear anything above the wind. The squawk of seagulls faded out, the soft wash of the sea too. Either side of me, the grass slanted away to the gravel and rocks that I'd seen on my approach, a grey stone beach that traced the circumference of the entire peninsula. Every time a gust jagged in, it almost knocked me off balance and I could feel the hardness of the ground beneath my feet. With the wind so brisk, with it still being so early, it was easy to forget that everywhere had been baked by the sun for months.

Within moments, the end of Stoke Point came into view, the tip of the headland marked by a signpost with writing on it. There was nothing else between me and it, just an ocean of undulating grass, jagged pockets of gorse, and knotted, ragged brambles. It was wild and bleak, but empty and featureless. There was no case-breaking piece of evidence on this finger of land. No smoking gun. The only thing this journey had reinforced was how untamed and isolated it all was out here; how, once you got on to the headland, the only way you got back off again was the way you'd come in. That made it the perfect place to disappear from if you were able to disguise your exit.

I headed back, windburn in my cheeks, sweat at the arc of my hairline, and climbed the steps up to the car park. Behind me, out in the Channel, the sun continued its ascent, changing the light on the peninsula again. There was an almost sepia quality to it, the headland bathed in its glow, the grass burnt orange like every blade had caught fire. In the car park, though – as I made my way back into the ring of trees – it was different. Shadows had formed and grown.

On the far side, the man who'd greeted me forty-five minutes ago was wearing a pair of gardening gloves and sweeping dead leaves into a pile next to the cabin. As he did, the wind picked up again, funnelling into the car park from the entrances at either end. Branches swayed around me. Foliage snapped. Shadows seemed to shift and twist as sunlight flickered through gaps in the canopy.

I got back to the car and grabbed some printouts I'd made of Lynda Korin's file. I flicked through to the official police investigation, to descriptions of how her purse and mobile phone had been found in the glove compartment, and her keys in the scrub beyond the vehicle. Looking out again at the lonely spaces around me, I watched trees lurch and roll in the breeze, and the shadows adjust again.

Gradually, everything settled.

Refocusing my attention on the paperwork, I zeroed in on a photograph of Korin's keys in situ, discarded in the grass. A computer illustration showed their exact position in relation to the car park.

It was off to my left, beyond a bank of long grass.

It was time to take a closer look.

9

With the file still in my hands, I passed through grass and into a tight nest of windswept alders, their branches crooked and gnarled. Sunlight dappled the dried mud at my feet, flickering into life and then disappearing again, and I followed the diagram to a spot where the even ground began sloping away, down to the peninsula.

It was colder under the foliage, the light hazier and greyer, and as I bent down at the location where the keys had been found – in a knot of roots at the foot of one of the alders – I found a blanket of discarded junk: a few old, rusted drink cans; some plastic sandwich wrappers; a crisp packet rinsed white over time.

I stayed where I was and reread the portion of the file dealing with the discovery of the keys, then looked at my surroundings again. The spot was maybe sixteen or seventeen feet back from the edge of the car park – the edge of the car park being the point at which its tarmac gave way to grass and trees. It was hard to appreciate it on the diagram in the file, but sixteen or seventeen feet made for a hell of a throw. I could see that now, standing where I was. It wasn't beyond the capabilities of Lynda Korin – it wasn't beyond the capabilities of any adult – but it was still a long way. If something about that bothered me, it didn't bother me as much as the place the keys were discovered, in among the drink cans and sandwich wrappers at the roots of the alder.

As I'd approached, I hadn't even been able to *see* the base of the tree, the point at which the roots were exposed and created a kind of natural pocket – and that was because, on a direct path from the car park, the roots were on the north-east side of it: the *opposite* side. They were all but hidden from view. The alder's roots faced in the direction of the Bristol Channel, not the car park.

Just to be sure, I returned along the path I'd come in on, and then walked it again, trying to keep the roots of the tree in view the whole time. It was impossible. A couple of times I caught sight of them as the path snaked right to left, but mostly the roots remained completely out of sight until I was right on the alder itself.

I paused there, file in hand, trying to take it all in.

DC White had proposed that Korin – or, if not her, someone else – had thrown the keys away. But if that *was* what had happened, I was being asked to believe that whoever had done so had not only thrown them that distance, but got incredibly lucky with where the keys had landed. It was certainly possible that it had played out like that. But it was equally possible that there was no luck involved at all. It was possible that a spot had been chosen and the keys had been placed there on purpose.

Crouching down at the foot of the tree, I looked around again, turning that same theory over in my head – that the location of the keys was too far from the edge of the car park, and too well hidden in the roots, to have been a fluke.

Question is, why would someone place them in this spot?

I glanced at the alder, and then at the one next to it.

The second tree was the thickest and biggest on this side of the car park, and its trunk was dotted with the scars of a hundred bored teenagers. All down the grey bark, kids had carved names into it, hearts, indecipherable graffiti that meant nothing. The same graffiti was in the background of the photograph of the keys in situ. As I thought of that, I opened up the file again and compared that shot to the view I had of the roots now. I looked from the photograph to the trees, to the file, and then back to the trees again.

Everything looked exactly the same.

I stood up and stepped across to the second alder, to its graffiti scars, twigs cracking beneath my feet, leaves vibrating as wind passed through them. Studying the hundreds of grooves and rifts made by knives and sharp-edged stones, my gaze eventually fell upon a small engraving, only a couple of inches high, about a third of the way up. It was easy to miss, almost hidden among everything else around it – but something immediately registered with me.

It was a film projector.

I double-checked the photograph in the file and saw that the engraving had already been there when the keys were found in November. So was it just a fluke? Could it really be a coincidence that a film projector had been carved into a tree, feet from where a former actress had last been seen, inches from where her keys were discovered?

I looked at the words to its right: *Lake Calhoun*.

Unsure where that was, I immediately headed back to the car, grabbed my phone and put in a search for it.

As soon as I looked at the first hit – a Wikipedia article – a charge of adrenalin grabbed me. I scrolled down, looking for more in the way of corroboration, and saw the same thing confirmed over and over.

Lake Calhoun was a four-hundred-acre body of water, south-west of Lakeville.

The city in which Wendy Fisher lived.

And the place in which Lynda Korin had grown up.

It was 7.50 a.m. in the UK, making it 1.50 a.m. in Minnesota, so Wendy was either asleep or at work. I fired off an email to her, remembering how her job as a nurse made it hard for her to take calls on the run, and told her I needed to speak to her as soon as possible. I wanted to know why the name of a lake – a lake local to her and her sister as children – might be carved into a tree, just feet from where Lynda Korin's keys had been found; and I wanted to know why a film projector had been scratched into the bark next to it.

As I thought of the projector, I thought again of the interview with Korin in *Cine* magazine, and grabbed my laptop off the back seat. I'd downloaded the digital edition of the issue the previous night but hadn't had a chance to read it yet. I'd been up too early, the article was too long and dense to do on a quick run-through, and I didn't want to miss anything. I'd planned to go through it once I got back to London. For now I just did a keyword search, hunting the PDF for any mention of Lake Calhoun. There were no matches.

Returning to Google on my phone, I tried to use the lake as a jumping-off point for stories that might be related to it – crimes, disappearances, things connected to Korin in some way – but there was nothing. Moments later, I noticed that the man at the gate was finishing up, his trousers hitched with a bicycle clip, the cabin beside him padlocked.

I started up the BMW and headed over.

As I got to him, I wound down my window. In my

rear-view mirror, I glanced back at the place where I'd found the inscription, and then to the top of the steps that led back down to the peninsula. The wind had calmed a little, and I could see the sun above the trees, a white disc against a flawless blue sky.

'You leaving already?' the guy said to me.

'I'm afraid so. This is the only way in and out of here, right?'

He frowned, looking towards the bridge binding the car park to the mainland, as if it might be a trick question. 'Yeah,' he said, frown still lingering, 'it's the only way in and out.'

I glanced again at my rear-view mirror.

'Do people ever moor boats off the peninsula?'

'Moor them where, exactly?'

'I didn't see a jetty.'

The frown stayed. 'That's 'cos there ain't one.'

Clearly, he'd marked me out as some sort of crackpot, so I tried to move the conversation on.

'I heard a woman disappeared from here last October.'

He seemed puzzled by the change of direction, but then his expression softened. 'Tragic,' he said. 'I was the one that called the police about it.'

'Oh, really?'

'Yeah. I told them she must have abandoned her car here.'

'That makes you Len Fordyce, right?'

His eyes narrowed. 'How do you know that?'

'My name's David Raker,' I said to him, offering him my hand, attempting to put him at ease. 'I've been asked to try and find out how the lady disappeared.'

'Oh,' he said, and we shook hands. 'You a copper or something?'

'More like an Or Something. I work for myself.'

'Like a private investigator?'

I gave him a business card and manoeuvred us back to Lynda Korin. 'So, you check on this place – what? – three times a week, is that right?'

'That's right. I'm not always here to open up at the start of the day like this, though. Sometimes I get here last thing at night, or at lunchtime. That's why the gate's on a timer – if I'm not here at this hour, it opens automatically five minutes after sunrise, and then closes again thirty minutes after dark. If your car gets stuck, tough luck. We warn people about it.' He gestured to the board on the cabin. 'It don't really matter when I come, as long as I make sure everything's in order when I get here. To be honest with you, I never even realized she'd left her car here permanently – *abandoned* it, I mean – until quite a while after.'

I nodded, looking back at the car park.

'Nice lady, that one.'

Instantly, I tuned back in again. 'What was that?'

'She came here a few times, is all.'

'You mean, before she disappeared?'

'Oh yeah,' he said. 'I saw her maybe five, six times.'

'Did you tell the police that?'

'Yeah, course I did.'

But that piece of information hadn't been in DC White's missing persons report. Why? Perhaps because he didn't think it was important. Perhaps because it *wasn't* important. She'd been here before – so what? *Because it meant she knew this place – or had got to know it. Or it meant she'd returned for some other reason.*

I thought of the engraving on the tree.

'Did she ever meet anyone here?'

'Not that I saw – but I suppose it might have been possible she did on the days I wasn't working.'

'So what did she do while you *were* here?'

He shrugged, looking across the roof of the car to where the steps led down to the peninsula.

'She'd go for walks out on the headland,' he said, 'or sometimes just sit in her car. She'd always say hello to me if we crossed paths, though, and a couple of times we had a nice chat. I liked her. Lynda, her name was.'

'Do you remember what you chatted about?'

'I don't know, really. Just stuff.' He paused, raising his left hand. There was a gold wedding band on his ring finger. 'Unfortunately, my missus passed on a few years back. Liver problems. So I like talking to people and getting to know them 'cos . . . well, y'know.'

I'm lonely.

'And you got to know Lynda?'

'I don't know about got to know her, but we talked.'

'Did she tell you much about herself?'

'She said she'd been married once, that she lived somewhere out on the Mendips. I think she said she was an accountant. We shared some coffee out of my flask one time when she turned up early in the morning and it was cold – but don't get me wrong, we weren't best of friends or nothing. We just chatted.'

'She ever mention anything about a Lake Calhoun to you?'

He frowned. 'A what?'

'Lake Calhoun.'

'Is that a lake round here?'

'It doesn't matter,' I said. 'So, soon after that, she abandoned her car?'

'Yeah. A few days after she disappeared, I came late in the day and it was parked up over there.' He pointed to the corner, close to where I'd followed the trail into the trees. 'It was a Thursday, I think. Anyway, I recognized her car, but couldn't see her anywhere. I didn't think much of it. I just figured she was out on the headland somewhere. I had a couple more calls to make on my rota, so I left pretty soon after. Week following that, I was on holiday, and then I came back on the Sunday; so – what? – nearly two weeks after she disappears. Again, I see her car, but there's no sign of her. So when I returned on the Monday and found her car in the same place and no sign of her, I went looking for her, out of curiosity, I suppose. I mean, I didn't think she'd just *leave* it here like that. But when I didn't find her, I started to worry for her, y'know? So I called the coppers.'

I glanced in my rear-view mirror again. I knew, from the police report, that Korin's Ford Focus had been towed away and impounded. It had never been claimed, because Korin was never found and she had no family to take ownership of it in her absence. After six months sitting in a pen, the Focus was eventually sold for scrap.

While I was still thinking of that, my eyes happened to move to the exterior of the cabin and I noticed a slim L-shaped tube made from black rubber poking out of the side of it. It was like a downpipe. Its end was embedded in a patch of concrete and secured there with rivets the size of ten-pence pieces. It took me a moment to realize what it was, but then I looked to the CCTV camera, mounted on a pole at the entrance, and saw wiring breaking out of the ground at its base from a similar rubber tube.

It's the wiring for the security system.

I remembered then what Ewan Tasker had told me. The security system here was old, disc-based, which meant the recording equipment must be inside the cabin.

I gestured to the downpipe. 'I don't suppose you'd be

willing to let me take a look at the CCTV footage from the day Lynda disappeared, would you?'

'If it were possible, son, you'd be welcome to it,' Fordyce said, producing a big bunch of keys from his pocket. Each one was marked with a number.

'But it's not?'

'We keep six months of discs inside.'

'And after that?'

'After that, they get dumped. The police might have a copy, though.'

I smiled, trying not to show my disappointment. I was going to have to find some magical way of building friendships with Avon and Somerset Police.

'Did you ever see the footage yourself?' I asked.

'Over someone's shoulder, yeah.'

'What did you make of it?'

He shrugged. 'It's like they said.'

'She just vanishes?'

'She comes into the car park here . . .' He paused, looking towards the peninsula. 'And she never comes back out again.'

11

The traffic was much heavier on the way back to London, but I still made it home by 11 a.m. My phone had pinged a couple of times on the way up, so I knew I had emails waiting, and when I sat down at the back of the house with my laptop, the sun beating down, I saw they were both from Spike.

I'd really been hoping for a response from Wendy, but it was still 5 a.m. in Minnesota, so I decided to give it another couple of hours before chasing her up.

In the end, there wasn't much to get excited about in what Spike had sent over, even though he'd collated information from a much bigger time period. He'd got me statements, financial history, phone records, emails, but – as I meticulously went through it all – it became clear that, if the search for Lynda Korin had stalled, it hadn't been because White had missed an email, or a phone call, or a clear and damning piece of evidence. That was a disappointment and a relief: it meant there were no new leads in what Spike had sent me, and he'd spent all night wasting his time on my behalf; equally, it meant the focus of the search had narrowed, and I could concentrate my efforts elsewhere. For now, that meant the inscription I'd found in the tree at Stoke Point, and the article in *Cine* magazine.

I spent some time doing the same searches for Lake Calhoun as I'd done earlier, making sure I hadn't overlooked anything. When it was clear I hadn't, I set that strand of the investigation aside until I could speak to Wendy, and switched tack. It wasn't just the name of the lake that had been carved into the tree, it was also the image of an old-style movie projector. I didn't know who had put it there or why, but the name of the lake was an obvious link to Lynda Korin – so it was logical to assume the projector was too. That made me think that I needed to know more about her film career, such as it was.

In the end, it took about five minutes to bring myself up to speed. I didn't need to read user reviews to know that Korin's films were bad – it was easy enough to come to that conclusion based solely on their titles. *She-Zombie* and *Dracula's Flesh* weren't going to be making a 'Best of' list any time soon, but – on the back of her fairly successful career as a catalogue model – I started to wonder if she'd just seen acting as a fun distraction. Whatever her reason for doing it, her sidestep into movies came courtesy of a working relationship she'd struck up with a producer called Isaac L. Murray, the brains – if that was the right word – behind a bunch of films with names like *Lust of the She-Wolf* and *B is for Blood*. More relevantly, he got *Ursula of the SS* off the ground in 1976, and offered Korin her first ever lead role. It was on the set of that movie that she met her husband, Robert Hosterlitz, although by then he was a shadow of his former self, penniless and desperate for work, borne out by the fact that he'd agreed to direct *Ursula* in the first place.

One site described the three *Ursula* films as 'cult seventies Nazi exploitation flicks about a sadistic, nymphomaniac female Kommandant who conducts experiments on her male prisoners'. The first made the infamous Video Nasties list during the 1980s, but – according to the same website – in reality, 'Ursula was banned more for the subjects it tackled (Nazis, sex, human experimentation) than its actual content. The truth is, the movie's actually trashy nonsense, made memorable by the busty, beautiful Lynda Korin.' Robert Hosterlitz had directed all three of the *Ursula* films his wife starred in, and then Korin had gone on to appear in another eleven movies Hosterlitz had made in Spain after that. She'd taken a mix of lead and supporting roles, but the movies were all of the same ilk, with names like *Kill!* and *Die Slowly*.

On paper, it was hard to see how any of this mattered, whichever way you approached it. Korin was having a bit of fun as a part-time actress; Robert Hosterlitz was in the dying embers of his career, just trying to make ends meet.

Even so, I spent twenty minutes seeing whether I could get hold of a few of Korin's films, just to get a sense of her, even from nearly forty years on. I also wanted to see if there might be something connecting back to what I'd found out about her already, or what I'd discovered carved into the tree. Instead, I found that only a couple of her movies were available any more – and the ones that were either had very long order times or were in the hands of specialist collectors.

Finally, I turned to Marc Collinsky's *Cine* article.

As Wendy had already told me over Skype, it wasn't really about Korin at all, but about her husband, and in particular his early career in 1950s America. Korin had simply been used as a way to understand him away from the camera.

The article began with how the Hosterlitz family, seeing the Nazi threat on the horizon, had emigrated from Germany to the US in 1933. Robert was eight at the time. His father, a minor actor himself, was friends with legendary director Fritz Lang and, eventually, that was what allowed Robert to grab a foothold in Hollywood.

'Robert had a difficult early life,' Lynda Korin says. 'His father died when he was thirteen, and Robert was diagnosed with a minor heart condition in 1943, when he tried to enlist. A lot of people didn't understand the reasons why he couldn't join up. They just saw this German kid, still with a little bit of an accent, who stayed at home when every other eighteen-year-old went off to war. I think that bred some suspicion, and the Robert I knew . . . that would have got to him. He would have *hated* the idea of being disliked. But, eventually, Fritz Lang managed to pull some strings and Robert got work editing scripts for propaganda films at the War Activities Committee. It was some time during that period that he wrote the script for *My Evil Heart*.'

In 1949, with Lang prominent in the background once again, Monogram was persuaded to give Hosterlitz a very small budget to make *My Evil Heart*. Against all odds, it was a critical and commercial smash and, off the back of it, Hosterlitz – just twenty-four at the time – signed a four-film deal with American Kingdom Inc. There, he made *Connor O'Hare* and *Only When You're Dead*, gaining two Oscar nominations, and then *The Eyes of the Night*. That was the game-changer. And not just for Hosterlitz either. His leading man in that movie, Glen Cramer, who'd already won an Oscar for his portrayal of the title character in Hosterlitz's *Connor O'Hare*, also went on to win his second Oscar for *The Eyes of the Night*.

In an interview with the *LA Times* in 1989, during the press for *Half-Light*, for which he won his fourth and final acting Oscar, Glen Cramer was quick to give Hosterlitz his dues: 'If it hadn't been for Bobby, I'd be serving hamburgers in McDonald's. I'll never forget, before he cast me in *Connor*, he came to see this show I was doing in New York. He waited outside the stage door, and I thought he wanted an autograph. I said to him, "This is the first autograph I've ever signed," and he said, "Well, it won't be the last." I'll never forget that. When he died last year, he left such a hole to fill. That HUAC bullshit back in the fifties has a lot to answer for. It was an absolute scandal.'

Accused of being a communist by the House of Un-American Activities, Hosterlitz fled LA for London, but he was soon in an irreversible slide. His career failed to ignite in Britain, he made three films in Germany, and then – eight years after he left, and no longer of interest to the HUAC – he returned to the US when his mother became ill. He got some TV work, directing episodes of *Bonanza* and *Petticoat Junction*, and then seemed to have manoeuvred himself back into the big time when he signed with Paramount to direct a western he'd also written the script for called *The Ghost of the Plains*. It was destroyed by *The Good, the Bad and the Ugly* at the box office. Hosterlitz's career was finished.

'He fell into more TV work to pay the bills,' Korin says, 'but then his mom died in 1969, and everything disintegrated. He got depression. He got addicted to painkillers, sleeping pills, speed . . . call girls.' Korin pauses at those last two words, then shrugs. 'He was lonely and grieving. He said the drugs made him paranoid, and he lost a lot of friends.' Disgruntled, unloved and alone, Hosterlitz moved back to the UK, where Hammer rival, Amicus, offered him the haunted house film *House of Darkness* (1971).

The production turned out to be a disaster.

'He was strung out on drugs most of the time,' remembers the producer Gordon Lem, 'and – even when he wasn't – everyone thought he was weird, all the way down to the woman who made the tea. To be honest, I felt sorry for him by the end. He was like the walking dead: gone behind the eyes.'

Three years later, Hosterlitz suffered a stroke. After a long recovery, and unable to get any work anywhere in either the UK or the US, Robert – now penniless – moved to Spain to direct the first *Ursula* film.

The grindhouse producer Isaac L. Murray offered to double his money if he directed back-to-back sequels to *Ursula*, so Hosterlitz made *Ursula: Queen Kommandant* (1978) and *Ursula: Butcher of El Grande* (1978), which switched the action to a South American prison. By that time, he and Korin were married. 'Those films were bad,' she says. 'If I tried to convince you otherwise, you'd laugh me out of the room. I mean, I spent most of the time in the buff. But if I hadn't done them, I never would have met Robert.'

It was at this point that Collinsky began to talk about Korin's own career, in particular the years after she married Hosterlitz. She seemed open and honest in her responses, always giving a straight answer to a straight question – but then Collinsky asked her about what had attracted her to Hosterlitz in the first place.

She thinks about it. 'He was clean by 1976 – he'd even given up smoking – and it was hard to tell he'd ever had a stroke. But there remained a sadness about him, and I guess that drew me to him. He wasn't attractive in the way I'd always *thought* of people as being attractive; not chiselled, or even that confident. I think his confidence had been beaten out of him by then. But he was mysterious. I used to think, "I bet he's got a secret to tell." And the more time I spent with him, the more I wanted to know what that secret was.'

'Did you ever find out?'

She doesn't answer.

'Is that a no?' I ask her.

Korin just looks at me. 'Next question,' she says.

I read the rest of the article but didn't find anything as interesting as what she'd said about her husband; about her belief that he was harbouring some sort of secret. When Collinsky had pressed her on what it was, she'd sidestepped it.

Why?

I read and reread the same section again, trying to figure out if it was directly relevant to this case, relevant to finding out what had happened to Lynda Korin after she'd driven down to Stoke Point ten months ago. It seemed unlikely, given that Hosterlitz had been dead twenty-six years by then.

But that didn't mean it was impossible.

12

At a couple of minutes before 1 p.m., Marc Collinsky emerged from an elevator on the ground floor of his office building. He may have been writing about film, but he looked like every music journalist I'd ever known: boots, skinny black jeans, a mop of messy hair and a leather jacket, despite the heat. He was about thirty-five, his blue eyes bright and youthful, his face covered in a fine scattering of stubble.

We shook hands.

'Thanks for sparing me the time,' I said.

He nodded. 'I don't know if I can help.'

He was Scottish and quietly spoken.

'Well, I appreciate it all the same,' I told him, and then asked where was good for lunch. He suggested a deli on Earlham Street, five minutes' walk away.

We headed there and he managed to find a table at the window, and once I'd paid for our food, I returned to him with two overpriced sandwiches and a couple of bottles of still water. Shrugging off his leather jacket, Collinsky uncapped one of the bottles and chugged most of it down in one gulp. 'Thanks for this,' he said, then pushed it aside, unwrapping a ham and pickle sandwich.

'I just finished your article on Hosterlitz.'

He looked up. 'Oh yeah?'

'I thought it was brilliant.'

His gaze lingered on me for a second, as if he thought he

might be the butt of some elaborate joke. 'Thanks,' he said, clearly still uncertain.

'I mean it.'

'Well, I appreciate it.' He shrugged. 'For me, it was about scratching an itch. Hosterlitz was a genius, a bona fide genius, and we're supposed to be a magazine about film, not just the last *year* of film. Sixty years on, those film noirs he made are works of art. Sixty years from now, they'll *still* be works of art.'

I got out a pen and a pad, and started to steer the conversation around to Lynda Korin. I gave him some background on who I was, why I wanted to speak to him and who I was working for. He listened, asking the occasional question, but mostly remained silent.

When I was done, I said to him, 'I don't think this is about some falling-out with her family, because her sister is back in the US. It's not about friends either, because – to be frank – Lynda didn't have that many. She seemed happy at work, didn't have any enemies, was in good health, physically and financially. So far, the thing that's most interesting to me is that, five days after your article was published, Lynda disappeared. That might be important or it might not. But if it was a catalyst for her going missing, I need to find out why.'

'Why would it be a catalyst for her going missing?'

I shrugged. 'That's what I was hoping to find out from you. Can you start by telling me how the article came about?'

He didn't reply straight away, clearly concerned that his article might be directly linked to Lynda Korin's disappearance.

'Marc?'

'Uh, well, I guess ultimately it came about because I met

her at a convention in 2011,' he said. 'Have you heard of Screenmageddon?'

'That's the horror and science-fiction expo, right?'

'That's right. Back then, I was a freelancer for a horror magazine, so, when I managed to get some time with her, I mostly spoke to her about the *Ursula* films. But, after we were done, she gave me her card. A couple of years later, in 2013, I got in touch with her again, because I was working for *Cine* by then, and it was the sixtieth anniversary of *The Eyes of the Night*, and I thought it might be cool to do a retrospective on it, and to have her talk about Hosterlitz, about his films, about him as a person. She wasn't keen on the idea at first, especially about inviting me into their marriage. I got the sense . . . I don't know, I just got the sense that her marriage was sacrosanct.'

'What makes you say that?'

He paused, tapping a finger against the table. 'I figured it had something to do with how she honoured her husband's memory. You know, that she wanted to protect the things they did in their marriage, certain special moments between them, and she didn't feel comfortable talking about any of that with a stranger. I understood that.' He stopped again, flicking a look across at me, clearly weighing up whether to say whatever was coming. 'When my dad was still around, he used to take me to Tynecastle to watch Hearts, and I'd come home and write these match reports for him, and I'd read them out to him – it was our little thing. I didn't show them to anyone. Those moments were between him and me and no one else.'

I could relate to that too, locking away the things that mattered from parts of your life you could never claim back.

'But then she changed her mind?' I asked.

'Eventually, yeah. We kept in touch, on and off, and last

summer I again floated the idea of doing a celebration of Hosterlitz's career. She was still reluctant, but she at least agreed to have a chat, and so I went to her house, and we got on really well, and it developed into something much bigger. In the end, it turned out to be the first of two interviews. She was brilliant, basically – really open about everything, surprisingly honest. I just kept pushing and she kept answering questions. She never batted an eyelid.'

'So you found her likeable?'

'Yeah, definitely. She was smart, witty, generous. She was confident and interesting. And, well, she was . . .' He smiled, but seemed uncomfortable for a moment. 'Basically, she looked bloody good for her age.'

I thought of the photograph I'd seen of Korin, taken for the magazine. He was right about that.

'Have you ever heard of a Lake Calhoun?' I asked, keeping things going. 'It may have been a place Lynda mentioned to you during your interviews.'

'Calhoun?'

'Yeah.' I spelled it out for him. 'That ring any bells with you?'

He shook his head. 'No, none.'

'It's probably nothing,' I said, although I didn't really believe that. The name hadn't been carved into a tree by chance. But, before we could get bogged down in a guessing game, I shifted things forward again: 'There's a section three-quarters of the way through your feature where Korin talks about what attracted her to Hosterlitz in the first place.'

'I remember that, yeah.'

'She said she thought he may have had a secret.'

Collinsky nodded. 'Yeah.'

'Did she ever say if she found out what that secret was?'

'No, she didn't.'

'Because she dodges the question in the interview.'

'Or she's embarrassed that she never found out.'

I studied him. 'Is that what you believe?'

He took a long breath. 'I don't know. Maybe. I just never got the impression she was lying to me. Not once. I've had lots of people lie to me during interviews, and I didn't get that vibe off her. I mean, why would she lie?'

Because people lie all the time, I thought.

'Was there anything you left out of the article?'

'I used most of what Korin gave me, especially about her years in Spain with Hosterlitz. That period of time – 1976 to 1984 – it's a big black hole, information-wise. They did all those films together, then they came back to England when he retired, he got cancer soon after that, and he was dead by 1988. But there *was* one thing.' Collinsky stopped and started to frown again. 'I don't suppose Lynda's sister ever mentioned the name "Ring of Roses" to you, did she?'

I shook my head. 'Should she have?'

'No. She wouldn't have known about it. I don't think *anyone* knows about it. That's the point.'

He stopped. Around us, the crowd in the deli had started to thin out.

'What's "Ring of Roses"?'

He didn't answer immediately, as if he were still trying to figure out the answer. 'I did two interviews with Lynda, and she mentioned it in the first, but only as I was just about to leave. By then, I'd already stopped recording. Anyway, I was heading out and she points to the window, the one into her back garden, at this big old shed she had out there. It was more than a shed, actually – more like a garden room. It had windows and hardwood walls, and the roof was tiled.

Anyway, she said to me, "In the years before Robert died, he started getting itchy feet. He missed it – the writing, the directing. So he'd sometimes take his typewriter out there, and he'd lock the door and he'd write – play around with ideas, experiment, whatever else. Those moments made him happy, even when he was ill."'

'Did she ever see what he was working on?'

'That's what I asked her. She said, no, she didn't. *Then* she says, "But he was always *talking* about this one idea."' Collinsky paused. 'Actually, I'm not sure if she called it an "idea" or a "project", but whatever it was, she said it was similar to the type of stuff he was making in the fifties, when he was winning all those Oscars. She said it had the title "Ring of Roses". At this point, obviously my eyes are lighting up, and I'm thinking, "I've got a potential scoop here." But, actually, that was it. That was all she remembered. I think it must just have been a concept Hosterlitz was playing around with.'

'Is that why you don't mention it in the article?'

'I thought seriously about writing a boxout on it. Like a "What is 'Ring of Roses'?"-style thing. And, when I did the second interview with her, I pressed her on it again. I mean, even if it was just a few lines on the back of a napkin, it was still a great exclusive – this idea that Hosterlitz had gone back to the beginning, to the type of film he was making at the height of his powers.' Collinsky stopped and took a drink of water. He shrugged. 'But she didn't know anything more than the name of it. I asked her if I could have a look at the shed, maybe take a few pictures, and she agreed, but it was just this dumping ground. There were still a few old movie props in there – a clapperboard, some bags of old junk with guff like vampire teeth, and blood, and make-up in them – but no sign of any scripts or equipment.'

'So you didn't do anything with that information?'

'With the "Ring of Roses" stuff? The second time I interviewed her, a photographer came along with me, and while she was having her picture taken I went online for the seven billionth time to try and see if I could find anything on "Ring of Roses". I'd spent the entire week preceding that trying to dig around for background on the name, to see if Hosterlitz had mentioned it before, or talked about the idea. I called up American Kingdom in LA – because they were who he worked with on *The Eyes of the Night*, *Connor O'Hare* and *Only When You're Dead* – and someone there put me in touch with the archivist they had here in London, at the European office. So then I spoke to *him* – but that was another dead end.'

'He'd never heard of "Ring of Roses" either?'

'No. I've got his details if you're interested.'

I told him I was and he found me the number for the archivist. I wasn't sure what he could give me that Collinsky hadn't already, but I was definitely starting to think that Korin's marriage to Hosterlitz, their time together, their history, wasn't the wild goose chase I feared it might be. While everything else in Korin's life was a dead end, there were unanswered questions about her career, about her husband's, about their years together and what he was doing in retirement. And all the time, something continued to rub at me: that five-day gap between the publication of the *Cine* article and Korin's disappearance.

'So what did you do after that?' I said.

'What *could* I do? For a while, I had this grand idea of making "Ring of Roses" the centre point of the feature, to kind of bring everything full circle: all the Oscars that Hosterlitz won, the lean period, the shite he was peddling in the seventies and eighties, the drugs, his depression, and then the promise of a new start. But I couldn't find anything about "Ring of Roses" anywhere. And even if I *had* managed to dig something out, from some corner of the Internet, I'd have got nowhere with Korin. She didn't know anything. That's the point. *No one* did.'

Collinsky shifted on his seat, his finger tracing patterns through the crumbs on the table. 'In the end,' he continued, 'I decided, without something meatier, vague speculation about what he may or may not have been working on in retirement didn't belong in the magazine. The magazine needs to be better than that. Or, at least, *I* believe it does. But then, me and my editor were chatting a few days after the issue went to press, and I happened to mention the thing about "Ring of Roses", and he said, "Why the hell didn't you put that in the mag?"' Collinsky rolled his eyes. 'So much for the integrity of print.'

'So what happened after that?'

'Long story short, my editor told me to write a separate piece for our website, and I ended up including "Ring of Roses" in that. We put it online a couple of days after the magazine went on sale – you know, in an effort to promote the print edition and try to drive people towards the issue. We're always doing that kind of thing. Airy-fairy, fact-free "Best of" lists are what the Internet drinks up these days, so I pulled a "Top 10 Best Unmade Films" list out of my arse to try and get some' – he made quotation marks with his fingers – ' "social media buzz".'

'So, wait – you *did* mention "Ring of Roses"?'

'Yeah, but only in that "Best of" list online, not in the magazine.'

'That was the first time anyone had ever run anything on it?'

'It was the first time "Ring of Roses" had been talked about, *ever.*'

'And the online feature went out a few days after the mag?'

'Uh, four, I think.'

Four days.

He didn't seem to realize the significance of what he'd just told me, but I saw it so clearly it could have been written in neon: the five-day gap between the magazine going on sale and Korin disappearing may not have been the thing that was relevant at all.

It may have been the piece Collinsky posted online – telling the world about 'Ring of Roses' – twenty-four hours before she went missing.

13

As soon as I finished up with Marc Collinsky, I called Louis Grant, the archivist at American Kingdom's European office, and asked if he could spare me an hour. I wanted to talk about Korin and Hosterlitz, and try to find out more about 'Ring of Roses'. Collinsky said Grant didn't know anything when the two of them had spoken, and had found nothing in the archives either – yet I still felt it was worth a shot. A polite South African, Grant said he was tied up until 5 p.m., but would happily meet me after that. He gave me an address in Southwark. Almost the moment I hung up, my phone rang again. It was a Minneapolis area code.

Wendy.

I grabbed my pad from my bag and pushed Answer. The line squealed briefly, then settled into a hum.

'Wendy?'

'David, hi. Sorry it's taken me so long to reply. I'm at work.'

'Are you okay to talk?'

'Sure. I just got on my break. Fire away.'

Very briefly, I gave her an overview of where I'd got to, without going into too much detail, and then asked her, 'What do you know about Lake Calhoun?'

She seemed slightly thrown. 'Lake Calhoun?'

'It's near you, right?'

'Yeah. It's forty minutes up the road from here.'

'Any idea why Lynda might be interested in that place? I found a reference to it. There's no evidence of her paying for plane tickets, and her passport was found at her house, but maybe she visited the lake some time before she disappeared?'

'No. No way. I mean, I guess we may have gone up on one of her trips out, but it's been a couple of years since she visited, and we've got a lot of lakes in this part of the world. I don't know why she'd only be interested in that one.'

'You never went there as kids?'

'Oh, sure. Mom and Dad would take us sometimes.'

'Nothing happened there when you were growing up?'

'One of us may have fallen over and grazed a knee or something – but *major* stuff?' She paused. 'Uh-uh. Nothing comes to mind, no.'

It wasn't what I'd been hoping for. I flipped back in my notes to the conversation I'd had with Marc Collinsky.

'What did you make of Robert Hosterlitz?'

'Bob?' She was surprised by the change of direction. 'I hardly knew him. We only met three times in the ten years he and Lyn were together. Most of the time, when Lyn came to visit, she came alone.'

'Did she ever say what attracted her to him?'

'To Bob? I don't know. I think she found him enigmatic.'

'Is that what she said?'

'No. Not exactly. But he was nearly thirty years older than her, a bit scruffy and unkempt, so it was hard to imagine it was physical. Lyn was gorgeous. She could have had any man she wanted. But she'd never had a long-term relationship with any-one until she met Bob. So he had something.'

'Something the other men didn't?'

'Right. Before him, she had this succession of boyfriends. Actually, even calling them "boyfriends" would be stretching it. She'd mention a guy to me on the phone, and then the next month it was someone else. She went through them quick and good.' She paused, playing back what she'd just said. 'That makes her sound slutty, I guess. But she really wasn't like that. She didn't go through them fast because she liked playing around, she went through them fast because she didn't want to let them into her life. I think, basically, they just weren't interesting to her.'

'But Robert was?'

'Well, she married him after six months.' She stopped for a moment. 'All I know is that she never talked about other men like she talked about him. Other men, she'd dismiss with a wave of the hand, but she was never like that with Bob. We only met him three times, but even then I could see a difference between the way she was around Bob and the way she was with other men she'd seen. Bob was *very* important to her. I mean, he must have been for them to get married so quickly. I'm just not sure if she saw him as a husband or some sort of father figure – or whether it was something more . . . unusual.'

'Unusual how?'

'I don't know.'

I waited her out.

'I think maybe she saw him as a challenge,' she said.

'In what way?'

'He was like her – he didn't give much of himself away – but whereas Lyn could disguise it well, Bob never could. Lyn always had something of the actress in her, but Bob was the opposite. He was quiet. He definitely *wasn't* the life and soul of the party. In fact, the first time I met him, I remember thinking he was boring as all hell. But Lyn wouldn't have dated him – and she *definitely* wouldn't have married him so quickly – if he was boring. She wouldn't have made that kind of commitment. She'd never made that kind of commitment to anyone else, *ever*. That's why I always thought there was more to Bob than met the eye – and I think Lyn found out what it was, and it really appealed to her.'

I thought back to the *Cine* article, to the section in it where Korin hinted at Hosterlitz harbouring a secret she wanted to get at.

'You couldn't tell what it was that appealed to her so much?'

Wendy laughed a little. 'No. I was blind to his charms, I'm afraid. But he made her happy, which was the main thing. He was clearly a smart guy, he loved her, so maybe it was that.' She paused. 'But he could be weird too, discourteous.'

'In what way?'

'Well, I remember when Lyn and Bob came out to us one year ... Jeez, this must have been Christmas 1984. Anyway, they stayed for a few nights, Christmas Day, and then Bob gets up on the twenty-sixth and just disappears for a week.'

'Really? Where did he go?'

'Northern Minnesota. Apparently, he went up to the state forests.'

'Is that what Lynda said?'

'She said he was scouting for work. I don't know if that was true or not – I don't even know if she really knew herself – but this was only the third time we'd ever laid eyes on him, and he couldn't be bothered to spend more than a few days with us before driving off to wherever he thought he was going to scout for work in rural Minnesota. I'll be honest, I thought he was damn rude.'

I started to remember her mentioning the same thing to White, in the interview transcript I'd read.

'That's what Lynda said – he was "scouting for work"?'

'I think so. I don't know. It was a long time ago. That's why I said we didn't ever really get to know him. We saw him three times before he died, and one of those times he spent most of his vacation on some sort of road trip.'

'Okay,' I said, trying to put things together.

Something's definitely going on here.

'Do you think this is about her marriage to Bob?' Wendy asked.

'No, I'm just trying to get some background.'

At best it was a deliberate fob-off, at worst a bare-faced lie, but I needed to know more before I made a commitment one way or the other.

'Can I ask you something else?' I said.

'Of course.'

'Have you ever heard of "Ring of Roses"?'

'The nursery rhyme?'

'I think it's more likely to have been a project that Robert was working on before he died.' I stopped, thinking. 'Maybe *project* is too grand for what it was. It's just . . . Lynda mentioned to the journalist who did that piece on Robert that he'd started writing again before his death, once they moved back to the UK. A name that came up is "Ring of Roses". It could have been a full-blown script or it could have been a name on the back of a napkin. I think a full-blown script is unlikely, but the name – "Ring of Roses" – is something I'd like to try and tie up.'

'"Ring of Roses"?'

'Right. This would have been in the years between 1984 and 1988.'

She paused. 'I'm trying to think . . .'

'If you're not sure, that's fine.'

I didn't want her misremembering something because I'd

pushed her too hard – or, worse, *pretending* to remember because she wanted to help.

Eventually, she muttered, 'I'm sorry.'

She sounded desperate to help, her voice emotional as frustration began to claw at it. I tried to come at it from a different angle. 'You talked just now about the trips Robert and Lynda took to see you out in Minnesota . . .'

'Sure.'

'You said that, during the Christmas 1984 visit, you found Robert a little discourteous because he just upped and left for the week.'

'Yeah. The scouting trip.'

'The name "Ring of Roses" never came up then?'

She took a long breath. 'I mean, it was such a long time ago, but I honestly don't remember that name – "Ring of Roses". I don't even remember if he took a camera with him, or a typewriter. He could just have been getting away from us all for a week. Like I told you, I'm not sure that even Lynda knew what he was up to while he was away.'

'What makes you say that?'

'I just remember asking her, "Where's Bob gone?" and she . . .' There was a crackle of air as Wendy made a noise. 'She just kind of shrugged.'

'Why wouldn't he have told her what he was up to?'

'I don't know.'

'The way you describe them, they sounded close.'

'They were,' she said. 'Honestly, they were.'

'Do you think it had something to do with his sickness?'

She considered it for a while. 'Well, Bob got told he had cancer a fortnight before he flew out to us in '84, so I guess it's possible, but . . . I don't know.'

I tried to match up the timings. As I understood it from

what I'd read in Marc Collinsky's feature, Hosterlitz shot his last film with Korin in Spain during the autumn months of 1983. After that, they moved to Somerset in early 1984, where he retired. Sometime in mid December 1984, he was diagnosed with cancer, and then – at Christmas – he and Korin visited Wendy in the US.

So did Hosterlitz disappear for a week because of the diagnosis he'd received before he left the UK? Was he simply trying to seek out some time by himself, away from the noise and commotion of a family Christmas? It would be understandable if that had been the case, but why keep it back from Korin? Why not just tell her the truth? If they were close, surely Hosterlitz would tell his wife that he needed some space, some time, to reflect upon news that would change everything – them, their marriage, their time together. It was literally life and death.

Ultimately, I couldn't plough a clear enough path through my thoughts to see the answer, and, after a while, wondered if that unaccounted-for week even mattered at all. Maybe, in a similar vein, 'Ring of Roses' didn't either. Maybe *none* of this mattered.

I just wasn't sure if I really believed that.

The 'scouting trip' to northern Minnesota, 'Ring of Roses', the carving of the words 'Lake Calhoun' and the film projector into the tree at Stoke Point – I didn't know what any of them meant or where they led yet, but I was pretty certain about one thing.

They were threads.

And threads always came loose from something bigger.

14

The address Louis Grant, the American Kingdom archivist, gave me turned out to be a crumbling art deco cinema in Southwark called the Comet that had been closed since 1998. It felt like a weird place to meet, but – as he'd agreed to see me so quickly – I went along with it. The cinema was next to the high belly of a rusting railway bridge, and though the building was old and decayed, the paint flaking, the bricks starting to crumble, I felt a powerful sense of nostalgia as I approached it, memories firing in my head as I remembered the one just like it that I'd gone to as a kid.

A door had been left open for me at the back, and inside the air was musty and stagnant, a corridor rolling ahead of me with two other doors off to the left, and a staircase at the end that wound up and to the right. The oppressive summer heat followed me in: sunlight glinted off the chipped floor tiles and the peeling vinyl wallpaper, and illuminated the dust in the air as I approached the stairs.

I headed up, following a vague hint of light, the smell closing in around me – old wood and furniture, and the whiff of stale cigarette smoke. At the top was an elegant foyer: marble floors with geometric squares, limestone stairs, balustrades made from chromed steel, and a ticket booth, standing alone like a lighthouse in the middle of the room. Beyond that was the auditorium itself. I stepped closer and looked in. The screen, taped in a couple of places and half hidden behind thick curtains, looked out over a sea of worn, red velvet seats.

There were three people in conversation halfway down, all with different accents: two men – one local, one South African – and an American female.

'Mr Grant?'

All three looked up.

'Ah, Mr Raker.'

Grant broke away from the group, moved up the aisle and shook my hand. It was clammy, but I didn't hold it against him. The auditorium was hot, the air dense, and Grant – a man of about fifty – was carrying a couple of stone of extra bulk. Sweat beaded his hairline, which was thinning, and his armpits were damp, but he was smartly dressed in black trousers, a black tie and a grey shirt, and had a trimmed silver beard that ran in perfect diagonals across both cheeks.

'It's nice to meet you,' he said.

'Thanks for seeing me so quickly.'

Behind him, the other man – in his late forties, stocky, with a shaved head and a tape measure clipped to his belt – headed off towards the front of the auditorium, while the woman approached us. She was forty, maybe a little older, and absolutely stunning: olive-skinned, slim, smart, dressed in a blue skirt and heels with shoulder-length black hair cascading against the white of her blouse.

'Mr Raker,' Grant said, 'this is Alex Cavarno.'

We shook hands.

'Alex is the COO of AKI Europe.'

I smiled. 'I didn't realize I was that important.'

She returned the smile. 'I wish I could pretend that was the reason, Mr Raker, or that it's because I attend every single meeting my staff schedule – but, the truth is, I dragged Louis down here this afternoon to talk about where our new archive is going to be. That's why you're standing in a dusty cinema at the moment, and not in our current office out in the Docklands.'

'I hope you don't mind meeting here,' Grant added.

'No, not at all.'

'It was just more convenient for me.'

I turned back to Alex Cavarno. 'So this is going to be . . .'

'Our new office,' she said.

'I *thought* that was what you meant.'

'Hard to believe at the moment, I know.'

We all looked around the auditorium.

'This place brings back all sorts of memories,' I said.

'Oh, really?' Cavarno said. 'Did you use to come here?'

'Not to this one, no. I grew up in a village where there were two shops and a pub and about eight other kids, so I'd get the bus into the next town. But we had an art deco cinema like this one.' I pointed towards the front of the room. 'You haven't watched a movie until you've watched one on a taped-up screen.'

She smiled again, more fully this time, revealing a perfect set of teeth. 'I grew up in East LA, next to the Santa Ana Freeway. That was literally the first thing and last thing I heard every day. My mom and dad, they had no money . . .' She shrugged. 'My dad spent a lot of my teen years off work – he had back problems, and then he got a knee replacement – and we never went on vacation, because we could never afford it. So the thing we did instead was watch movies. I'm that rare thing among studio executives – I actually know something about films.' She paused for effect, and started grinning again. 'That was obviously a joke. Well, sort of.'

Her handbag and laptop were perched on one of the seats nearby. She reached into the bag and took out a business card. 'Louis tells me you're trying to find Robert Hosterlitz's widow. I can't claim to be an expert on Hosterlitz's films, I'm afraid, as bad as that sounds coming from someone in American Kingdom management, *and* someone who just told you they know about films. But if you need anything else, let me know. I have a great team here in the UK.' She handed me the card and looked at Louis. 'Not that I'm suggesting for a minute that Louis won't have it covered. This guy knows more about films than *anyone* I know.'

'Thank you,' I said, holding up the card.

'Sure. Well, I'll leave you two to it. We've got a launch party for the new season of *Royalty Park* on Monday and I'm supposed to be taking an interest.'

Royalty Park was a television costume drama, co-funded by the BBC and American Kingdom, the third series of which had been the UK's most-watched TV show of 2014. I'd only ever seen it in snatches, but there were adverts for it everywhere in anticipation of its return.

'I hope you don't mind my architect being here,' Alex Cavarno said, looking past me, and I remembered the other man. He was measuring up some panelling on the front stage. 'Billy,' Cavarno called out to him. 'Please get me that drawing for the projection room tomorrow morning.'

'Will do,' the man said, holding up the tape measure.

'Yeah, well, that's what you said last week,' Cavarno muttered under her breath, and rolled her eyes. She shook my hand again. 'Pleasure, Mr Raker.'

'David,' I said.

She nodded. 'Alex.'

Her eyes lingered on me, her smile still evident at the corners of her lips, and, out of nowhere, I felt a sharp fizz of electricity scorch my veins. My gaze drifted to her left hand, automatically, without thinking, searching for a ring. It was a movement that – when I looked up at her again – she seemed to be aware of, because, when I found her ring finger empty, it was like she gave a little shake of the head. *I'm not married, I'm not engaged, I'm not seeing anyone.* We remained like that, caught in a silent conversation neither of us appeared to be quite sure was happening, and then I shuddered out of the moment, grabbed a hold of myself and thought of Melanie Craw. What the hell was I doing?

'Anyway,' Alex said, 'you have my number.'

'I do,' I said, just for something to say.

Her eyes lingered on me for a moment more – and then she was gone. It was almost a relief. I felt embarrassed, thrown, guilty.

'Don't worry,' Grant was saying, and I realized he was directing me to a line of seats in the back row of the cinema. 'I cleaned all the cobwebs off these.'

I got out my pad and pen, then spent a moment trying to clear my head, pretending to leaf through my notes. When I was ready, I explained about my meeting with Marc Collinsky, how the subject of 'Ring of Roses' had come up, and how I wanted to find out more.

'Well, I can tell you everything I know about Hosterlitz,' Grant said, 'which will take us some of the way into his career, but not all of the way. I'm afraid, like most people, I have a bit of a blind spot when it comes to his horror films.'

'You mean the ones he made in Spain?'

'Particularly those, but also the ones he made here in the UK too, during the early seventies. I've seen *House of Darkness* because that became quite infamous – he was turning up drunk, or spaced out on painkillers, every day during that.'

In Collinsky's article, I remembered the quote from the *House of Darkness* producer that claimed the same thing. The late 1960s and early 1970s seemed to have been when Hosterlitz was at his lowest – depressed, addicted, bankrupt.

'I'm happy to tell you what I know, though,' Grant said.

Although his South African accent was close to estuary English – no doubt softened over time – it was still peppered with hard vowels and *Ja* instead of *Yes*.

'Great,' I said.

'Okay, so I'll give you the brief A to Z. Hosterlitz made his debut in 1949 with *My Evil Heart*, made for a company called Monogram. After that, he shot three of the greatest film noirs in the history of cinema, one after the other, all for American Kingdom. *Connor O'Hare* in 1951, *Only When You're Dead* in 1952, and then the biggie: *The Eyes of the Night* in 1953. That won seven Oscars, including Best Picture, Director and Screenplay, and also Best Actor for Glen Cramer. What makes that win extra special is that Hosterlitz was just twenty-eight at the time. Incredible when you consider how good it is. Have you seen any of his early films?'

'*The Eyes of the Night* – but a while ago.'

'Well, you can get them all on Netflix, so they're easy to find. The original negatives are in our LA vault, and we maintain a pristine distribution print of all three here in London. We obviously don't own the rights to *My Evil Heart*, but in terms of style you can lump that in with the other three. They're all of the same ilk and explore the same classic noir themes. My personal favourite is *Only When You're Dead*, but the Oscar wins obviously made *The Eyes of the Night* the most notable. Anyway, given all of that, Hosterlitz *should* be up there with the biggest names in movie history. Instead, he's barely a blip on most people's radars.'

'Because of the HUAC hearings?'

'Right, *ja*. I don't know how much you know about it, but the House of Un-American Activities was a committee that was set up to investigate allegations of communism among US citizens during the Cold War. In the late forties, it started targeting Hollywood professionals. Its power began to wane by the sixties – that was why Hosterlitz felt safe coming *back* to the US in '62 – but the damage was already done for him. Instead of staying and clearing his name – or attempting to – he packed his bags and headed to the UK.'

'So *was* he a communist?'

'Never proved one way or another, as far as I know.' Grant shrugged. 'You can understand why he decided to leave the States, though. You didn't even have to be a *confirmed* member of the American Communist Party to be subpoenaed to appear before the committee, or to face potential blacklisting – or even a prison term if it *really* went south for you. It was little better than Nazi Germany. Just a witch hunt, all based on rumour and counter-rumour.'

Grant continued: 'So, anyway, he fled to the UK in 1954 and made one film here, but it was all downhill after that. He went to Germany for a while and then returned to the US in '62 and ended up directing episodes of TV shows like *Bonanza*, *Petticoat Junction* and *The Defenders*. His TV stuff's not bad, actually. Some of it, anyway. But he always loved movies – TV just paid the bills. Unfortunately, his comeback, *The Ghost of the Plains*, was a bit of a disaster. People are sniffy about it because it bombed at the box office, but it has its moments. Have you seen it?'

'No. It's a western, right?'

'Right. It's not *The Searchers*, but it's pretty good. Anyway, that's the point at which it gets a bit cloudier for me, as he did some more TV stuff for a couple of years after *The Ghost of the Plains* bombed, then returned to the UK to make some budget horror movies, *then* ended up in Spain making even *lower*-budget horror movies. They were basically like production lines. He made fourteen in seven years.'

'That's where he met Lynda Korin.'

'Correct. Have you seen the *Ursula* films?'

'No. I was going to ask you about those Spanish films, actually. I've been trying to find some copies for reference, but they're pretty hard to get hold of.'

'You should be able to find the *Ursula* films on DVD somewhere, but I agree: the ones he made after that are much harder to track down.' He stopped, his fingers drumming on the arm of his seat. 'There's a place called Rough Print, just off Charing Cross Road. The owner is a kind of collector of rare films and books. He might have something. I know he's a big fan of Hosterlitz.'

Grant found the number in his phone and gave it to me.

'What are the *Ursula* films like?' I asked.

'Garbage, really,' Grant said, 'but not without small moments. The saddest thing about it is that you can see these very short, very brief sights of Hosterlitz's talent shining through, but most of the rest of it is borderline unwatchable.'

'Do you know much about them as a couple?' I asked.

'Hosterlitz and Lynda Korin?'

He looked out at the auditorium, thinking. The architect was on the opposite side of the room, using his tape measure at the stage and scribbling the measurements on to a notepad.

'Not much,' Grant said. 'However, I *did* meet Korin at a convention a few years back.'

'Was that Screenmageddon?'

'*Ja*,' Grant said. 'That's the one.'

I remembered Collinsky mentioning the same event. He'd told me that it had been the first time he'd met Korin, and that she'd given him her card.

'It's a sci-fi, horror and fantasy thing – you know, paradise for geeks like me.' He smiled and got out his phone again, searching for something. 'Anyway,' he went on, continuing to search, 'it's massive – like, 200,000 visitors – and they have some big guests there, but they have tons of minor ones too; the sort of people who were in the cockpit of an X-Wing for five seconds in the original *Star Wars*.' He stopped searching and handed me the phone. 'They always have this European horror section as well. That was where I met her.'

I looked at his phone.

It was a photograph of Lynda Korin sitting at a table, a few copies of the original *Ursula* fanning out from her elbow in an arc.

'What was she like?' I asked.

'She was really lovely, actually, but she seemed a bit over-whelmed by the whole convention thing. She told me she'd never done anything like it before and said that she agreed to do it because she thought it might be fun, and because she was surprised anyone still remembered her. This was – what? – 2011. In truth, I hadn't seen any of her films, even *Ursula*. I just knew about her because she was married to Robert Hosterlitz. That was why I wanted to talk to her.'

'So did you two talk about Hosterlitz?'

'Oh, man. I can't remember exactly. Probably, *ja*. I imagine I told her I was a huge fan of her husband's work. I couldn't, in all good faith, tell her that I loved the *Ursula* trilogy, or pretend to her that they were "cult" films.'

'What about "Ring of Roses"? Have you ever come across this idea that Hosterlitz may have been working on something towards the end of his life?'

But Grant was already shaking his head.

'Honestly?' he said. 'No. Never. I find the idea hugely exciting, but, when Marc Collinsky originally phoned me, I went through both our physical archives here, and digitally searched the AKI master vault in LA, and it's just a dead end.'

Grant took a long breath, the sweat at his brow reflecting the dull yellow glow from the auditorium's lamps. We both watched the architect for a moment, the metallic snap of his tape measure carrying across the room to us.

'The fact is,' Grant said, 'if Hosterlitz *was* working on something at the end of his life, I think it's highly likely that he didn't tell anyone the full story.'

15

Rough Print, the shop that Louis Grant suggested might have some hard-to-find copies of Lynda Korin's horror movies, was already closed for the day by the time I got there. It was frustrating because I'd planned to head back to Somerset first thing in the morning to take a look at Korin's house, and didn't want to have to make a detour into central London again. All I could do was give them a call as soon as they opened and see if it was worth a return journey.

There was better news from Marc Collinsky, though: he'd emailed through the audio files for both interviews he'd done with Korin. On the tube back to Ealing, I plugged in my headphones and began listening to the first one.

As Collinsky had suggested, Korin was a good interviewee. Forthright and engaging, she still had an American accent, despite years in south-west England, although she seemed to have lost a lot of her Minnesotan twang. There was a hushed quality to her voice too, a crackle that made me wonder whether she was, or had been, a smoker, as well as frequent, considered pauses – some quite long. She wouldn't be hurried into answers, conducting everything at her own pace: after Collinsky asked something, she always considered it carefully before giving flight to her words.

The conversation they had about 'Ring of Roses' the first time wasn't on tape, because it had happened after Collinsky had stopped recording, but his efforts to press Korin for more details in the second interview were. In the end, she didn't really know enough for the conversation to go anywhere, and – in terms of my search for Korin – it was hard, for now, to see any line that directly connected her to 'Ring of Roses'. There was *something* in their marriage, some half-submerged piece of evidence, waiting to be unearthed – I could feel it. But I couldn't say for sure if 'Ring of Roses' was it.

When I got home, I made myself something to eat and then took it through to the back deck to enjoy the last of the day's sun. As I ate, I listened to the interviews for a second time. I wasn't necessarily looking for fresh insight in the conversations she'd had with Collinsky. Instead, it was an effort to familiarize myself with her: the way she spoke, answered questions, her idioms, choices of vocabulary. That was also why it was going to be important to get hold of her films – or as many as I was able to. She'd be much younger in them, but it would continue to help build a picture of who she was.

What was clear from the interviews was that questions about Hosterlitz, about working with him, didn't seem to faze her at all. I didn't ever get the sense she was dancing around an answer, or trying to suppress something. If anything, she was more open and honest than I expected. Collinsky asked her about the nudity in her films, about what it was like having her husband direct her in sex scenes with other men, and she told him it was just acting – it was weird, but it was what she was being paid to do.

'I was pretty confident in my own skin by then,' she said. 'I'd been standing around in the buff for years in photo shoots.' She laughed a little. 'I'm under no illusions: most of those films were terrible, and I didn't get cast in them because of my acting talent. But you take what opportunities come your way, and you make the most of them.'

'Did it ever bother Robert?' Collinsky asked.

'That I was naked? No, it never bothered him. At the end of the day, I was just doing what he told me to.'

'In terms of his direction?'

'Exactly, yeah.' There was a long pause. 'Do you know what he called me the first time he met me?' She stopped again; Collinsky must have shaken his head. 'He said to me, "You are an angel."' Korin was attempting to do an accent, a mash-up of German and American. '"I think you are the most beautiful woman I've met in my life. You're a work of art."'

That same laugh.

'What did you say to that?' Collinsky asked.

'What was I supposed to say?'

'Thank you, I guess.'

Korin laughed again. 'He meant it, that's the thing. Up until that point, a lot of men had said the same thing to me, but most of them were trying to get their hands up my skirt. As a woman at that time, especially in the industry I was in, men were basically trying to molest you every day, and you couldn't do a damn thing about it. It was a male world, top to bottom. But Robert said it, just once, and never followed up on it – at all. I mean, he never touched me, never even asked me out. I had to make the first move. That sadness he had that I talked about, that was powerful. But so was the moment he said those things to me. After the first *Ursula*, he did all his own cinematography. He told the producer on those movies that it was because it would save money, but it wasn't that. It was because he wanted to see me through the lens.'

She stopped, clearing her throat. The tone of her voice was softer, more reflective. 'That probably sounds creepy, but it never felt like that. Sometimes he used to spend hours setting up shots that I was in, even unimportant scenes, trying to frame them just right. No one would care or even notice, but when I watched the rushes back, or I saw it up on screen, I noticed. He never got weird or inappropriate. He never tried to come on to me. This wasn't an obsession. It was simple: he just loved the way I looked.'

The interview continued, Korin and Collinsky's conversation fading into the background as I tried to make some sense of what she'd just said.

' . . . women like Maria Hadak and Veronica Mae.'

It snapped back into focus. I stopped the recording, rewound the audio and listened again. Korin was talking about other women who'd starred in Hosterlitz's Spanish horror movies. I'd heard this once already on the train back home, but on a second listen something registered with me that I'd missed first time.

Veronica Mae.

' . . . Hadak and Veronica Mae,' Korin repeated. 'Veronica did six films with Robert and me, so we were all quite close back then. She got to know us very well.'

'I read that she doesn't live too far away from here,' Collinsky said.

'That's right. She was from Bristol, although you'd never be able to tell. We used to tease her about her plummy accent. But I liked her. We both did. She was the one who actually persuaded Robert and me to buy a house in this area.'

I recalled the scan of the Polaroid that Wendy Fisher had emailed to me, of Korin and Hosterlitz sitting together in Madrid in 1983, his arm around her, her leaning into him. The back of the photo had been scanned in too, where 'Madrid 1983: Bob and Lyn, by Ronnie M' had been written. I'd assumed that Ronnie M was a man. But what if Ronnie M was Veronica Mae?

If she lived close to Korin, if they still spoke, she might be able to provide some insight into Korin as a person. I made a note to track down her address and then listened to the rest of the files.

By the time I was done, I felt jaded. I'd been up since 3.30 a.m. and had spent half the day in the car and the other half in the heat of the city. At 9 p.m., as the light escaped from the sky, I collapsed on to the bed and tried to sleep.

An hour later, I was still awake.

Eventually, I got up again, went to the TV and started trawling Netflix for Robert Hosterlitz's noirs. All four were on there, alongside his western, *The Ghost of the Plains*. Making myself a coffee, I set his debut, *My Evil Heart*, going.

Before I knew it, one film had turned into four.

Over the course of the next six and a half hours, I watched *My Evil Heart*, *Connor O'Hare*, *Only When You're Dead* and *The Eyes of the Night* back to back, only getting to bed at just after five. All four were mesmerizing. But as I lay there in the dark of the bedroom, still unable to drop off, I found it difficult to articulate *why* they had such power. I just knew they did.

The longer I chased an explanation, the more I concentrated on what connected them, the themes they shared. There were the world-weary protagonists: a small-time gangster in *Connor O'Hare* who had become tired of the game; downtrodden cops in both *My Evil Heart* and *The Eyes of the Night*; a private detective struggling for work in *Only When You're Dead*. There was always a murder at the centre of the plot, and the murder always brought the male leads to the doors of a femme fatale. All the men were portrayed as corruptible and weak, the females as liars and seductresses, and Hosterlitz used his Los Angeles settings like labyrinths – an unending maze of streets, of bars, clubs and lounges; of identical houses – that the male characters finally became lost in, unable to distinguish right from wrong. All four used flashbacks – and all ended on a downbeat note.

Each of them was immaculately shot too, a beautiful marriage of light and shadow, the action choreographed and edited with such precision. There were no rough edges, not a single bum note. It was slick, handsome and smart.

There was something in Hosterlitz's dialogue too, the way sentences were constructed and words were used. It was like the characters who populated those four films had some kind of unique vocabulary, a way of speaking and interacting that marked them out as being Hosterlitz creations. It didn't ever feel unnatural or wrong. In fact, quite the opposite: it was almost lyrical, like poetry.

Close to 6 a.m., having not slept at all, I got up again and decided to start streaming *The Ghost of the Plains*, Hosterlitz's western – his fifth studio picture. It had never been rated in the same way as his noirs. It had a bad reputation because it had tanked at the box office in 1967 and ruined any pretensions Hosterlitz may have had about being restored to the A-list. Yet, while it wasn't as good as his earlier films, something echoed through it that I recognized instantly – something unique to the way that Hosterlitz shot his films.

And, eventually, after the sun was up, peeking through the curtains at the living-room windows, it hit me. I finally understood why the movies were so potent and compelling. *It's the way he uses the camera.* He didn't ever utilize fast cuts, rarely panned, never zoomed. Instead, he stationed the camera in one place and *watched* his actors, only tracking slowly, drinking in the intricacies of their performances, the beauty of the scenery surrounding them, the sets, the lighting.

His films weren't ever uninteresting but they *were* static.

He examined. He observed. Sometimes it was even like he'd crept into the scene unnoticed, filming from afar without anyone realizing. In *The Eyes of the Night*, there was a scene where he filmed a two-minute conversation between two actors through the gap between a door and its frame. It gave the whole thing a strange, detached feel. In a way, it made it seem like he was intruding on something – or hiding from view.

As that idea came to me, as I began to imagine the camera as an uninvited guest, that scene grew to become something else. Something discomforting. I started to see the lens as a watcher, a prowler, a voyeur. The concept stayed with me as I lay back on the sofa and closed my eyes, bone-tired. This time around, I dropped off quickly, even while cubes of sunlight filled the room – but my thoughts trailed me into sleep.

My dreams became full of distorted faces, of actors repeating lines, of black and white cities whose streets seemed to go in circles, spiralling further and further towards the centre of their maze. And then, just before I woke again four hours later, sweat-stained and disorientated, the dreams abruptly seemed to darken, and I found myself bound to a chair, in a house I didn't recognize, gagged and frightened, being made to face something in the corner of the room.

Silent, motionless, hidden by shadows.

It was a camera.

16

Any plans I had to leave early for Somerset were over before I even fell asleep, not least because I'd only dropped off at 8 a.m. When I woke again at midday, my head fuzzy, I picked up the phone and called Rough Print to see if they had any copies of the films Lynda Korin had made with her husband in the late 1970s and early 1980s. It turned out I was in luck. The owner of the shop said he had four: *Ursula: Queen Kommandant*, the second of the three *Ursula* films; *The Drill Murders*; *Axe Maniac*; and Hosterlitz's last movie, *Death Island*.

'The only issue,' the owner said, an old man with a slight wheeze, 'is that two of the four films aren't in English. They're dubbed into Italian and Spanish. In fact, English versions of the two dubbed films don't exist any more. Does that matter to you?'

I thought about it. 'That's fine. I'll still take all four.'

'Excellent,' the shop owner said. 'I really am quite pleased. I'm a big fan of Hosterlitz's early work, so I picked these up at an auction in Bilbao about six months ago for next to nothing. But no one has shown the remotest interest in them until you called me. It's so sad how it ended up for him, don't you think?'

I agreed that it was and headed to the Tube.

By the time I was back home from Rough Print, it was after two-thirty. I thought about getting into the car and heading down to Somerset, about paying for a room in a hotel somewhere so I could make sure I got the early start I'd wanted to get today. But then my phone started ringing.

It was Melanie Craw.

'At the risk of sounding like an old, nagging wife,' she said, by way of a greeting, 'you have a doctor's appointment in an hour. You remembered, right?'

I'd forgotten all about it.

'Yes,' I said.

'Don't bullshit me, Raker.'

I was in the kitchen now. From where I was, I could see the untouched bottle of antidepressants on a shelf in the kitchen.

'Do you want me to drag you down there?' she said.

'Look, Craw, I —'

'Let's not forget, at the end of last year, you hit the deck like a rag doll. You need to check in with someone, Raker, just to get the okay. If you *don't* do this, if you keep on pretending that what went on last year didn't happen, next time you might black out and not wake up again.'

'I think that's unlikely.'

'You're a doctor then, are you?'

'Craw, I'm not going to the —'

'Stop being so bloody selfish.'

Her words hung there on the line between us. For a second I thought of the moment with Alex Cavarno at the Comet cinema the day before, and then the guilt started to pool in my stomach again.

'Okay,' I said.

'Good. Let me know what they say.'

And then she was gone. Basically, it was Craw in a nutshell: five seconds after telling me my health was both our concern, she'd hung up on me. I looked at the time, and then over at the four horror films.

For now, they'd have to wait.

My doctor was a small Indian man in his late fifties called Sunil Jhadav. He had an immaculate silver beard and old-fashioned, horn-rimmed spectacles. The first time I'd been in, after I'd blacked out, he'd set up an appointment for me every three months, ostensibly so he could write me a fresh prescription for the antidepressants I never took. But I missed the last one, and I'd only made the one before that because Craw had happened to have a day off and told me she was going to drive me.

'How have you been since February?' he asked.

If it was a jab at me, he'd disguised it well.

'Fine,' I said.

'Headaches?'

'No.'

'Any difficulty speaking, or understanding people?'

'No.'

'Ever feel like you're going to be sick?'

'No, I'm fine.'

He checked my heart and then moved on to my blood pressure. After that, he looked over some scarring I'd sustained to the head, shone a penlight into both my eyes, and then stepped back, rolling his chair out from under his desk.

'Any more blackouts, Mr Raker?'

'No.'

He sat down. 'I'm not sure we ever discussed your medical history.'

I just looked at him.

'It makes for colourful reading, I must say. Injuries to

your back, your hand, you've been stabbed in the stomach, you even had your heart stop on the operating table. Did I ever ask you what it was you did for a living?'

I briefly considered lying about my line of work, but he'd read my medical history. He was smart enough to know that I wasn't holding down a job in retail.

'I find people,' I said.

'Find them?'

'People who are missing.'

'I see.' He adjusted his glasses and slid back in his seat. 'And that appears to be quite dangerous work.' He studied me. 'Are you having trouble sleeping? You look . . . tired.'

I shrugged, recalling the night I'd spent watching Hosterlitz's movies, and the way I couldn't stop thinking about them afterwards – their themes, what linked them, the way the camera sat there and watched, the dream I'd been left with afterwards, when I'd dropped off.

'Is that a yes?' he said.

'I happened to have a bad night last night.'

'I see. Any particular reason?'

'Just work.'

'I see,' he said again. 'Are you feeling depressed at the moment?'

'No.'

His head rocked to one side and he pursed his lips, like he was having a conversation with himself. 'Do you mind if I ask whether you have any family?'

I frowned. 'I have a daughter.'

'Anyone else?'

'No.'

'No wife or partner?'

'My wife died.'

'I'm sorry to hear that. What about brothers or sisters?'

'No.'

'You're an only child?'

'Yes.'

'Parents?'

'What's the relevance of this?'

He nodded again, this time more forcefully, as if my answers were helping cement whatever conclusion he'd reached. 'How long ago did your wife die?'

'That's got nothing to do with anything.'

'Mr Raker,' he said, his voice suddenly softer. 'I don't know how honest you've been with me, but I'm guessing not very.' He waited for a response, as if he expected me to fight him on it. 'You're alone, you're tired, you can't sleep, you may even be having a delayed reaction to the trauma of burying these people you cared about. You were diagnosed with PTSD back in November, you had chronic fatigue, were probably depressed. As a result of that, you were referred to a psychologist, yet I can see from your notes that you never turned up to any of those appointments at the hospital.' He stopped again, steepling his fingers in front of his face. 'It's difficult to move forward if we don't know precisely what is wrong with you, and earning a living in a world where, as a matter of course, you're attacked with knives, and sustain blows to the head . . . well, I can assure you, that isn't going to help you recover what you've lost.'

'What I've lost?'

His eyes strayed to the scarring on my head, to other scars he knew I had on my body. 'I used to have a friend, back in Mumbai, who worked as a detective for the Indian Police Service. He joined after his brothers were killed in a house burglary. He never wanted to be a policeman, not really, although I dare say he was good at it, but he thought the police service might bring him some answers; maybe he thought it would address the emptiness he felt. But you can't bring back the dead, Mr Raker, and trying to do so . . . well, that will make you careless. My point is, this job of yours might cost you your life. And maybe it won't be because you get stabbed. Maybe it will be because you're sick.'

'I'm not sick.'

'How do you know if you don't turn up for your appointments and don't take the pills I prescribe you? Mr Raker, I don't know you. I don't know how long your wife has been dead. But the only reason to do the kind of work you do is to make something right.'

He looked at me, almost as if he pitied me.

'Grief is a sickness, Mr Raker. My friend – the one I was just telling you about – he was so devastated from the loss of his brothers, he felt so much the need to avenge them, the grief he carried was so heavy, that he tried to take down a gang of four thieves one night in November 2010, entirely on his own.' He shrugged. 'They lured him into a dead end, and then they shot him in the back of the head.'

We stayed there in silence for a moment, looking at each other, and then Jhadav opened up his hands. 'In the end,' he said quietly, 'my friend chose not to see what was coming. Just make sure you don't do the same thing.'

PART TWO

'You know what they used to call this place?'

Ray Callson is looking out of a window to the left of him. Five floors below, traffic is backed up along Wilshire Boulevard in a long, unbroken line. Nothing moves out there. It's just late-afternoon sky and the shimmer of exhaust fumes. Above the whirr of the camera and the hum of air conditioning, it's possible to hear car horns and police sirens in the distance, and there's music closer by – the deep thump of a bassline.

He turns back to the camera. 'Do you know?'

'Do I know what?' a voice responds.

'What they used to call this place?'

'You mean, Los Angeles?'

'Right.' Callson glances out of the window again. 'When my old man moved here – back in the early twenties – they used to call it the "white spot of America". Did you know that?'

'No.'

'Yeah. LA was billed as this Protestant promised land where you could live in peace and harmony among your own kind. But it was all bullshit. Blacks, Latinos, Asians – they were already here. I mean, this place doubled its population in the twenties – you think that happened because only white people came to live here?'

'Do you think it's better or worse now?'

'LA?' Callson tears his eyes away from the view and looks back at the camera. 'I don't know. All I know is that everything in this place is a lie. Always has been, always will be. By the middle of the twenties, they had six hundred brothels in the city. You could get your dick sucked by another man at a Ninety-Six Club a few blocks from City Hall. We had communists running around Boyle Heights. We had elephants and circus freaks luring people out to housing developments with the promise of a free lunch, and people gawping at the corner of Wilshire and La Brea because they'd never seen neon signs before. Some white Protestant promised land, huh? All it was, all it is, is a magic show. LA was a lie back then, and it's a lie now. There's no black or white here. There's just grey.'

'You sound frustrated.'

Callson smirks. 'Yeah, I guess I am. That's something you learn to get used to as a homicide detective. The frustration. Thirty to forty per cent of all the cases you take on, you won't solve. That's just a fact. You gotta face reality.'

'Is that because people lie?'

'Not always.'

'But most of the time?'

'Yeah, most of the time people lie. You spend enough time in this city, I honestly think it gets into your blood. It becomes a part of who you are. You're lying without even realizing. I mean, what do you expect from a place where men and women stand around on studio lots, in make-believe sets, and get paid to pretend they're someone else? Of course they're gonna lie. They're doing it every day of their lives. It becomes second nature.' He shrugs. 'This city is just a magic show. Everyone's got a trick.'

17

In the end, I decided to get out of London.

I stayed in Bristol, at a hotel near Temple Meads station. It was one of the last rooms I could find, as the bank holiday weekend had accounted for everything else. After checking in, I took a walk through the crowds at the Harbourside, found something to eat, then returned to the room, keeping the lights off and the air conditioning on, and sat at the window, looking out to where the spire of St Mary Redcliffe rose upwards like a pale blade out of the earth. Six floors up, everything below me seemed stilled, more obscure; all suggestion and shadow.

After a while, I made myself some coffee and grabbed my rucksack off the floor. Inside were the four horror films Korin had made with Robert Hosterlitz.

The set had cost me £44, which seemed steep for four movies no one else in the city had even looked at in the entire time they'd been on sale at Rough Print. The owner suggested a book too, *Dia de los Muertos*, about the European horror movie industry in the 1970s and 1980s, which included a section on Hosterlitz – or, rather, Bob Hozer, the alias he'd gone by during that time. I'd decided to take it when I saw that it had a chapter on the *Ursula* films and a transcript of the panel Korin did at the Screenmageddon convention in 2011. That had been the same panel that both Marc Collinsky and Louis Grant had attended. In the end, it proved to be the only public appearance Korin would do at an event like that in the years after she walked away from acting.

The four films were all shrink-wrapped and sported equally lurid covers. *Ursula: Queen Kommandant* had a full-length colour photograph of Lynda Korin in her mid twenties, in a ridiculously tight shirt, buttons open far enough to reveal the curves of both breasts, a swastika stitched on to one of her pockets. Above a title awash in blood was a tagline: *She'll make you scream for more!*

The cover for *The Drill Murders* was grisly – a close-up shot of an unseen assailant, just his hand visible, about to start drilling into the head of a screaming woman. It was the Italian version of the film, so I understood nothing of the copy on the back, but a ridiculous tagline on the front, written in English – *Drill, drill, drill! Kill, kill, kill!* – helped to offset the gratuitous, somewhat distressing nature of the photo. When I checked the credits, I saw Hosterlitz again listed as Bob Hozer – as cinematographer, editor, writer and director – and another name I recognized in the cast: Veronica Mae. Out of interest, I logged on to IMDb again and found a photo for her, taken in her twenties. She was petite, pretty, with long, sandy hair and a tiny beauty spot at her nose. It was her eyes that stood out, though – they were a startling green, like chips of jade.

The covers of the other two films I'd bought – the English version of *Axe Maniac*, and *Death Island* in Spanish – were basically just repeats of each other: both featured a generic, buxom woman running away screaming, one in a forest, another on a sandy beach fringed with palm trees.

The room came kitted out with a DVD player, so I removed *Ursula* from its case and dropped it into the tray, flicking through *Dia de los Muertos* while it loaded up. In the section on Hosterlitz's years as Bob Hozer, there was a page examining his shot composition. One section in particular caught my attention:

Most critics agree that Hosterlitz was never the same film-maker once he was forced to flee the US in 1954, even when making his comeback as a writer-director in 1967 for big-budget western *The Ghost of the Plains*. But, in truth, even when you examine his horror films, beyond the shambolic nature of the acting, his loss of confidence as a writer, the illness, addiction and depression that skewed and neutered his talents, Hosterlitz was still showing flashes of that same innate brilliance during the 1960s, 1970s and 1980s: in the beauty of his shot composition, in the way the camera lingers and reveals, in the minute expressions he captures in trademark close-up, or in the scenes he watches from a distance.

That description of his shot composition all rang true based on what I'd seen of his noirs the previous night, and while the second *Ursula* film proved to be an absolute mess – violent and tedious, ramshackle, full of gratuitous nudity and toneless acting – once you set your mind to it, it was easy to start locating those same Hosterlitz trademarks, even while they were more infrequent. The difference was, in his noirs, the observation of the scene, of the characters and their stories, was supported by actors like Veronica Lake and Glen Cramer. By the time he made *Ursula*, Hosterlitz's gift for dialogue was gone, ground out of him during his decline, and he no longer had the actors for it, anyway.

I sat through countless shots of women showering, a couple of prolonged sex scenes, a disembowelling, a man being stretched on a torture rack, and then decided to fast-forward through the rest, only stopping when a moment arose that I recognized as truly belonging to Hosterlitz. The more I watched, the easier they became to spot, flourishes that were like ghosts from another time.

When I was done with *Ursula*, I grabbed the copy of *Axe Maniac* and set it running. It was easily as terrible, maybe even a little worse. Korin's performance turned out to be the best of an awful bunch, but again there were glimpses of Hosterlitz's identifying style among all the chaos: individual scenes – flawless, coherent – that stood out a mile. The moment I spotted them, I paused the action and watched them properly, and then hit Fast-Forward once they were over.

Gradually, something started to dawn on me.

There was a pattern, a connection between all the moments that I chose to pause on: it was that the best scenes, the ones where the genius of the man rose above the artlessness of the films, were always the ones featuring exactly the same person.

Lynda Korin.

In *Ursula*, and even more in *Axe Maniac* where she just had a supporting role, any time Korin was onscreen by herself – alone, or away from the rest of the cast – Hosterlitz got his act together. He treated her scenes with a reverence and care that he never bothered to apply to any other part of the movie. She was lit perfectly, he reduced the dialogue she had – so she wouldn't be shown up as a mediocre actress – and he simply watched her.

When he filmed her from a distance, he'd use wide shots and little in the way of music or sound effects, concentrating on her, on things like her humming to herself, or the sound of her footsteps as she wandered around the rooms of a house. Or he'd do the complete opposite and come in tight to her and listen to the rhythm of her breathing, repeatedly using a device where her eyes acted as a mirror, reflecting back other people in the same scene – as if she were the window to the whole movie. But anything else in the film, any time the other actors were involved, it changed. The rest of it was subordinate to whatever he did with Korin. He'd whip through reams of dialogue, even if other actors were mumbling or delivering lines with zero expression, and scenes without Korin were never lit as well, or framed as exactly as hers. Yet the minute Korin had a scene where she was alone, there was a complete reversal of quality. *That* was when you caught a glimpse of the man Hosterlitz had been; the director whose film had won seven Oscars.

Pausing the action on a close-up of Korin, I shuffled forward on the bed. Her profile was frozen onscreen, the vague hint of the film's deranged killer in the background, the contrast between the dark of his silhouette and the flawless, snow-white of her skin so stark and beautiful it could have been a still from one of the noirs. The more I looked at the perfect composition of the shot, the more I wondered whether Hosterlitz's approach in these scenes simply came down to nepotism, to a husband favouring the contributions of his wife, or whether it was something even more deliberate.

When I allowed the scene to snap into life again, something Korin had said in the interview with Collinsky came back to me: *Do you know what he called me the first time he met me?* she'd asked. *He said to me, 'You are an angel . . . You're a work of art.'* The more I thought about that, the more I started to recall about the rest of her interview: *He wanted to see me through the lens. Sometimes he used to spend hours setting up shots that I was in, even unimportant scenes, trying to frame them just right.*

This wasn't an obsession, she'd said to Collinsky.

Except now, in this moment, it felt like that was *exactly* what it was. It was eerie and slightly discomfiting knowing how he'd felt about her, and seeing the results playing out. As the camera lingered on her, it was almost like a soundless conversation between them; between the stillness and lure of Korin's beauty and the constancy of Hosterlitz's camera. I felt like an uninvited stranger standing at the window of a house, straying into the privacy of someone else's life.

I continued to watch, the film rolling towards its conclusion. The axe maniac of the title had noisily butchered eight people at a dinner party and was now pursuing Korin's character and her onscreen boyfriend, the hero of the movie, through the rooms of a house. The film had regressed again now that other characters had become involved, a mess of confused camerawork, bad editing and worse acting.

But then, as the hero sacrificed himself for his girlfriend, as Korin finished off the killer with his own axe and stood there, breathless, bloodied and alone, it all started to change again. The music dropped out. The camera started to move.

And something weird began to happen.

18

It started with a wide shot, inside a living room, with Korin perched on the edge of an armchair, spattered in blood, and the killer lying on the floor at her feet.

Slowly, the camera began dollying in towards her, in profile, motionless on the edge of the chair, her eyes downcast. There was no music, no sound at all except Korin's breathing, which got louder and louder the closer the camera got to her. Halfway between the camera's starting position and Korin, the sound of her heartbeat began to fade in too, thumping in the spaces *between* breaths, like the distant pulse of tribal drums. I'd seen continuous evidence of Hosterlitz's fascination with Korin throughout the movie, in *Ursula* too, but this was different: it was a truly incongruous moment, a much longer, slower, more intense movement in towards her – almost like we, as the audience, were creeping up on her, unseen. There were no other actors left to disturb her, no lines left to speak, no scenes to play out, nothing that could draw the camera's attention away from her.

It was just her and us.

I expected the camera to come to a halt once it reached her – but it didn't. Instead, it inched right past Korin, towards the corner of the room, where a walnut-cased television set was playing soundlessly. The TV was showing footage from the inside of a car as it drove slowly along a nondescript street. I could make out the upper windows in a series of three-storey buildings, the camera tilted so that only the very tops of people's heads were visible at the bottom of the shot. The footage ran for ten seconds and then ended.

The titles came up.

As the credits rolled, I sat there in the silence of the hotel room, unsure of what I'd just watched. Rewinding the film again, I played it from the moment after the killer was offed, when the movie seemed to switch tone, the camera began its slow dolly in towards her, and Korin's breathing faded in, her heartbeat. Once it was past her and zeroing in on the television set in the corner, I inched closer, remote control in hand, ready to stop it. As soon as I had a clear view of the footage on the walnut-cased TV, I hit Pause.

Whoever had taken the footage seemed to be deliberately angling the lens upwards, only the heads of occasional pedestrians drifting into view. Nothing else at street level was visible, just the upper-floor windows on a road full of unrecognizable buildings.

I watched it again from beginning to end.

The whole scene lasted ninety seconds, the slow dolly in towards Korin *so* slow that it took two-thirds of that time before the camera actually passed Korin at all. A shot lasting a minute and a half was a long time when nothing was actually happening – no movement of people, no dialogue – and it seemed especially frivolous when it was tagged on to the end of a film whose total running time was a fraction above eighty minutes.

It was more than the weird dissonance of the footage too; it was the fact that it was so beautiful, elegant and composed.

I picked up the copy of *Dia de los Muertos* and skipped to the chapter on Hosterlitz, searching for anything related to the scene, any discussion of it at all. There was nothing; no mention of it. However, in the transcript of the panel that

Korin had done at Screenmageddon, something caught my eye.

MODERATOR: Next question. Uh . . . the guy in the red shirt.

JOURNALIST: Hey Lynda, how you doing? I'm Bill Martinez from CinemaTechniques.com in San Diego. Big horror fan, big fan of your work. Huge, huge fan of your late husband as well.

KORIN: Oh, thank you. That's really kind.

JOURNALIST: You're welcome. Anyway, uh . . . my question is about a film you did with Robert in 1982 called *Die Slowly.*

KORIN: I remember it, yeah.

JOURNALIST: Great. I managed to get hold of a dubbed version of *Die Slowly* at a market in Barcelona, on a trip out there in May. What I wanted to ask you about, if you can even remember it, was one of the scenes in that movie.

KORIN: I'll try my best.

JOURNALIST: It's right at the end of the film, after the monster is dead, when your character is looking out from the cabin at all the dead bodies scattered in the forest. Anyway, there's this amazing shot where the camera starts at the back door of the cabin and moves in towards you at the front windows. You're side-on to the audience – you know, in profile – and the camera keeps on dollying in towards you, and then goes right the way *past* you, and there's no music any more, just your breathing.

I stopped for a second and returned to the start of the question, double-checking that this guy wasn't talking about *Axe*

Maniac, the film I'd just watched. He wasn't. He was talking about *Die Slowly*, which had come out two years *after* the release of *Axe Maniac*. I had to reread the same section a third time, just to be certain I'd understood it correctly: Hosterlitz had included a virtually identical scene in two of his films, two years apart – both featuring Lynda Korin.

KORIN: I think I remember that scene, yeah.

JOURNALIST: It just felt so odd – in a good way! The rest of the film is so frenetic and bloody, and then you've got that scene, which feels like it's been transported in from a Hosterlitz picture of old. You know, like *Connor O'Hare* or something.

MODERATOR: So have you got a question for Lynda, sir?

JOURNALIST: Sorry. I guess my question is . . . Why wasn't *all* of the film shot like that? It seems like that scene was singled out for special treatment – I was just wondering why, basically.

KORIN: I'm not sure.

JOURNALIST: There was no special reason for it?

KORIN: Not that I remember. It was a long time ago.

JOURNALIST: Do you remember the bit with the TV?

I could hardly rip my eyes away from the page now.

KORIN: The bit with the TV?

JOURNALIST: Yeah. That was also quite weird.

KORIN: No, I'm not sure I do.

JOURNALIST: The camera passes you and moves right into the TV in the corner of the room, which is playing footage shot from inside a car – it looks like a residential street maybe.

KORIN: Really? I don't remember that.

JOURNALIST: There's a similar section at the end of another movie you did with Robert, in 1979 – *Hell Trip*. People tell me there's one in *Axe Maniac* too, although I've never seen that.

I was stunned.

If the journalist was right, that made three films now – *Hell Trip*, *Axe Maniac* and *Die Slowly* – each with the same scene of Korin repeated at the end.

The question from the journalist never really got properly answered. Korin apologized again and repeated that she didn't remember the scenes, that she barely remembered a lot about the actual movies themselves, only the time she spent with Hosterlitz making them. It was hard to tell from the transcript whether she was sidestepping the question or answering it honestly, but I didn't know why she *wouldn't* have had a conversation with her husband about what exactly the scene was about.

Grabbing my pad and a pen, I started to make some notes, attempting to put my thoughts into some sort of order. The first two *Ursula* films were set during the Second World War, and the third just after it – before the advent of television in homes – so despite some trademark Hosterlitz moments, as the camera lingered on Korin alone, watched her, followed her, there had been no replication of the scene in *Axe Maniac*, or of the ones that the journalist had referred to in *Die Slowly* and *Hell Trip*. But what about the other eight films that Hosterlitz had made with Korin between 1979 and 1984?

I grabbed the copy of *The Drill Murders*, removed the wrapping and fired it up. I didn't bother watching it properly, not least because it was in Italian and I wouldn't understand a word of it anyway. I just kept my thumb on

Fast-Forward and an eye out for anything that looked like an echo of the scene I'd watched in *Axe Maniac*. I knew if it was going to be anywhere, it would be at the end.

Which was exactly where I found it.

Korin, who barely seemed to have featured in the movie at all, was in the kitchen of a house, a knife in her hand. Her face, neck and vest were all covered in blood. Again, the final scene of the movie began with a slow dolly in towards her, across a kitchen this time. As in the others, there was no music – just her breathing and her heartbeat. Behind her, on the counter, a television was playing – and onscreen was exactly the same footage of the street, shot from inside a car.

What the hell is going on?

I unwrapped *Death Island* and did the same, fast-forwarding through the entire film. At the very end, just like the others, I found the same scene *again*. The fact that the movie was in Spanish made no difference; at this point, there was no dialogue anyway, just a near-identical sequence.

Pulling my laptop towards me, I went online to see if I could find any discussion of the repeated scene, because I had a hard time believing no one else except a journalist, maybe a few hardcore Hosterlitz fans, and now me, had taken note of it. His noirs got mentions on a number of forums, while his horror films were listed on a site that detailed every movie that made it on to the Department of Public Prosecution's Video Nasties list in the 1980s – which included Hosterlitz's *Ursula of the SS* and *Savages of the Amazon*. I found various mentions of him on Wiki and list sites, but none dealt with the particular scene I was interested in.

At the point of giving up, I finally stumbled across an American horror movie forum called Darker Screen. That was where I found something.

19

A forum thread titled 'Ursula of the SS, Directed by Robert Hosterlitz AKA Bob Hozer – THIS FILM ABSO-LUTELY STINKS!' had been created on 22 October 2008, and was set up by someone who had clearly just watched the film for the first time, and whose exposure to Hosterlitz's horror movies had been limited.

#1 | Posted by ListicalNinja on 10/22/08 | Member since 2002

Picked up a copy of 'Ursula of the SS' yesterday from a secondhand store close to where I live (Milwaukee). Has anyone else seen it? Hard to believe it's directed by Robert 'The Eyes of the Night' Hosterlitz. It's TERRIBLE.

I continued down the page. People were slow to respond, which suggested that either the forum didn't get a lot of traffic, or the subject matter had failed to ignite the imagination of the people posting. When I took a look at some of the other threads, I quickly decided it was the latter. Hosterlitz wasn't a big draw, and even among this community, neither were his horror films.

#2 | Posted by MickeyMooney on 11/03/08 | Member since 2003

Saw it ages ago and I agree it sucks a fat one. Have you watched any of the films he made AFTER that? They're supposed to be even worse.

#3 | Posted by CollarMeBaddUK on 11/03/08 | Member since 2000

I've seen 'Axe Maniac', but most of them you can't even buy any more. Not sure about in the States. Maybe you can still get all of Hosterlitz's Spanish-made films there, ListicalNinja . . . ?

#4 | Posted by ListicalNinja on 11/03/08 | Member since 2002

Nah. It's the same here too. I can only find a few of his films in English. There might be some dubbed versions available somewhere, but most of his movies are vapour – the original negatives have probably been lost forever.

#5 | Posted by PinheadMcTavish on 11/03/08 | Member since 2002

Yeah, those films are gone and they ain't coming back. In fact, rumour has it that the last time anyone saw them, they were in a plain brown envelope being mailed to 'XXXL Landfill Site, Siberia' ☺

A user called MelissaA posted about the availability of Hosterlitz's horror films, informing the thread that, of the movies he'd made after he left the States for the final time in 1970, only *House of Darkness* – which he shot in the UK in 1971 and whose troubled production Collinsky had referenced in his article – the *Ursula* trilogy and *Axe Maniac* were still available to buy in English. Four others were available in Europe – three in Spanish, and one in Italian – but most users on the forum seemed to agree copies would be rare, and difficult to locate. It tallied with what the guy from Rough Print had told me.

After MelissaA talked briefly about Hosterlitz suffering a stroke in 1974 and his addiction to painkillers in the years before he moved to Spain, the subject shifted to Lynda Korin – and, among male posters, the size of her breasts.

#33 | Posted by CollarMeBaddUK on 11/05/08 | Member since 2000

Lynda Korin = ☺ AM I RIGHT?

#34 | Posted by PinheadMcTavish on 11/05/08 | Member since 2002

Yeah, she's definitely a contender for a BREAST Actress Award. ☺ ☺ ☺

#35 | Posted by MickeyMooney on 11/05/08 | Member since 2003

She would have been great in a remake of The TIT and the Pendulum.

#36 | Posted by PinheadMcTavish on 11/05/08 | Member since 2002

ROFL. Wonder what a woman like that ever saw in Hosterlitz?

My gaze lingered briefly on that last post.

Pretty soon, the thread fizzled out and remained entirely dormant for over two years. But then, at the start of 2011, someone posted about Korin's upcoming appearance at the Screenmageddon convention.

#58 | Posted by CollarMeBaddUK on 01/22/11 | Member since 2000

If anyone out there is still interested in Robert Hosterlitz's career, Lynda Korin is appearing at Screenmageddon in London on 7 July. She never does public events so could be worth a look. Tickets available <u>here</u>. I'm going!

#59 | Posted by PinheadMcTavish on 02/04/11 | Member since 2002

Shit! She's still pretty hot. How old is she now?

#60 | Posted by CollarMeBaddUK on 02/04/11 | Member since 2000

58, believe it or not. Hope my wife looks like that when she's 58 ☺

#60 | Posted by MickeyMooney on 02/05/11 | Member since 2003

Man, I hope my GF looks as good as that when she's 28!!! LOL. If it wasn't gonna cost me $$$$$, I'd be in London faster than the Flash.

After that, there was another long gap between posts – over three years. But then, in June 2014, the thread suddenly got bumped, thanks to a fresh post.

It was from Marc Collinsky.

#61 | Posted by MarcCollinskyCine on 06/12/14 | Member since 2014

Hello everyone. Not sure if this is going to be seen by anybody, as there doesn't seem to have been much activity on here since 2011, but my name is Marc Collinsky and I'm a writer at Cine Magazine in the UK. Good news: I'm interviewing Lynda Korin about Robert Hosterlitz in a couple of weeks, and being a big fan of Hosterlitz's early work, this is VERY EXCIT-ING. Bad news: I know his film and TV work back to front up until the third 'Ursula' film in 1978, then it all gets a bit fuzzy. I've managed to get hold of a copy of 'Axe Maniac', which I've never seen before, but I haven't been able to find a trace of the others anywhere. Does anyone know where I can find them?

#62 | Posted by MickeyMooney on 06/14/14| Member since 2003

Welcome aboard Marc! Yeah, you're shit out of luck if you're hoping to find copies (in English) of anything other than 'Ursula 1–3' and 'Axe Maniac'. Even eBay don't have them. You might have to find a specialist collector somewhere – otherwise it's Hozer and out ☺

#63 | Posted by MarcCollinskyCine on 06/14/14 | Member since 2014

Appreciate it, MickeyMooney. If anyone has any sugges-tions for questions, then feel free to put them out there. I can't promise I'll ask them but I'm especially thinking in terms of the 11 films he made after 'Ursula 1–3'.

#64 | Posted by PinheadMcTavish on 06/14/14 | Member since 2002

Number one priority: let us know if Lynda Korin is still hot!!!!!

I scrolled through the rest of the page, and through the next one too, the subject returning to Korin's nude scenes, to predictable discussions about the size of her breasts and how good she looked in 2011, in her late fifties.

But then I got to the bottom of the page.

Here, someone new had posted.

#76 | Posted by Microscope on 06/15/14 | Member since 2014

I've got a question you can ask Lynda Korin: why does every film she made between 1979 and 1984 have exactly the same ending?

20

The poster was someone calling themselves 'Microscope'. They'd never posted on the forum before and appeared to have joined solely to raise the question of the repeated ending. MelissaA – the most sensible of the regulars – responded first.

#77 | Posted by MelissaA on 06/15/14 | Member since 2007

Welcome Microscope! What do you mean, 'the same ending'?

#78 | Posted by Microscope on 06/15/14 | Member since 2014

Which of Hosterlitz's films have you seen, MelissaA?

#79 | Posted by MelissaA on 06/15/14 | Member since 2007

All of them up to 'Ursula 3', as well as 'Axe Maniac'.

#80 | Posted by Microscope on 06/15/14 | Member since 2014

Then you won't know what I'm talking about.

#81 | Posted by PinheadMcTavish on 06/15/14 | Member since 2002

Psycho alert!

#82 | Posted by MelissaA on 06/15/14 | Member since 2007

Uh, OK. So why don't you TELL me what you're talking about?

#83 | Posted by Microscope on 06/15/14 | Member since 2014

All 11 films he made in Spain after 'Ursula 1–3', from 'Cemetery House' in 1979 to 'Death Island' in 1984, have the same last scene in them. The only reason no one on this forum realizes that is the case is because 'Axe Maniac' is relatively easily available, and in English, whereas four other films are only in Italian or Spanish and much harder to track down, and the other six are gone for ever. Trust me, the last 90 seconds of all 11 films he made during that time – but for some minor differences – are the same.

#84 | Posted by MelissaA on 06/15/14 | Member since 2007

Are you serious?

#85 | Posted by Microscope on 06/15/14 | Member since 2014

100% serious.

#86 | Posted by MelissaA on 06/15/14 | Member since 2007

How have you managed to see all 11? Very few places have copies of ONE of those foreign language films, let alone all four. But not only are you telling us you've seen those four, but you've seen the other six 'lost' films as well? I call bull-shit, sir! You said yourself, the six lost films are gone for ever.

#87 | Posted by CollarMeBaddUK on 06/15/14 | Member since 2000

You tell him, MelissaA! Yeah, it seems unlikely. As I under-stand it, re the six 'lost' films, it was a combination of a lot of the distribution prints not being returned, and then the production company going up in smoke in '86.

#88 | Posted by Microscope on 06/15/14 | Member since 2014

Believe whatever you want to believe.

#89 | Posted by CollarMeBaddUK on 06/15/14 | Member since 2000

Why would he repeat the same scene in all of his movies, Microscope? That makes about as much sense as an episode of 'Geordie Shore'. I think people might have noticed if a scene had been repeated 11 times.

#90 | Posted by Microscope on 06/15/14 | Member since 2014

People have noticed. Ask Bill Martinez at CinemaTech-niques.com. The problem is, me, Bill, and the six or seven people that have been posting on this thread for the last six years make up the 00000000.1% of the Earth's population who actually still give a shit about what Hosterlitz did after

'The Ghost of the Plains' bombed. So if none of you noticed, how was the rest of the world supposed to?

#91 | Posted by MarcCollinskyCine on 06/15/14 | Member since 2014

Hey Microscope! Is there some way we can talk on email? Marc C.

#92 | Posted by Microscope on 06/15/14 | Member since 2014

No. I'm not emailing you, DMing or anything else. Just ask Korin this: why did Hosterlitz repeat the same scene 11 times? See what she says.

#93 | Posted by MarcCollinskyCine on 06/15/14 | Member since 2014

And what do you think she'll say?

#94 | Posted by Microscope on 06/15/14 | Member since 2014

I don't know. But she knows more about Hosterlitz than the rest of us can ever hope to learn. Those films have the same ending. Same soundtrack. Same voice-over. Are we seriously suggesting she didn't notice?

Same ending. Same soundtrack. Same voice-over.
What voice-over?
No one really picked up on the comment about the VO. It got lost among a discussion about the repeated scene, about Korin, about Hosterlitz as a director. I looked at my

TV, where *Death Island* was paused on the credits, picked up the remote control and rewound it. I stopped it just before the beginning of the end sequence, where the ninety-second dolly began. Pulling a chair in close to the TV, I plugged my headphones in and pressed Play. I wanted to cancel out as much peripheral noise as possible – from the hotel room, from the people passing in the corridor, from the traffic rumbling past outside. All I wanted to hear was the film.

The sequence began.

I listened hard as the sound of the heartbeat and Korin's breathing began to get louder. That was all I'd heard on the soundtrack up until now, and it was all I could hear again. There was no voice-over. The heartbeat and breathing reached a crescendo about halfway between the camera's starting point and where Korin was positioned, and then it began to drop off a little as the camera finally reached Korin and manoeuvred past her towards the TV set.

I rewound it for what felt like the hundredth time and played everything over again. This time I didn't watch the sequence, I just ducked my head away from the TV so the images wouldn't distract me, pressed my headphones deeper into my ears and listened. I heard the familiar sound of her breathing fading in, her heartbeat. I tried to will myself to hear beyond them both.

Then, vaguely, I caught the tail end of something.

Like a whisper.

It was the first time I'd heard it. It was so soft I wasn't sure if I'd even heard it at all. I hit Rewind on the remote and spun the film back ten seconds. This time, as the camera drew level with Korin and began heading towards the TV set, I turned the volume right the way up.

My head thumped in protest.

But this time the whisper was even clearer. It was the softest of voices, half hidden within the breathing and the heartbeat, like the glimpse of a silhouette. I couldn't quite pick up what was being said, so I rewound it again. On the next play, I realized it was a man, but his voice was so delicate, so deliberately gentle, it was almost feminine.

I rewound it yet again, playing it through, and this time I picked up the hint of an accent in the man's voice.

He was saying, 'You don't know who you are.'

He was saying it over and over. 'You don't know who you are. You don't know who you are. You don't know who you are.' He was repeating it constantly behind the noise of the heartbeat and the breathing. 'You don't know who you are.' He did it all in the same, soft timbre, and it didn't stop until the credits rolled.

You don't know who you are.

The voice belonged to Robert Hosterlitz.

21

After a restless night's sleep, I woke up after seven, showered, and headed down to breakfast. The restaurant stank of fried food, the buffet loaded with trays of oily bacon, eggs and hash browns. I stuck to cereal, fruit and coffee, then took my laptop to a table in the far corner of the room.

At just gone eight, I tried Marc Collinsky.

He was in Berlin, but I hoped by calling early I'd catch him before he headed out to whatever event he was there to cover. It worked. He said he was about to board a train, so I got right to the point and gave him an overview of what I'd discovered the previous night – including the voice-over.

'Voice-over?' Collinsky said.

'You didn't know about that?'

'I remember that person on the forum – Microscope – they said something about a voice-over, but I never really followed it up because they were just so weird and unhelpful. You said you think the VO is actually Hosterlitz himself?'

'It sounds exactly like him. I watched a documentary about him that was floating around on YouTube. He speaks in an American accent but it's got that slight Germanic tone. He keeps saying, "You don't know who you are" over the film's ending. Does that mean anything to you? Is it related to any of his movies?'

'No. Well, not that I can think of. When I interviewed Korin that first time, I'd only managed to see *Axe Maniac*, so

I had nothing much to go on – in terms of the stuff about the repeated scenes – other than a weird theory some stranger online was pushing my way. But, in between the first interview and the second, I got in touch with a journalist in our Spanish office and she managed to track down a copy of *Hell Trip*, through a collector.'

'That was when you realized the same scene was repeated?'

'Right. Near identical in both movies.'

'Did you bring it up with Korin in that second interview?'

'Not *during* the interview, but I did afterwards,' he said, which explained why I hadn't heard him pose the question on either of the audio files he'd sent over. 'She said she just went along with whatever Hosterlitz asked. She wasn't an actress, she was a model, so she never questioned the direction she was given.'

'Did you believe her?'

'Yeah, I think she was being honest. She was always the first person to tell you that her acting abilities were limited. She just did what Hosterlitz asked her.'

'But being asked to do the same scene eleven times?'

'Maybe she just never thought that hard about it, or maybe she figured it was some kind of calling card for Hosterlitz. You know, something he included to identify the film as one of his – like a Saul Bass title sequence, or the Kubrick Stare.' He stopped, sighed a little. 'But I don't know. Maybe she *was* lying to me. I just never got that sense from her. I really didn't. I honestly believe that she respected Hosterlitz's artistic vision.'

'Okay,' I said. He didn't feel like she was lying and maybe she wasn't – but something was going on. I changed direction. 'So what do you think they mean?'

'Mean?'

'Those scenes. The films I watched last night, they're terrible. They're full of sloppy editing, shrieking music, there's no subtlety or craft to them – apart from those scenes with Korin when she's alone. Those moments feel completely different.'

A tannoy started up in the background of the call. When it was over, Collinsky said, 'I don't think there's any doubt that their inclusion was completely intentional. He must have been aware that he could get away with putting them in, because no critics were reviewing his work, and punters at the time didn't care about the story because they were too busy getting their fill of blood and boobs. And then, almost as soon as those films were out, they were forgotten again, and Hosterlitz was prepping his next, terrible horror movie. He wasn't as prolific as some of the European horror directors like Franco or Fulci, but he was making them fast enough that they came and went in the blink of an eye.'

He stopped, but I could tell he wasn't finished. 'I need to get the train in a minute, but if you want my opinion, I think those scenes are some kind of allegory, probably for the way he was treated by Hollywood. The dolly into her represents the path of his career. The blood on Korin symbolizes the way he was stabbed in the back by the HUAC hearings, the way Hollywood fed him to the wolves. It's a statement on the death of his career, and probably – given the lurid red of the blood – some sort of comment on him being labelled a communist as well. Did you listen to the interviews I sent you?'

'Yeah, a few times.'

'Then you would have heard Korin talking about how Hosterlitz called her an "angel". A lot of people say he was obsessed with her, and I think they're probably right, but I don't think it was in a scary, stalkerish way. Why would she marry him if he was some psycho? I think he was obsessed with her *beauty*, the way she looked. And so he used her as a sort of canvas to paint everything on, because she was a part of his life too, like the HUAC. Maybe the major part. After all, when everyone else turned their backs on him, Korin didn't.'

Some of that felt like a stretch, but what Collinsky had said about Korin, about Hosterlitz being obsessed with her, resonated with me. I'd thought the same thing the night before.

'All right,' I said. 'So what about the television?'

'The one that plays that footage being shot from inside a car?'

'Yeah. What do you think that's about?'

'Absolutely no idea.'

'No theory about what street it's showing?'

'Sorry.' Collinsky paused. I could hear him moving, the squeal of train brakes, the hum of people's voices. 'But there might be someone who does.'

'Microscope,' I said.

'Right. I just don't know how the hell you find him.'

I called Louis Grant at AKI and asked him the same questions I'd asked Collinsky, but he was similarly unsure, so I returned to my room to get my things together, then sat down in front of my laptop again. Going to the forum I'd looked at the night before, I found the Hosterlitz thread and the posts from Microscope, and clicked on the name. It took me to a public profile. When users signed up to the forum, they had to provide some personal information – but it amounted to very little, and there was nothing to stop them from lying about who they were. Age, sex, location – it could all have been faked.

I studied Microscope's profile.

Male. Forty-five. He'd listed his location as London W1. That was it. A man in his mid forties from central London. There was no way to tell if that was true. I had no idea if he had posted from an apartment he was renting, a house, a place of work, or if he had just been passing by – he could have posted from a hotel room, or a coffee shop. He could have posted from another city, or country.

It was a dead end for now; another loose thread.

I gathered my things together and headed to the car.

22

Once I was out of Bristol, the traffic started to melt away and the grey of the city became the green of the country. It was hot again, the sky an immaculate blue.

Veronica Mae, the actress that Korin had mentioned in her interview with Marc Collinsky, and also the woman who'd taken the Polaroid of Hosterlitz and Korin in Madrid in 1983, lived about a mile south of the village of Litton, right on the edges of the Mendips. I planned to call in on her before heading to Korin's place, a few miles down the road. In truth, I didn't know what I expected to get from Mae – or even if she would be home – but it felt like it was worth a journey.

I followed the A37 south through a succession of villages, until it became the A39 and cut across a high sweep of sun-drenched pasture, divided up by drystone walls and criss-crossed by telephone poles. A few minutes later, in a cleft a couple of villages on, I found Mae's cottage. I parked up, got out and rang the bell.

After the call with Collinsky over breakfast, I'd done a little more digging on Mae and had managed to find some other pictures of her from the early 1980s. Her career had broadly mirrored Korin's: she'd made low-budget dross – mostly horror films – and her fame, such as it was, had been built on the notoriety, and minor cult status, of one project in particular. For Korin, it had been the *Ursula* trilogy. For Mae, it was a 1984 horror film called *Mr Crow*, about a scarecrow that comes to life and starts murdering people with a corn scythe.

The front door opened.

The second she appeared, I knew it was her. She was fifty-five, a little plump, her hair short and bleached an ash colour – but it was her. I recognized the beauty spot to the left of her nose, but mostly it was those green eyes, as perfect now as they had been three decades ago. She wore a pair of unflattering, baggy tracksuit trousers and a vest which accentuated every crease of flesh at her waist, but as her eyes caught the fringes of the sun moving over from the back of the house, their colour like a sheet of emerald glass, it became easy to see the visual potential Hosterlitz had glimpsed in the younger version of her.

She was holding the door open with her right hand, her left on her hip. I couldn't see a wedding ring on her finger, so I played it safe.

'Ms Mae?'

She eyed me with suspicion. 'Yes.'

'My name's David Raker.' I already had a business card out and handed it to her. 'I find missing people – and at the moment I'm looking for Lynda Korin.'

Her expression changed instantly: surprise, then concern. 'Oh. Right.'

'I don't know whether you're aware, but Lynda has been missing for ten months – since last October.'

'Yes, I heard.' She looked from me to the business card again. 'I haven't seen Lyn for . . . oh, I don't know – eight, nine years. I used to live out near Chew Valley Lake for a long time, so we'd still bump into each other. But then I moved into Bristol for a job, and then back down here, and we just kind of lost contact.'

'I totally understand,' I said. 'But if you've got a spare half hour or so, it would be useful to talk to you. I promise not to take up too much of your day.'

She looked like she might be trying to come up with an excuse, but then acquiesced, stepped back further into the hallway behind her and invited me in.

The cottage was tidy and smartly decorated, the hallway running through to a modern kitchen and a conservatory with two big leather sofas and bi-folding doors. She led me to the conservatory – cooled slightly by a breeze coming in off the farmland – and asked if I wanted something to drink. Once she'd returned with two mugs of tea, she sat on the other sofa and I talked a little more about my line of work and about my search for Lynda Korin. When I was done, she started filling me in on how she'd first met Hosterlitz and Korin.

'After I did my A levels,' she was saying to me, her accent elegant – Korin had joked that it was 'plummy' in the interview with Collinsky – 'I took a year out and went travelling around Europe with a friend of mine. We started in the south of Spain and the idea was we were going to go in a loop: Spain, France, Belgium and Holland, then back down through Germany – West Germany as it was then – into Switzerland, and then finish up in Italy. But we ended up staying in Madrid.'

'Because that's where you met Robert Hosterlitz?'

'Right. My friend and I were in a bar near Atocha station because we were due to head down to Valencia, and Bob, Lyn and some of the other cast and crew from the third *Ursula* film were in there. They'd just wrapped up the shooting.'

'How did you get talking to them?'

'Lyn came up to the bar to buy a round and my friend and

I were there. When she heard us speaking English, she started talking to us, and before we knew it she was buying us beer and we were sitting with her and the crew. It was a fun night. My friend and I were pretty drunk by the end of it and we didn't have anywhere to stay because we'd planned to be in Valencia. So Lyn said we could crash at the place she and Bob were renting in Alcobendas. Next day we wake up and wander through to the living room and there's a photograph of Bob – this old black and white shot – and he's holding all these Oscars. He'd told us the night before that he was a director, but I didn't recognize any of the cast, and I didn't recognize him either, so I didn't think much of it. But then I started to quiz him about the photograph and he told me this film he'd made had won seven Oscars, including Best Director. I couldn't believe it. I mean, *seven* Oscars. You just never would have believed it. The place they were renting – it was a complete dump.'

'So how did you end up working for him?'

'He was due to start shooting on the first of – I don't know – ten or eleven films he'd agreed to make for Mano Águila. Have you ever heard of Pedro Silva?'

'I've seen his name mentioned.'

'He was a producer. Mano Águila was his company. Anyway, the first film Bob made for him was . . . Goodness, it was so long ago. *Cemetery House*?'

'That's right, yeah.'

She nodded. 'He told me he needed victims – you know, people who could be killed off by the monster. My friend and I thought it'd be fun being slathered in fake blood, it was a chance to be in a film, and they paid us ten thousand pesetas, which was, I don't know, forty, fifty pounds. He asked if we had any acting experience. I said I'd done a bit of drama at school, so he gave me a couple of lines and then we bomb up to this old warehouse north of Madrid and the cameras start rolling – and that was that. The whole thing was laughable, really. Pure amateur hour. I was a terrible actress and my friend was even worse, but we were young and we had a great time, and by that stage of his career I'm not sure Bob's quality control was particularly high. When he finished the film, he said I looked great on camera, and would I consider doing another movie. I told him I'd think about it, finished travelling around Europe with my friend, and then returned to Madrid a year later to work on . . . I think it was *The Drill Murders*. My friend had to get back to the UK for university, but I had no course to return for and no job waiting for me, so I figured, what the hell? I ended up staying in Spain until 1983, when Bob decided to retire. Pedro Silva wanted him to do more films, but Bob said no. That was how they ended up in Somerset. I told them it was beautiful, that they'd love this part of the world, and so they bought their house here.'

'That's the place a few miles up the road?'

'Right. It's gorgeous. They lucked out.' She stopped, taking a sip of her tea. 'We used to see a lot of each other for a while because I was in a teacher training programme here – that's what I'd always wanted to do – so I just stayed with my parents while I was studying. But then my first placement was in London for a couple of years, and by the time I returned, Bob had been dead for six months.'

'That must have been a shock.'

'Yeah,' she said. 'It was.'

'You were close to them?'

'Yeah,' she said, but then stopped.

Something lingered in her face.

'Ms Mae?'

She looked away for the first time, out through the doors into the garden, her gaze following the path of a butterfly as it settled on the conservatory doors.

'Don't get me wrong,' she said, 'I liked them both a lot – I really did – but I was just thinking about some of the . . . I don't know.' She shrugged. 'They were . . .'

'What?'

'Well, they were a little odd sometimes.'

'In what way?'

Mae was silent for a moment, a look of anxiety on her face, as if she was uncomfortable talking about them in this way. 'I guess we all have quirks,' she said softly, pressing her lips together so hard they blanched.

'What quirks did they have?'

Another long pause. 'Bob was ultra-quiet, sometimes to the point of being completely mute, at least until you got to know him a little bit. Even then, it wasn't going to be a conversation for the ages. It was hard to imagine him as this successful Hollywood director. He seemed to have lost all his confidence, his spark. In the time that I knew him, he'd sit there at the table, in the corner of the room, and he'd listen to everybody else talking – just watching them. He was always pleasant enough, but even by the time I'd done the third film with him, I honestly couldn't say I knew all that much about him. Not really. Part of me wondered if he might have been that way . . .' But she stopped.

'Deliberately?'

She looked at me; nodded once.

'You mean, he didn't *want* you to get to know him?'

She didn't answer immediately, and I thought of something Wendy Fisher had said: *Bob was quiet . . . I always thought there was more to him than met the eye.*

'Ms Mae?'

'Yes,' she said. 'Yes, I think that's exactly what it was. You'd just catch him looking at you sometimes.'

'Looking at you how?'

'When he was on his own, and even sometimes when they were together, this other look would come across his face. You'd catch him staring at you but there wouldn't be anything *behind* the look. Does that even make sense?'

'Like his mind was on something else?'

'Exactly. For people who didn't know him all that well, I think he probably came across as impolite and aloof.' As she paused, I remembered Wendy – who'd never really got to know her brother-in-law – saying exactly that: *I'll be honest, I thought he was damn rude.* 'But I don't think he was being impolite,' Mae went on, 'I really don't. When he was quiet like that, I often thought that it was something much more complicated than that.'

'Complicated in what way?'

'It was like something was weighing on him,' she said, and then stopped again. 'Something was weighing on him – and, whatever it was, he found it impossible to let it go.'

'You never found out what it was?'

'No. But I always felt with Bob and Lyn ... I don't know ... I think there were things going on in their private life.'

'You think they were unhappy?'

'Actually, the total opposite of that.'

I frowned. 'I'm not sure I follow.'

Mae pursed her lips again, changing position in her chair. She had the uneasy air of someone who hated the idea of gossip, of discussing other people – their decisions, their choices. 'Look, Lyn was a very attractive woman, clearly, so on-set she tended to be right at the centre of everything. And, you know . . .' She shrugged. 'It wasn't always unwanted, I guess.'

'In what sense?'

She shrugged again. 'I mean, I think most days she enjoyed the attention. I'm not judging her, but she would play up to the crowd. You must have seen photos of her, so you know what I'm talking about: she had boobs all the way out here' – she paused, holding both hands an arm's length away from her chest, exaggerating for effect – 'a face like a china doll, this hourglass figure most of us would need a corset to get *close* to . . .' She stopped again, this time for longer. 'But, despite all that, she was never interested in other people – only Bob. He would sit there watching her, never saying boo to a goose – and not because he was powerless to intervene, but because I think he liked it. Watching her, I mean.'

She didn't continue for a while, as if gathering her thoughts, and I flipped back in my notes to where I'd quoted Korin's interview with Marc Collinsky: *You are the most beautiful woman I've ever met in my life. You're a work of art.* As I stared at the quote from Hosterlitz, I recalled the way he'd treated Korin in the films I'd watched: his fixation on her, the obsession with the way she looked.

I prompted Mae. 'Why do you think he liked watching her?'

'I think he got off on people's reactions to her. Sometimes I'd catch sight of him watching other men watching her. It's not like he sat there with this leering grin on his face, like some dirty pervert. It was more that he was enjoying the fact that *they* were enjoying *her.* Never once did I see him tell her to stop.'

'Do you think they were faithful to one another?'

'Oh yes,' she said. 'Definitely.'

She was vehement about it, and I remembered something she'd told me just now. I'd asked her if she thought they had been unhappy.

Actually, the total opposite of that.

'What you've got to understand about Bob and Lyn is that, if they chose to do those things, it was because they *both* chose to do them. As a unit, they were incredibly tight. In fact, they were so well suited to one another that they could sometimes come across as rude. They could appear to be almost paranoid about letting other people in. I mean, Lyn always did such a good job of disguising it – she never made you feel uncomfortable or unwelcome. She was lovely. But I got closer to them than anyone, and I'd watch them sometimes, and they'd look at each other, and it was like they communicated without speaking; and if you got too close, you'd be able to . . . to kind of . . .' She stopped. 'I don't know how to explain it, really. You'd just be able to feel them back away from you.'

'What sort of things would make them back away?'

'Anything, nothing – I don't know. It was a long time ago. There were just certain things, certain discussions, that made me think, "That was weird."'

I wrote some notes and we talked a little more, but the subject seemed to plateau, so I changed gear. 'Do you remember anything odd about the end of the films you shot with Robert and Lynda back then? Specifically, a ninety-second scene with Lynda that seems to have been repeated a few times.'

She looked at me blankly. 'No, not really. I mean, I haven't seen those films since the eighties. To be honest, a few of them I never even bothered watching when they came out.' She broke into a smile. 'I told a lot of my family I was working in Spain as an English teacher for those years, because I didn't want them watching films like *Die Slowly* and seeing me running around stark naked and screaming.'

I returned the smile she gave me, but kept pressing: 'You never felt like Lynda's scenes got treated differently?'

A frown. 'How do you mean?'

'Maybe Robert spent more time on them?'

She eyed me, as if she guessed I was trying to lead her somewhere, but it was obvious she had no idea what I was talking about – not least because those films were made over thirty years ago. I decided not to risk losing her courtesy and backed away from the subject.

'In the report into Lynda's disappearance, there's a photograph of Robert and Lynda that I think you took of them – a Polaroid.' I grabbed my phone, went to Photos and showed her the picture. 'Do you recognize this?'

Her face brightened. 'Wow.'

'Do you remember taking that picture?'

'I do, yes.'

'The police found it in Lynda's house. Anyway, I'm interested in that part of their lives – the eleven or so years between the time they met to the time Robert died. I don't suppose you've retained anything from that period yourself – you know, photographs, letters, things you brought back from Spain?'

She frowned. 'Not that I can think of.'

'Maybe something they gave you, or another photograph you took of them? Anything that might help me, really.'

I could already see it was a lost cause. She was still frowning, trying to recall something, anything, but it was a part of her life long consigned to history.

'Final few questions, I promise. Did either of them ever talk to you about a place called Lake Calhoun?'

'Calhoun?'

I spelled it for her.

She shook her head. 'No.'

'You don't remember anything like that?'

'No, definitely not. Where is it?'

'It's in the States.'

It clearly meant nothing to her.

'What about the name "Ring of Roses"? Does that mean anything to you? Did either of them ever discuss a film idea that went by that name?'

'No, but the police officer also asked about that.'

I looked up from my notes. 'About "Ring of Roses"?'

'Yes. When he came to speak to me about Lynda, he asked me quite a few times if I knew what it was.'

'The police came to see you?'

'Yes.'

'That was Detective Constable Raymond White?'

'Uh . . . I think so.'

'But you're not sure?'

'I can't remember what he said his name was.'

An alarm started going off in my head.

'Was it just one police officer?'

'Yes.'

'And he asked you about "Ring of Roses"?'

She nodded. 'It was all he seemed interested in, really.'

I felt my fingers tighten around the pen. 'Did he show you a warrant card?' I asked. 'You know, his police ID?'

'Uh, I think so.' But her eyes spoke of conflict, of confusion, of a difficulty in remembering. 'Or maybe he didn't, I don't know.'

There was no record in White's report of him ever visiting Veronica Mae at home, so I was betting on *didn't*. And that really only meant one thing.

The man who had visited her wasn't a cop at all.

Sirens drift across the afternoon.

In front of the camera, Ray Callson is seated cross-legged, his eyes on the windows. Sunlight shines on his skin. The finger and thumb of his right hand are gently rubbing together — a nervous tic maybe, or the sign of a smoker aching for a cigarette. He takes a long breath and then his eyes shift from the windows to a space just off camera.

'Anyway,' he says, a little wearily, 'I was going to tell you about that one case I had. What do you want to know about it?'

'You said, in your thirty-two years of being a police officer, it was one of the cases that stuck with you.'

Callson just nods.

'Can you describe it?'

To start with, it's unclear whether Callson has heard.

'Mr Callson?'

'We got a call to go to the Pingrove,' he says quietly.

'That's how the case began?'

'Yeah.'

'What's the Pingrove?'

'It was a hotel, not far from here. On the corner of Wilshire and North Camden. It doesn't exist any more, but back then it was a pretty famous spot. The place to be seen, I guess you could say.'

'You said "we" got the call — who's "we"?'

'Me and my partner, Luis. Luis Velazquez. He's gone now. Been gone a while, actually. Had a heart attack four or five years back. He was a good man.'

There's a short, respectful silence.

'So what happened when you two got to the Pingrove Hotel?'

Callson sniffs, adjusts himself in his seat. 'It was weird. Everything in there was completely normal – except for the manager. The people behind the desk were carrying on with their jobs, the bellboy, concierge; there were guests milling around all over the place. They didn't have the first idea what was going on. But the manager – he was out front, waiting for us. He hadn't told any of his employees what he'd found yet. He was the only one who knew what had happened on the eighth floor – apart from the maid who'd reported it in the first place. I remember he was white as a sheet and he'd sweated through his shirt. He looked like my son used to look when he was a kid – you know, after he'd woken up terrified from some nightmare.'

'He was emotional?'

'Emotional. Yeah, that's one word for it.'

'How would you describe him then?'

'No, emotional's right. He was in shock.'

'Because of what he'd found?'

Callson nods.

'What happened after that?'

There's a pregnant pause. Callson's eyes are now fixed on a space low down, beyond the camera. 'If I remember right,' he says, 'he told us what he found up there, and Luis started speaking Spanish.'

'Spanish? Why?'

Callson looks up. 'He was reciting the Lord's Prayer.'

23

I was still thinking about what Veronica Mae had said – about someone coming to the house, pretending to be a cop, and asking about 'Ring of Roses' – when my phone started ringing on the seat beside me. It was Melanie Craw. The line popped and then buzzed as I answered, and I heard Craw saying, 'Raker?'

'Yeah. Can you hear me?'

'Just about.'

Ahead of me, the road bisected a thick beech forest, like a canyon carving its way through a set of cliffs, and I managed to find somewhere to pull in, next to a gate and a stile. Above the stile, a Forestry Commission sign marked *Sherborne Woods* was pointing in the direction of a path winding beneath the dense canopy of trees.

The call cut out.

I slid out of the car and wandered up the road, hoping it might flicker back into life. Wind moved silently through the forest as I dialled Craw's number.

Click. 'Raker?'

'Sorry about that. I'm out in the sticks.'

'How did it go at the doctor's yesterday?' Craw said, cutting to the chase.

'Everything was fine.'

'Did he examine you?'

'Yeah.'

'And?'

'He said things were good.'

'No chance of you keeling over again any time soon?'

'No. Sorry to disappoint you.'

'Did he prescribe anything else?'

'Just more of the same,' I lied.

As I turned back towards the car, the faint breeze died away, the branches settling, the leaves doing the same – and, as everything hushed, I thought I saw something move out of the corner of my eye; off to my left, deep in the forest.

There was a drystone wall separating the road from the trees. I stepped up to it and watched the forest for a moment. Leaves and branches began moving again, thin shafts of sunlight appearing and vanishing, pale amber strands criss-crossing along the forest floor.

'Raker?'

'Yeah,' I said, my eyes still on the trees. 'I'm here.'

'I'm finishing work at seven tonight and the kids are with my mum. I was thinking of getting a takeaway.'

'Okay, well, I'll wait for an invite.'

'Ha ha,' she said. 'I need to talk to you about something.'

'That sounds ominous.'

She didn't respond.

'Is everything all right?' I asked.

'Like I said, I need to talk to you.'

I looked at my watch. It was almost midday.

'I'm down in Somerset at the moment, and I'm not sure what time I'll be back tonight. But I can give you a call when I'm an hour away.'

'All right. Don't get yourself killed in the meantime.'

'I'll try my best.'

I looked into the forest again, my eyes moving between trunks and branches, across grass and beds of fallen leaves.

There was no one around.

All I could see was a bird – a rook – on a branch about twenty-five feet from where I was standing, its black eyes and silver beak trained on me.

It squawked once and took off.

24

It took me a while to find the house that Lynda Korin had lived in for thirty-one years. West of the village of Hinton Blewett, it was tucked away on its own at the end of a short country lane, hidden from the road by plump hedgerows, its old, rust-speckled front gate pretty much invisible until I was almost upon it.

Getting out of the car, I fanned the gate open, its hinges moaning, and swung the BMW in through the gap in the hedge. At the end of a sand-coloured driveway pitted with small, uneven holes, a beautiful grey stone cottage laced with ivy came into view. It sat on an incline and looked out across the Mendips. The view was like a shot from a postcard: a carpet of green and yellow squares outlined by stone walls, Chew Valley Lake sitting like a thousand acres of blue ink about three miles away.

There was no alarm on Korin's place, or at least not one that I could see, which made my life easier. Leaving the car door ajar, trying to keep it as cool as possible, I went to the front of the cottage. It had three windows on the ground floor: one on the left, which looked through to a small sitting room, and two on the right – one, a bedroom, the other a study.

I carried on around to the right, following a flagstone path between empty flowerbeds to a door on the side of the house that led to a utility room. Further around still was the back garden. A raised patio sat directly outside a pair of French doors, stone steps dropping down to a lawn that rolled at a marginal slant because of the way the hill sloped. It was hard to get a sense of whether Korin loved gardening, because it had clearly been untouched in ten months: the grass was knee-length; weeds were crawling up the steps and out between patio slabs; flowerbeds were either empty, like the ones at the side of the house, or overrun, rampant and unchecked.

However, it didn't take much imagination to envision what it might once have been like; how an immaculate garden at the back of a beautiful cottage, with the still of the countryside and sweeping views of the valley, would transform it all. I began to understand why Korin hadn't left this place, even after Hosterlitz had died.

My gaze finally settled on the far corner of the garden. Sitting there in a sea of grass was the shed that Marc Collinsky had described to me. As he'd said himself, the word 'shed' didn't really do it justice. It was a garden room, hexagonal in shape, with a slate-tiled roof and three windows at the front.

I moved through the grass and stepped up to its windows. Collinsky had described it as a dumping ground when he came out here. But whatever Collinsky had seen inside, however messy it had been in October, it wasn't now.

It had been cleared out.

I removed my picks and went to work on the lock and, twenty seconds later, the door sprang out from its frame. Inside, the building was about ten feet in diameter, but felt bigger because it was empty. I could see where shelves had once been screwed into the walls, and scratches on the floor where a table, or a workbench, had stood before being moved. On another wall panel there was the echo of a tool rack, the outlines of hammers and wrenches left behind. In specks of red, I saw where paint pots had once been stacked.

The only one of the garden room's six walls that didn't

appear to have any kind of history was one at the back and to the left. There was no indication of shelves having been screwed into it, no hint of what had once hung there. Instead, the wall panel had been given a fresh lick of paint, the same soft grey as the other walls in the shed, but clearly added more recently. Its surface was smooth and unblemished, and because the garden room had been closed up for so long, the vague whiff of paint still lingered. In Korin's financials, there had been nothing to support the idea of a sale, no chunks of money coming into her account to indicate that she'd got rid of everything before she vanished. So where did the contents go? I looked back at the freshly painted wall panel. And why only paint this one? Did she start but not get the chance to finish it?

Or had she been trying to cover something up?

On my keyring was a penknife. I selected it, popped the blade out and gently tried to scrape away at the top layer of paint, trying to get at what might be underneath. I didn't expect it to work and I wasn't disappointed. Paint came off easily enough, but even when I barely applied any pressure to the knife, all I ended up doing was picking through to the wood below.

Painting just the one panel didn't necessarily mean she was trying to cover something up. I knew that.

Yet something didn't feel right.

Grabbing my phone, I went to my inbox and drafted an email to Collinsky, asking him about his recollection of this room: what he saw, what had been kept here, whether he remembered if one of the panels had been painted recently. That last question was a long shot, but I took a series of pictures of the room anyway, and then messaged them all across to him, hoping one of them might jog his memory.

After that, I headed to the house.

25

I made my way through the long grass, up on to the patio. To the left of the house were two windows, side by side, looking in at different ends of the kitchen. It was long but narrow, and finished in a farmhouse style. On the wall was a clock that had come to a halt at two forty-two.

Moving across to the French doors, I could make out a second living room, bigger than the one at the front, and decorated more attractively. Sun poured in through a window at the side, revealing leather sofas and cane furniture laid out across white wood floors. Built around the window was a made-to-measure shelving system, a TV sitting inside it, a DVD player, countless books and films. There were ornaments too, trinkets, photos.

I went to work on the French doors with the pick, eventually managing to pop the lock, and then pulled one of them open. I paused for a moment, just in case there *was* an alarm and I'd missed it, then stepped into the house. Like the garden room, weeks of sun had baked the interior, dust barely moving, the air stagnant.

I tried the light switch closest to me, but nothing happened. There was no hum from the refrigerator in the kitchen, no buzz from the TV or a slim decoder tucked away in a space beneath it. The electrics had obviously been turned off.

Moving through to the kitchen, I opened up the fridge, expecting to be hit by the stench of long-expired food.

Instead, I found it had been cleaned out. When I checked the freezer, it was the same – defrosted and completely spotless.

After that, I started going through the cupboards. They were mostly full of cutlery and kitchen equipment, but when I came across food it was tinned or in packets, and had been left tidy: lined up, or stacked two or three deep, or – if it was dry food – decanted into separate, sealed containers. I opened up the oven and could see it had been cleaned. The inside of the microwave smelled of disinfectant. It was like some sort of show home – pristine and flawless.

As I went through the rest of the house, I found it in a similar state and could only really think of two reasons why. The first was that Korin had tidied the house before driving out to Stoke Point, knowing she wasn't coming back. Maybe that was why DC White eventually let the case drift: because he thought that all of this, the neatness, pointed to Korin disappearing on purpose – coming up with a plan, executing it perfectly. People had the right to go missing. There was no crime in that.

Or there was another, more disturbing reason it was so clean: someone else was trying to disguise their part in whatever had gone on. I thought again of the cop Veronica Mae had referred to, and then headed upstairs.

It was in exactly the same condition. Two bedrooms, as well as Korin's, and then a separate bathroom, all orderly and uncluttered. Sinks had been cleaned, bath, toilets, shower. There was an attic as well, accessed via a ten-step staircase on the landing. It was light and airy, the ceilings high, its four windows facing out in four different directions. Some old boxes filled with junk had been stacked against one of the walls: musty clothes, blankets, books, a broken record player, a cracked wristwatch. As I looked through them, I remembered pictures of the boxes, of the attic, of all the rooms in the house, in White's official report. But then my attention switched again: right at the bottom of the last box, just as I was about to close it, I found a scrapbook, water-wrinkled and laced with cobwebs.

Inside were photographs of Robert Hosterlitz.

There were no dates anywhere, but as I started to flick through the first few pages, it was relatively easy to get an idea of when the pictures were taken.

One was a faded black and white shot of him outside a cinema in Los Angeles, the RKO Pantages, the marquee overhead announcing it as the location of the 26th Annual Academy Awards. Dressed in a tuxedo, smiling, clean-cut but a little overweight, he was holding an Oscar in each hand. I figured this must be his Best Director and Best Picture wins for *The Eyes of the Night*, which meant the photograph was taken in March 1954. There were others dotted around it: a picture of him and Barbara Stanwyck, smiling for the camera, on the set of *Only When You're Dead* in 1952; one of him arched over a typewriter in a small office at what I assumed was the American Kingdom studio lot in LA; and him perched on a wall at Victoria Embankment, cigarette in hand, looking towards Big Ben. At the bottom it was stamped *Wick Films, 1957*, making this a publicity still, taken by Wick, the UK production company he'd signed with after fleeing America. He looked good: handsome, slimmer. At the time, he probably saw this as a new dawn for himself. In reality, it was the beginning of the end.

Then, five pages in, something unexpected happened: Hosterlitz suddenly vanished from the scrapbook entirely, and was replaced by hundreds of shots of Lynda Korin.

There were photographs of her everywhere, crammed into every available space – haphazardly, untidily. Despite that, there seemed to be a vague chronology, starting when she was in her mid twenties – which put it at about the time she'd first got together with Hosterlitz – and carrying on into her mid thirties, which would have been around 1988, when he'd died. It made me wonder whether he might have taken these, and not just because the decade-long time frame of the shots fitted the ten-year period the two of them were married. It was also because they seemed to echo the films I'd seen the night before. He was fascinated with her in the same way.

Every single picture was perfectly framed, the lighting exemplary, her skin flawless, her eyes such a deep, resonant blue they seemed to come alive in front of me. Every time I turned a page, there was another shot of her; occasionally, there were so many of them on a single sheet of the scrap-book that they overlapped each other or had begun to come loose. Then, halfway in, three of them cascaded out from a page towards the back, the glue long since dried out, and scattered across the floor of the attic.

I picked them up.

Except these weren't of Korin at all.

Instead, they were pictures of an intricately carved angel, perhaps eight inches high and made from wood, hands together in prayer, its head bowed. As I flicked forward in the scrapbook, I found more at the very back: two pages of the same angel, shot from different angles and distances. It was hard to tell where they'd been taken, although the angel was sitting on the same table throughout.

I checked back, making sure I hadn't missed anything similar, but it was just the countless pictures of Korin.

Returning to the rear of the scrapbook, I counted up the shots of the angel. There were twenty-one of them.

Confused, I returned to the three photos that had come loose, zeroing in on the one that provided the clearest, front-on close-up of the angel. The wood had been carved to make it look like the figure was wearing a long, flowing gown, and its face was minutely detailed, its eyes closed, nose and lips visible. On its neck, I noticed a mark had been made in black felt tip. It was a crucifix.

Someone had drawn it on.

Wondering if it was Hosterlitz or Korin who had taken the photographs of the angel, and whether one of them had added the cross – or someone else entirely – I suddenly recalled what Hosterlitz had said to Korin: *You are an angel. I think you are the most beautiful woman I've met in my life. You're a work of art.* Was his choice of words just a coincidence? Or was there a connection between what he'd said and the photographs I had here?

Unable to decide for certain, I set aside one picture of the angel, slid the rest of them into the scrapbook and returned everything to the box again.

By the time I got back downstairs, though, a vague air of familiarity had started to eat at me. I began wondering if I'd seen the angel somewhere before. I searched the house for a second time, ending up in the living room I'd started out in, where the shelves were dotted with ornaments and keepsakes.

But there was no angel.

I headed back to the car and fished out White's file, going back over his account of when he'd taken a look at this place himself. It was short and sweet, which was why I'd failed to recall much about it:

Nothing of note at house. Three-bedroom cottage, attic, two living rooms – one large, one small. House clean.

The first time I'd been through it, I thought he meant the house was clean, as in clean of any evidence. But now I was starting to think he probably meant it was *literally* clean. Spotless. Wiped down. That meant the house had been this way when White had come to take a look at it two weeks after Korin vanished. Knowing that for certain didn't make much difference: there was still no telling whether Korin herself had cleaned the house down in the days before she disappeared, or if someone else had come back and done it before White arrived on 11 November. Both made me uneasy.

I lingered on the file for a moment, going through the pictures White had taken of the house himself, and a few others he must have found here in frames and in drawers and then added to the report. I'd looked at them all before, many times over, but I went over them again.

There was one of Korin in her early fifties at some kind of fete, smiling for the camera next to a bunch of older people, presumably from the local village. Another of her with the ladies of the book club she attended, and a third of her in the living room – she was standing at the doors, the garden visible behind her, shelves to the left of her, smiling for the camera. Wendy had also sent me the same picture.

I moved on. White had taken shots of all the rooms, and also a few top-down pictures of the storage boxes in the attic. Did that mean he'd looked inside the scrapbook? What had he made of it? I could phone him and try to find out, but it was safe to assume that he'd made little of it, because there was no mention in his investigation of how Hosterlitz had photographed Korin over and over, or of the weird, repeated shots of the angel in the –

I stopped.

Wait a second.

I flipped back to the photograph of Korin in her living room. It must have been taken recently, because she looked in her early sixties. But it wasn't that.

It was something on the shelves beside her.

Getting out of the car again, I returned to the house and made a beeline for a shelf full of DVDs, perched above the television. They were all Hosterlitz's films. His noirs. His western. The horror films that were still available to buy in English. They were stacked horizontally now, one on top of the other – but in the photograph of Korin with the shelves, they'd been stacked vertically.

They've all been moved.

I slid out one of the cases and opened it up. It was empty. When I tried the next one along, it was exactly the same. I tried some more and found the discs missing from all the cases. Every single Hosterlitz film had been removed.

But that wasn't the only thing.

In the photograph of Korin, an ornament had been sitting at the end of the shelf to the left of her shoulder, almost acting as a bookend for the DVD cases.

It had been the wooden angel.

Now that was gone too.

26

I took a step back from the shelf.

Had Korin taken the wooden angel and Hosterlitz's films with her? They were there in the shot that Wendy had sent me, the one White also had in the file, and the picture couldn't have been more than twelve months old. But why take the angel? Why take the films?

Unless *she* didn't take them at all.

Someone else did.

I thought again of the police officer that Veronica Mae had described, a man who hadn't identified himself but had come asking questions about Lynda Korin. Was it him? Why did the films and the wooden angel matter?

I headed outside into the long grass, trying to think, the sun immediately beating against my back. As I looked across the valley, the lake winking under the heat of the day, I closed my eyes, listening to the far-off drone of a plane passing high above me. When I couldn't come up with anything, I returned to the doors of the living room and looked inside, back to the shelf that had been next to Korin in the photograph. Instantly, something else registered with me there.

A six-inch-by-four-inch photograph in a silver picture frame.

My gaze had passed it countless times as I'd searched the room earlier, but it was only now, looking at the frame from outside rather than inside, that I could see something on it: a series of marks, like fingerprints, dotted across the rear of the frame, where someone had been holding it. The marks were grey.

I looked across at the garden room.

Grey – like paint.

I reached in and picked up the frame. It *was* paint. Someone had come in here and handled the photo frame while they'd still had paint on their hands.

But then my attention switched again.

Inside the frame was a photograph of Korin and Hosterlitz. They looked younger than in the Polaroid that Veronica Mae had taken, Hosterlitz especially, and were on the fringes of a shore. It was a bright summer's day, both of them in shorts, Korin with sunglasses perched on top of her head. As I took that in, I thought back to something Wendy Fisher had told me, about how Hosterlitz had only been out to Minneapolis with Korin twice – once in the summer of 1979, once for Christmas 1984 – and then my eyes settled on the corner of the shot. There was a wooden sign next to them.

It said: *32nd Street Beach – Lake Calhoun.*

A charge of adrenalin almost knocked me off balance. Quickly, I turned the photo frame over, pushed the catches open and removed the back section. Inside, a piece of brown cardboard had been used to keep the photo in place and to fill the quarter-inch gap between the back of the frame and the glass. I took out the cardboard, set it aside and grabbed the picture. There was nothing inside the frame except the photograph. I ran my fingers beneath the edges of the interior, just to make sure, but all I found was dust.

Pausing there, I looked at the frame again, at the same grey paint that was on the garden-room wall, and then finally at the photograph of Lynda Korin and her husband at Lake

Calhoun. What had I been hoping to find? A suicide note? A confession? Some damning piece of evidence? Frustrated, feeling a little foolish, I started to put the thing back together again, my eyes straying from the picture to the frame – and then finally to the piece of cardboard I'd set aside.

I turned the cardboard over.

Taped to the back of it was a key.

27

I ripped the key away from the cardboard.

It was for a meter box.

Heading outside, into the garden, I hurried across the lawn to the side of the house and found it next to the utility-room door: a white box, at ankle level, with a slanted lid. Kneeling, I used the key on the lock, twisted it and hoisted the lid up. Inside was a gas meter, encased in re-inforced plastic. Cobwebs formed a fine grey blanket across everything, but when I pushed them aside, I saw something underneath. Roughly the size of a brick, it had been wedged into the space between the bottom of the meter and the edge of the box, and was wrapped in black plastic.

Once I had it out, I returned to the house, laid it on the living-room table and used my penknife to cut along the strips of brown packing tape. The package had been secured so tightly, it took me a minute to unravel it all. Once I had the plastic off, I started to see what had been wrapped up.

A teak box.

Inside were four items: a red USB stick; a business card, with a yellow Post-it note folded around it; and another key, but in brass.

As I removed them one by one, my eyes lingered on the key. It was a Yale, with a number 6 scratched into it on both sides. It was wholly unremarkable, and yet I felt as if I'd seen it somewhere before. Unable to place where, I shifted my attention to the Post-it, and then to the business card. Unfolding the Post-it, I found four lines in black felt tip:

> X CADAAH
> E OECGEY
> _____
> KILL!
> 1h 19m 7s

I zeroed in on the bottom half: *Kill! 1h 19m 7s*.

Was that a reference to *Kill!*, the film that Hosterlitz had made in 1981? It seemed like a logical leap to make, especially with the timecode attached to it – but I had no idea what the two lines of letters above it meant. The other problem was that, even if I was right about the *Kill!* timecode, six of the eleven films that Hosterlitz had made between 1979 and 1984 were history. *Kill!* was one of them.

As I pondered that, I thought again of the guy who'd posted on the forum under the handle Microscope. He claimed to have seen all eleven films, so short of Korin herself sitting down with me, he'd surely stand the best chance of being able to interpret this for me. But how the hell did I find him?

Frustrated, I took phone pictures of each of the items, in case I lost the physical versions, and then turned to the business card.

The name on it was Tony Everett. He was listed as the general manager at a firm called Roman Film. They were based on an industrial estate in Bath. On the back of the card, Everett had written: *Great seeing you yesterday! I'm in Friday, TE.* He, his company, and the message he'd written meant nothing to me, so I grabbed my laptop from the car and moved on to the USB stick. Setting the laptop down on the living-room table, I slotted the USB into it.

The stick contained four video files.

They'd been labelled *August20.avi, September2.avi, September15.avi* and then, finally, *October28.avi.* My pulse started to quicken as I looked at the name of that last one: 28 October was the last day Korin was seen alive.

I opened the 28 October file.

It started playing automatically and, inside a second, I knew exactly what it was: CCTV film from the camera mounted outside Stoke Point.

Footage from the day Lynda Korin disappeared.

I tried to think straight. What was the footage doing on this USB? Who did the USB belong to? Was it Korin's? Someone else's? Why had it been wrapped up and hidden inside the meter box?

Initially, the video was confusing, and when I looked at the readout of the time in the corner, I realized why: it began in the middle of the night, at 12.01 a.m. on 28 October. It was almost entirely dark. The only thing I could make out was a low-level lamp, halfway along the bridge, which cast a grey pool of light. It wasn't much, but it would be enough to make out any cars or people; anyone approaching or coming back out.

Yet, as I moved the footage on, apart from the occasional flicker as a bird swooped past or a mouse scurried from one side to another, there was nothing. At about 6.30 a.m., the light slowly started to change, and by 7 a.m. it was clear the sun was up, even if I couldn't see it. It illuminated leaves on either side of the bridge and cast shadows across the tarmac. But still there was no one – not until just before 9 a.m., when I saw a black Ford Focus come into view, a flash of someone at the wheel. The Ford crossed the bridge and disappeared out of shot, into the car park.

Korin.

Rewinding the video, I watched again, but this time inched it on frame by frame. A couple of seconds later I had the perfect shot of her, unmistakable and distinctive: both hands on the wheel, her face fully turned in the direction of the camera, her white-blonde hair tied in a ponytail. I recognized the image I was looking at immediately: it was exactly the same frame that had been included in the official police paperwork. If I'd had any qualms about it somehow not being her at Stoke Point that day, they were dispelled. It was definitely Lynda Korin.

I inched it back again, watching her for a second time, and then let it run on at normal speed for a while, wanting to see how the day had unfolded. But it was so tedious and uneventful, I soon found myself fast-forwarding through it at 4x speed, then 8x when even that felt too arduous. No one else turned up at the peninsula for another two hours, until an old couple in a pale blue Golf entered Stoke Point. Another car – a Renault people carrier, with a mum and two kids inside – arrived half an hour after that; and then a red Vauxhall Insignia – with two older women in it – fifty minutes later. Just after 12.30 p.m., the mum in the Renault left, the Golf exited half an hour after that, and the Insignia was gone by 2 p.m. No one else arrived until after 3 p.m., when another old couple in a bottle-green Rover turned up. Fifteen minutes later, a man entered on a motorbike. By 4 p.m., both the couple in the Rover and the man on the bike had left.

Korin had never reappeared.

I watched the rest of the day through, until the sun set at just after five o'clock. As darkness descended, and the light at the gate fluttered into life, I knew this would be the most effective time to make an escape on foot, using cover of night as a disguise. But the gate snapped back on its automatic timer, and Korin didn't come out. There was no sign of her. When I hit the end of the video at exactly midnight, I brought it all the way back to sunset and watched it again.

I knew for a fact there was no way out except across the bridge, because I'd seen it for myself – so where could Korin have gone?

As soon as the video was over for a second time, I closed it down and switched to my phone, using the web to find tide times for 28 October. But, deep down, I knew she couldn't have left by boat, just as I knew it from the very start. Low tide was 10 a.m., high tide 4 p.m. Bringing a boat in risked being seen; wading out to one risked getting stuck.

I glanced at the Yale key again, troubled by it, troubled by all of this. As I mentally played back the image of her on the security camera, I started to wonder whether she'd slept over in her car and exited the next day, or in the early hours of the morning – after all, there was no footage on the USB from 29 October. But then I remembered there had been a reference to 29 October in the police report; of the video from that day being checked as well. The police had found nothing.

So could she have been smuggled out?

She wasn't lying flat on the back seat of any of the vehicles, I knew that for sure, because the position of the camera made it easy to see down into the rear of the cars that had passed in and out on 28 October. But what about in the boot? I couldn't see into any of them, which made it impossible to know for sure.

I returned to the footage and noted down the registration of each of the cars that had come into Stoke Point on 28 October, thinking I could use Ewan Tasker to get me backgrounds on the owners if need be, then opened up the next file. This one was for 20 August.

That was two months before Korin vanished.

It began at the same time, 12.01 a.m., and I ran it on at the same speed – not so fast that I wouldn't spot anything suspicious, but fast enough to whip through the lack of activity. As it was summer, the light began to break early and, by 6.30 a.m., everything was visible. At just before 9 a.m., the first visitors arrived – a family of four in a Volvo – and, as the day progressed, more and more people joined them. It was sunny, it was the school holidays, so it was much busier than 28 October. By midday, I'd counted fifteen cars; between midday and 3 p.m., there were another fourteen.

But, just after 3 p.m., something strange happened.

A bottle-green Rover, with the same registration plates that I'd seen on 28 October, turned up. It had the same old couple inside it. They passed over the bridge, into the crescent of trees, and were gone from view. I rewound it and played it again.

The same couple were at the peninsula – so what?

In White's report, he'd mentioned that he'd talked to all of the drivers of the cars that had entered Stoke Point on 28 October, and they'd all been frequent visitors there. There was no crime in returning to a place you liked.

An hour later, just before 4 p.m., the old couple in the

Rover appeared again, exiting across the bridge and out of shot. This time, I paused it as they left. Even given the rinsed-out nature of the security feed, it was a clear picture of them. They looked like they were in their eighties, him hunched over the wheel slightly, her in the middle of saying something. Neither of them was familiar.

I ran the footage again, watching a succession of families leave through the gate, until I'd accounted for every vehicle I'd noted on the way in. Shortly after that, the gate swung closed and the sun started to set.

Once the video from 20 August was done, I moved on to 2 September. Just like the others, it started at one minute past midnight, and while I kept a close eye on the shadows, watching for anyone using them as a hiding place to get in and out of the car park, nothing of note happened until 11 a.m.

That was when a pale blue Golf entered.

Recognition hit me immediately: *it's the same blue Golf I saw enter the car park on 28 October*. When I paused the security feed to check, the car had the same number of people in it as it did on the day that Korin disappeared. It was another older couple, but not the same couple that was in the Rover. What tethered the two couples and the two vehicles together was obvious, though: they were both in footage from separate days, saved to this USB – and they'd both returned on 28 October, the day Lynda Korin had disappeared.

As the security feed continued to roll on, other cars arrived, but I wasn't interested in them any more. I was interested in the couple in the Golf. I kept my eyes fixed on the screen, only breaking off to glance at my pad, to look for where I'd written down their registration number, to remind myself of it – but then, the third or fourth time I looked at my notes, something leaped out at me. The entry and exit times I'd written down for the Golf on 28 October: *11.12 to 13.02.*

As I turned back to the screen, I saw the timecode in the corner tick over to 13.02 and the Golf emerged from the car park again.

I froze.

It's the same footage.

The Rover and the Golf both entered and exited Stoke Point at *exactly* the same time on 20 August and 2 September as they did on 28 October – because the footage from those days had been edited into the video for 28 October.

The video from 28 October wasn't an original.

It was a composite.

The whole thing was a lie.

28

I looked down at the Yale key, at the business card, at the Post-it, and then back to my laptop. My stomach turned as I started putting it together. The whole thing was a lie – and Lynda Korin had constructed it. When I played the last file, just to be sure, I found exactly what I expected: on 15 September, as well as the other vehicles that came and went, I spotted the red Insignia with the two women in it, the mum and her kids in the Renault people carrier, and the guy on the bike. The arrival and departure of all three had been taken from this footage and spliced into the video for 28 October, along with the pale blue Golf and the bottle-green Rover from the other dates. But the truth was, none of the vehicles had ever been there on the twenty-eighth – it was just made to look like it.

I remembered again how, in White's original report, no one he'd talked to – not the owners of the Golf, the Rover, the Insignia, the people carrier or the motorbike – could remember much more than being at Stoke Point at *around* the time Korin went missing. It was two weeks between the disappearance and the case finally landing on White's desk, which wouldn't have helped – but, as well as that, all the people interviewed were frequent visitors to Stoke Point.

That was why none of them could be one hundred per cent certain if they were there on the twenty-eighth or not. Even if they told White they were pretty sure they *weren't*, he would have told them they'd been caught on CCTV camera on the day, and they'd have just put their recollection down as an error. They were at Stoke Point all the time – they would just assume they'd got their days mixed up. Out of all of them, there had only been one person adamant he wasn't there, and he'd told White as much. In my notes, I'd written, 'Man, 80+, says he wasn't there on 28/10, even though he's on tape. Mistake? Forgetful?' But it wasn't either of those things. The man was the one who'd been driving the Rover. He'd told White he wasn't there that day, but White put it down to the same reasons as I had in my notes. A mistake. An error. A forgetful old man.

We'd both done him a disservice.

The five vehicles had been cut into the footage because they were the five vehicles most frequently seen by Lynda Korin at the peninsula in the months leading up to her disappearance. The guy I'd talked to at Stoke Point, Len Fordyce, had told me about how he'd got to know Korin a little, how they'd chat, how she'd returned a number of times to the car park before she vanished on 28 October. She'd been doing reconnaissance. She'd been watching the cars coming in and out, seeing who arrived most often. Eventually, she'd narrowed it down to five vehicles in the footage, and the whole time Fordyce thought she was talking to him because she was just that type of person. Maybe she was. But it wasn't *just* that. She'd talked to him, got to know him, using his loneliness as a way to lower his guard. And as I looked at the brass key again, with the number 6 etched into it, I knew why I recognized it, why the number had disturbed a memory that I couldn't quite place. It belonged to Fordyce. It was for the cabin at Stoke Point.

I'd seen him carrying a set of identical keys when we'd been talking to each other, numbers etched into them in the same way, each one presumably unlocking similar cabins at each of the locations that were on his route. He must have thought he'd lost this one somewhere, somehow, and he had. But it wasn't down the back of the sofa. Korin had removed it from the ring, and then she'd gained access to the cabin – and that was when she'd gained access to the security system.

The DVR inside. The discs full of footage.

I drew the business card towards me. At the bottom, beneath the name of Tony Everett, his job title and the name of his business, Roman Film, was a URL. I entered it into the browser on my phone, and soon had exactly the answer I was expecting: they were a video production company. They produced high-end content for big-name international businesses. Cutting together elements from four different CCTV videos, editing it, making it impossible to see the joins, the borders between one piece of footage and the next, would be a walk in the park for them. If the police had been fully focused on Korin, if they'd put more than just a single man on to her disappearance, maybe someone, somewhere, would have noticed the footage was an amalgam. But they didn't.

I looked at the message on the back of the card.

Great seeing you yesterday! I'm in Friday, TE.

It was a message to Korin. Everett was like Fordyce: he thought he knew her – but he didn't know her at all. I doubted if he'd had a clue what he'd signed up for, maybe still didn't, but I could imagine how Korin had made it work. There was six months' worth of security footage on disc inside the cabin. Once she had the keys, she got inside and took the DVDs she needed, handed them to Everett, and he cut together the footage for 28 October. She'd have told him the footage was for an advert, for a corporate video, for a presentation; she'd have told him it was somewhere other than Stoke Point, some other part of the country. She might not have even given him her real name, so when she vanished, it was never a blip on his radar. When Korin had disappeared, it had barely been reported, even in the local press, so he wouldn't have put it together. When I went to the 'Who are we?' tab on their website, I found pictures of the staff, and I saw Everett at the top: a man in his early sixties, smiling but awkward; plain, ordinary, unmemorable. Korin was the same age, but she was anything *but* ordinary. She was beautiful, confident.

Manipulative.

I remembered what Wendy had said to me – *Lyn always had something of the actress in her* – and then filled in the rest. Once Everett had done what she'd asked, she must have returned the discs to the cabin, as well as the recut footage for 28 October. She must have put them back in the days after she disappeared, when Fordyce wasn't around, when no one else was parked up at the peninsula who could place her there. The recut footage no longer included her leaving on foot, which is what she must have done the day she abandoned her car there. She *was* caught on camera leaving that place – but no one would ever see it. The original DVD recording from 28 October was gone for ever.

Her exit had been completely erased from history.

I looked around the spotless house. If she'd planned her disappearance, then it confirmed why the house was so neat, why even the fridge had been wiped down. She must have placed the car keys deliberately at the foot of the tree in Stoke Point too – but to what end? To draw attention to her message about Lake Calhoun? To help make the connection to the photograph, to the meter key? Why? The message in the tree was so small it might never have been seen. White missed it altogether; I nearly had too. Certainly, without the engraving of the film projector, I definitely wouldn't have looked twice.

So if she was going to lay a trail of clues, why make it so obscure? Why try to hide it so well? Why do it at all? I didn't understand why she'd so meticulously planned a disappearance, and then led someone like me back to her front door, to a box showing the lies she'd built, to the men she'd influenced and taken advantage of. Why have Everett make digital copies from the physical DVDs and then leave the files on a USB stick to be found?

Nothing about that made sense.

I tried to clear my head, to put everything into some sort of order, but as I did, my phone beeped once. It was an email from Collinsky. He was replying to my message about the garden room, to the pictures I'd sent him of how it looked now – how it had been cleared out, repainted, fixed.

Subject: Re: Garden room
Date: Saturday 29 August 2015 – 16.13
From: marcc@cinemagazineuk.com
To: raker@davidraker.com

Looks completely different. Wonder why she cleaned everything out, even the tools etc? Back wall wasn't like that when I saw it, at least as far as I can remember. That looks like the original wall panel that she's repainted there (is that right?) – 90% sure there was no wall panel on view when I saw it, and that a piece of plain plasterboard had been covering it. Think she'd attached shelves to the plasterboard, and the shelves were full of junk.

M

I left my laptop where it was, heading out across the garden to the shed. Once I was back inside, I returned to the repainted wall panel. In the very top and very bottom corners, I found slight indentations where screw holes had been plugged with Polyfilla and painted over. The work was good. Even in the right light, it was hard to see where the plasterboard had once been secured.

One possible explanation for the wall panel being repainted was obvious: Korin had prised the plasterboard from it when she'd cleared it out, and the wall panel underneath had discoloured more than the others. Its need for repair was greater.

But somehow, given what else I'd just found out – the deceit, the carefully constructed lies – I doubted that was the real reason.

29

Just as I'd suspected, Tony Everett – the MD of Roman Film – didn't even know Lynda Korin by that name. To him, she'd been Ursula Keegan, a marketing manager for an advertising firm in London, who was looking to use the security footage in a pitch she'd be making to the Department of Transport.

It was hard listening to Everett talk about her, not least because – in not so many words – it sounded like he thought they'd had a connection, beyond just client and customer. I hadn't told him the truth about who she was, because it invited fewer questions that way and because it felt cruel to twist the knife. He said he'd asked her out for a drink when the work was complete, and she'd told him the next time she was down in Bath, she would love to do that. But, like everyone else in the world, he'd heard nothing from Lynda Korin for the past ten months.

In truth, this whole thing left me cold: it wasn't the direction I'd expected the case to take, it wasn't the person I'd expected Lynda Korin to be, even as both her sister and former friend talked about her being hard to break down, about her and Hosterlitz being odd as a couple, having secrets, behaving strangely. Those things hadn't rung alarm bells the first time I'd heard them, because a lot of missing people were like that. All of them had quirks, and they all had secrets. But this was more than that. This was deceit.

By the time I got off the phone to Everett, I was halfway

back to London, the motorway less affected today by the crush of bank holiday traffic. On the seat beside me was the box I'd taken from Lynda Korin's, the photograph of the angel I'd removed from the album, and the DVDs of Korin's four horror films.

As I ate up the miles, I thought about those films, about the ending that connected them all, about Hosterlitz's strange, whispered repetition of 'You don't know who you are' hidden on the soundtrack. I thought about the Post-it note that Korin had left in the teak box too, the timecode for *Kill!* on it, and the two lines of letters above that. XCADAAH. EOECGEY. Were the letters related to *Kill!*? How was I ever going to find out, even if they were? Without a clear line of sight on whoever Microscope was, I had no idea who else might know, especially as six of the eleven films Hosterlitz had made in Spain after 1979 were gone for ever.

I decided to phone the guy at Rough Print again.

After reintroducing myself, I cut to the chase: 'Any idea where I might find copies of any of Hosterlitz's so-called "lost" films?'

'Hmm' was all he said.

'That doesn't sound good.'

He chuckled. 'Those films . . . well, the general consensus seems to be that they're unrecoverable. The original negatives – basically, what Hosterlitz shot – got lost when the production company closed in 1986. It's not necessarily the end of the matter if you've still got, say, distribution prints – they'll be inferior in quality, but you can still make a dupe negative from a print – it's just that this didn't happen either. Those films were designed to be made quickly and on the cheap, and one of the results of that, I'm afraid, is that the places that showed them at the time didn't treat them with much in the way of reverence. That included returning them in a decent state, on time, or – in this case – at all. It happens more often than you might think. There's a film called *Symptoms . . .*'

But I'd already tuned out and started thinking about my next move. In the copy of *Dias de los Muertos*, there had been the transcript of the panel Korin had done at Screenmageddon. Someone from a movie website in San Diego had asked her a question. Maybe I could get in touch with him next.

' . . . all sorts of other examples as well. The British Film Institute have got a list of seventy-five lost films on their website which they want to find, preserve and make available. Quite a few of them ended up going the same way as Hosterlitz's horror movies.'

'That's really interesting,' I said, trying to sound genuine. 'So how likely do you think it is that someone could have copies of all eleven of those films?'

The man blew out a jet of air that crackled down the line. 'I mean, I guess it's *possible*. Even the six "missing" films existed at some point, and no one knows for sure what happened to them. Not one hundred per cent. If the negatives didn't just get thrown in the bin when Mano Águila closed, maybe they got passed on to someone – a collector of some sort – but how you even *start* to look for that person, I don't know. Plus, if someone *has* those films, why sit on them for thirty years? Why not share what you have with the world?'

We chatted a little longer and then I thanked him and hung up, frustration starting to eat at me. As it festered, I noticed something in my rear-view mirror.

A black Mercedes, about five cars back.

It had got on to the motorway behind me at Bath, but that

had been ninety minutes and eighty-five miles ago. I was skirting the northern edge of Windsor now, an hour from home, and it was still there.

It had been there the whole time.

I let a couple of miles pass, keeping an eye on the vehicle. Its windscreen was reflecting back the bright sun and the blue of the sky, so it was impossible to see who might be inside. But the further I went, the less concerned I became by it, the Mercedes slowly dropping back, cars changing lanes in front of it. Before long, it was eight cars behind me, a blob in the shimmering evening heat.

I glanced at the clock. Five forty-five.

I pulled into the middle lane and eased the accelerator down, wanting to get home now, to shower, to change, to get something to eat.

As I did, the Mercedes started pulling out too.

It was mirroring my movements.

30

A mile ahead of me was Heston services.

I kept my foot to the floor, flicking a look behind me at the Mercedes. It was subtly trying to close the gap between us. As the sun went behind a cloud, I caught a glimpse of a shape at the wheel – a man, broad, darkened by the shadows of the interior – and then the sun appeared again, and all I could see was a windscreen full of sky. As it did, my mind spooled back to what Veronica Mae had said about the cop who'd come to see her; and then to the forest I'd stopped at on my way out from her house, to the flash of movement I'd seen among the trees.

At the turn-off for the service station, I waited for as long as possible and then pulled a left, coasting up the slight rise and slowing down to see whether the Mercedes reacted. It did. As it pulled off the motorway, I rounded a corner – following a curved road into the car park – and the Mercedes disappeared from view. Accelerating, I whipped into a parking space as close to the service station building as possible, got out of the car and immediately popped the boot. I started going through my rucksack, pushed aside my clothes, washbag, a second notepad – and then finally found what I was looking for: a spare mobile phone. I always brought it with me as back-up, just in case my current one packed up.

Pocketing it, I slammed the boot shut, checked to make sure the Mercedes hadn't arrived yet, and headed inside the service station.

It was busy. I made a beeline for the main shop and soon found what I was looking for: packing tape. Duct tape would have been better, but I'd make do. Paying for the tape, I headed out of the opposite side of the building, on to a small paved area with a few wooden benches and a dreary-looking Travelodge. As quickly as possible, I worked my way around the back of the motel, tracing a very rough circle until I was in the car park again, looking across at my BMW.

The Mercedes was about twenty-five feet away from me, slightly off to my left, parked under the shade of a tree.

There was no one inside.

Keeping my eyes on the service station entrance, I approached the vehicle at a half-run and cupped my hands to the glass as soon as I got to the driver's side. In the passenger footwell I could see a red card folder, white paper edging out from it. I made my way around the front of the car, checking for the returning driver – even though I had no idea what he looked like – and then peered inside the Mercedes for a second time. Closer up, I could see the sheets of white paper had handwriting on them, and that there were two, maybe three photographs stapled to a sheet of pale yellow card. I tried the door in the vain hope that it had been left open, but it was locked, so I started to rock the Mercedes gently instead, hoping not to set the alarm off. I was aiming to shuffle some of the paperwork out from under the card covers.

A few seconds later, I had something.

The white paper was a diary, or a table of some description. There was handwriting inside boxes, some numbers too, and although it was untidy and difficult to make out, the longer I looked at it, the more it began to make sense. It was a time chart. I leaned even closer to the window, my breath fogging up the glass, trying to read the entries on it. Then I realized something: the same word was repeated over and over again.

Raker.

I felt something curdle in my stomach. There were mentions of the Mendips, the address of Veronica Mae's house, my hotel in Bristol. Whoever the Mercedes belonged to, they'd been following me the entire time.

Stealing a quick look at the entrance to the service station, I gave the car another rock, harder this time. The piece of yellow card strayed further beyond the perimeter of the file, two of the photographs stapled to it coming into view.

It took me a second to process what I was seeing.

The first one was a photograph of Alex Cavarno, the COO of AKI Europe. I'd met her in the Comet cinema two days ago. I paused there, a little thrown. Why the hell was there a picture of her? It had been taken without her knowing, outside the entrance to the Comet. She had a takeaway coffee in one hand and was talking on her mobile. As I looked at her, frozen within the boundaries of the snapshot, I remembered the short, unspoken moment between the two of us, the fizz of a connection. Dismissing the feeling, and then forcing the memory away too, I tried to concentrate, to connect the dots, to work out why she was being followed, just the same as me, but I couldn't put it together.

I switched my attention to the second photograph.

It sat adjacent to the one of Alex Cavarno, half still hidden beneath the cover of the folder. I tilted my head, trying to work out what was going on in it, and realized it was a blurry shot of an old man, slightly crooked, at the front door of a house. The walls either side of him were constructed in London stock brick, so it must have been somewhere in the capital.

The man was probably in his nineties, although it was difficult to tell for certain. He was very tall, had a thin covering of white hair, and was smartly dressed in a navy jacket and brown trousers. He had a walking stick pressed between his arm and his ribcage, and was half turned to the door, as if locking up.

Just like the picture of Alex Cavarno, this one had been taken without the subject knowing, cars out of focus in the foreground, as if the photographer had been stationed across from the old man, on the other side of the street.

I glanced towards the service station again, and then back to the picture, and – when I looked at it a second time – something clicked into place. Immediately, like a match igniting in the darkness, I was transported back to Hosterlitz's noirs, to the actor I'd seen in *Connor O'Hare* and *The Eyes of the Night*.

It was Glen Cramer.

This was the person Hosterlitz had discovered in an off-Broadway show; the man who had won two Oscars for his roles in Hosterlitz's noirs. In fact, Cramer was unique, a record-breaker – the only male actor in Hollywood history to have ever won four Academy Awards for acting. But why would anyone want to photograph him like this, as an old man? Why do it in secret? What connection did he have to Alex Cavarno? To me? To any of this?

I finally stepped away from the car, knowing that I had to get clear of the vehicle before the owner came back. Looking around to make sure I wasn't being watched, I moved to the rear bumper.

Tearing off a strip of packing tape, I turned the phone on and then taped the handset to the underside of the Mercedes, making sure the mobile was out of sight. I then layered the phone with more packing tape, ensuring there was no give and that it was properly secured to the belly of the car. Once I was satisfied, I headed back across the car park to the side of the Travelodge, retreating into the shadows, still trying to work out what I'd seen.

Cramer had been signed to AKI in the early 1950s, and he'd returned to do films with them over and over again throughout his career. But he hadn't *just* worked for AKI – he'd done work across all the Hollywood studios. So why was he being photographed now? Why was Cramer even in London in the first place? He was American, he lived in LA.

But then another memory started to form, a shape gliding towards the surface of a lake.

Royalty Park.

The blockbuster television show, co-funded by AKI and the BBC, had been the most-watched programme of 2014, and the fourth series was just about to drop. It was filling ad breaks, billboards, web pages – and, when I'd talked to Alex Cavarno, she'd said the launch party for the new series was on Monday. *That* was why. Cramer had come out of retirement in 2010 to play the role of a retired American ambassador. I wasn't a regular viewer of the show, which was why I hadn't made the leap straight away – but that was the reason he was living in London. So why was he being followed? Why was Alex? Why was I?

Suddenly, I clocked movement near the Mercedes.

The driver.

He was approaching the vehicle, but not looking in my direction. Instead, his eyes were on my BMW, parked thirty feet from him. He looked from my car back to the entrance, and then out across the rest of the car park. He'd clearly looked for me inside but been unable to find me.

I stepped back even further into the shadows, slowly, so he didn't register the shift, and then he came around to the front of the car and got inside.

Wait a second, I thought. *I know this guy.*

Yet, because I wasn't immediately sure where I knew him from, I began to doubt myself. He was wearing a baseball cap, a tan jacket and a black turtleneck, none of which rang any bells. He had a shaved head. He was stocky, like a boxer gone to seed, in his late forties, with grey stubble. He was chunky and powerful, craggy and unattractive. Did I *really* know him? From where?

He glanced across at my BMW again, and then he finally fixed his gaze on the entrance to the service station, his face turned further towards me.

Shit. I know where I've seen him before.

I know who he is.

He'd been inside the Comet cinema the day I'd first met with Alex and Louis Grant. He'd been at the front of the auditorium with a tape measure. He was supposedly drawing up plans for AKI's office renovation – except he hadn't been doing that at all.

He'd been listening to my conversation.

The man in the Mercedes was the architect at the Comet.

31

I left a message with Alex Cavarno's PA and told her I needed to speak to Alex as soon as possible. But, the moment I hung up, I was gripped by panic. What if she was involved in whatever this was? What if the architect was there that day on her instructions? Every case I'd ever worked had been populated by lies and liars – what if she was the same?

But if that was what was going on here, it didn't make any sense. If she knew who the architect was and why he was following me, then why was he taking photos of her without her knowledge? Why invite him to the Comet so that I could see what he looked like? As I retreated further into the shadows, beneath the rattle of an old air-conditioning unit at the side of the Travelodge, my phone began buzzing again.

It was her.

I let it ring a couple of times, trying desperately to draw links between the things that I'd found out over the course of the last few days, but nothing led me back to her. The only link I could see was American Kingdom itself: Alex was running the European office, Cramer had starred in some of its most-renowned films, and I was trying to find the wife of a director who once worked for them.

I pushed Answer. 'David Raker.'

'David, it's Alex Cavarno.'

Her accent sounded stronger over the phone, the hint of her West Coast roots coming through, and I replayed an image of her walking towards me inside the Comet: olive skin, shoulder-length black hair; a blue skirt and white blouse.

'Thanks for calling me back so quickly.'

'Sure,' she said. 'I'm really glad you got in touch.'

She thought this was about something else. I had to manoeuvre us away from here. It was dangerous ground, but not as dangerous as allowing myself to become distracted. I was trying to find Lynda Korin. That was all that mattered.

'David?'

'I'm sorry,' I said. 'This is slightly awkward. You remember I told you I was trying to find Robert Hosterlitz's widow, Lynda Korin?'

'Sure, I remember. Did you get everything you needed from Louis?'

'Yeah, I did, but . . .' I stopped. *I've just got to tell her.* 'I'm being followed,' I said.

A confused pause. 'I'm sorry?'

'Someone is following me.'

'What are you talking about?' She sounded genuinely disconcerted. 'What do you mean, you're being followed?'

'The guy who was there when I met you and Louis in the Comet the other day. I think you said he was your architect. What do you know about him?'

She seemed thrown. 'Uh . . .'

'Did he tell you his name?'

'Are you saying *he's* following you?'

I didn't reply for a moment, giving myself time to think. Her responses felt genuine, but there was no way to tell for sure. I either backed away and played it completely safe, or I opted to trust her and found out what she knew about the architect. For now, I didn't know which one was the right choice.

'David?' she said, sounding irritated for the first time. Her voice had begun to harden. 'What the hell's going on?' She sounded pissed off, misled.

'Your architect's got pictures of you and Glen Cramer in his car.'

A stunned silence, punctuated only by a series of words that seemed to catch in her throat. 'What?' she said finally – and then, more forcibly, as if the idea was really hitting home: '*What?* What the hell are you talking about?'

I glanced at my watch. Six-fifteen. As far as the architect was concerned, I'd been inside the service station for half an hour. It was time to wind my way back around to my car if I didn't want to arouse his suspicions.

'What's his name?' I asked.

'Uh . . .' She still sounded confused. 'Uh, Billy Egan.'

I remembered her calling him Billy at the Comet.

'Have you used him before?' I asked.

'No,' she said, gathering herself. 'We invited local businesses to pitch for the work because we thought that would play out well with the community and the press. Seriously, David, this is right out of left field, don't you think?'

I entered the rear doors of the service station, into the crowds of people.

'Why would he be taking pictures of me?' she said. 'Of Glen?'

'I don't know yet.'

'But his credentials were impeccable. He had photographs of all the work he'd done before, he had brilliant references, he even gave me the numbers of ex-clients of his – I chatted to them and they said he was . . .' She paused, as if holes were opening up in front of her eyes. *He showed her photographs of buildings and projects – but none of them were really his work. He showed her references — but they were fake. She spoke to ex-clients of his — but they weren't ex-clients at all.*

'Son of a bitch,' she said softly.

A second later, I emerged into the late-afternoon sunlight at the front of the service station, and immediately kept my focus on my car.

'Did he have a website?' I asked.

'No. He said it was in the process of being rebuilt.'

'Did you ever go to his office?'

'No. He always came to me.'

'Did he ever give you an email address?'

'No. He just gave me a phone number.'

'Can you text it to me?' I asked. 'I can't write it down now.' The architect's Mercedes was in my peripheral vision now. 'Weird question, but did he ever mention *Royalty Park* or maybe the launch party?'

'No, of course not,' she said. 'Why would he mention that?'

'I'm trying to think of why he'd be interested in Glen Cramer.'

I opened my car and slid in at the wheel.

'Could you email me over the guest list for the party as well?'

'Yeah, sure. I'll get my PA to send it to you.'

I pulled my pad across from the passenger seat and made some notes. 'You said you invited local businesses to pitch for the contract at the Comet?'

'It was America's idea.'

'The US office?'

'Yeah. To be honest, the whole thing was driven by the US. They suggested getting people to pitch, the pitches were sent out to them for approval, and they were the ones who selected Egan. I just met up with him so he could show me his portfolio and make sure I was in the loop. Everything else was done out of LA.'

I paused, pen hovering just above the page.

'So who in the US office set this whole pitch process in motion?'

'Ultimately, it was Saul Zeller.'

'The guy who runs AKI?'

'Wait a second, wait a second.' She was clearly trying to pull it all together. 'Are you saying that Saul lied to me?'

I paused for a moment, thinking. Switching the phone to speaker, I asked Alex to give me a second, then backed out of the call and went to my web browser. I put in a search for 'Billy Egan Architect'. There was nothing.

'So your part in all of this was what?' I asked.

'You mean the selection process? My admin staff compiled all the pitches and mailed them off to the US. We waited a couple of weeks, and then Saul got back to me and said, "This is the guy. Chat to him, to the people he's done work for, see if you agree." I chatted to Egan and he seemed smart. I liked his ideas. That was the end of it.'

The lack of a website, an email address, the fact that he always came to her office, not the other way around, hadn't registered with her at the time. I didn't blame her for that. She rightly would have assumed that Saul Zeller – or, rather, his team in the US – had done the necessary checks at their end.

Something else occurred to me then. 'Who called you to give you the go-ahead on the office move? I mean, who in the US specifically?'

'Saul.'

'Zeller himself? Not his staff?'

'No. Him.'

'But he must have a ton of people working under him?'

'Yeah, he's got a massive team out in LA.'

'So you didn't think it was slightly odd that he got so personally involved in this whole Comet cinema thing – even down to selecting the architect?'

'It probably sounds weird, but when you're on the ground it's really not. He's super hands-on; like, *over the top* hands-on. He's nicknamed the Eye of Sauron because he always has to know what's going on. But it works. You can't argue with what he's done – when he took over AKI, it was minor league. Now it's one of the biggest entertainment companies in the world. All big expenditure – and we're talking almost ten million pounds to convert that cinema – ultimately gets signed off by Saul. More day-to-day stuff he'll obviously leave to me.'

But even if that *was* the case, some measure of doubt still lingered in her voice. Something was going on here, something anomalous. We both knew it.

'When did this whole process start?'

'You mean, when did we invite people to pitch?'

'Yeah.'

'I don't know. Last year – the beginning of November, maybe.'

'Were you expecting it to start then?'

'No. The whole thing had been dragging on for months, and Saul seemed reluctant to sign off on it. The "okay" just came out of the blue, really.'

Except she seemed to catch herself a moment later and we both filled in the gaps: *Zeller had spent months refusing to sign off on the expense – but then, all of a sudden, at the beginning of November, he did.*

The beginning of November.

Only days after Lynda Korin went missing.

'How well do you know Glen Cramer?' I asked.

'Glen? Pretty well.'

'I need you to set up a meeting – today, if possible.'

'It's Saturday evening, David. I can't –'

'This Egan guy has photographs of Cramer and you in his car. He's been following me for at least twenty-four hours, maybe longer. I really need you to set up a meeting, Alex.'

I'd said it softly, but I could feel her bristle.

'And what exactly do I tell him?'

'Whatever you think is the best way to get him to say yes.'

'You don't just drop in for afternoon tea at Glen Cramer's house. This is one of the world's biggest movie stars.'

'I know,' I said again.

She didn't reply for a moment.

'Fine. I'll see what I can do. Anything else?'

'I think it would be a good idea if you *didn't* mention this to Saul Zeller for the time being. Let's just keep it between the two of us until we find out more.'

'Okay,' Alex said, and then paused.

'Are you all right?' I asked.

'Why would Saul lie to me?'

She sounded worried, a little spooked, which was understandable. I felt the same way.

'I don't know,' I replied. 'Maybe he isn't.'

But I wasn't sure she believed that.

And I wasn't sure I did either.

32

Egan tailed me for the next eight miles, all the way to my exit, always at least six cars back. But as I came down the ramp towards Chiswick roundabout, he broke off and headed towards central London. It made me wonder where he was going. It also added to the concern that was building in me: for now, the tail was passive – but at what point would that start to change? When he realized I was on to him? When he next talked to Alex and started to get the sense she might know something? I didn't have a clue who Egan was, had no idea about his background, what sort of person he might be, what drove him, or how he'd react to being exposed, whereas he knew plenty about me. He knew what case I was working.

He probably knew where I lived.

When I got home, I pulled into the driveway, switched off the ignition and waited there for a moment. The alarm was still blinking and there was no indication it had gone off while I'd been away. But, just to be on the safe side, I did a quick circuit of the house before heading inside.

The first thing I did was grab my phone, go to a device location app and log in. A list of my three connected devices rolled out beneath a map that was busy generating a location for each of them. My main mobile and my laptop were with me, so two pins dropped at my home address. A third pin dropped at the western end of Wandsworth High Street. Egan was moving east.

Leaving the phone where it was, I grabbed my laptop, went to my inbox and found a message waiting from Alex. She'd emailed through the table plan for the *Royalty Park* launch party. It was a simplistic, top-down line drawing of the layout, with twenty tables and ten people per table. Each seat had been allocated a name. I didn't recognize all of them, but I recognized a lot: actors and directors, producers, BBC management. Glen Cramer was on a middle table close to the stage. Alex and her European management team were among some more *Royalty Park* actors one table along. Then my focus switched to a table right at the front. It had more of the show's cast members on it, as well as another name I'd come to know better in the past few hours.

Saul Zeller.

He's flying over for the launch party.

Why would the President of AKI fly halfway around the world for a party? *Royalty Park* was a huge success, but it was a fraction of what the company put out in terms of films, TV, music and videogames every year. They must have been laying on parties and launch events all the time.

Trying to fill in the gaps in my knowledge, I put in a web search for him and quickly found a profile piece.

Saul Zeller is the legendary industry heavyweight who, after taking over from his father, Abraham, as President of American Kingdom Inc. in 1970, transformed the company into a major competitor to the likes of Fox, Universal and Warner Bros. He is one of the longest-serving studio heads in Hollywood history.

Joining the company in 1951 as a fresh-faced 24-year-old, Saul was hugely influential at AKI from the get-go. His tenacity and hard-headedness, especially when it came to what worked commercially, won him enemies in the industry, but he enjoyed immense success from early on, persuading his father to make bold – and successful – moves into TV and music, and personally green-lighting box-office hits like *Department Crime* and *The Man with No Mouth*. But his judgement wasn't just confirmed at the tills. He personally signed off on AKI's first Academy Award winner, *Connor O'Hare*, in 1951 – legitimizing the company in many observers' eyes – and then followed that with director Cornell Graham's *The Last Days of the Empire* in 1952, and seven-time Oscar winner *The Eyes of the Night* the following year. As early as the mid 1950s, with Abraham Zeller suffering from ill health, most people believed that Saul was, in actual fact, running the company as the de facto President.

Having threatened to retire many times, Zeller has never *quite* been able to let go of the reins, saying it comes down to 'being a total control freak and not wanting the fun to end'. He often jokes that his long life and good health are down to the 'Prolong' pills used in the company's billion-dollar science-fiction franchise, *Planet of the Sun*. 'I've been taking them every day since 1982,' Zeller told the *LA Times* last year. 'They're like Viagra, but they don't make me feel like I've got three legs.'

Leaving everything where it was, I showered and changed, and – after returning – checked my phone again and saw that Egan's car was slowly inching south along Trinity Road, heading towards Tooting. I grabbed something to eat and, while I ate, I flicked back through the notes I'd made. Mostly they were details I'd garnered from Alex about Saul Zeller, but I also added what I remembered from my chat with the guy at

Rough Print, and began compiling a filmography for Glen Cramer. My hope was that Alex would be able to arrange a meeting with him in the next couple of hours and, if she did, I wanted to be prepared.

His career turned out to be a long and impressive history of success – four Oscars, record-breaking openings, iconic roles as everyone from Abraham Lincoln to the Nazi doctor Josef Mengele, and then even more awards and critical acclaim after he came out of a nine-year retirement in 2010 to star in *Royalty Park*.

It was only after I'd finished and was reading back what I'd written that I felt something gnawing at me: a detail on the page that I wasn't seeing clearly yet. I went back and forth through my notes and eventually returned to the conversation I'd had with the guy at Rough Print, to something he'd said about how lots of films went missing in the way Hosterlitz's horror movies had. He talked about the British Film Institute compiling a list of seventy-five 'lost' films they were keen to get their hands on. Was it something in that?

Unsure, I used my laptop to put in a search for 'BFI lost films'. A couple of moments later, I was on a page headlined 'BFI's 10 Most Wanted'. A few seconds after that, my phone burst into life.

It was Alex.

'Okay,' she said, after I'd answered, 'Glen's agreed to meet up at 8 p.m.'

I looked at the clock. It was 7.15 p.m.

'Fantastic.'

'Thing is, though, he's old but he's not stupid. If you go in there pretending this is about the launch party or something like that, and then start asking him questions about Saul

Zeller, he's going to know this isn't about where he is on the table plan. So I told him a version of the truth – you're doing some work for AKI, and looking into the possibility of undiscovered material from Hosterlitz.'

That was closer to the truth than she realized given Korin's admission that Hosterlitz may have been working on a project called 'Ring of Roses'.

'Okay,' I said, 'that's smart.'

'You've only got an hour, though. That's all I could organize. After that, a limo's picking him up and we've got to run him out to a photo shoot that *Vanity Fair* have organized with the show's cast at Osterley Park.'

'The sun goes down in an hour.'

'It's a night shoot. Please don't be late.'

I thanked her again, ended the call and phoned Melanie Craw. When I'd talked to her earlier, she'd invited me over to her place for something to eat. I felt a pang of guilt as she answered, even though any opinion I had of Alex Cavarno, any connection we shared, had so far gone unspoken.

'I'm not going to be able to make it tonight,' I said to her once she'd picked up. 'I'm really sorry. Something's come up and it won't wait.'

'Okay.'

That was it. I listened to the silence on the line, then remembered what else she'd said to me on the phone before: *I need to talk to you about something.*

'We can chat now,' I said.

'No, not over the phone.'

'Are you sure everything's all right?'

'Just give me a shout when you're free,' she said.

I waited for a moment, trying to imagine what she might want to talk about – but then I let it go.

Using the mobile again, I double-checked Egan's position. The pin had finally come to a halt in a street called Bradbury Lane, just off Streatham High Road. That was eleven miles south-east of where I was. I watched for a while, ensuring Egan had definitely come to a stop, my eyes flicking between the phone's display and the notes I'd made on the laptop, still feeling like something was staring me in the face. The harder I looked, the fuzzier the words became.

It doesn't matter. All that matters is Egan.

But as I went to close my laptop, my eyes strayed across the BFI's '10 Most Wanted' page again – and, at the bottom, I fixed on their address.

21 Stephen Street. London. W1T 1LN.

The postcode. I felt an internal shift.

It's their postcode.

Feeling a charge of electricity, I put in a search for a list of curators – the people at the BFI who maintained and catalogued the organization's collection – and found a list of nearly thirty people, divided into Fiction, Non-Fiction, TV, and Special Collections. There were seven names in the Fiction section, four men and three women. I started going through the men, reading each of their biographies.

At the third one down, I stopped.

His name was Rafael Walker. He looked to be in his mid forties. His work for the BFI had involved curating exhibitions on American film noir and European horror movies from the 1970s. He'd contributed articles on those subjects to *Sight & Sound* magazine and had written the BFI Classics book on *The Eyes of the Night*. He knew Hosterlitz's work intimately, both his noirs and his horror films.

Male. Forty-five. W1, London.

I was starting to wonder if I'd just found Microscope.

33

Glen Cramer lived in a detached, four-storey townhouse in Bayswater. It was a beautiful building, a mix of London stock brick and white render, with ivy covering an entire flank of the building. Immediately outside its set of six-foot steel gates, a group of four girls in their mid-to-late teens were chattering to one another. On the opposite side of the street, eight other people were gathered, some taking pictures of the house. Two of them, smoking and leaning against the bonnet of a grey van, were press photographers, cameras hanging from their necks. It made me realize how easy it would have been for Egan to blend in here.

As I arrived, Alex Cavarno was already waiting for me in her Range Rover. I parked behind her and she started to get out, dressed for the weekend in a pair of red leggings, a white vest and flip-flops, her dark hair braided to one side, her face free of make-up except for a hint of mascara. Casual or formal, it didn't seem to make much difference – she looked just as good as the first time I'd met her.

'Hey,' she said.

'Hey.' I gestured to the house. 'Thanks for organizing this.'

'Sure.' She stopped in front of me – her eyes on the photographers, on the girls gathered at the gates – and cut to the chase: 'Do you think we're in danger?'

My head was still filled with noise – with Egan, with the idea that I might have located the man known as Microscope, with the prospect of interviewing Glen Cramer – but, when I looked at her, everything seemed to fall away for a moment. Without her heels, she was shorter than me by about six inches, so, even from four feet away, her chin was tilted slightly as she looked up at me. I could see the lines of her neck, the ridges of her collarbones, the bronze of her skin; and I could see the worry in her face, the tautness of her expression.

'I don't think so,' I said.

'How do you know?'

'If Egan was going to make a move, he would have already.'

'I'm glad you're so confident.'

'He's been watching me for at least a day. He's almost certainly been watching you for longer than that. If you were any immediate danger to him, he wouldn't be stalking around in the shadows taking your picture.'

She frowned. 'So what's he waiting for?'

'That's what I need to find out.'

Alex eyed me for a moment. 'You're asking me to put my trust in a guy I only met for a couple of minutes two days ago.' She looked from my car, to me, to the pad I was holding, and then a smile traced her lips. 'That's you, by the way.'

I returned the smile. 'I realize that.'

'Can I trust you, David?'

'If I told you that you could, would you believe me?'

Her gaze lingered on me.

'Yeah,' she said. 'Yeah, I think I probably would.'

I could feel the heat of her eyes on me, but I focused my attention on the house instead, on Cramer, on everything I needed to cover in the next hour. A second later, we were crossing the road towards the gates, shutters buzzing like a field of crickets, as the celeb-spotters took camera-phone pics of us. They didn't recognize us from *Royalty Park*, from

TV, from the movies, from anywhere – but they still took their shots, just in case.

It felt weird being there. I found myself wondering what Cramer would be like, how he would come across, how different he would be from the characters he played onscreen. I thought about what my daughter would say when I told her I'd interviewed one of the world's biggest movie stars. Briefly, I even thought about asking Cramer for a photograph afterwards, so I could message it to Annabel in Spain. I smiled at the idea of writing something casual like 'Me with my best pal Glen' or 'Glen Cramer says hi', and smiled again at the thought of her response. But then the intercom at the gate buzzed into life, and all of that seemed to drop away again, and I was back in control and felt ridiculous for getting carried away.

'Hello?'

'Anthony, it's Alex Cavarno.'

A second later, the gate hummed once and bumped away from its frame. Alex moved through ahead of me as I pushed the gate shut again, and then we made our way across the driveway to the front steps. As we started the climb up, the front door opened and Glen Cramer emerged from inside.

Even though – at ninety-one – this wasn't the same version of him that I'd seen in Hosterlitz's noirs, it felt strangely like I knew him already. He remained tall, but he'd become very thin and, as I'd seen in Egan's photograph, he now had a veil of chalky hair. It was fine, almost like thread. I'd seen a crookedness to him too in the picture, and that was clearly evident now, his spine curving at the halfway point, so the top third of him teetered like a building on the brink of collapse. Elsewhere, his face was criss-crossed with lines and folds of skin, his complexion a mesh of tiny blood vessels, and his trademark blue eyes had lost some of their lustre. But the echoes of the man he'd been, square-jawed and stately, were still there, and age had robbed him of none of his presence.

He kissed Alex on both cheeks and they both looked at me as Alex said, 'This is David Raker, Glen. He's the man I was telling you about.'

Cramer held out his hand. 'Nice to meet you, David.'

'A pleasure, Mr Cramer.'

We shook and then he said, 'Please, come in.'

He looked beyond us both and waved to the people waiting outside. One of the teenagers squealed with delight. I saw that she was wearing a *Royalty Park* T-shirt. The press photographers were already on our side of the street, cameras in front of their faces. Cramer gave them another wave before we stepped past him and he closed the door.

He rolled his eyes at us, good-naturedly. 'I'll admit,' he said, 'until I started on *Royalty Park* I thought my days of screaming teenagers were over.'

We followed Cramer into a gorgeous airy foyer with a chequerboard-tiled floor and an ornate oak staircase on the right. A man in a navy-blue blazer, built like a gorilla, was sitting in an armchair close to the stairs.

Cramer said to Alex, 'You've met Anthony, my security man.'

'I have,' Alex replied.

'Vera?' Cramer said, shuffling to a stop.

A few seconds later, a short woman in her late fifties emerged from the kitchen, an apron on, a pair of Marigolds dotted with soapsuds on her hands.

Cramer looked at us. 'Can I offer you something to drink?'

'Coffee for me,' said Cavarno, and – to make things easy – I said coffee was fine for me too. After the housekeeper had disappeared back into the kitchen, Cramer led us into the living room, another impressive space full of original Georgian flourishes, and a set of rear doors that opened on to an emerald-green square of lawn, dappled with late-evening sun. The house looked the part, but it was obvious he was renting. There was none of his history here, no photographs, no cabinets full of awards, or reminders of the life he'd enjoyed. I watched him shuffle to one of the sofas and topple back into it, and then I sat down on a second sofa, opposite him. Alex took an armchair.

'So,' he said, hands planted either side of him, veins worming their way beneath ivory skin, 'Alex tells me you're an investigator, David.'

'That's right.'

'"Forget it, Jake. It's Chinatown."'

I smiled. 'I'm not quite Jack Nicholson.'

Cramer laughed. 'I actually read the *Chinatown* script when they were still casting it, but Robert Towne told me that they'd already got John Huston in mind for Noah Cross.' He grinned, his teeth the only part of him that hadn't really aged – bleached, artificially perfect. 'I haven't many regrets, but that's one of them.'

'You still made some pretty good choices.'

'I did okay, I think. You a fan of the movies, David?'

'Very much so.'

'This must be an interesting project then?'

Alex leaned forward. 'I told Glen that you're looking into the possibility of there being some undiscovered material from Robert Hosterlitz's AKI days.'

Cramer nodded enthusiastically.

'That's right,' I said. I felt bad about lying to him, but I went with it for now. 'Is it okay if I ask you some questions?'

'Of course,' he said, opening out his hands. 'Ask me anything you want.'

34

I eased Cramer into it with something straightforward.

'What do you remember of Robert?'

'What do I remember of him?' He took a long breath, as if there was too much to recount, the question too vague. 'He was a good man. Intelligent and reputable. I felt honoured to call him a friend.' Cramer stopped, looking out over my shoulder to the rear doors, where the sun spilled a rectangle of tangerine light across the living room. The more thought he gave it, though, the more sombre he seemed to become. 'Oh, Bobby,' he said eventually, quietly, almost to himself. 'Those HUAC hearings back in the fifties . . . Man, they were such bullshit. Just random target practice for assholes on Capitol Hill with a God complex. I knew him for over four years before he was being defamed in that disgusting pamphlet the *National People*, and I'm telling you, Bobby Hosterlitz wasn't any communist. No way. He was a moderate. Most of the time, I never even heard him talk about politics. All he really cared about was movies.'

I pulled my pad towards me and made a couple of notes. 'The *National People* was a US magazine back in the fifties and sixties – is that right?'

'Sorry, yeah,' Cramer said, holding up a sinuous hand in apology, 'I forgot you guys have probably never heard of it. Lucky you.' He shook his head. 'It was a tabloid, kind of like the *National Enquirer*, feeding on sex, violence and scandal. Nothing else. It was just full of hateful lies. They broke the story about Bobby supposedly being a communist, and – as soon as they did – the vultures at the HUAC were circling him, and that was it. "Sex-obsessed Hosterlitz outed as a Red".'

'That was the headline?'

'Correct.'

I thought of Hosterlitz's trademark style – the lingering camera, the secret watcher – then of what Veronica Mae had said about his relationship with Korin.

'Why "sex-obsessed"?' I asked.

Cramer shrugged. 'There always had to be some sex angle to everything. It was all about sex. And if it wasn't about sex, then they just made something up.'

'Did they make something up about Robert?'

'They said he had a taste for prostitutes.'

Cramer obviously saw that element as another part of the hatchet job the *National People* did on Hosterlitz, but Lynda Korin had admitted in the interview she did with *Cine* that Hosterlitz had paid for sex during his struggle with booze and painkillers in the 1970s, in the years before the two of them had met. It didn't seem like much of a stretch to suggest that he might also have done the same in the 1950s. The question was whether it was in any way relevant.

'Do you ever remember Robert dating anyone?'

'In the fifties?'

'Yeah. Girlfriends, relationships.'

'I guess he must have.'

'But you don't remember anyone specific?'

'He was a young, successful director, so there were always hangers-on. But if you're asking me if I specifically remember *individuals*, then I'd have to say no, I don't. It was a long time ago, and I'm an old man, so that doesn't help.' He smiled again, although I could see that he wasn't finished. 'But if I'm being honest, Bobby was always something of a lonely soul. I never really figured out if it was being an only child that did it, or whether it was a German thing, some product of how he'd been brought up. But he was comfortable in his own skin, his own company. He didn't go looking for relationships. I remember he used to tell me how, growing up, he'd spent hours on the sets of Fritz Lang's pictures, observing how Lang worked, how he directed, and he would compile these reams of notes. *That* was what interested him. I mean, does that sound like the kind of thing *you* were doing as a teenager, David?'

'Not really, no.'

He held out his hands. 'Nor me.'

'When was the last time you saw him?'

'Oooh,' Cramer said, pressing a couple of fingers to his head. 'I don't know. I didn't see him for a long time after he moved here. I was born and raised in the San Fernando Valley, I've spent most of my working life in LA, and he was on the other side of the world – here in the UK, in Germany, in Spain – so we kind of lost touch with one another after a while. I don't think he wanted anything to do with Holly-wood after what had happened – and who could blame him? The industry sold him down the river. They fed him to the sharks. All the crap on the front pages, all the lies in those HUAC hearings, and no one – not studio execs, not direc-tors, not producers, not a single actor he worked with – ever went out to bat on his behalf.' He paused, blinking slowly, smaller somehow, as if the colour had been rinsed from him. 'I'm embarrassed to say, that also includes me.'

The housekeeper entered, carrying a tray with three cof-fee mugs on it and some biscuits, but Cramer didn't look up. He just stared into space, quiet and far-off, and the remorse didn't leave his face for a long time. Eventually, Alex stepped in and began talking about the launch party, about some of the people who were going to be there, and then Cramer got on to the subject of this series of *Royalty Park* being his last, about how audiences might react to him being killed off in the last episode. He turned to me quickly after he said that and apologized for giving the plot away, but I told him not to worry, and he and Alex picked up the conversation again. He talked about the lease running out on this place, how he planned to move back to LA, how he was going to miss London but not the weather, and then everything came full circle and they were back on to the party.

Despite the expensive sheen of his surroundings, it was easy to forget that this man had once been one of the biggest movie stars on the planet, and maybe still was. No male actor had ever won more Oscars than him. No one had been as critically acclaimed *and* as commercially viable, and now he was bowing out from what might currently be the biggest television show in the world. As I chewed on that, I thought of how Cramer's experiences contrasted so dramatically with those of Robert Hosterlitz, the person who had plucked Cramer from obscurity, who had waited for him at the stage door of an off-Broadway play and told Cramer he could be a Hollywood star. They'd both won Oscars for *The Eyes of the Night*, but while Cramer had gone on to become a phenomenon, Hosterlitz had died on a hillside in Somerset, alone except for the love of one woman, with thirty years of movies and TV behind him that no one remembered, much less cared about.

I gently returned Cramer to our conversation. 'Did you ever see any of the other movies that Robert made after he left the US in 1954?'

'I saw *The Ghost of the Plains*.'

'His western?'

'Yeah. When was that released? Mid sixties?'

'Nineteen sixty-seven.'

'I remember seeing that at the pictures. I loved it. I know the critics were sniffy about it, and I know it didn't make Paramount a whole bunch of money, but I preferred it to the spaghetti westerns that Clint was making. Bobby's film had real class. Although, well . . . I guess he made *Ghost* after he *returned* to the US.'

I nodded. 'What about the movies he made in Europe?'

'Um . . .' He frowned, his fists balled up as if he was trying to force himself to remember. Or maybe he was trying to force himself to remember their titles, because it was obvious he hadn't seen anything else Hosterlitz had made.

'It's okay if you didn't,' I said.

He let out a coarse breath. 'I feel bad.'

'Don't worry.' I pressed on. 'I'm not sure if you know this, but he made eleven horror films in Spain between 1979 and 1984, and they all have a ninety-second scene at the end featuring his wife Lynda and some footage of a residential street.' I paused, searching his face, but he just stared at me, clearly unaware of where this was going. 'What I mean is, except for some tiny details, that scene is reproduced almost identically in every film he made during that time.'

Alex was frowning. 'Are you serious?'

I nodded and we both looked at Cramer, but he was glancing between us as if this were some joke at his expense. 'The same scene?' he said uncertainly.

'That doesn't mean anything to you?'

He shook his head, a confused frown etched into his face, and he suddenly looked his age. I decided to change direction before I lost momentum.

Removing the picture of the wooden angel, and passing it across to him, I said to him, 'This is going to seem weird, but does this photo ring any bells?'

He held it between his finger and thumb and fiddled around in the breast pocket of his blazer for a pair of glasses. He was wearing a blue shirt under it and a pair of cords, and he eventually found his glasses in the pocket of his trousers.

'Is this an angel?' he asked.

'Yes. It's carved from wood. Do you recognize it?'

'No.' He looked up. 'What's that on its neck?'

'A black crucifix.'

Cramer tilted the photo, as if he were hoping it might form into something three-dimensional that he could move and manipulate. Eventually, he handed it back to me. 'Did you find this among Robert's things?' he asked.

'Among his wife's. Do you recognize it?'

'No,' he said, 'I'm afraid I don't.'

I checked my watch. As Alex saw me doing that, she said, 'We're going to have to wrap this up before too long, David.'

I turned to Cramer again. 'Do you still have many dealings with Saul Zeller?'

'Saul? Ooh, not for a long time.' He looked confused again by the change of tack. 'The last picture I did for American Kingdom was *D* back in . . .' He turned to Alex. 'When was *D*?'

'Mid nineties?' she said. 'Ninety-four, maybe?'

'Yeah, 1994 sounds about right. Saul had been running things, officially, since 1970, but unofficially from way before that, and I did a lot of films for AKI during the fifties, sixties and seventies, so I got to see him – on and off – plenty of times, in that period.' He paused. 'But after *D* came

223

out . . . Ooh, I don't know when I last actually spoke to Saul. Could be five years. Could be ten. I mean, I was fully retired by 2001 and, when I came back to do *Royalty Park* in 2010, it was Alex that I dealt with because the show was being made out of London, not LA.'

I wrote down a couple of notes.

He was still frowning. 'Why do you ask?'

'Oh, it's nothing,' I said, dismissing it all with a wave of the hand, trying to give myself some thinking time. 'I might get a chance to meet him while he's over for the launch party, is all. From what I've read, he's got a fierce reputation. I just wondered whether to take a flak jacket.'

That seemed to relax Cramer, who laughed gently, and said, 'Oh, he's not that bad. I've been in meetings with him where he's chewed someone out – but that's normal for these high-powered execs.' He glanced at Alex and winked at her. 'No, Saul's okay. I've talked to him at dinner parties, at functions, and had lovely conversations with him. I'm sure he'll be on his very best behaviour.'

'So you've never fallen out with him?'

'No, Saul and I have never had any cause for pistols at dawn.' He was still smiling, seeing this as part of the same joke about Zeller's fierce reputation.

'What about the name Billy Egan – have you ever heard of him?'

He looked at me, as if unsure whether this was a continuation of the joke about Zeller or not. 'No,' he said, 'I haven't. Is he someone I *should* have met?'

'No,' I replied, making light of it, 'just a loose end.' I changed the subject before he could ask a follow-up. 'Did you ever meet Robert's wife, Lynda Korin?'

'No, unfortunately I didn't. I would very much have liked

to, though. Like I said to you, Bobby was a lonely soul, so for him to have made the leap in that way and commit himself to someone . . . well, she must have had something special.'

'What about the term "Ring of Roses"?'

He seemed temporarily thrown and, when I glanced at her, I could see a similar expression on Alex's face too.

'"Ring of Roses",' he repeated. 'Like the nursery rhyme?'

'Exactly. Does that mean anything to you?'

'You mean, *apart* from it being a nursery rhyme?'

'Right. Maybe it was a script you read?'

'No,' he said. 'No, I don't think so.'

This was going nowhere. Cramer had probably read thousands of scripts over the years. I dropped it and got ready to move on.

'We're *really* going to have to wrap this up, David,' Alex said.

'Okay, just one last thing.' I had maybe three minutes. 'You told me earlier you didn't see Robert for a long time after he moved to the UK. Does that mean that you *did* see him again after he left the US in 1954?'

He nodded. 'Yeah. But only once. No, twice.'

'Do you remember when those times were?'

He narrowed his eyes, thinking. 'The first time was when he was shooting *The Ghost of the Plains* at Paramount, because I was shooting *Saints of Manhattan* at the same time, and I had no idea he was back making films. I don't think anyone did, really – or, at least, Bobby didn't announce it to the world. I think he wanted the picture to come out and speak for itself.' A flicker of a smile: sad, distant, but then it began to warm. 'I can't remember all the details, but I recall I was out on the studio lot somewhere and I looked up and thought, "That guy looks just like Bobby Hosterlitz." He was sitting there, side-on to me, smoking a cigarette, had this great, thick script' – Cramer indicated how big with his forefinger and thumb – 'resting there on his lap, and he was furiously scribbling all over it. I wasn't sure if it really *was* him or not, because he'd lost a lot of weight since the last time I'd seen him – but the closer I got, the more I realized it definitely *was* him. I said to him, "Bobby? Is that really you?" and he looks up at me, and this great big smile blooms on his face and he says to me, "Glen, I was hoping I might run into you."'

Cramer paused, staring off into space, absorbed by the memories. 'He was renting this crappy apartment in East Hollywood, so I invited him to come and stay with me for a few weeks while I helped him look for something better. I did it automatically, without thinking, and then a part of me started to worry that, after however long it was – twelve, thirteen years – we might not have anything to say to one another. But, actually, it was lovely – like no time had passed at all.'

'What about the second time you saw him?'

His face darkened.

'Mr Cramer?'

'The second time wasn't quite as nice.' His lips flattened in a grimace, and I could see he was trying to be diplomatic, trying not to paint Hosterlitz in a bad light. 'I can't remember when the second time was exactly. A good while after that, though. Years.' He paused, eyes screwed up, trying to remember a date. 'I think it must have been a December, because I got home one night and there was this guy – this bum – slumped outside the gates of the house, beneath a tree my maid had decorated with lights.'

'Are you saying the guy was Hosterlitz?'

He nodded. 'It wasn't a bum, it was Bobby. He looked terrible. He'd lost so much weight, he was so gaunt. I pull up next to him and put down my window, and I say, "*Bobby?*" – and all I can smell is booze. It's coming off him like cologne. I say, "Come on, let's get you inside, let's get you cleaned up," but then he staggers over and starts pointing his finger at me, swearing at me. It was . . .' He'd already started shaking his head. 'It was unlike him. I mean, there were rumours – especially when he returned to the States to do *The Ghost of the Plains* – that he had a problem with drink. I know the death of his mom hit him hard shortly after that too. But I'd certainly never seen him as bad as this. Definitely not as aggressive.'

'What was he saying?'

'Some of it was hard to make out.'

'Can you remember anything?'

'He was slurring a lot. But I think what sticks with me the most is him telling me I didn't deserve anything I'd achieved.'

'Why would he say that?'

'I've literally no idea. Silly thing is, those words actually hurt. They hurt a lot. Coming from him, from someone I'd been so close to at one time, someone who was basically *responsible* for my entire career being what it was, they stung me. I've had a few bad reviews, and I don't spend a second worrying about what the *LA Times* thinks of my movies. But what Bobby thought, that was different. I respected him. I don't know what I'd done to upset him – but his words hurt.'

Cramer shrugged. 'I don't know if he was drunk, or high, or just confused – but whatever was wrong with him, he was seriously screwed up. Eventually, I managed to calm him down, I took him inside and he fell asleep on my couch. I'll admit that took a fair degree of soul-searching on my part, to take him inside like that and let him sleep it off in my home when he'd been so vile outside it. But the alternative was calling the cops and them throwing him in the drunk tank, and that just didn't seem like the right way to treat a friend, even one who was behaving as badly as Bobby was. I remember the woman I was dating at the time – her name was Gloria – she chewed me out the next morning when she came through and found puke all over the couches, over the floor, all over the house.'

'Did Robert apologize to you the next day?'

'No. He was gone before Gloria and I had even got up.' He attempted a smile, but it wasn't much of one. He looked pained and hurt. '*C'est la vie*, I guess – but I can't pretend that I wasn't angry at the time. And that was the last memory Bobby left me with: shouting outside my house, the swearing and ranting, and my maid on her hands and knees the next day, sponging his vomit out of the couch.'

'You didn't see him again after that?'

Cramer shook his head. 'No,' he said, quiet, melancholic. 'The next time I saw Bobby Hosterlitz was in an obituary column.'

35

A limousine came to pick Cramer up a couple of minutes later and, after he was gone, Alex and I stood beside her Range Rover, the sky dark, the stars out, the tourists and photographers long gone.

'I've got some work I need to finish off,' she said.

'Thanks again for organizing this.'

'Did it help?'

'Yes,' I told her, although I wasn't sure if that was really true or not. I needed some time to process everything Cramer had just told me, because at the moment I was struggling to see how it all connected. Cramer hadn't seen Saul Zeller for five years, maybe even longer than that, and he hadn't seen him with any frequency since before Cramer did his last film with AKI – and that was over twenty years ago. It wasn't like they were friends, or colleagues, or even enemies. They were just people who'd worked together once. Likewise, Alex spoke to Zeller at least once a week on video call, as an employee of his. I wasn't sure what would motivate Zeller to have Alex – and Cramer – followed with a long-lens camera.

At the same time, the only reason I could come up with for Zeller having *me* followed was if he had a vested interest in what I might find during my search for Lynda Korin. But was his interest in my case to do with Lynda Korin – or Robert Hosterlitz? He'd had a working relationship with Hosterlitz once upon a time, he'd had one with Glen Cramer until 1994, and now he had one with Alex Cavarno, so those links at least made some sort of sense. But Korin? As far as I was aware, the two of them – Zeller and her – had never met. Which was why I was starting to think that Zeller needed Korin in order to get at something in Hosterlitz's life. Something hidden in his past.

'So should I call the police?'

I tuned back in. The street was quiet except for a couple of birds cooing on a telephone wire high above us. Alex was standing at the door of her car, her fingers on the handle, looking up at me. From three feet away, I could smell her perfume, her eyes like embers under the orange street lights.

'Call the police?' I said.

'About being followed by this Egan guy.'

'I don't think you need to do that yet.'

'So you think I'm safe?'

'I've got his address, and I'm going to find out who he really is, so I think he'll be more interested in what *I'm* doing.' I gestured to the mobile she was holding. 'You've got my number, though. Call me if you're worried.'

'Okay.'

'I mean it.'

She nodded, her gaze lingering on mine, and I felt that same buzz along my spine, across my chest, behind my eyes.

'I don't have to finish off my work tonight,' she said.

I knew what was coming.

I just looked at her, her skin an autumnal brown, her eyes a dark amber. She looked beautiful.

'Do you fancy getting a drink?' she asked.

Yes. No. I don't know.

'David?'

'I can't,' I blurted out, and I felt the breath leave

me – relief, guilt, regret. 'I can't,' I repeated, the words clearer, stronger, now that I'd committed myself to them. 'It's not that I don't want to . . .' *Because I do.* I stopped, swallowed. 'It's just . . . I'm seeing someone else.'

'Oh.'

'I don't want to hurt her.'

'No, of course,' she said quickly, embarrassed now. 'Of course you don't. I didn't mean to . . .' It was her turn to stop this time. 'I'm sorry. I didn't . . .'

I held up a hand.

'I misread the situation,' she said.

'You didn't misread it.'

The implication was obvious, but it did nothing to stifle her discomfort. She pulled at the door of the Range Rover.

'I'd better be going.'

'Okay.'

'Give me a call if you need anything else.'

'I will. Thank you again, Alex.'

It was only as her car disappeared from view and the burn of the guilt and regret began to ebb away that a thought popped into my head: What if all of this was about 'Ring of Roses'?

What if that was the reason Saul Zeller brought Egan into the fold at the beginning of November? Completely out of the blue, he'd given Alex the go-ahead on the Comet refurbishment, after months of stalling on it, and told her to invite local businesses to pitch for the work. What if he did that because, a few days before, Zeller had come across Marc Collinsky's web article?

The timings fitted.

Late October was the first time 'Ring of Roses' had been mentioned anywhere, in any form. Collinsky had left all mention of it out of the print edition, which was why that wouldn't have rung any alarm bells with Zeller. Plus, as a UK magazine, it wouldn't even have been available in the States on export until January or February. But the Internet was different. It was instantly available. The article was there, for everyone to see, as soon as it went up on 27 October.

Maybe Zeller had found the article online himself. Maybe Egan had brought it to his attention. Maybe someone else did. However it had happened, it *had* to be why Zeller had signed off on the Comet plans so suddenly. He wanted Egan close to AKI Europe – in and around it. But to keep an eye on Alex? On Cramer? Or to follow a trail back to Korin and Hosterlitz, to whatever 'Ring of Roses' was? Egan was either following me because he hadn't found Korin, or because he had. So did that mean he was trying to stop me – or use me?

Even without the answers I craved, I felt something grip in my stomach, an intuitive feeling that this was going somewhere bad. It was instinct kicking in from years of having followed missing people into the darkness. As I got out my phone and went to the location app, the same map of the same area in south London appeared, the pin dropped outside the same house as earlier on.

It belonged to Billy Egan.

I had to find out who he really was.

36

Bradbury Lane was an L-shaped cul-de-sac midway along Streatham High Road. The cul-de-sac consisted of an odd mix of 1930s houses, a couple of boxy, pebble-dashed bungalows, and a series of small businesses – a corner shop, a car workshop, a tailor, a chip shop. At the bend in the street, I spotted the Mercedes for the first time: it was half hidden by a tree at the gates to one of the bungalows, and sat parked on the drive, its black paint melding with the dark of the night. I pulled a U-turn and found a space away from the house, right at the mouth of the road.

The bungalow outside which the Mercedes was parked was probably the least attractive of all the houses. It had a single bay window at the front, a black door, an ugly brown colour to its pebble-dash, and a wooden fence that had gone a long time without being treated. Halfway along, the fence bowed slightly, as if either it had been battered by a strong wind, or someone had driven a car into it.

I checked the time. It was 10.30 p.m.

Angling the rear-view mirror so I had a clear view of the house, I used the time available to me to start searching for Rafael Walker, the man I hoped might be Microscope. The unusual, European spelling of his first name, combined with his very English surname, meant the hunt didn't last long. Pretty soon, I had both Facebook and Twitter accounts for him, Instagram too, and the bones of a website he'd tried to get off the ground – and given up on – when he'd started writing for *Sight & Sound* and the BFI Classics range.

On Facebook and Twitter, he was careful not to give too much of his personal information away; his posts were about films, TV, or work he was engaged in at the BFI. There were pictures from the American film noir exhibition he'd curated, but not a lot else. He loved his job, he loved movies. That was about the sum total of it.

On Instagram, however, he'd been marginally less cautious. I searched for his name in an online phone directory, found twenty-four R. Walkers in London, and then started going through his pictures individually, trying to look for any indication of where photos had been taken, and whether those photos might give me an idea of obvious life patterns, routines, where he liked going, and in what area he might live. After a couple of minutes, I found a shot of him with two other people in some kind of park. There was a series of small white boulders surrounding them; a sort of stone circle. Behind them, the sun had started to set, and – as I studied the photograph more closely – I realized I recognized the layout of the stones.

It was Hilly Fields in Lewisham.

I returned to the online phone directory. The twelfth R. Walker on the list had an address on Prendegast Avenue, half a mile from Lewisham High Street.

I thought briefly about calling him and double-checking he was definitely the person I was after, but it was ten-thirty on a Saturday night, and cold-calling him at home and firing questions at him about Hosterlitz and Korin seemed like the wrong way to play it. If he was smart, he'd probably figure out that I'd stalked him through social media, using it in the worst way possible, but that was just something I'd have to tackle once I got him on the phone – or saw him in person.

Monday was a bank holiday, which meant he wouldn't be back in work until at least Tuesday – and there was no way I was waiting two days just so I could turn up at the BFI offices and make it all look official.

Setting aside thoughts of Walker for the time being, I reached into the back seat, removed my pad and all the files I'd collected over the past few days, and started leafing through them again. It didn't take long before I returned to Glen Cramer, to my short-hand version of the interview, rereading the same things in the same order, and turning them over in my head. Pretty soon after, I hit the section where he'd talked about Hosterlitz coming to his house, to the gates of his home, and my eyes came to rest on a line I'd added right at the end.

2nd time – December WHEN ??

It referred to the second and last time Cramer had seen Hosterlitz. The first time had been on the Paramount lot in 1966, when Cramer had been filming *Saints of Manhattan* and Hosterlitz had returned to make *The Ghost of the Plains*. The second time, according to Cramer, had been December in some unspecified year.

I flipped back in my pad, all the way to notes I'd made while speaking to Wendy Fisher on video call, and then drew my laptop towards me, loading up a full interview transcription I'd typed up. I started going through it line by line. It didn't take me long to find what I was looking for.

WENDY: I remember when Lyn and Bob came out to us one year . . . Jeez, this must have been Christmas 1984. Anyway, they stayed for a few nights, Christmas Day, and then Bob gets up on the twenty-sixth and just disappears for a week.

ME: Really? Where did he go?

WENDY: Northern Minnesota. Apparently, he went up to the state forests.

ME: Is that what Lynda said?

WENDY: She said he was scouting for work. I don't know if that was true or not – I don't even know if she really knew herself – but this was only the third time we'd ever laid eyes on him, and he couldn't be bothered to spend more than a few days with us before driving off to wherever he thought he was going to scout for work in rural Minnesota.

Cramer had remembered how the tree outside his home had been decorated in lights the night that Hosterlitz had come to his house, and that it had been December.

So what if Hosterlitz's scouting trip wasn't to northern Minnesota at all?

What if he'd gone to Los Angeles instead?

I went through the interview a second time, a third time, but my attention kept returning to the same section: *She said he was scouting for work. I don't know if that was true or not – I don't even know if she really knew herself.* Was it possible that Korin genuinely didn't know where her husband had been that week in December 1984? If that were true, why would he choose to keep it from her? Why would he make a trip to LA in the first place? Was it simply to confront Cramer?

It surely couldn't have been to actually *look* for work. By that time, he'd been retired for nearly a year and was living with Korin on the Mendips. But even if he'd changed his mind about retiring, no studio would hire him, so hoping to find work of any kind was surely a wasted journey. Korin had talked about Hosterlitz starting to write again in retirement, to find happiness in it, but Cramer had never heard of 'Ring of Roses', and Korin had never seen as much as a partial script, so it seemed unlikely Hosterlitz had flown out to LA brandishing a finished screenplay.

Equally, it seemed an extreme course of action to fly fifteen hundred miles just to have a go at Cramer. Why bother? Was he looking for someone to blame for the demise of his career? Was it jealousy? Spite? All he'd ended up doing was embarrassing himself, and near destroying whatever affection Cramer still held for him. Perhaps, by that stage, Hosterlitz could see the end coming. He'd been given the devastating news that he had terminal cancer just weeks before he flew out to the US to see Wendy and her family, so he knew he was ill. Maybe that, combined with years of feeling victimized, the drink, the pills, the bitterness and resentment he must have felt, didn't make it seem like an extreme reaction to him. Maybe it felt rational.

The last act in one long tragedy.

My gaze returned to the quote from Wendy Fisher – to the possibility that Korin had had no idea what Hosterlitz had been up to that week – and it made me wonder what other aspects of their marriage had been like that. What else had he kept back from her? Had she, in return, done the same to him? I thought of the conversation I'd had with Marc Collinsky, about how Korin had told him she'd never questioned Hosterlitz's direction, even the repetition of those same, ninety-second scenes. But what if she *had* asked about it and he'd given her a reason, just not one that was the truth? Nothing in any piece of paper I'd read, or interview I'd done, suggested to me that they were unhappy. But if he'd lied to her about his so-called scouting trip in 1984, why not lie about other things?

Maybe he wasn't the man Korin thought she knew.

Maybe he wasn't a man anyone knew.

As I traced the lines of the interview for a fourth time, trying to find more of it that I could get into and prise open, I caught movement in the rear-view mirror and realized I'd become so consumed by the idea of Hosterlitz going to LA and lying to his wife that I'd shifted my attention away from the house.

Someone was coming out of the bungalow.

37

Snapping the laptop shut, I sank into my seat, eyes on the mirror. It was Egan. He came out of the front door and pulled it shut behind him, took a cursory glance out into the street, then unlocked the Mercedes. The indicators flashed twice. I caught a brief glimpse of his shaved head as he leaned forward, checking something on the dash, and saw that he was wearing the same clothes as earlier – a tan jacket, a black turtleneck. But then the shadows took him.

I'd parked close enough to the car behind me for him not to be able to see my registration plates when he passed, and far enough away from the nearest street light for the grey of my BMW to look black, silver or dark blue against the colour of night. But as he switched on his headlights and bumped off the drive, he headed towards me and then straight past without even giving me a sideways glance.

As he paused at the top of the road, indicating left, the car lit by the glow from Streatham High Road, I looked at my phone and saw the pin mirroring the movements of his vehicle. The phone was still in place, taped to the underside. He hadn't realized it was there yet – which meant he still didn't know I was on to him. I needed to make use of that advantage while I could. Once he was gone, I threw everything into my rucksack, swung it over my shoulders and headed down to the house.

As I approached, I saw that a gate at the side had been padlocked shut. I looked up and down the street, checking for twitching curtains, and then eyed the bay window at the front of Egan's bungalow. The blinds were drawn and, through the mottled glass panels in the front door, there was no sign of any internal light. Checking again that there were no eyes on me, I slipped along the pathway running parallel to the house, climbed up and over the gate, and dropped down on to the other side. I paused, listening.

Everywhere was quiet.

At the back of the house was a small garden, basic, perfunctory: a two-foot brick wall hemmed in a patio full of uneven, moss-covered slabs, and a square of lawn that looked like it had recently been treated with weedkiller. There was nothing in the beds, no pots, no trellising. On one side the garden was overlooked by a bigger, two-storey house, and on the other side I could see the back of the tailor's shop. There was no activity in the shop, which wasn't a surprise, but the lights were on upstairs in the house next door, so I kept to the rear wall of the bungalow and tried to stay out of sight.

There were two windows and a door. The door led into the kitchen, one of the windows also giving a view of it, while a second belonged to the living room. The room was small and had one two-seater sofa in it, an open fireplace, and a television on a three-legged stool in the corner. There was no wallpaper, no pictures, no shelving. As I leaned in against the glass, I could see a DVD player as well, the wires from that and the TV snaking across the old carpet to a plug point next to the hearth. Beside the sofa were remnants from a takeaway. Otherwise, it was empty.

Egan must have been renting this short-term.

Returning to the door, I took out my picks and went to

work on the lock. It was an old-fashioned tumbler, the pins full of rust, but – after a couple of failed attempts – I managed to get it open. I checked the tailor's shop and the windows in the house next door, and then headed in.

Once I pushed the kitchen door shut again, the traffic on Streatham High Road became a dull buzz, like a dying insect, and the soft sounds of the house started to emerge: the hum of a refrigerator; the gurgle of a water pipe; an occasional, faint creak from somewhere as the house contracted in the cool of the dark. I hadn't used the torch yet and there was enough light escaping in from the street for me to work with, so I left the kitchen and made my way into the hall.

It was short and sparse. There was paint on the walls but it had long since started to flake away, and the carpet must have been thirty years old: at the very edges it was still intact, but along the middle of the hallway, where thousands – perhaps tens of thousands – of footsteps had passed back and forth, it had worn down to the weave, bits of stray thread exposed. Off the hallway, there were three doors: one into the living room, one into a bedroom, one into a small bathroom.

Pausing halfway along, I removed my phone and checked on Billy Egan's whereabouts. The device location app put him two miles north of me, moving up Brixton Road. Pocketing the phone, I stepped into the living room, taking a closer look, but it was exactly as I'd seen it from outside: unloved, unfurnished.

The bedroom was equally small and just as sparse. There was a single bed, a fold-up wooden table being used as a place to stack toiletries, and a set of built-in wardrobes. The same carpet that was in the hallway and living room had made it in here too, thinned, dusty, frayed. I was more certain than ever that the house was only a temporary stop-off for Egan, just a roof over his head.

I went to his wardrobes. Some clothes on hangers, separated into smarter wear – suits, shirts – and more casual stuff like T-shirts and jeans. A jumble of shoes, thrown into a heap. An empty suitcase. And then a pile of old books, their covers lined and spines creased, and some DVDs. I dropped to my haunches and went through both piles, but the books were mostly fiction – horror novels, sci-fi, thrillers from the 1970s and 1980s – and the DVDs were movies that had long since been confined to bargain bins. It suggested long hours of waiting, filling his down time with books and films.

I pushed the wardrobe doors shut and looked around the bedroom again, trying to imagine what Egan's story was. If he was renting short-term, and he was working for Zeller, did that mean he'd come from the States?

Back in the hallway, I paused again to check Egan's location, and saw that he was at the Elephant and Castle roundabout. That was thirty minutes from here on a clear run, even if he turned around right now. But he didn't. Instead, he continued north-west on London Road, past the South Bank University campus.

I glanced at my watch and saw that it was after 11.15 p.m., and as I did, I became aware of something in the bathroom, adjacent to where I was standing.

The door was moving slightly.

There's a breeze coming from somewhere.

I edged closer. The bathroom was tiny, a bath on the right, a toilet in the middle alongside a basin and a mirror, and a wall decorated with neither shelves nor tiles. I stepped fully inside the bathroom and pushed the door shut behind me. The other sounds of the house – the refrigerator, the gurgle of pipes, the soft creaks – were silenced; all that remained was the faintest whistle of wind. It had been coming from directly behind the bathroom door.

Now I could see why.

There was an entrance to a cellar.

38

The padlock on the cellar door had been left unlatched.

I removed the torch from my rucksack and flicked it on. A set of polished concrete steps dropped down into darkness. Pulling the bathroom door open again, so I would be aware of any noise from the house, I double-checked Egan's position. He was on Blackfriars Road, still heading north towards the bridge.

Squeezing behind the open bathroom door, I took a couple of steps down and stopped again. The walls of the cellar had been boarded with plywood, and a series of wires – pinned with tacks – snaked up from under the carpet and climbed towards the ceiling. The further I went, the more of the cellar I could see. It was big, maybe half the length of the house, and – like the rooms upstairs – furniture was sparse: a desk in the centre, with a brand-new iMac on it, a scanner and a printer; a big leather sofa, papers scattered across it, as if Egan had been in the middle of looking through them; a single shelf, full of ring binders. Below that was a filing cabinet.

I searched for a light switch on the walls next to me and couldn't find one, but as I swung the beam of light around, I noticed that – beyond the desk – a felt pinboard had been screwed to the far wall. There was a map of London attached to it. A waterfall of photographs were at either side, pieces of string coming from individual pictures to points on the map, indicating where the photos had been taken. There were six of Alex Cavarno: one a repeat of the picture I'd seen inside Egan's car of her at the Comet; three outside the AKI office near the Docklands; and two outside what I assumed was her home. There were three more of Glen Cramer as well: the one I'd seen already of him locking up his house, one of him getting into a limo, and another of him having dinner, alone, at a restaurant in Mayfair.

All nine of the pictures had been taken with a long lens. More disturbingly, on the shot of Cramer getting into the limo, and in one of Alex outside the AKI offices, targets had been drawn on to their faces with a red pen.

There were a couple of photographs of me too. One was a fuzzy picture of Alex and me, quickly taken, talking to one another in the auditorium at the Comet. It was from our first meeting, when Egan had been there at the front of the cinema, posing as an architect. The second hadn't been tagged to a location in London. It had been taken from behind a tree, through a forest of leaves, and I was talking on my phone. I felt a flutter of alarm as I realized where I was: a few miles from Veronica Mae's house. At the time, I'd sensed someone was watching me, even though I hadn't been able to see anyone. But Egan had been there. Until I'd spotted him on the motorway, he'd stalked me like a shadow.

I refocused, waking the Mac from its slumber, but it was password-protected, so I moved beyond the desk to the leather sofa, and to the paperwork scattered across it. As I pinched the torch between my teeth and gathered up the papers, I realized what I was looking at.

Lynda Korin's missing persons file.

I checked that it was exactly the same as the version I had – that he hadn't had access to anything I hadn't already seen – and then put the file down again, returning the pages to an approximation of how they'd been before. When I was done, I got an update on Egan's position and then went to the filing cabinet.

The top drawer wheezed on its runners.

Inside was a series of vertical card files, each one containing paperwork. I pulled some of the papers out. They were a mix of photographs and printouts. The photographs were of Lynda Korin's house. Every corner had been documented, every room, external wall, the attic, the lawn, the view, the shed. I checked the shots of the living room to see whether the angel was in place. It wasn't. There was no angel and the DVD cases of Hosterlitz's films were placed horizontally. That meant, whenever Egan had arrived at the house, the angel and the films were already gone. So did that confirm that Korin had taken them herself?

I kept going through the drawer, and then the next one down, and found the same financial information and phone records for Korin that I'd already obtained myself. There were photocopies of paperwork Egan must have taken from Korin's house too, as well as countless time sheets for Alex, for Cramer, for me, detailing exactly what all of us had been up to. In Alex and Cramer's cases, the reconnaissance went back months. There were printouts of individual IMDb pages too – one for every film Korin had made with Robert Hosterlitz – even when all that page amounted to was a poster, a cast list and a limited synopsis.

I pulled the last drawer all the way out on its runners, and heard something roll away from me with a soft *thunk*. I reached in. The first thing I found was another photograph.

It was a shot of the wooden angel.

It was from the album in Lynda Korin's home. I knew it straight away. I recognized the style of the photograph, the lighting – it echoed the one I'd taken and the others I'd found inside. But then I turned it over and realized this wasn't the same. Not quite. On this one, something had been written on the back.

I hope you can forgive me, Lynda.
   Robert x

Hosterlitz.
But forgive him for what? I checked the front of the photograph again but didn't see anything that I hadn't already seen. It was the same angel in the picture, the same drawn-on black crucifix, the same discoloration on the ornament, the same minor chips and hairline cracks in it. I took a picture of this photograph, as a back-up, and then checked Egan's position.

He'd finally started heading home.

Unzipping my rucksack, I put the new photo inside with the one I already had, then checked the filing cabinet again. Something had made a noise in there, something heavier than just a piece of paper.

Right at the back, I found out what.

It was a book.

The front cover had mostly been torn away, but the back was still intact, even if the colours had long since faded and some of the blurb was hard to read. At the top I could make out the tagline 'Twenty of History's Most Infamous Crimes!' and when I lifted up what remained of the front cover, I found another dedication, faded a pale brown over time, this time from Korin to Hosterlitz.

My dear Robert,

Happy birthday! (I hope this is the one you asked for!)

L x

February 1983

Egan must have gone to the house in the days after Korin went missing and taken the photograph and the book. I stared at Korin's dedication, at the coffee-stained, dog-eared book, the whiff of cigarettes and mildew coming off the pages. But why take them at all? Was it something to do with the messages on them?

I began leafing through the book and, on the copyright page, saw that it had been published in 1982. I turned to the title page, where the name of the book – *Criminal History* – was revealed, and then stopped at the contents page, rust-brown and creased, the bottom half of it missing. Not knowing what lay in store didn't make much of a difference in terms of surprises: the book was filled with the stalwarts of true-crime literature – the Manson Family, Bonnie and Clyde, Ted Bundy, the Zodiac Killer, John Wayne Gacy, the assassination of JFK.

But then I got to the fifteenth chapter.

It took a couple of seconds to register with me before I realized what had happened. The book had made a twelve-page leap from the last page of one chapter on the killing of John Lennon, to the last page of the next one on some unspecified case. The entire chapter was missing, bar the last three lines.

where he died in San Quentin State Prison, aged thirty-nine.
It remains one of the most brutal and controversial cases in a
long history of notorious Los Angeles crimes.

I reread the remaining lines again. Had Egan taken the other pages out himself? If so, why? I looked around the room for any sign of them, couldn't find anything, and turned my attention to the book again. The contents page was torn, so I flipped to the back, hoping to find an index or a bibliography, an author's note – anything that might help me to pinpoint what case the missing pages related to. But there was nothing. I went to my phone and put in a search for the book title, hoping to find it on sale somewhere online, or – if I really lucked out – uploaded to Google Books in its entirety. But the book was thirty-three years old. It was out of print. It was gone, forgotten.

But not by Billy Egan.

I put in a second search, for 'San Quentin prison 39 years of age', but the term was too vague. There were too many results, tens of different names and dates, so I dumped the book into my rucksack along with the photograph and made sure everything else in the cellar was exactly as I'd left it.

Upstairs, the house was silent, street light seeping inside via the glass panels on the front door. Switching off the torch, I moved into the hallway and looked out through the living-room windows to the vacant driveway, to the road beyond. It was well after midnight now. Most of the houses were dark.

Returning to the location app, I saw Egan was about fifteen minutes away. I wasn't about to take any more chances, either here in the house, or with the phone stuck to the underside of Egan's Mercedes. If he discovered the mobile, the first thing he'd do was try to get into the handset. It was password-protected, but that wouldn't keep him out for very long if he – or anyone he knew – had any sort of expertise with technology. It wouldn't take much imagination for him to start looking in my direction when he found it either, even if I remote-erased everything on it, which I planned to do. But minus any of my information, he couldn't be one hundred per cent sure the phone was mine.

I set the remote-erase going.

Outside, the night was cool and, for the first time in days, it felt like rain might be in the air. Pulling the door shut, I made my way back along the edge of the property, close to the wall, staying out of the sightline of the house next door. Slipping the torch into the rucksack, I zipped it up and turned the corner.

Then it felt like I got hit by a train.

It took me a second to realize what had happened and, by the time I did, I was on the floor, flat on my back, blood running out of my nose. I looked up, slightly dazed, my vision blurring, and saw a figure loom over me, fists clenched.

It was Billy Egan.

I tried to scramble to my feet, but – in one swift, powerful movement – he'd pushed me down at the shoulder and jabbed me in the neck.

He's injected me with something.

'Nighty night,' he said softly.

I blacked out.

00:09:03

Silence, except for the whir of the camera.

There's a moment more of quiet, and then — somewhere beyond the office windows — a car horn blares and it's like the volume snaps back to normal: engines, sirens, music, shouting, the hum of four million people living inside five hundred square miles, travelling sixteen million miles of road. Ray Callson leans forward for his glass of water, takes a sip, then places it down in exactly the same spot as before. There's a reluctance to him now, wedded to the lines of his face.

'Are you okay?'

He shrugs. 'Sure. I guess.'

'You were telling me about what happened in the Pingrove.'

'Yeah,' he says. 'Room 805.'

'You and your partner went up in the elevator?'

He runs his tongue around his mouth. 'Yeah,' he repeats, then heaves a long sigh. 'Yeah, Luis and I rode the elevator up to the eighth floor and the whole time the manager was just talking at us, trying to fill the air with words. He was talking about absolutely anything except what he'd found up there. I mean, it was like I said. He'd sweated through his shirt. He was frightened. He didn't want to be there. He just wanted us to go in there and do what we do and make it all magically go away.'

Callson pauses, frowning to himself. 'I'm trying to remember exactly how it all went down after that. I remember, on the eighth floor of the hotel, they had these expensive penthouse suites. Couldn't even tell you how much they cost a night, but it was a lot. Gold handles on the door and what have you. And there was definitely a maid outside the room. She'd been crying. There might even have been another manager there too — the maid's boss. I don't recall. But Luis was kind of like the junior partner at the time, so I told him to wait outside with everyone. Once I went inside the room, I didn't want the manager or the maid or whoever bursting in and disturbing my train of thought. At crime scenes, I always liked to have space to think. I liked quiet. I needed time to interpret everything. That's just how I was. Anyway, the manager had locked the door from the outside, so he handed me the key, and I unlocked the room, and I went in by myself.'

Callson reaches for his water again, but this time, after taking a mouthful, he doesn't put it down. He just cradles it in his lap, sniffs, clears his throat.

'It's crazy,' he says. 'Do you know the first thing that came into my head when I opened the door to that suite? It was totally irrational. I thought to myself, "This'll be the first and only time I ever get to set foot in a place as expensive as this."' He smiles. His eyes aren't on the camera at all now. They're on the floor. The smile fades. 'Like I said, before we went up, the manager had explained to us what the maid had found when she'd gone to clean the room, so I guess — in my head — I'd built up a picture of what to expect in there. And you know what? I'm not sure I felt any different about going into that room than I felt about going into other places I'd been into as a cop. Even by that time, I'd seen my fair share of repugnant shit.'

'So what you're saying is, you weren't scared?'

He shakes his head. 'Not at first.'

'But after you went in?'

Callson is still staring into space.

'Mr Callson?'

'What he'd done didn't frighten me,' Callson says, 'if that's what you mean. Why would it? He was just sitting there, on the edge of the bed, *crying like a baby. Minute I come in, he looks up and starts saying to me, "I didn't do this, I didn't do this," and I'm thinking, "Sure you didn't, buddy."'*

'*Are you saying you didn't believe him?*'

'*That's exactly what I'm saying.*'

'*Why?*'

'*Because he stank of booze. Because he had her blood all down his shirt, his pants, all over his face. And because I could see he had these long strands of hair between his fingers that he'd torn out of her fucking scalp.*' *A beat. Callson glances at the camera.* '*I've seen that sort of thing — and a lot worse — a million times over. I was seeing them, every day, right up until I retired. One person killing another? That stopped scaring me about a minute after I joined the department. No, it wasn't what he'd done that frightened me. It wasn't the act itself.*'

'*So what was it?*'

'*It was who he'd done it to.*'

PART THREE

39

I opened my eyes.

It took me a couple of seconds to get a sense of where I was, and then my surroundings began to shift into focus. I was in a Portakabin, brushed aluminium blinds at windows either side of me. They were closed most of the way, but I could see that it was still the middle of the night, the dark absolute beyond the glass, except for a single lamp, some-where outside, that burned yellow. It sent shallow sheets of light into the Portakabin, layered one on top of the other.

I'd been left on the floor at one end of the room, and one of my boots had been taken off and dumped out of reach. It didn't take me long to work out why: my left ankle had been handcuffed to an old metal radiator. As I tried to move my leg, the cuffs seemed to lock even tighter, the radiator not shifting an inch. It was screwed to the wall with bolts the size of pound coins. There was no give and no escape unless the whole radiator – and probably the wall itself – came with me.

I looked around the Portakabin. It must have been twenty-five feet long. At my end of the room, there was a big desk, substantial and heavy, that had been cleared of any-thing I might be able to reach and use. I could see the stationery that had once been on it, plus the computer and in tray, on a second desk at the other end. In between were the windows either side of me, the door, and a series of wood-veneer shelving units. Everywhere had a slightly untidy, dishevelled look about it. The paint was peeling and the carpet was dirty. There was a sink stacked with dirty coffee mugs and old, food-encrusted plates. I could smell the toilet from where I was, a mix of stale urine and toilet spray.

I shifted from side to side, checking my pockets, but my wallet was gone, my phone and my car keys as well. My rucksack was nowhere to be seen. Even my watch had been removed. I couldn't see a clock on the wall, so I had no idea how long I'd been out, or what the time was now – only that it had to be before 6 a.m., because the sun wasn't up yet.

Leaning forward, I started fiddling with the handcuff at my ankle, trying to see if there was any give in it, but it was secure. I looked around for anything I might be able to repurpose into a makeshift pick, but Egan had done a good job of neutering me here too: there was nothing usable within at least fifteen feet.

I leaned back against the wall, rolling my neck, trying to ease some of the stiffness out. Egan had caught me totally on the hop at the house. I'd been watching his car almost the whole time and, according to the location app, he'd still been fifteen minutes away. The fact that he wasn't suggested that he'd spotted the phone on the underside of his car some point after he'd left. He'd either moved the phone to another vehicle, or it had just remained there on the Mercedes as a new driver took over, and Egan returned to the house on the Tube. Whichever it was, I felt angry at coming off second best.

But then, after a while, the anger started to become exhaustion – my eyelids struggling to stay open, like the wings of a doomed butterfly – and whatever Egan had injected me with began to take hold again. Slowly, I could feel it dragging me down.

Sometime after that I drifted off to sleep.

*

It felt like only a few seconds passed, but when I woke, I saw sunlight squeezing past the blinds at the windows. To start with, I wasn't aware that anyone else was inside the Porta-kabin with me – but then I felt hands slide under my armpits and lift me roughly off the floor. When I tried to move my hands, to bring them around from behind me, I realized they were now bound with duct tape.

My ankle, still attached to the radiator, sparked with pain – the handcuff gripping tightly – as I was dumped into a chair. I had to sit on the edge of it, with my leg straight and at an angle, or the joint felt like it might pop from its socket. A moment later, a roll of tape wheeled off across the floor of the Portakabin, in the direction of the other desk.

'Wakey wakey, asshole.'

Egan came out from behind me.

At the Comet, from what I could remember, he'd had a hard south London accent. But it had all been an act. He wasn't from London. He was American.

His name probably wasn't even Billy Egan.

He took a couple of steps back until he hit the edge of the sink, then stopped, china coffee mugs pinging and rattling against the surface of the draining board. He studied me for a moment, his mouth turned up in a hint of amusement, before reaching to the back of his jeans. He pulled out a long hunting knife.

I tried to conceal my alarm by turning to the windows, to see if – with daylight – there was a view beyond the blinds, but Egan had closed them even more, only the tiniest slivers of light escaping through.

He laid the knife down on the edge of the sink, the blade catching a finger of sunlight, and removed his beanie. His shaved head glistened with perspiration. I'd put him in his late forties when I'd seen him before, but it was harder to be sure now. Grey stubble dotted his jawline, yet the destructive bent that lingered in his face and eyes seemed to smooth away some of the evidence of age. He watched me for a moment more before reaching into his jacket pocket and taking something else out. It was the mobile phone I'd taped to the underside of his Mercedes.

'Very clever,' he said. 'What's also clever is that you had the brains' – he tapped his head with it – 'to wipe it clean.'

I didn't say anything.

'*Oh*. You're smart, is that it? Is that your thing? You think you're smarter than me?' He held up the phone again. 'I found out about this fifteen minutes after I left the house. Does that make me smart too?' This time he paused, watching from under his brow, his eyes small and dark. 'So, if you're so smart, how come you're in the corner of the room, chained to that radiator like a fucking dog?'

He tilted his head as he studied me.

'Look, I'll make this easy. What's going to happen is that I'll ask you some questions, and you'll give me some answers, and if you don't do that, I'll start carving pieces off your body.'

He grabbed the knife, turning it so I could see both sides of the blade. I did my best to suppress the panic that was building in me, at the idea of being chained up in a room with one exit, facing down a man on the fringes of losing control.

'Where's Lynda Korin?' he asked.

So they don't know where she is either.

His eyes were fixed on me, his body becoming still as he waited for an answer. I looked at him. He must have guessed that I didn't know where she was, otherwise I would have already closed the case. What he was really trying to find out was how much I knew – about Korin, about him, about what I'd found in his cellar.

'I don't know,' I said.

'Where is she?'

'I don't know. That's the truth.'

He studied me, sniffed. 'What did you find in the cellar?'

'You know what I found.'

'You found that photograph of the angel.'

'Yes,' I said, watching his face.

But Egan gave nothing away, just carried on rolling the knife against his hand. In between us, as the sun got stronger outside, a sea of dust emerged.

'What's so important about the angel?' I asked.

'Well, that's the thing, isn't it? You and me, we're both trying to figure that out. And you know who might have the answer?' He stopped turning the knife. 'That stupid bitch you're trying to find.'

I processed that for a moment.

The angel mattered. It mattered to this case. Korin had taken it with her, but Egan didn't know why. Neither did Zeller. *Neither do I.*

I thought of something else. 'Why take that true-crime book from her house? Why tear those pages out? What case is it that you –'

'Enough.' He moved towards me; his legs were either side of my knee, the point of the knife about an inch from my throat. It all happened so quickly. 'Let me ask *you* something,' he said.

I swallowed.

'I've been going through the notes you've made, through your phone, and I've found a few things. Names, items of interest . . . well, that makes me a bit nervous.' With his spare hand, he reached into his pocket and took out a scrap of paper, his eyes pinging between me and what he'd written. 'Who's Rafael Walker?'

Microscope.

In my notes, I hadn't directly attached Walker's screen name to his real name, so Egan wouldn't make that connection. But Walker was innocent. He didn't deserve to be sucked into this mess.

'He's just a film historian I was going to speak to.'

'About what?'

'About Korin and Hosterlitz's films.'

Egan eyed me for a second, looking for a trace of a lie, then – presumably unable to see one – glanced at the scrap of paper again. 'X-C-A-D-A-A-H,' he read, referring to the Post-it note I'd found at Korin's house. 'E-O-E-C-G-E-Y. Kill, one-H-one-nine-M-seven-S. Now I'm assuming that last part is a reference to the film *Kill!* – to a specific point in it. One hour, nineteen minutes, seven seconds – right?'

I nodded.

'Is that a yes?'

'There aren't any copies of the film left to check.'

He nodded again, clearly up to speed on which of Hosterlitz's movies were available and which weren't. 'And all this other shit above it? All these letters?'

'I don't know.'

Again he eyed me, but more suspiciously this time.

'It's the truth,' I said.

'Where did you find the Post-it note?'

'At Lynda Korin's house.'

Again he spent a long moment studying me, and then his eyes switched back to the scrap of paper in his hand.

'Craw,' he said.

'She has nothing to do with this case.'

'So why have you written her name down?'

'She's just a cop I know.'

He studied me for a moment more, the knife inching even closer to my left eye, as if he thought its proximity to my face might force me to admit that I'd lied. But eventually he shoved the paper back into his pocket.

'Do you know what I do for a living?'

His voice was quiet, but it bristled with menace. The knife was so close to my face now that all I could see was a blur: his arm, the blade, merging into one.

I shook my head.

'Well, I'm not an architect,' he said. For the first time I could see one of his front teeth had discoloured to a grey-blue, dying below the arc of the gum. 'I sort things out. I know people. I suppose I'm what you might call a "fixer".'

I felt the tip of the blade nick the skin next to my Adam's apple, and when I looked up at him, I had a horrible feeling he might be waiting for me to reply; that he was going to cut me off by jabbing the blade through my throat. Instead, he leaned in closer, so I could smell the sweat on him, feel his breath on my face, and said, 'You know, when I found out that you were working Lynda Korin's case, I looked you up on the Internet and saw all the headlines about you. And I said to the boss – and I remember this, clear as day – I said, "He's good. He'll be dangerous." And the boss says to me, "Dangerous? How can he be dangerous?" And I said, "Look at these cases he's solved. He probably *will* find out where Lynda Korin is – but it'll come at a cost."'

I felt a trickle of blood inch towards my shirt.

'And here's the cost,' he continued. 'That brain of yours,

whirring and clicking, dancing around the edges of what's going on. You shouldn't have gone into that cellar, *David*.' He leaned closer to me. 'Not that it matters any more. In a couple of hours, you'll be nothing but worm food –'

'All right, that's enough.'

Egan backed away from me, surprised by the sound of another voice behind him. As he shifted out of the way, I saw the door – saw it was open, and that a woman was standing there, backed by shafts of bright sunlight.

It was Alex Cavarno.

40

My heart sank as she moved further into the room, almost reluctant to cross it, as if she were wading into a swamp she knew there was no escape from. Her eyes shifted from me to Egan and then back to me, and she said, 'That's enough.'

Egan made an incredulous noise.

She turned to him again. 'I mean it.'

I just gazed at her, unable to understand why she was here, why she was involved with Egan, with Zeller, with whatever this was. She seemed to pick up on what I was thinking, like she was seeing right into my head, and she perched herself on the empty desk, about six feet from where I was, and just sat at its edge and stared into a space between us. Finally, when she looked up, she had an apologetic slant to her face, a tight-ening of the lips that said *sorry* clearer than any words ever could. Egan was behind her, unable to see her expression, and probably thought the two of us were just staring at each other, sizing each other up. Or maybe he didn't. Maybe he knew everything – how she'd played me from the first moment we'd met. I thought I was better than that – too strong to fall for those tricks, too wise. But in the end she'd reeled me in. I'd been as weak as the next man.

Just bait on the end of a line.

She was wearing a dark blue skirt-suit, tailored to follow the curves of her body, and as she sat there, legs crossed, she removed her jacket and placed it beside her. She looked from my wrists, my arms still bound behind me, aching, numb, to the handcuff at my ankle – and then she started checking her pockets.

'I never wanted any of this, David,' she said quietly, and produced a packet of cigarettes. 'Once the police investigation hit a dead end, I hoped that would be the end of it. I hoped that no one else would get involved in the search for Lynda Korin. No one would get hurt.' She stopped, shrugged. 'Unfortunately, that's not what's happened. We've been monitoring Wendy Fisher's calls, just in case she ever decided to get someone else involved, but somehow we must have missed her call to you, because the first time I ever heard so much as a mention of your name was when I was at the Comet, talking to Louis, and he told me that you were meeting him, and that you wanted to talk about . . .' She stopped, swallowed, the words seeming to stick in her throat. 'Robert Hosterlitz,' she said finally, quickly, wanting her lips to be rid of his name. 'I felt deflated. I felt even worse when we met.'

'I'm sorry to have upset you,' I said, my words shot through with such a sense of betrayal, it was like they were wrapped in barbed wire.

'I understand why you're upset.'

'Do you?'

She nodded. 'I do, believe me. You told me you were going to find out who Billy Egan was, that you had his address, and so I called him and told him you were coming.' She gestured to Egan, and I remembered what he'd said to me earlier: *I found out about the phone fifteen minutes after I left the house.* 'It was how he was able to turn the tables on you. So, yeah, I understand, I really do. Thirty-six hours ago, I asked you out for a drink. This morning, you're chained to a radiator.'

Thirty-six hours ago. That made today Monday. I'd been

here two days, not one. They'd kept me chained up since Saturday night.

I looked up at her. 'Have you ever been in Egan's cellar?'

The air seemed to cool. Alex glanced over her shoulder at Egan, he looked back at her, and though he hardly moved, I could see a flicker of anger in his eyes at the fact that I would even think to bring it up.

'He's been following you around for months,' I said. 'He's got your picture all over his walls. He's *targeting* you. Do you even know who this guy really is?'

'I didn't know he was told to check up on me,' she said. 'But unfortunately, yes, I *do* know who this guy really is.'

'And you're *still* working with him?'

She removed a cigarette from its packet and propped it between her lips. 'They don't give you a receipt for family, David.'

That stopped me.

'Yes,' she said. 'He's my brother.'

'Half-brother,' Egan muttered from behind her.

As I tried to process that, and what it meant, she ignored Egan and took a long drag on her cigarette, blowing out a flute of smoke. She was harder to read now, her face more ambiguous. After watching the smoke dissolve, she picked a sliver of tobacco from her tongue, gesturing with her cigarette to the handcuff, and said, 'I don't like this stuff. Chaining a person up like a dog – I don't believe in it. That's why my brother doesn't trust me, it's why he keeps me under surveillance, even though we're both tied to the same man. He thinks I'm a weak link.'

'Tied to the same man? You mean Saul Zeller?'

She didn't respond, but I knew I was right. I watched more ash fall away from the end of the cigarette like flakes of snow. 'That story I told you, about how I grew up next to the Santa Ana Freeway. That was a lie. I'm sorry. I grew up in a seven-bedroom house on Mulholland Drive, with my *half*-brother and my father and whatever woman Dad brought home that week.'

I studied her. *With my half-brother and my father.*

She could see that I'd put it together.

'Zeller's your *father*?'

'Yes,' she replied. 'Cavarno's my mother's name, but she died when I was young. I never knew her. We don't really talk about our family history, which is why most people aren't even aware that Saul and I are related. In fact, we don't really talk about anything.' She opened out her hands. 'Now you understand why my life's so screwed up. I've got him as a brother and Saul as a father. I don't trust them and they don't trust me, but somehow we make it work.'

I glanced at Egan. He just stared back.

Alex took another drag on her cigarette. 'Anyway, when this started, I thought we'd find Lynda Korin within days and then it would all be over. I mean' – she jabbed a thumb in Egan's direction – 'he's not one for great dinner conversation, but, in his own way, he's quite talented. Hollywood's an ocean full of sharks, and if you stay in the same place, trying to tread water, you drown. So sometimes you need someone who can get things done, because you need problems to disappear. You use what leverage you can, to get you to where you want to be. We're not living in some black and white sitcom where everyone's tipping their hats to one another on the edges of their manicured lawns. LA's a cesspit. You sink or you swim.' She stopped again, realizing that she'd strayed off course. 'Point is, someone like Lynda Korin, with no particular skills? Finding her should have been a walk in the park.'

Her gaze idled on me for a moment and then she shuffled along the desk and reached for an empty mug at the sink. She set it down beside her and tapped some ash into it. I wanted to ask her about Korin, about why they were so desperate to find her, about whether it had anything to do with 'Ring of Roses'. I wanted to ask her about the true-crime book I'd found in the cellar, about why the angel mattered, about a million other things. But it wasn't the right moment. Not yet.

She spent a long time studying me, her dark eyes fixed on mine, as if she could see me working things through, and then very quietly, very evenly, said, 'My brother told me he went through your car and found CCTV footage from the day Lynda vanished. *Wow.* You've got to admire her. I always wondered how she did it. Though the question I'm trying to figure out for myself is, did she hide those discs, and that business card, and the key for the cabin at Stoke Point, in that box for you *specifically* to find? Or did she just do it in the hope that *someone* would find it and figure out what's going on? The distinction is important. See, if she did it for you, then that suggests she's buzzing around somewhere close by and knows that you've picked up the case; if she hid it way back when she first disappeared last year, then that's different. It means ten months have passed without her ever coming up for air – which, in turn, raises the question of why she's been so quiet.'

'Maybe she's dead.'

Egan snorted, a smile worming its way across his face. 'Listen to Columbo over there,' he said, looking at his sister. 'I think we'd probably know if she was dead or not, don't you? *We're* the ones trying to put her in the fucking ground.'

I felt a coolness travel the length of my spine. Alex closed her eyes, as if she hated hearing him talk like that, as if she were trying to push the words back.

We're the ones trying to put her in the ground. I'd seen the evidence of Lynda Korin's deceit in the CCTV footage, in the way she'd used the men she'd befriended to cover her tracks. I'd seen the stage on which she'd built her disappearance, and been impressed by its sophistication and disquieted by its cunning. But in everything I'd read about her, in all the testimony I'd heard on audio and listened to in person, the thing I'd always found difficult to accept was the idea she would do any of this malevolently. She hadn't struck me as that type of person. Her inability to open up to people completely, the vagaries of her relationship with Hosterlitz, neither of those things made her malicious, they just made her good at keeping secrets – and she had a secret Alex Cavarno, Billy Egan and Saul Zeller needed to get at. Even if she'd run because she was scared of them, they were just as scared of her – or, at least, scared of what she knew. So what was it she'd found out? The truth about what 'Ring of Roses' was? The truth about those repeated scenes in the horror films? The wooden angel? The case in the true-crime book? All of them?

'I saw the true-crime book,' I said.

Alex shook her head, her eyes full of pity, as if I were a child who had disappointed her. 'You don't know anything, David. Don't embarrass yourself.'

'Is that why you want Korin dead?'

'Because of some book?'

'Because she knows the truth about the case you tore out of it. She knows how it connects to you and your brother, to Zeller. She knows what that angel means.' I paused, watching her for a sign that I'd hit upon something. When she gave me nothing, I threw her the only thing left. 'She knows about "Ring of Roses".'

Egan moved against the sink. It was a flicker, a moment of discomfort that he'd just as quickly tried to disguise. When I looked at Alex, her expression hadn't shifted an inch.

'I'm right, aren't I?' I said. 'It's about "Ring of Roses". This is about whatever Hosterlitz was working on at the end of his life – about the script he was writing.'

Instantly, something changed in their faces, but this time I'd missed the mark somehow. Egan started smiling. They both seemed to relax.

'What do you know about "Ring of Roses", David?'

I looked at Alex, her question hanging there between us, and then turned to Egan. The relief was so clear in his face.

'You think all of this is about a film?' she said, and glanced at Egan. 'He doesn't actually realize yet. I thought you said he'd figured it out.'

'I thought he had,' Egan replied.

I glanced between them. 'What are you talking about?'

'"Ring of Roses",' Alex said.

'What about it?'

'Hosterlitz's great, unfinished masterpiece – is that what you think this is about?'

'Are you saying it's not?'

'I'm saying it's bullshit.'

I felt my chest close. 'What?'

'He wasn't working on a film, David. He wasn't working on a script. There never *was* a script. "Ring of Roses" isn't a movie – and it never was.' She leaned into me, her perfume coming with her, its odour catching in my throat. 'It's something much more dangerous than that.'

41

'You genuinely believed that Hosterlitz started writing again in retirement – is that it?' Alex looked at me, sympathy in her face. 'I mean, who knows? Maybe he did. But he didn't finish any script. Way I heard it, after he got diagnosed with cancer, he went back to hitting the booze, and hitting it hard. Painkillers too. By all accounts, he was completely fucking loaded most of the time. The pretty picture of married life that Korin painted in *Cine* – it was rose-tinted bullshit. Most nights, he was down the local pub cleaning out their whisky supply. Ask my brother . . .' She gestured to Egan. 'He spoke to some of the people in the village when we started trying to find Korin back in November, and do you know how they remembered the great Robert Hosterlitz, Oscar winner and cinematic visionary?' She took a drag on her cigarette. 'As a sad old drunk.'

'Why would I believe anything you say?'

She shrugged. 'Believe what you want to believe, but – deep down – you know it's true. I mean, let's pretend for a moment that Hosterlitz *was* working on a film in the last, miserable, sickness-affected years of his life. Where the hell is it? It's twenty-seven years since the old man died. Where's the script? Where are the sketches, and the notes, and the ideas? Where are the actors he spoke to, or the producers he pitched it to? Where's the evidence that it ever existed, in any form? Do you think Lynda has just been sitting on it for over a quarter of a century?'

I didn't reply – didn't know what to say.

'There *is* no movie,' Alex said. 'There never *was* a movie. We should know. My father's been watching Hosterlitz from before Korin ever came on the scene.'

I frowned at her. 'What do you mean?'

She shrugged again.

'Zeller had been watching Hosterlitz since the seventies?'

'Since *way* before that.'

'Why?'

But Egan stepped in. 'That's enough.'

Alex didn't look at him, wisps of smoke curling past her face. 'Point is, no script was written at that house. Nothing was made there. All Hosterlitz was doing in retirement was drinking and dying.'

'But why was Zeller watching him?'

'Dad likes to know his enemy.'

'Hosterlitz was his enemy?'

'Robert Hosterlitz isn't the man you think he is.'

'Meaning what?'

She didn't reply this time. I looked at her, my mind spooling back to what Hosterlitz had written to Korin on the back of the photo of the angel (*I hope you can forgive me*), and then to what Veronica Mae had said about Hosterlitz, about the way he always behaved as if something was weighing on him.

'Is "Ring of Roses" related to that case in the true-crime book?'

The two of them just looked at me.

I thought of the pages that had been torn out of it. Had Hosterlitz known what they related to? Had he told Korin before he died? Somehow I doubted it, because if he had been telling her everything, he wouldn't have lied to her about his trip out to LA in 1984, and he wouldn't have asked for her forgiveness on the back of a photograph. But *why* keep something important from her? Because he hadn't thought she needed to know? Or because he had been trying to keep her safe?

Alex tapped some more ash into the coffee cup. 'The truth is, David, the best you can hope for – I mean, where any film is concerned – are some scrawled notes Korin may have kept, that Hosterlitz had *maybe* written on the back of a napkin while loaded up on bourbon and tramadol – and you really think my father's losing sleep over that? Hosterlitz was finished. No one took him seriously. No one was interested in any script he was writing, even if he *had* completed it. This isn't about a film, it's about what Lynda found out about her husband.'

'Found out about him?'

'Bobby was keeping secrets from her.'

Something curdled in my guts.

She paused, as if she thought she might have said too much. Then her eyes moved to the handcuffs, to my bound wrists, and she seemed to figure it made no difference now. But, as her eyes met mine again, an idea started to form. I thought of Korin. I thought of the surveillance tapes from Stoke Point – how she'd manipulated them, how she'd planned everything out.

'Korin found out what "Ring of Roses" really means,' I said. 'That's it, isn't it? She must have found out in the weeks after she did that interview for *Cine*. That's why she chose to disappear – and that's why you're trying to find her.'

Neither of them reacted.

But I knew I was right.

Except something didn't make sense. 'If she's got something on you, if that's the reason she vanished, why the hell has she been sitting on it for the past ten months? Why not tell the world what she knows?'

Finally, Alex moved, rubbing at an eye.

'Well,' she said, 'that's the big question, isn't it?'

She wasn't toying with me now. She genuinely didn't know why Korin had so flawlessly planned her departure, knowing that – eventually – she would be hunted, *then* proceeded to spend the last ten months doing absolutely nothing in response. Maybe Korin was ill. Maybe she was quietly wasting away somewhere.

Maybe she really *was* dead.

Alex took a last drag on her cigarette and dropped it into the empty mug. 'You know, I *am* genuinely sorry, David,' she said softly, almost tenderly. 'I know it doesn't mean much, but the couple of times we've met over the past few days, I've come away thinking, "I hope he gives up. I hope he fails to get anywhere," because I didn't want to see this.' She opened and closed the lid of her cigarette packet. 'My brother did warn us about you. He said you'd become a problem. Your stubbornness, your tenacity. I looked at your history, and I'm not saying you don't have a very strong, very worthy moral centre – I can see that you do – but some of the stuff you've done down the years, some of the risks you've taken?' She shrugged. 'I guess my brother was right. It was always going to come to this.'

Egan took a step forward.

'I have to go,' she said. 'I wanted to come here and look you in the eye, because I felt you deserved that. I'm a pretty good judge of character these days. You tend to get good at picking liars when you do a lot of lying yourself.' A smile – small, almost contrite. 'I had to be sure you didn't know more than you were letting on.'

She meant Korin. She meant she needed to be sure I hadn't actually found out where she'd holed up, or what 'Ring of Roses' really was. The finality to her words sent nerves scattering along my back, and my heart started to pump hard in my chest. I looked around me, realizing I was out of time. I tried to seek a way out, a plan, a strategy. But there was nothing.

I was handcuffed to a radiator.

She stared at me, her eyes lingering on me for the last time, and then got up, walking to one of the windows. She parted two of the slats with her thumb and forefinger. 'You know what the irony is? My brother will make you disappear like the people you find. You, any trace of the life you lived, your car, your belongings, this case. It'll all be gone. *You'll* be gone. There'll be nothing. And you know what? That's going to upset me. I like you, David.' She let the slats snap back into place and then returned to the desk she'd been sitting on, not looking at me, but reaching for her jacket and shrugging it on. 'In a different life, I'd have loved to have got to know you better.'

She returned to the door without once making eye contact with me. It was a weird, discordant moment: it felt like she genuinely meant what she was saying – and yet she was reading me my last rites.

'You know what the old man told you,' she said, talking to Egan this time. For a second she stood there, staring at the floor of the Portakabin. 'Wherever you put him, make sure he never gets found.'

42

After Alex was gone, her heels clinking against the Portakabin steps, Egan just looked at me, almost sizing me up: a
mortician at a slab; a butcher at a carcass. A moment later, he
said, 'I need to go and get my tools.'

His tools.

The words seemed to hover there, a noxious cloud of
smoke, and then, with a smile, he added, 'Don't go anywhere, okay?' He exited the room, blocking my view of what
lay outside, and slammed the door behind him.

Do something. Do something now.

My wrists were bound at my back – my hands level with
the base of my spine. Keeping my eyes fixed on the door, I
tried prising my hands apart, pulling them in opposite directions, but Egan had bound them so tightly I wasn't only
failing to shift the tape, I could feel it cutting off my blood
supply. I pulled again, teeth clenched, muscles taut, every
ounce of energy focused in my fingers, my wrists, my arms,
but my skin needled with pain and I started to feel
light-headed. I shifted on the seat, trying to clear the haze
behind my eyes – and, as I did, I felt something cool tug at
my ankles. Dread filled my guts like a sludge. I'd forgotten
about the handcuffs.

I stood up, keeping an eye on the door – turning as best as
I could with a handcuff clasped around my ankle – and
looked at the chair I'd been sitting on. Was there anything I
could use? Any sharp edges I could try to snag the duct tape

on? There was a tiny screw halfway up one of the legs, rusty and frilled at its circumference, and not sitting quite flush to the frame. But it was difficult to get at, and when I sat again I struggled to even find it with my fingers.

Eventually I did, and with the handcuff tugging at my ankle, I tried to get a clumsy sawing motion going. If Egan walked in now he'd know instantly what I was up to. I was at a forty-five-degree angle, with my wrists three-quarters of the way down a chair leg. He'd see what I was trying to do. But I was out of options.

It was this or nothing.

I sawed as fast as I could, repeatedly catching my skin on the edges of the screw. Before long, I'd opened up cuts on both arms, and there was blood in the creases of my palms. Undeterred, I kept going. The faster I went, the less accurate my movements got, and the more damage I was doing to my skin. When I slowed, I gained back accuracy but ate into whatever time I had left. I tried to mix it up – fast and then slow, repeat, repeat – and a minute later, I could feel the first tentative signs of give in the binds. I fumbled around with my thumbs, running them both along the edges of the duct tape. I'd torn it slightly – but, when I tried to prise my arms apart, the tape still didn't budge.

I started again, slowly getting into a rhythm, the chair wheezing under my movements. I'd been going about a minute when there was a subtle shift in the shadows around me. I glanced through the mottled glass of the door and heard Egan coming back up the steps, his silhouette distorting as he reappeared there.

Come on.

I kept going, even faster now, feeling the screw shredding my skin, the leg of the chair slick with my blood. *Come on, come on.* I closed my eyes for a second, trying to fixate on the movement of my wrists, on catching the screw against the edges of the duct tape – and then, suddenly, pain seared up my arm. I stopped, sucking in a breath. When I opened my eyes again, I saw Egan right outside the door, his silhouette perfectly formed, the handle starting to turn. Yet it was hard to fully focus on that because my left arm felt like it was on fire. I could feel blood all over it, carving a series of trails down the inside of my forearm – over the duct tape, into the lines of my hands, along my fingers to the floor. I'd ripped something, lacerated skin. I didn't need to see it to know that it was bad.

The door opened.

Egan appeared in the doorway, the knife in one hand, some sort of rolled leather pouch in the other. Inside, I could hear tools clinking against each other.

'It's time,' he said.

43

I sat up straight and tried to erase all emotion from my face. I wasn't sure if Egan could see any blood from where he was standing – I wasn't even sure how much blood there was – but, as he entered and clicked the door shut behind him, he eyed me without paying particular attention to the carpet or the chair.

Instead, he ran his tongue along the top of his gums, like he was trying to rid himself of the lingering taste of something sour, and waved the knife in front of him, disturbing the still air, testing it out. He held it up to the sun coming through the blinds, the blade winking in the dusty light, then placed it on the desk nearest to him along with the leather pouch. The pouch rattled, clanged.

'My sister is more emotional than me,' he said, looking down at it. He undid a tie and it unfurled like a blanket. I could see scalpels and pliers, a hammer, clamps, strap wrenches. I swallowed, trying not to show him any fear, but he didn't look at me. 'Thing is, emotion can cloud judgement. She was quite taken with you, so when she said she had to look you in the eye to make sure you weren't lying to her, I'm sure she believed that you really *weren't* lying about what you'd found out.' He stopped, wriggling a scalpel free of its binding. 'Unfortunately, I'm not as trusting. So you're going to tell me what you know about Lynda Korin's location.'

'I told you, I don't know where she is.'

He turned, the scalpel clasped inside his hand.

'Are you listening to me?' I said. 'I don't *know* where she is.'

'I love cooking.' He paused, watching me. 'But have you ever cut yourself chopping vegetables? You know the type of cut I mean: the ones where you just nick the skin. Man, those cuts hurt the absolute worst. Those really painful *small* cuts – the ones here, right on the end of your finger – they throb for *hours*.' He held up his other hand, revealing the flat of his palm. 'Now imagine one cut on every finger. Imagine twenty. Imagine an arm full of them, a leg. Imagine them all over your face.' He smiled at me, the dying tooth visible at his gum. 'And you know the *really* bad news? By the time I'm done showing you what else I've got in that pouch, you'll be begging me to go back to this scalpel.'

'No,' I said, looking beyond him, searching for a plan – for *anything* – but then I looked down at my ankle chained to the radiator, and I realized there was no way out. My heart began a savage thump against the inside of my ribs, battering the bars of its cage like an animal trying to escape. I felt weakened and tired. I felt woozy.

Focus.

Egan moved closer, the scalpel out in front of him like an extension of his body. I went to hold up a hand, an automatic reaction to the weapon, to Egan, to everything that was about to come – but then I felt the binds tug. They locked in place and pain flashed through my left arm, shoulder down to hand. I twitched, sucking in a breath, listing slightly to the side.

As I did, I felt something tear.

The duct tape.

Some of it had come away – a fractional abating of the pressure on my right wrist. I straightened as adrenalin charged through my body.

'Wait a second,' I said.

Lightly, I pulled my wrists apart, disguising the movement behind a roll of the shoulders. Egan paused briefly, then came forward again, the tip of the blade no more than four feet from my body. I shifted from side to side, as if scared, and used it to hide another attempt to pull my hands apart. This time, I felt more of the duct tape split, my right hand dropping away, as if totally freed, my body lurching. Egan stopped, frowning, eyes flicking to the floor beneath me.

For the first time, he saw the blood.

I sprang from my seat, whipping my right arm round from behind me, and drilled a punch into the centre of his throat. As Egan staggered back, clutching his neck, air wheezing out of him, the handcuffs locked against the radiator and hauled me back towards them. I fell clumsily, into the radiator, into the wall, and then into the chair I'd been sitting on. It tipped as I hit it, and I tumbled across it.

Scrambling to my feet, I looked for Egan again.

He was beyond my reach – bent over about five feet from me – fingers at his throat, the scalpel still in his right hand, its point dragging against the carpet. I looked around me, desperate, knowing I couldn't get to him, knowing that all I was doing now was waiting for him to regain control – and then I thought of something.

The chair.

I picked it up, gripped the legs and drew it back. Egan glanced up, his eyes – marbled with blood vessels – widening as he saw what was coming. Swinging with every ounce of energy I had, I felt the impact tremor up my arms as it caught him in the head. He staggered sideways into the desk, the pouch shifting, its tools rattling, and the scalpel dropped to the floor with a faint *ping*. As he rebounded, his back leg seemed to collapse from under him and he folded.

He hit the floor face-first.

Pausing there for a moment, chair still gripped in my hands, I watched for any sign of movement, any indication this was part of the game. But he was out cold. I could see him breathing, a mixture of blood and saliva bubbling at his lips.

I need to get the hell out of here.

Putting the chair down, I checked my left arm. There was a four-inch gash gouged into it, the wound still oozing, blood criss-crossing like routes on a map. My hands and wrists were all marked with smaller cuts, bruises and grazes, dirt and grease from the screw smudged among them. Dropping to my hands and knees, I shuffled in Egan's direction as far as the handcuffs would allow me to go, then got down on to my belly. Flat on the floor, I could reach his midriff, his arm, his waist.

I checked his jacket. His phone, a set of car keys, my wallet. Removing them and setting them aside, I tried his trouser pockets. In one I found my own mobile. In the other was a silver key with a distinctive O head. It had to be for the handcuffs. I shuffled back towards the radiator and then slid the key into the lock. They popped open.

Getting to my feet, I moved to the sink – keeping half an eye on Egan – and washed down the wound on my arm, then headed to the toilet to get some paper towels. Wrapping my arm to try and stem the blood flow, I used an elastic band from the other desk to keep everything in place, and then returned for my phone and wallet, Egan's mobile and his keys. I had no idea where he'd put my own car key, but I wasn't going to stick around to find out.

Grabbing my boot, which they'd removed, I glanced back

at Egan again. He was starting to stir, his breathing becoming less cadenced, his eyelids flickering. Hopping into my boot, I laced it up and headed to the door, yanking it open.

Sunlight erupted past me, painting the interior of the cabin a chalk-white and blinding me for a moment. It took me a few seconds to realize where I was.

A scrapyard.

Towers of vehicles, cadaverous and rusting, rose like metal buildings. I stepped on to the stairs and tried to get a sense of where I was, in what direction I should be heading, but it was like a maze. Rutted mud tracks wove in and out of countless vehicles, some of the stacks eight or nine cars high, huge pieces of scaffolding erected with more cars lying inside – as well as doors, tyres, wheel trims, bonnets.

I moved down the stairs, looking left and right. It was a labyrinth, nothing visible beyond the scrapyard except the vague hint of distant rooftops. I began moving right, towards the place where the rooftops seemed closest. The tracks had been baked in months of summer sun, hardened and calcified, and a couple of times I almost turned my ankle. But the further I went, the more something else started to dawn on me. There was no one around. No employees, no customers.

Because it's bank holiday Monday.

It was why they'd brought me here. This place was shut for the weekend. No one was working today, no one was coming. No one would hear me, see me.

Egan had this place to himself.

I glanced at my watch, and then recalled that Egan had removed it – he'd kept it, dumped it, got rid of it somewhere. I wasn't sure which and I wasn't going back to check, so I got my phone out instead. There were twenty missed calls, a mix of friends and potential clients, a central London number I didn't recognize, and three from Craw. I remembered, then, how she'd wanted to talk to me about something. She'd also sent me a text.

> Where are you? We really
> need to talk asap x

It was 10.52 a.m. She hadn't heard from me in nearly forty hours. I hadn't returned her calls or her texts. But I couldn't worry about that for now.

I had to get out of here.

In front of me, the tower of cars finally ended and a massive corrugated-iron fence emerged. This close to it, the rooftops beyond the scrapyard, the ones I'd glimpsed earlier, had disappeared and all I could see were the bones of the dying vehicles that encircled me. I tried to listen for telltale sounds beyond the fence, but there were no voices, no hint that this place was close to suburbia, to houses, to people, to signs of life. Instead, all that came back was the distant hum of traffic, a monotonous rumble that made me think it might be a motorway.

I got out my phone and went to Maps and, as it loaded, I looked along the fence, trying to figure out a plan of attack. If I followed it around, there had to be an entrance somewhere. This place was big, but if we'd come in, I could get back out again. Returning my attention to the phone, I watched as the map continued its slow load in, chunk by chunk, a weak signal making the process a frustrating crawl. And then, out of the corner of my eye, I saw something else – a movement from light to dark.

I glanced back at the Portakabin.

Egan, knife in hand, was coming for me.

44

I headed right, following the path of the corrugated-iron fence. In front of me was a canyon of cars, a stack of six propped against the fence itself, another tower of eight – windowless, engineless – slotted into holes in purpose-built scaffolding.

As I sprinted between them, shadows started to settle around me, the sun vanishing behind barricades of oxidized metal. The track softened beneath my feet where the sunlight couldn't get to it and, in this stretch of scrapyard, the path was littered with small, shallow puddles, grey with mud. At the end, the canyon kinked left like a turn in a maze, and I glanced back over my shoulder to see how far behind Egan was. Except he wasn't there.

He's not following me.

I stopped, my pulse starting to quicken. I should have been able to see him by now. Edging to the corner of the next turn, I looked along it. It ran for a long way, perhaps two hundred feet, endless vehicles stacked up on either side. At the end was an opening, a yellow flash of a crane and the side of another machine. *The crusher.* Long bits of metal poked out from a gap close to the top of it, like arms reaching for help. As I kept my eyes on both directions – the way I'd come, and the path down to the crusher – I got out my phone again and returned to the map.

It had loaded.

I was on an industrial estate in a barren patch of land

three miles west of Ealing. It was why I could hear cars but no domestic life: to the south was the M4, to the east was the River Brent, to the west were patches of park and woodland. It was a smart place to bring me: no one lived close enough to hear anything, and as it was a bank holiday weekend, the whole industrial estate was a ghost town.

I put the phone away and listened. There were gaps in vehicles that I could see through, windows without glass, and bodywork punctured with jagged holes. I could hear the popping and groaning of the cars, a choir of old frames creaking and expanding under the sun, as they climbed their way to the sky. But I couldn't see Egan, and I couldn't hear him either.

Quickly, I searched for something I could use, and found what looked like a drive shaft with part of the transmission still attached, sitting discarded under the shell of a purple Vauxhall Cavalier. It was black and flecked with rust, but it was heavy. Gripping it tightly, I began moving in the direction of the crusher.

More puddles littered this area of the yard, collecting in the grooves of the track like spores. I tried not to land in them, to disturb the water, to give any sense of where I was located. Despite the heat, goosebumps scattered across my back and the throbbing pain of my left arm faded in, reminding me that I was carrying an injury; if it came to it, I couldn't rely on my left being as strong as my right. I looked down at the paper towels, bound to my arm with an elastic band, and tore them away. Blood was caked to my skin, the gash raw and angry, but it had dried.

I got closer to the crusher. It was huge and ugly, like a shipping container with a mouth torn along it. To its left was the gap in the maze that I'd seen earlier.

It led through to a small car park.

This, I started to realize, was why Egan hadn't followed me. He knew I'd end up here. As I stood there, I thought briefly about a retreat, but mostly all I could think about was getting the hell out of there as fast as possible. I needed to regroup, reorganize.

If there was a car park, then it was a safe bet I was somewhere close to the exit. But it was also a safe bet that Egan was waiting for me, that – familiar with the layout of this place – he'd made it look like he was coming after me, then made a beeline for this end of the yard instead. I might have been closer to the exit here, but one bad decision and I'd be leaving with a knife in my back.

I paused there, trying to think through my next move, my arm throbbing, the drive shaft greasy and becoming more difficult to hold – and then I clocked movement through the gap. I took a couple of steps back, trying to seek refuge in the shadows, expecting to see Egan emerging into view.

But it wasn't Egan.

45

It was a man I didn't recognize. He was dressed in blue overalls, the front stained with a mix of engine oil and mud. He must have been in his fifties, was grey-haired and corpulent, and wore a pair of glasses too small for his face.

He had an odd gait, his right arm hidden from me and pressed to his body on that side. I wasn't sure whether it was due to his weight, his caution, or some injury that he'd never fully recovered from. I shifted left, behind a column of cars, using a window to look over to where the man was. That was when I saw his right hand. It wasn't his weight or an accident that was making him walk that way. It was what he was holding close to his leg.

A gun.

He stopped. I felt my heart shift as his eyes zeroed in on a spot close to where I was hiding. The silence seemed absolute for a second: no hum from the motorway, no birdsong, no pops or groans from the cars piled up around us. It took everything I had not to make a break for it, the instinct to take flight was so powerful. But I couldn't outrun a bullet. Instead, I stayed exactly where I was, gripping the drive shaft harder than ever, and watched as the man headed right, in the direction of the cabin.

Wait until he's out of sight – and then run.

He was almost completely gone from view when, somewhere above me, I felt a change in the stillness of the air – and then a low, doughy moan, as if one of the cars was about to come loose.

I looked up.

Egan seemed to come from the sky somewhere, his entire weight behind the leap. I had a split second to realize he'd got on top of the crusher without me ever noticing him – and then he smashed into me and everything became a blur.

He took me with him, his knees in my ribs, in my stomach, and – as we landed, him on top of me – every ounce of air exploded out of my body. Egan fell away from me, unbalanced from the landing, and I knew I had to stand, to fight back, to prepare for whatever he was going to throw at me next. But when I tried to get up, when I staggered to my feet, it felt like I was going to vomit. I dropped forward again, back on to my hands and knees, winded, shaken, and another wave of nausea crashed into me. I began retching – my throat like an overfilled balloon – and just about managed to spot Egan scrambling to his feet beside me, blood streaked across his face, his hand trying to grasp at his waist, where the rubberized grip of his hunting knife showed above his beltline. I started to see him more lucidly: teeth clenched, jaw tight, his face coloured.

'I've got him!' he screamed.

There were footsteps, dull at first but then louder. Looking around on the ground, I tried to find the drive shaft and saw it an arm's length away from me, to my right. I scrambled across to it, battling my nausea, and shifted on my knees, gripping the drive shaft as tightly as I could.

Egan came at me again. He crossed the distance between us in two or three strides. I rocked back as his knife whipped through the air in front of my face and nicked the very tip of my chin. As the momentum carried Egan to my left, I desperately swung the drive shaft at him, trying to hit whatever part of him I could.

The steel tube reverberated hard in my hands.

Egan staggered away from me, his legs quickly giving out from under him, the knife pinging against the shell of one of the nearest vehicles as his arm flailed around at his side. He hit the floor. I heaved myself up, feeling like a drunk: there was blood on my chin, saliva on my lips, and my vision was blurring in and out. I readied myself for Egan's attack.

But it never came.

He was belly down, arms splayed, his face battered and bloodied. I'd got him in the side of the head. One of his eyes was already closing up. I wasn't sure if he was breathing or not.

Shit. *Shit.*

Almost immediately, the other man appeared, the quickness of his movement belying his size. I swung the drive shaft around again, catching him in the top of the arm. The gun spun out of his hands and the impact forced him into a series of quick sidesteps, his foot landing in the cleft of a puddle, unbalancing him. I darted towards him and took a second swipe at him, this time catching him in the neck. He jolted, as if he'd suffered an electric shock, landed against one of the cars with a crunch, and slid down into the mud.

Silence.

I stayed rooted to the spot, waiting for him to come at me again. But he didn't. Neither of them did. I doubled over, trying to catch my breath, feeling a twist of guilt at the damage I'd caused. I hadn't wanted to hurt anyone, but I'd been left with no choice. It was survival. They'd been armed with a knife, with a gun, and wouldn't have spent a single second feeling sorry for me as I bled out at their feet. But the thought didn't make me feel any better. I found no pleasure in hurting people.

That was what made me different from them.

I started to check them both over, bending down next to Egan, his skin slick with blood and sweat, trying to find a pulse. I found one, but it was faint. The old man was conscious but groggy – so much so that he put up no fight as I tossed his gun away and started to go through his overalls.

I found his wallet first, a faded, dog-eared business card inside revealing that his name was Geoffrey Barneslow, the scrapyard was called Barneslow Scrap, and he was the owner. He had a pre-touchscreen mobile phone, the last number that had called it matching the number for the Barneslow Scrap landline on the business card. I'd taken Egan's phone with me when I left the Portakabin, which meant Egan must have called Barneslow from a landline inside, requesting back-up. There was no way to tell for sure, because there was no one left to ask, but I could guess at what arrangement they had: Egan brought people here when it was closed and then cleaned up after himself; Barneslow cashed the cheques and didn't ask questions.

I stood again, then headed out in the direction of the car park. I needed to find my keys. I needed to find my car.

I needed to get out of there.

46

I found my car a minute later. As I looked at it, I recalled what Alex Cavarno had said to me: *My brother will make you disappear, like the people you find. You, any trace of the life you lived, your car, your belongings, this case. It'll all be gone. You'll be gone. There'll be nothing.* The BMW was in the crusher, completely destroyed.

For a second, I felt an odd, irrational sense of loss. I'd bought the BMW at a time in my life when I'd never thought I'd be anything other than a journalist; a time when Derryn had been alive, when I'd spent nights beside her on the sofa, in front of the TV, not handcuffed to a radiator in a Porta-kabin in a corner of London where no one would ever find me. Derryn and I had travelled miles in that car, been all over Europe in it, to the north of Scotland, to Ireland; it had been just one small part of my life with her, insignificant in the grand scheme of things, but a constant nonetheless. I'd lived through her death and then slowly emerged out the other side – and the car had remained a part of my existence the entire time.

Now, like her, it was a memory.

I thought of everything that I'd left inside it – my laptop, my rucksack full of case notes, the photos of the angel, the true-crime book, the DVDs of Lynda Korin at Stoke Point – and then, next to the crusher, spotted a caravan.

I headed for it.

Inside it was a mess. A bed, the sheets twisted and

unmade; evidence of food, of things having been cooked, of dishes in the sink. There were clothes in the wardrobe, a tablet, a toilet that stank of urine. Barneslow lived on-site.

Next to the caravan was Egan's Mercedes – and, between where the car had been left and the main gates of the scrapyard, under half a tin roof that looked like a collapsing bus shelter, I spotted two big oil drums.

They were still smoking.

On the floor, beside them, was my discarded rucksack – unzipped and emptied. Inside the drums, I found the melted remains of my laptop and the DVDs. I saw what was left of my notepad's leather covers. But as I tried to look for the true-crime book and the two pictures of the angel among all the rubble, I realized it was too late for both. They'd long since turned to ash.

I felt for my wallet and my phone and took them both out. *So why hadn't he burned these too?* He must have been planning to go back through my calls and texts, my search history, the life that existed in the cards and receipts of my wallet, to make sure there was no link back to him, to Zeller, to Alex. After that, he would have thrown them into the fire, just like the rest of it.

Grabbing my empty rucksack, I went back to the Mercedes, slid in at the wheel, started it up and headed east out of the scrapyard. My left arm was still sore, so I tried to avoid using it as much as possible, perching it against my thigh. I could smell sweat and blood on myself, and could see grime in my skin that would only come out with soap. I needed a shower and a change of clothes.

I needed a pharmacist too. The inside of my arm down to my wrist throbbed, the cuts like strips of red ribbon. Halfway down Uxbridge Road, my prayers were answered. I found a chemist with a bank holiday service operating out of a slide window. I bumped up on to the pavement and rang the buzzer.

While I waited, I took a look at Billy Egan's phone – but it didn't take me long before I realized it was a dead end. He'd been smart. He had no numbers in his address book, he'd cleared out his Recent Calls list, and he'd deleted texts as he'd sent and received them. There was no Internet history either. The phone was a shell; a hollow piece of plastic. I could have called Spike again and got him to go hunting around at Egan's network, because there would be a record of the calls and texts on a server somewhere, a browser history too. But it was complicated work. It would take time.

Time I didn't have.

Stuck in traffic a couple of minutes later, I tried phoning Melanie Craw, but it went to voicemail. I left a message for her, promising that I'd call her again later. I'd missed a call from a central London number too, one I didn't recognize, so I dialled that as well. It just rang and rang without anyone answering.

After that, I started going through the navigation system on the Mercedes. I was trying to trace back Egan's routes over the past couple of days, to see where he'd been. Instead, I came across a reference to a satellite tracking system.

They can find me through the car.

Pulling off Uxbridge Road and heading south, I made for the northern fringes of Ravenscourt Park. Finding as conspicuous a spot as I could, right outside a bank of shops, I bumped up on to the pavement. It was double yellows for as far as the eye could see. I locked the Mercedes, tossed the keys and Egan's mobile into a nearby drain, and made a call to the police from a phone box to tell them that an illegally parked car on Goldhawk Road was creating havoc.

If everything went to plan, the next time Egan saw his vehicle it would be clamped or impounded.

I headed to the Tube.

47

An hour after dumping Egan's Mercedes, I emerged into the heat of the afternoon at Lewisham station, the air thick with exhaust fumes. About eighty yards down the high street, between the back of the police station – a huge red-brick building, with cream render and blue-framed windows – and a grim piece of 1970s architecture, which now housed a shuttered bowling alley, was Prendegast Avenue.

Number 47A was halfway along. It was the bottom floor of a three-storey terraced house, each floor split into flats – A, B and C. I made my way down some stone steps, and although I wasn't able to see much through the only window at the front, I could see enough: a living room with old film posters on the wall and, towards the back, the shadows of a man in a kitchen, sitting at a small table.

Microscope.

I pushed the buzzer and made sure I wasn't visible to him at the window, so he'd have to open up to see who it was. Before getting the train, I'd found a public toilet and washed myself down, cleaning the blood and grime from my arms and dressing my wounds properly. I'd bought some fresh clothes too – a long-sleeved T-shirt, a new pair of jeans, a cheap watch. In the shade of the front porch, I hoped the cuts on my face would be less noticeable to him.

The door opened.

Rafael Walker was dressed in a pair of red shorts and a white T-shirt with a faded *American Werewolf in London* film poster on it. He was just over six feet tall, and had black hair that was greying around the ears. Tall and skinny, he'd grown a beard in the time since the photograph of him on the BFI site had been taken. He ran a hand through it, gathering it into what was almost a tail at the front, and then briefly looked me up and down, his eyes lingering on a cut at my cheekbone.

'Can I help you?' he said.

'Mr Walker?'

He automatically went on the defensive. 'Yes.'

'My name's David Raker.'

I removed a business card from my wallet and handed it to him. He took it. I was cold-calling him at home on the Monday of a holiday weekend and had no idea how much time I had before Egan woke up and crawled to a phone to call Alex and Zeller. The fact that Egan had asked me about Rafael Walker at the Portakabin made things worse because it meant Walker was on his radar now, however obscurely. It meant Egan could come here. That might give me three or four hours with Walker, or it might give me thirty minutes. I didn't have time to dress this up as something it wasn't. I needed him to answer my questions.

'Okay,' he said, still studying the card.

'I find missing people.'

'I can see that.'

'I'm looking for Lynda Korin.'

His expression changed instantly, his frown dissolving, surprise taking hold. 'Oh,' he said. 'As in Robert Hosterlitz's wife?'

'Exactly.'

'She's missing?'

'It wasn't really reported in the press, but yes, she is. She's been missing since the end of October last year. I think you might be able to help me.'

He didn't respond for a moment, as if his mind was elsewhere.

'Mr Walker?'

'Help you how?' he said.

'Help me find her.'

The frown returned. 'I'm not sure how you think I can help.'

He had an elegant accent. There was a hint of mainland European to it – perhaps Spanish or Italian – but it was hard to tell. His English was immaculate.

'You work at the BFI, right?'

He didn't seem disturbed by the fact that I knew. Perhaps he just figured it was a by-product of an investigator turning up unannounced on your doorstep.

'Yes, that's right,' he said.

'I'd like you to tell me about the horror films Robert Hosterlitz made in Spain between 1979 and 1984. I'm particularly interested in the way they end.'

He glanced at my business card. 'The way they end?'

'The last ninety seconds.'

I saw it before it arrived. For whatever reason, he was going to deny that he knew anything. Sure enough, he said, 'I'm not sure I know what you're talk–'

'I saw your posts online.'

He looked at me straight – but his eyes gave him away.

'I know you're Microscope,' I said.

48

His living room was small and compact. Two bookcases almost filled one wall, their shelves lined with novels, reference books and Blu-rays, and where there was space either side there were film posters, or photographs of what I assumed was Walker's young son. Thin, four-foot-high surround-sound speakers sat in the corners of the room, like black plastic totem poles, and a fifty-inch LCD was perched on a cabinet and paused on a scene from a film I didn't recognize.

One wall of the living room had been knocked through to the kitchen. As I continued scanning the room, I noticed another long row of DVDs beside the TV cabinet, some silver film cans, and a laptop being recharged.

'Do you want something to drink?' he asked.

'Water would be great.'

As he went to the kitchen, one of the bookshelves caught my eye. Any Hosterlitz film available on DVD, Walker had, including the ones that had starred Lynda Korin. But as far as I could see, he didn't have any of the six 'lost' films. I thought of the Post-it note I'd found in the box at Korin's house, with the *Kill!* timecode on it. *Kill!* was one of the lost films. If Walker didn't have access to all eleven films, he didn't have access to *Kill!*, and that meant what Korin had written on the Post-it note – the two lines of random letters – would still be unresolved.

That last thought lingered as he returned with my water,

offered me the sofa, then dragged a chair across from the kitchen and perched himself on the edge of it. Reintroducing myself, I gave him some background on the search for Lynda Korin. Anything he didn't need to know, I left out. Anything that might make him jumpy, I left out. Anything that I thought might compromise him in any way, I left out. He asked occasional questions, but mostly he just listened to me.

'Which brings me to the films he made between 1979 and 1984,' I said.

Walker nodded.

'I've seen three of them: *Axe Maniac, The Drill Murders* and *Death Island.* They've all got the same ending – or, at least, an ending that's almost identical.'

He nodded a second time.

'I understand he made eleven films during that time, and six of those are gone for ever – the so-called "lost" films. But, on that forum, you said you've seen all eleven, including the six that are unavailable. Were you telling the truth?'

'Absolutely.'

I looked at him. 'I don't see them on the shelves here.'

He was already shaking his head. 'Because you can't get them on DVD. They're called the "lost" films for a reason – they're lost to the general public.'

'But not to you?'

'No, not to me.'

'Are they at the BFI?' I asked.

'No.'

I glanced around the room and my eyes came to settle on the film cans near the TV. 'Is that them?'

He laughed, as if I'd insulted him. 'No.'

'So where are they?'

'With respect, why would I tell you anything?'

I eyed him, annoyed by his tone, irritated by his obstinacy. While I was sitting here, trying to negotiate answers out of him, Egan and Alex and Zeller would be regrouping. I glanced at my watch. It was after 2 p.m. already. I tried to strike a conciliatory note. 'I just want to find Lynda Korin. That's all.'

He looked at me for a moment.

'Mr Walker?'

'I don't even know who you are,' he said.

'I've told you who I —'

'A business card doesn't tell you who a person is.'

I thought of Alex Cavarno. He was right about that.

Gesturing to the laptop he had recharging, I said, 'You can read about some of my cases online. I'm not trying to dupe you here.'

He got up and grabbed his laptop, yanking the power lead out of the side and returning to his seat. It took about half a minute before his eyes flicked up from the screen to where I was sitting. He'd obviously found a press report about one of my better-known cases.

'You were the one who found the Snatcher?' he asked, referring to the case, in 2012, through which I'd first come into contact with Melanie Craw.

'Yes,' I said.

'Who's employing you to find Lynda Korin?'

'Her sister.'

His eyes remained on the laptop.

I pressed on. 'Have you ever heard of "Ring of Roses"?'

He looked up at me again. 'Yes. I read something about it online.'

'At the end of October, on the *Cine* website?'

'Yes, that's right.'

'Was that the first time you'd heard the name?'

'Yes. Do you know anything about it?'

'I'm not sure it exists.'

He looked taken aback. 'What?'

'I don't think Robert Hosterlitz was writing a script – or, if he was, he never finished it. He had no production facilities at his home – not even as much as a camera – so he wasn't shooting something on the cheap either. He was diagnosed with cancer in December 1984. People tell me he was a drunk, addicted to painkillers, sick . . . I think whatever he told his wife about "Ring of Roses" being a film was basically a lie.'

I thought of what he'd written on the back of the angel photograph. *I hope you can forgive me, Lynda.*

'Why would he do that?' Walker asked.

'I'm not sure. That's what I'm trying to find out.'

His eyes returned to the laptop screen, rereading whatever article it was that he'd found online about me. Then he snapped it shut.

I tried again. 'Like I said to you, I'm not attempting to hide –'

'I'm writing a book.'

I stopped, puzzled. 'Okay.'

'I've been working on it for years. It's about Hosterlitz.'

I came forward on the sofa. 'About his films?'

'About his life.'

'A biography?'

'Yes.'

I studied him, waiting for him to continue, remembering how – when he'd answered the door to me – he'd denied that he knew anything about the repeated scenes in Hosterlitz's movies, until I made it clear that I'd found out that he was Microscope. I recalled too that there had been posts on the forum where Collinsky had asked if he could get in touch directly with Microscope, to talk about the repeated scenes – and Walker had shut him down straight away.

He was trying to protect his book.

'You're trying to keep the book secret?' I asked.

He shrugged. 'I don't know about secret. But I've been trying to chart the course of Hosterlitz's life and there are things in it that . . . they just . . .' He stopped for a moment. 'There are things in his life that just don't make any sense.'

49

'What do you mean, "things that don't make sense"?'

'I don't know exactly,' Walker said, 'and until I've figured out the truth, I'm keen to keep my work under wraps.' He hesitated, as if he wasn't sure whether he could trust me or not. 'Okay, look,' he continued softly, a little guarded. 'Did you know that his father, Hans, contributed money to the Nazi Party in 1930?'

I shook my head. 'No, I didn't know that.'

He nodded. 'He renounced the Nazi ideology only a couple of years later – it was part of the reason why he moved the family out to the States in 1933. He claimed that he was drawn in by Hitler's promise to revive the economy and tear up the Treaty of Versailles, but when he saw what the Nazis *really* stood for, he said he was ashamed to have contributed a single penny to their cause. Anyway, there's an interview with Robert Hosterlitz in the *LA Times* in 1954, just after he won all those Oscars for *The Eyes of the Night*, where he talks about his father.' Walker paused, going to his laptop. 'Let me just find it.'

I wondered where he was going with this.

'Here,' Walker said. 'Hosterlitz says, "My father wasn't a fascist. He *hated* fascism. He made an error of judgement at a time when Hitler hadn't been clear on the full extent of his beliefs, and my father admitted as much every day of his life until he died in 1938. I think if he were alive today, he would have voted Republican – but he would have looked at a lot of

Democratic policies and thought, "That really makes sense to me." I feel like I maintain those same political views.' Walker stopped; looked at me. 'Does any of that seem a little off to you?'

Immediately, I thought of something Glen Cramer had said: *I'm telling you, Bobby Hosterlitz wasn't any communist. No way. He was a moderate.* I looked at Walker. 'Hosterlitz seems to be describing himself as centre-right.'

'Correct.'

'But he was accused of being a communist.'

'Exactly. That was the whole catalyst for him leaving the States in the first place. It was why his career was flushed away.' He gestured to the screen. 'But how could he have been a communist if he was voting Republican?'

'Maybe he wasn't. Maybe he lied to the journalist.'

Walker was shaking his head. 'I've spent over a decade trying to put this book together. I've spent half my holiday entitlement flying out to Los Angeles to make Freedom of Information requests. I've tracked down anyone from the time who might remember *anything*, and eighteen months back, I found some documents dealing with Republican Party donations between 1950 and 1960. None of that sort of information had to be officially disclosed before the law changed in 1971, so it took me three years to find those records. Hosterlitz is in them.'

'He was a Republican Party contributor?'

'Correct. He made a three-thousand-dollar donation in the run-up to Eisenhower's 1952 election campaign. That would be over twenty-five thousand dollars today. That's not exactly a small amount of money.'

'That doesn't necessarily change anything,' I said, although I wasn't sure if I believed what I was saying now or not. 'I guess there's an argument that maybe he contributed to the Republican campaign as a way to hide his real views.'

'Or maybe he wasn't actually a communist.'

'Sixty years on, I'm not sure if we'll ever get to find out.'

Walker was shaking his head again. 'How did he even end up on the radar of the House of Un-American Activities in the first place?'

I shrugged. 'The committee had been all over Hollywood like a rash since 1947. Sooner or later they were bound to get around to Hosterlitz. That article in the *National People* just helped them focus their attention.'

'Exactly,' Walker said. 'It was the article in the *National People.*'

I looked at him, momentarily confused.

He shuffled forward. 'You said yourself, the HUAC had been going after Hollywood since 1947, yet Hosterlitz was never named by anyone who took the stand, and the HUAC never subpoenaed him until the article came out a couple of months after the Oscars in 1954.'

I started to see what he was driving at. 'So what are you saying? That you think the article in the *National People* was a plant?'

He nodded. 'That's exactly what I'm saying.'

'Someone was setting him up?'

'Yeah. Someone phoned the *National People* – and they fed them the story about Hosterlitz being a communist.'

'Why?'

'They knew, at worst, he'd be dragged before the committee and have his credibility destroyed in front of the nation. At best, he'd be blacklisted. At the *very* best, he'd get sent to prison, or would choose to flee the country. Whatever happened, whether he was guilty or not, he'd end up tarred as a communist and his career would be finished. His work, his life – it would all be ruined.'

'But why would someone want to destroy Hosterlitz's career?'

Walker shrugged. 'Jealousy. Spite. Money. There are all sorts of reasons.'

Could it have been Zeller who set him up? Cramer?

I felt a dull thump behind my eyes. They were both around at the time of the HUAC hearings in the 1950s – but what exactly did they hope to gain from planting the story? Back then, Hosterlitz was one of the hottest directors in Hollywood. He'd just come off *The Eyes of the Night*, he was a multiple Oscar winner, he was still contracted to AKI for another movie. Saul Zeller, as de facto president of the studio, would want him tied to American Kingdom for as long as possible. Cramer himself had said many times over, in many different interviews, that without Hosterlitz he never would have had a career. Neither man should have been hostile towards Hosterlitz. And yet, hours earlier, I'd been handcuffed to a radiator while Zeller's son told me he was going to torture me, kill me, and bury me where I would never be found.

'Mr Raker?'

'David,' I said softly, but my thoughts had already shifted forward again, to the true-crime book I'd found in Egan's basement.

Maybe it's to do with that.

I looked at Walker, recalling the section that had been left behind in the book.

where he died in San Quentin State Prison, aged thirty-nine. It remains one of the most brutal and controversial cases in a long history of notorious Los Angeles crimes.

A man dying in San Quentin aged thirty-nine, at some point before the book's release in 1982. A reference to a Los Angeles crime. I'd done a web search already using all of that information and it had taken me nowhere.

'David?'

I turned to Walker. 'Do you know anything about San Quentin?'

He seemed momentarily thrown by the change of direction. 'Are you talking about the prison?'

'Right.'

'Yeah, it's north of San Francisco, I think.'

'There's a case that might be relevant to Hosterlitz . . .' I stopped. *It might be relevant to Egan, to Alex, to Zeller. Maybe to Cramer too.* I pushed on: 'Thing is, I don't know what the case is, or even when it took place. All I've got to go on is the death of an inmate at San Quentin, aged thirty-nine.'

Walker was frowning, clearly confused, and as I played back what I'd just said to him, I understood why: I sounded vague, borderline incoherent.

'I'm trying to think of notable San Quentin inmates,' I said.

He was still looking at me like I might be losing it. After a while, he said, 'Charles Manson?'

The Manson Family murders had all happened in and around LA. But that couldn't be what the torn-out pages had been about. I'd found an account of Manson's crimes earlier on in the same book. The case wasn't anything to do with Manson.

It was something else.

I sat there for a moment, trying to come up with something, and then my eyes fell upon the DVD cases of Hosterlitz's films.

'Have you really seen all of the films he made after 1979?' I asked.

'Yes,' he said. 'All eleven of them.'

Walker studied me for a moment, concern in his face, perhaps thinking that he'd entrusted the secrets of his Hosterlitz biography to someone unstable; a man for whom there was no clear path from one question to the next.

'What do you make of the way they end?'

'The repeated ending? I don't know. That's why I wanted that journalist to ask Lynda Korin about it.' He paused for a moment, considering me. 'But I'll tell you this: the footage that plays on the TV set at the end – that's California.'

'The section filmed from inside the car?'

'Yes.'

'What makes you say that?'

'At one point, if you study it closely, you can see a slight reflection in the window of the vehicle that the footage is being filmed from. The reflection is of a Cadillac Coupe DeVille – and it's got blue and yellow Californian licence plates. That was the type of plate they used out there between 1969 and the mid eighties.'

'So it's California, but not LA?'

'It probably *is* LA,' Walker said, 'but there's not really enough to go on, so I can't be one hundred per cent sure. It's kind of a best guess.'

'Do you think Hosterlitz shot the footage himself?'

'That would be the natural assumption.'

I tried to imagine *when* he might have shot it, and there was really only one possibility: in the time before he left the States in 1970. He couldn't have recorded it during his trip out to LA in December 1984 because the footage appeared in all eleven films he released in the five years before that. In theory, at least, he might have been able to do it during his and Korin's original holiday in Minnesota, during the summer of 1979, but if he'd disappeared for a week, just like he did that Christmas, Wendy surely would have remembered it.

What interested me more than all of that, though, was how Walker knew the films in such detail, right down to the reflections that were visible in windows for fractional periods of time. It suggested he really *had* seen all eleven films, over and over again. It suggested he had access to them. It probably meant they were close by.

He just didn't trust me enough to show me yet.

I went to my phone and found the photographs I'd taken of the wooden angel pictures, then handed him my mobile.

'What's this?' he asked.

'Do you recognize the angel?'

He shook his head.

'It never featured in any of Hosterlitz's films?'

'No,' he said.

'It belonged to Lynda Korin. Or maybe Hosterlitz himself. Swipe through to the next picture.'

He did as I asked. '"I hope you can forgive me, Lynda."' Walker looked up. 'Is that Hosterlitz's handwriting?'

'I think so. He wrote it on the back of one of the photos.'

'What is he asking forgiveness for?'

I thought of what Alex had told me in the Portakabin. *Robert Hosterlitz isn't the man you think he is.*

'That's what I need to find out,' I said.

He handed me back the phone, and I went to the picture of the Post-it note I'd discovered at Korin's house. The original was gone – Egan had burned it while I'd been out at the scrapyard – but he hadn't got around to deleting the digital copy from my phone. I needed to figure out what the letters meant, but I also needed to get a fix on the timecode too.

'Does this mean anything to you?' I asked, holding up the screen.

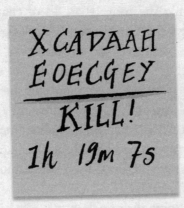

Walker leaned in and took the phone again. 'The two lines of letters? No.'

'What about under that?'

'Is that a *Kill!* timecode?'

'I think so. Do you know what it might be referring to specifically?'

He pressed his lips together. It clearly meant nothing to him, but his eyes continued to switch between me and the phone display, as if he was thinking.

'No,' he said after a while.

'You've no idea what the timecode means?'

'No,' he repeated. 'But there might be a way of finding out.'

50

He got up, gestured for me to follow him, and led me into the kitchen. In the corner, out of sight, was a set of five oak drawers.

He pulled at the middle one.

Except they weren't drawers at all. The whole thing was a single oak panel, made to look like a series of drawers. Immediately inside, filling the entire space, was a dark grey steel safe. It had a number pad on it and a turning wheel.

Walker put in a code.

The safe made a short buzz and then he spun the wheel until the door bumped away from its frame. Wisps of smoke escaped through the gap – and then I realized it wasn't smoke at all, but tendrils of freezing-cold air.

The safe was a refrigerator.

Inside were two big metal drawers, stacked on top of each other. Each had a handle. Walker grabbed the top one and pulled, and the drawer slid smoothly out from the space it had occupied on a set of runners.

'These things were originally built to hold six 2,000-foot reels of 35mm film,' he said, turning to me. He seemed nervous, as if I might be about to push him aside and start tearing into them. 'They were transportation cases. I bought them in auction – I don't know, six, seven years ago. At work, we've got a vault that stores master material at a constant temperature of minus five, but as I haven't got one of those and won't be getting one any time soon, I've made do.'

'You built this yourself?'

'The cases came as is. Everything else, yes.'

The top case had a latch on its flank, which he flipped, and then he hoisted the lid up. I stepped closer and looked inside. There was a row of five silver film canisters, each one slotted into a moulded foam base, end up. 'I've got all eleven of the films that Robert Hosterlitz made between 1979 and 1984,' he said. He ran a hand along the canisters. 'There's five here and six down there.'

I glanced at the case below.

'These aren't the dubbed versions either. They're the original negatives, in English. The only one of these films you can buy now in English is *Axe Maniac*, and that DVD version is made from a distribution print. Same deal with the other DVD releases that have been dubbed into Spanish and Italian. All are distribution prints, not originals. I know, because I've had the original negatives since 1987.'

'How?'

He pushed the top case in slightly and pulled the bottom one out, opening it to reveal the other six canisters. 'I was born in Madrid,' he said. 'My father was a film projectionist at a cinema in Salamanca that used to show English-language films. My mother was a doctor, so she worked a lot of nights, which meant I usually tagged along with Dad. That was how I fell in love with cinema – and where my interest in Hosterlitz started. I used to watch his movies, even though I must have only been ten or eleven, and every time they showed, my father would try to shield my eyes from them. "These are junk," he used to say to me. "But his early films, now *they* were good." Most people watch Hosterlitz's noirs and work forward, losing interest in his movies after *The Ghost of the Plains*. I started at the end and worked back – and if anything, it only made me more interested in him.'

Walker looked at me, then down at the canisters again. 'Mano Águila, the production company Hosterlitz worked for between 1979 and 1984, they didn't close in '86 because they weren't making money. They closed because they *were*. The guy who was running it, Pedro Silva – he owed about seventeen million pesetas in unpaid tax. So when the taxman closed in, he shuttered the premises and fled to Argentina. A couple of months after that, I got inside the Mano Águila building.'

'You stole these?'

He nodded. 'They'd just been left there. So I grabbed them, chucked them into the car, and I never mentioned it to anyone. My father was English, although he'd lived in Spain for years, and he used to call petty thieves "toerags". That's what I was, I suppose – but I've never regretted it.'

He leaned down and removed a canister from the bottom case.

'This is *Kill!*,' he said.

There was no writing on the canister, just a number 6 on the side. *Kill!* had been the sixth film that Hosterlitz had made for Pedro Silva.

I looked around the room. 'Have you got a projector?'

He pointed towards the bedroom and led me there. It was semi-lit, a blind at the window keeping the sun out. Walker opened up all the doors on a row of built-in wardrobes. Filling the space was a huge 35mm projector, facing out at the white wall above Walker's bed, on the opposite side of the room.

He was projecting across to there.

'This was my father's,' he said, laying a hand briefly on the machine. 'It's the 35mm projector he used at the Royale in Salamanca. They let him keep it when the place went belly up in the early nineties. I took it on after he died.'

A moment of sadness flickered in his face as he talked about his father, and then he held up the canister with *Kill!* in it: 'The film is made up of six different reels, because all Silva's movies were shot on "short ends" – the ends of rolls of raw negative stock left over from bigger productions. Because of that, and because I don't have a platter to make the switch between reels easy, if you want to see the whole thing, start to finish, I'm going to have to load it all in manually, one reel at a time. That means there'll be five breaks as I do.'

'How long's the film?'

'About eighty-five minutes – and that includes the credits.'

The timecode on the Post-it was one hour and nineteen minutes, which put it very near the end of the movie.

'Just go straight to the last reel,' I said.

'You don't want to see the whole film?'

I shook my head. 'Just how it ends.'

51

'Before 1951,' Walker was saying, leaning over the projector, 'the industry standard stock was nitrate.' He was inching the reel through some sort of roller. '*My Evil Heart* and *Connor O'Hare* would have been shot on nitrate. That stuff was lethal. It would catch light at the drop of a hat, go off like a box of fireworks, and it was near impossible to put out. But after 1951, everything was shot on safety stock. That'll burn — but not like nitrate.' He paused, struggling with something. 'This reel is Eastmancolor,' he said, teeth gritted, still struggling. 'It's safety stock, so it won't go up in flames as easily, but it suffers from something called magenta bias. That means, over time, colours fade, leaving only the red hues, especially if it's not stored properly.' Something snapped into place. '*Finally,*' he muttered, and then straightened, wiping his hands against his shirt, trying to rid them of sweat. 'My point is, I've done my best to preserve these, but they're not pristine.'

'It's fine,' I said. 'Honestly.'

The projector hummed and then rattled into life, a cone of light erupting from its lens, an image immediately cast on to the far wall. The reel made a soft, familiar chatter as the sprockets fed it through the machine, and I was taken back to my childhood, to the cinema I'd gone to as a boy. There was a pop from the audio and then the film's sound launched from the speakers.

'How far in are we?' I asked Walker.

'This is the seventy-first minute of eighty-five,' he said.

As the movie began playing, I set the timer going on my watch so I'd have a rough idea of when we got to seventy-nine minutes, and – impatient now – considered getting Walker to wind the reel on quicker. But then a female actor I instantly recognized as Veronica Mae appeared onscreen, and I held off.

Without the benefit of a decent speaker system, because the audio levels hadn't been properly balanced at the time of production, and because the acting was so bad, it was sometimes hard to follow the dialogue. Onscreen, Mae was joined by two male actors, even worse performers than her, as they sought shelter in an abandoned shop. I listened hard to their exchange and managed to figure out that they were, predictably, escaping the clutches of a deranged killer who had already killed at least three of their friends. The male actors spoke in awful American accents, and the shop had been set-dressed with an American flag.

Eventually, the killer managed to catch up with them as they tried to find an exit at the back of the shop. Dressed in a long hooded raincoat, he sliced one man's neck, decapitated the other, then chased Veronica Mae into a large upstairs room filled with storage shelves and bric-a-brac. The film was chaotic and badly lit, and backed by a horrible, screeching soundtrack. When I glanced at my watch, I saw we were sixty seconds away from the seventy-ninth minute.

I took a step closer to the projection on the wall, watching as Mae tried, in vain, to show the terror her character was feeling – and then the camera lurched up to the right to show the killer beside her, knife in his hand. But that was when the twist came: as the hood fell away, the killer was finally revealed – and it wasn't a man at all. It was a woman.

It was Lynda Korin.

I glanced at my watch. The twist had happened at the start of the seventy-ninth minute – so was that what the timecode on the Post-it had been referring to? As I considered that, the two women briefly fought some more in a nearby office, and then Korin threw Mae against a wall, where she was impaled on a large shard of glass. After that, something more familiar took hold: the action cut to a wide shot, Korin the central focus, and the soundtrack dropped out.

It was the start of the ninety-second end sequence.

The slow dolly towards Korin began. I couldn't hear Hosterlitz's voice-over this time – not because it wasn't there, but because the quality of the projected sound wasn't good enough. After sixty seconds, just like all the movies I'd already seen, the camera inched past Korin and moved towards a walnut-cased television sitting in the corner. In this film the TV was off to start with, just a black screen, but then it popped into life and the same footage kicked in: the same video, shot from inside the same car, of the same street.

Ten seconds later, the credits rolled.

I looked back at Walker. 'Did you see anything?'

His eyes were still on the wall. 'What if the timecode you have for *Kill!* is a reference to the film's reveal?' he said. 'What if it's pointing to the fact that the killer is a woman, not a man?'

His thoughts were echoing my earlier ones.

'Maybe,' I said, and thought about the VO again. 'There's something else I wanted to ask you about. When the heart-beat and breathing come in, there's –'

'"You don't know who you are."'

I nodded. 'You've definitely heard it, then.'

'Yes.'

'Do you know what it means?'

He shook his head. 'No. It's so difficult to even hear him. I only really found it by accident, through repeated viewings of this sequence.'

I'd done the same with the DVD versions.

'Can you play it over again?' I asked.

Walker leaned over the projector and began reversing the reel. It kicked into life about a minute prior to the twist. I took a couple more steps towards the wall and then, as we got closer to Korin's appearance, Walker began slowing the whole thing down, feeding the reel through the projector at half-speed. We moved past the point of the reveal and into the struggle between Korin and Mae, and nothing caught my eye – not about the construction of the scene, not about the women involved. Once Mae was dead, the repeated sequence began.

This time, I noticed something.

'Wait,' I said. 'Wait a second. Can you take it back to the moment when Mae is killed by Korin?'

He did as I asked.

'That's it. Pause it there.'

Again, he followed my lead.

'How long between Mae's death and the start of the end sequence?'

Walker shrugged. 'I don't know. Five seconds maybe.'

'Can you play the film frame by frame from here?'

He looked dubious, and I understood why: the film had been shot at the standard twenty-four frames per second, so even five seconds of the film equated to one hundred and twenty separate frames. But he did as I asked and I waited, quietly, while he set it up. Pretty soon, the film began again.

I was watching the scene so closely now, analysing every frame – even when one was almost identical to the next – that, after a while, I began to feel the pressure of it building behind my eyes. My head thumped and my vision blurred. It was a bizarre, unnatural way to view the movie, like watching the pages of a flick book shift at an infinitesimally low speed.

In these final few moments before the switch to the end sequence, the movie seemed darker than ever, as badly lit as anything Hosterlitz had ever put on to film.

Except maybe it wasn't badly lit at all.

It had taken three viewings – once at normal speed, once at half-speed and once frame by frame – for it even to click. At first, the poor lighting had just seemed like a by-product of the way the movies were made – quick and on the cheap. But now, slowing it right down, everything became clearer.

When Hosterlitz started the end sequence, when Korin became the sole focus for him, he got his act together and the scene was shot impeccably. But, before that, in the preceding seconds, the frames were so poorly lit and inadequately photographed that they were reduced to near black.

'Because he's doing it on purpose.'

Walker frowned, looked at me. 'What?'

'He's poorly lighting these final moments before the repeated sequence on purpose. This last second is so dark it's almost impossible to see what's going on.' I paused, thinking. 'What if he's hiding something?'

'Hiding something? Where?'

'Can you rewind it?'

Walker's gaze lingered on me, as if he feared once again that I was losing it, but then his curiosity got the better of him and he changed the direction of the reel. He took it back two seconds. Korin, having killed Mae, played out a series of minor actions in reverse, and then – with a snap of a switch – Walker began moving forwards again, frame by frame.

Two seconds of film comprised forty-eight individual frames. The closer to the forty-eighth we got, the harder it became to see anything, as if Hosterlitz had deliberately and rapidly faded out the lighting. In real time, the two seconds passed so quickly that the change in light would barely register as anything other than an amateurish moment in a movie littered with them – but slowed down to this pace, it felt completely deliberate. In the forty-sixth and forty-seventh frame, there was hardly any light at all. In the forty-eighth and final frame – before the switch to the wide shot that marked the start of the end sequence – Hosterlitz went even further than that: there was no hint of the scene at all.

The frame was just black.

'Why has he done this?' Walker said quietly.

'You've never noticed this before?'

'No,' Walker said. 'I've watched all these films countless times, but I've never watched them frame by frame like this. How have I never seen this?'

He sounded frustrated, understandably, but the answer seemed obvious. The finale of *Kill!* was so badly lit, in fact the entire *film* was so badly lit, that it would have been impossible to pick out a single frame of black. But, as I stepped away from the wall in an attempt to see things clearly, I started to realize something: the frame wasn't *entirely* black.

There was some grey in it.

'You see that?' I asked, tracing a series of vague swirls with my fingers.

'Yes. What are those?'

I squinted, willing myself to see better.

'They're words.'

Walker glanced at me. 'Words?'

'The same three words, repeated over and over.'

He just continued looking at me, like I might be joking. 'I haven't got my glasses,' he said, turning his attention back to the wall. 'What do they say?'

'They say, "Ring of Roses".'

52

The two of us were silent for a moment, our eyes on Walker's bedroom wall, on the black frame filled with the same three words, repeated over and over again. I was caught halfway between elation and horror, buzzing from having followed the rabbit hole this deep, anxious and alarmed about what it might mean.

'We need to do the same thing for the end sequence,' I said.

Walker tore his eyes away from the wall. 'What?'

'We need to go frame by frame.'

'You're talking well over two thousand frames.'

'I know.'

We stared at each other for a moment, Walker looking like he wanted to protest, but then his interest in Hosterlitz won out. The frustrated author in him, the man who had spent so many years trying to understand the director, trying to finish his book, was never going to be able to let this one go. He set it up and we began.

Forty minutes in, we found something.

It was a single frame, embedded in the moments after the camera had dollied past Korin and started focusing in on the television. At full speed, watching it with the naked eye, its screen time would have amounted to a twenty-fourth of a second. In real time, it would have come across as a pop, a jump, a rogue frame.

But it wasn't any of those things.

It was a photograph.

Taken in black and white, the tones had been deliberately adjusted, the blacks blacker, the whites greyer, allowing it to be disguised within the shadows and half-light of the end sequence. But frozen here, on the wall of Walker's house, we could see everything – the detail, the background, the woman in the centre of the shot.

'Who's that?' Walker asked, pointing to her.

She was in her mid thirties, was slim and about medium height, although it was hard to be entirely sure as she was sitting on the top step of a clapboard house, its porch extending out either side of her, her legs tucked into her body.

'This is old,' I said.

'What do you mean?'

'I mean, even in 1981 – when *Kill!* was released – this was already an old photograph.' I paused, studying the woman more closely. She was beautiful. 'Look at her hairstyle. Look at the kind of clothes she's wearing.'

Her jet-black hair was cut into an Italian style that recalled Elizabeth Taylor in *Cat on a Hot Tin Roof*. Her clothes were an even better barometer of when the picture was taken: she wore a full, gathered skirt, a petticoat visible underneath, and a pale blouse and dark neck scarf. She looked like she'd just come from a dance hall – or was about to leave for one.

'This must have been taken in the fifties,' I said.

Walker studied the image. 'So who is she?'

'I don't know,' I said, and my eyes drifted to the edges of the photograph, where the number 117 was fixed to the house, in a space next to the front door – and then to what lay beyond the house, further in the background.

'What are those things?' Walker asked.

He was pointing to the far right-hand side of the

photograph, where my own gaze had already settled. There was the hint of a dirty-looking canal, overgrown and dark. But that wasn't what Walker had been referring to, and it wasn't what I had my gaze fixed on either. We were both looking at the same thing: silhouettes on the horizon, one next to the other, like a forest of electricity pylons.

'I think they might be oil derricks,' I said.

'Oil derricks?'

I looked at the woman again, at the way she was dressed, at the clapboard house, at the canal, at the derricks, trying to put it together.

'Venice,' Walker said.

I turned to him. 'What?'

'It's Venice in Los Angeles. It's got to be. I've done so much research on the city for the book, I know it inside out. They struck oil in Venice in the twenties. It was like a fifty-year boom or something, and then the wells ran dry in the seventies. At one stage, they would have had these derricks all along the coast.' He stopped, eyes still fixed on the photograph. 'The clapboard house, the canal, the oil derricks, it's *got* to be Venice. It's got to be LA in the fifties.'

As I processed that, I thought of those lines in the true-crime book. *A notorious Los Angeles crime.* Was that where this woman fitted in? Was she where this all ended up? I continued to stare at her, the altered monochrome of the photograph taking nothing away from her. In fact, in an odd way, it made her even more striking – more ethereal somehow, her pale skin reduced to a grey mask, her lipstick a dark, perfect oval.

'So who is she?' Walker asked again.

'I don't know,' I replied, taking a camera-phone shot of her. 'But we need to check some of the other films you've got. We need to see if Hosterlitz included this photograph, and the black "Ring of Roses" frame, in those too.'

Walker did as I asked, grabbing another film at random from cold storage and loading it into the projector. This time it was *Beware of the Woods*, made the year before *Kill!*. The negative wasn't in as good condition, magenta bias evident in a pinkish tinge to some of the actors' faces – but it was easy to ignore now.

'How will we know where to pause it?' Walker asked.

He meant, watching it at normal speed, how would we know if there was a single black frame like the one in *Kill!*.

'I think he'll put it in exactly the same place,' I said.

Walker stopped it before the end sequence, inching it back to the moments just before the wide shot. We found the black frame quickly after that. It was in exactly the same place as *Kill!*: embedded before the first frame of the wide shot, like a title card announcing a new scene. After a while, we found the photograph of the woman too, slotted in before the walnut-cased television became the sole focus of Hosterlitz's camera.

'It must be in every film,' I said.

'This is insane,' Walker replied.

'Can we check some of the others?'

'Which ones?'

'Any. Just select a couple at random.'

Walker headed back to the kitchen.

As he did, I felt my phone go off in my pocket. When I got it out, I saw that it was Melanie Craw. She'd tried calling me while I'd been chained up at the scrapyard. I'd called her back after I got out, hit her voicemail and promised to try again later. But I never had.

Next to me, the woman in the photograph remained

frozen on the wall. The ashen tint of her skin, the darkness of her lipstick, the lightness of her clothes. But, this time, as I stared at the snapshot of her, the phone still going off in my hand, I began to see something new. Something I hadn't spotted until now.

A tiny shadow, cast across her neck.

I felt the phone stop buzzing, and then Walker returned with two more film cans and made a beeline straight for the projector.

'Wait a second,' I told him, holding up a hand. 'Wait a second.'

He looked at me. 'What?'

I found the pictures of the wooden angel on my phone, and then held one of them up beside the woman on the wall. I looked at the woman again, and then back to the angel. The woman. The angel. The photograph. The phone.

Shit.

It wasn't a shadow I was seeing on her neck.

It was a tattoo of a crucifix.

'Shall I change the reel?' Walker asked.

I nodded, but I wasn't really listening now. I wasn't really listening even as we got confirmation that the black frame and the photograph were in exactly the same place in two other films, and probably the rest of the horror movies too. All I could think about was that someone – *Hosterlitz? Korin?* – had drawn the cross on to the wooden angel in order to exactly mirror the tattoo on the woman. Why?

Who was she?

If she was in her mid thirties back then, she'd be in her nineties now. Lynda Korin, Veronica Mae – neither of them was the right age to be the woman in the picture.

So who the hell *was* she?

'I've got to go,' I said to Walker, looking at my watch. It was 5 p.m. I needed to get out of here, clear my head, think through my next move.

In my pocket, my phone started buzzing again.

I took it out, expecting it to be Craw a second time. But it wasn't. It wasn't any number I had logged – but it *was* one I recognized. It was the same central London landline that had phoned me while I'd been kept at the Portakabin. I'd tried calling it back once I was out, but no one had picked up.

Confused, cautious, I hit Answer. 'David Raker.'

'Mr Raker.'

The voice on the line sounded taut and frightened. I'd heard it before, many times over – but, out of context, it took me a couple of seconds to place it.

Glen Cramer.

'Mr Cramer?'

'Yes,' he said, wheezing a little. 'Yes.'

'Are you okay?'

'I need to see you. I need to tell someone before it's too late.' His words were weak and smudged, as if he'd just been crying. 'I can't keep this a secret any longer.'

53

The idea that it might be some sort of trap occurred to me the moment I ended the call. I wasn't sure if it was because I actually suspected Cramer of being involved with Zeller and Egan – he hadn't wanted to say much more over the phone, but I'd seen no flicker of deceit when I'd interviewed him face-to-face – or whether, after years of being lied to in my job, by families, by the victims themselves, suspicion had become my reflex state of mind. Either way, I wasn't about to take a chance.

Cramer had wanted to meet somewhere close to the hotel at Blackfriars Bridge where the *Royalty Park* launch party was going on, but I told him that wasn't going to be possible. I needed him in a place he didn't know and hadn't chosen – ideally, somewhere public. But putting one of the world's biggest movie stars in a crowd immediately raised a separate set of problems, so I told him to get a taxi from the hotel to Limehouse, without telling anyone, and I'd meet him outside the DLR station at 11 p.m., once the party was over. There was a location just around the corner where I used to meet sources during my newspaper days.

I got there early, the sun still warm, the heat like a fever, and did a circuit around Limehouse station, checking entrances and buildings, getting a sense of the layout, the residents, the passers-by. Once I was done, I retreated to a shabby twenty-four-hour café on Commercial Road. The café was run-down and empty, its tables covered in sticky sheets of plastic, its walls ingrained with the stench of smoke and grease. I found a table by the window and got out my phone.

The woman in the photograph. The angel.

The crucifix tattoo.

The case in the true-crime book.

Was this what Glen Cramer had been talking about when he'd called me? Was this what he meant when he said, *I can't keep this a secret any longer?*

I put in a Google search, throwing 'Angel crucifix tattoo Venice crime' at it – and then hit Return. The page loaded in.

At the very top was a Wikipedia entry.

The Venice Angel – Wikipedia, the free encyclopedia
https://en.wikipedia.org/wiki/The_Venice_Angel_(case)
The '**Venice Angel**' was a nickname given to Életke Kerekes (b. 22 December, 1918, in Budapest) . . . lived in **Venice**, California . . . the house at 117 Regency Road was demolished after her death . . . small **crucifix tattoo** on her neck . . . the **crime** . . .

Underneath that were additional links, related to the search.

Martin Nemeth – Pingrove Hotel – Crimes in Los Angeles, California

I clicked through to the Wikipedia page. I'd never heard of Életke Kerekes before. I wasn't familiar with the name Martin Nemeth in the link below hers either, but I'd heard of the Pingrove Hotel. It had been a famous landmark in LA until the late 1960s, a place where Hollywood royalty used to gather, its location on the corner of Wilshire Boulevard and

North Camden Drive making it local to many of their homes in Beverly Hills, or out in nearby Holmby Hills and Bel Air.

The page loaded in. On the right-hand side was a photograph of Életke Kerekes.

It was her.

It was the woman that Hosterlitz had hidden in his films.

This picture was in black and white again, but she wasn't on the steps of her house this time, she was in front of a white, nondescript building, smiling at someone off camera.

She looked startling, the contours of her face like the strokes of an artist. Her eyes were bright, pools of clear water, her nose small and perfectly aligned, and – just above the neck scarf she was wearing – I could see the very top of the crucifix. It was hard to judge, but it must have been about an inch high, and sat exactly halfway between her collarbone and the line of her jaw. It was delicate, the upright thicker than the horizontal part of the cross.

The caption underneath the picture read:

Életke Kerekes on the American Kingdom Inc. lot, 1949.

Immediately, without having to read anything else, I knew this had to be the case that had been torn out of the true-crime book. I knew that this woman, hidden in a split-second of a lost Hosterlitz film, had to be at the centre of whatever was going on – of Zeller and Egan's attempts to get to Korin; of Korin's decision to vanish in the first place. Maybe the woman was the secret that Glen Cramer had talked about. Maybe she was where everything began.

Maybe she's where everything ends.

I paused for a moment, lingering on that last thought – and then I started reading the article.

PART FOUR

Ray Callson shifts his weight on the chair and crosses his legs, running the back of his hand across his mouth. Outside, the light of the day is fading fast now, and a fully formed reflection of him has emerged in one of the windows.

'I've seen a lot of murders,' *he says.*

'But this was the one you couldn't let go.'

He shrugs. 'Like I said, it wasn't what the kid had done. It wasn't the blood. It wasn't him sitting there in that hotel room, on the edge of that bed, crying like a baby. It wasn't that.'

'It was his choice of victim?'

'Yeah.' *Callson sniffs.* 'That was the first time I ever saw a murder like that. Actually, come to think of it, over the years, I maybe only saw one or two like that. There were other guys who caught cases like it, so I heard about them, but I rarely saw them myself. Mostly you were dealing with husbands who'd offed their wives. This . . . I don't know . . . It was like something got all screwed up.'

A darkness forms in Callson's face, pooling there like ink.

'Can you tell me about the victim?'

Callson heaves a long sigh, his expression softening. 'She was one hell of a nice-looking woman, I'll tell you that much. She was from Hungary originally, but emigrated to the US after the Second World War. Once she got here, she anglicized her name to Elaine Kinflower, and that's what everyone knew her as – I guess it was easier to pronounce – but her birth name was Életke Kerekes. In 1953, she would

335

have been . . .' He blows out his cheeks. 'Thirty-five. Something like that.'

'You said she lived in Venice?'

Callson nods. 'Back then, it was a fucking dive, though. At the time she was there, the whole area had hit the skids. It used to be called the "slum by the sea". All the souvenir shops, the bingo parlors, they were now pawnshops and liquor stores. The canals looked like rivers of shit. The tourists were gone. The only people living in Venice at that time were immigrants or the so-called "counter-culture" – writers, poets, artists, those sorts of people. She paid next to nothing to live in this run-down bungalow – but you know what? I remember going to her house and thinking to myself, "Actually, this place is real nice." She'd made the best of what she had.'

'You didn't expect that?'

'In Venice at that time? No, I didn't.'

'What was so nice about her house?'

'She'd just worked real hard on it, is all. I gotta couple of daughters. I know what it's like out there, and I know what it was like back then. Women at that time, they were treated like second-class citizens. Still are, if you ask my girls about it. Életke Kerekes probably put in twice as many hours as some of the pricks that were pinching her ass all day, and probably got half the pay in return – but she made her money count. I liked her place. It spoke well of her.'

'So why is it this case in particular still eats at you?'

He says nothing to start with as he looks off to his left, his gaze settling on the windows. But then something unexpected happens. The glare from the camera's light attachment catches his eyes – and they flash with tears.

'Mr Callson?'

'There was just something wrong about it,' he says. 'I mean, look at me.' He gestures to his eyes, to his tears. 'Do you think I got like this every time I turned up at a crime scene? Do you think I was blubbing *like a child every time someone got their face turned to paste? I went to a million crime scenes. I saw a million things that should never have happened. No.' He shakes his head. 'No, it wasn't that.'*

'So what was it?'

'Maybe I've just gone soft. That happens when you get old.'

'Do you really think it's that?'

He shakes his head again and leans forward to where his water is. When he's sunk the last of it, he holds it up and says, 'Can I have a refill on this?' His voice is quiet, a piece of string reduced to its final cord. The glass is taken away, refilled and brought back to him, and he drinks half the water in one go. When he's done, he places the glass down in front of him.

'The press called her the Venice Angel. It was that crucifix tattoo she had.' He gestures to his neck. 'Back then, a woman having a tattoo like that, it was pretty unheard of. Racy, I guess, or vulgar, depending on your point of view. The media cottoned on to that. It was the way she looked too – beautiful, almost angelic. She went to some convent school back in Hungary, so that all played into it. One of the papers – the National People *– gave her that nickname, and it stuck.'*

'Was she married?'

'She arrived at Liberty Island in 1946, moved to Kansas for a time, then ended up in LA, and a year later – this would be 1948, I guess – her husband walked out on her and their young son to chase some piece of skirt to the East Coast. After that, she anglicized her maiden name and started having to make ends meet as a single mother.'

'How did she cope with a young kid?'

'We asked around in the days after she was found, and it turned out that she had a neighbour down in Venice who helped her out with her son. This neighbour would look after the boy – pick him up from school, give him dinner, that sort of thing – when Életke, Elaine, whatever you prefer, went to work.'

'What did she do for a living?'

'She had a job at American Kingdom. Started there as a typist in 1947, the year before her husband left her. Eighteen months later, she moved to Abraham Zeller's office to work as his secretary. But she was smarter than that. By then, she was fluent in English and writing these children's stories. We found a ton of them in her house. They were good. Real good. Her son told us she would read them to him at night, before bed. He told us his mom's imagination was amazing.'

Callson joins his hands across his belly, his elbows on the arms of the chair, his eyes on the ground, as if pulling the memories out of the floor. 'Anyway,' he says, 'doesn't take long for Zeller Senior to notice she's got talent, above and beyond what she's doing as his secretary. Probably helps that she looks a million bucks. I mean, that sort of thing tended to get you noticed in a world like that, with all that testosterone kicking around.' He stops and looks up, past the camera. 'You ever heard of a movie called Tiger Goes to Town?'

'It was an animated film.'

'Right. You probably know that it was made in 1950 by AKI, then. I read up about it too. It was one of their first ever animated movies. They were trying to compete with Walt Disney at the time. Guess where the idea for it came from?'

A pause. 'Életke Kerekes?'

'Right again,' Callson says. 'I don't know if this is actually how it happened or some Hollywood-fabricated bullshit, but the way I heard it, Zeller Senior happens to be at her desk one day, going through his appointments, and he sees this story she's written for her son. He reads some of it over her shoulder and thinks it's brilliant. He asks to see more, and so she brings in a bunch of them from home for him, and he picks out Tiger Goes to Town. They give it to some screenwriter to adapt, they pay her a fee, and – voilà – a year later it's up there onscreen.'

'Did she make much money from it?'

Callson shrugs. 'She was still living in Venice, right up until she died, so I'm guessing not – or, at least, not enough to move her and her son out to somewhere better, and keep them fed and watered. But she got a "Story by Elaine Kinflower" in the credits, and Zeller Senior – and then Saul Zeller when he joined in 1951 – started using her to bounce ideas around, especially where their kids' films were concerned. She understood kids. She had this flair for what they liked. As I said, she was smart.'

'What happened after that?'

'For a while she was still making the coffees, and typing up letters, but then, in 1952, the Zellers gave her this junior writing role, working under some of the guys they had on staff there. Didn't pay much, but she could see it for what it was – a bridge to something better. This was the fifties, remember. Back then, you could count the number of female screenwriters on one hand. That's another reason why I think the papers had such a thing for her. The Angel stuff – that all helped the, uh . . .' He rotates the forefinger of his right hand, searching for the word. 'The, uh . . . the . . .'

'Narrative?'

'Right. The narrative. "The Venice Angel" was a hell of a lot easier to process than "Életke Kerekes". But, from what I've read, there was a lot of fascination with her too. Lot of jealousy, lot of criticism, but a lot of praise, approval and whatnot. The idea of an immigrant, a single mother, a widow, escaping the typing pool and trying to make it as a screenwriter.' He shrugs. 'That never happened then.'

'Wait a second, you said a widow.'

Callson nods.

'Her husband died?'

'The asshole who left her and their boy in 1948? He died a year later in New York. Got stabbed with a box cutter in a bar. But it's not him I'm talking about.'

'Are you saying she got remarried?'

'Yeah. She met this guy, John Winslow. He came back from the

Second World War and got a job as an investigator at an insurance firm. The two of them met at a party, I think. Anyway, they dated for a year and, November 1951, they got married. He moved in with her because his office was in Culver City, so Venice was closer than Echo Park, and by all accounts they were real happy. Eleven months later, he's dead.'

'How did he die?'

'Car accident. Old woman in a Studebaker. Mounted the sidewalk, hit him square on. Paramedics arrived at the scene and he was already dead.' Callson falls into silence. 'Year after that,' he says quietly, 'Életke Kerekes went the same way.'

'You haven't really talked about how she died.'

Callson hesitates again, a flicker in his face. His eyes shift from the camera to the windows. Through the glass, the sky is a deep red.

'Can you describe the scene you found in Room 805?'

He shifts on his chair, straightening the jacket he's wearing. 'Sure,' he says, after a long breath.

'You told me you left your partner, Luis, out in the corridor with the hotel manager and you went in by yourself. What did you find?'

'I found her killer, sitting on the edge of the bed.'

'He was crying.'

'Yeah. The tears had made trails through the blood on his face. Weird what you remember, but I remember that. He had blood all over his shirt, all over the front of his pants. He worked in the kitchen at a diner a couple of blocks from the hotel, this dive of a joint called Mulligans. Cleaned floors, washed dishes, whatever else. He was wearing this white shirt and it was just soaked through. But it was the hair that got to me.'

'The hair he'd torn out of her head?'

'Yeah. He'd ripped it right out. When we found her, her head was full of these bald patches. Just these spots where he'd grabbed and pulled.

I mean, that's one thing, right? That's pretty messed up. But this kid never got rid of it. Never tried to wash her hair away. He just woke up, realized what he'd done, and then sat there on the edge of the bed, her hair stuck to his fingers, crying.'

'Woke up?'

'He'd been loaded the night before. He must have grabbed her hair when she fought back. He had scratches on his arms from where she'd obviously tried to defend herself – but he said he didn't remember any of it. The moment I got the tox report back, I could see why. He'd sunk half a bottle of whisky. He'd taken enough sleeping pills to bring down a bull, and there were traces of amphetamines in his system too. You know much about speed?'

'A little.'

'While you're up, it's great. You're the life and soul. You got energy and you don't get tired. You feel like the man. Come out the other side and you start to feel like shit. Low. Agitated. Irritated. Depressed. Some people, like him, they go full-on psychotic. That scene in there, what he'd done – that was psychotic. The kid was psychotic. There must have been a moment, some time before we got there, where he woke up and was lucid and was, like, "What the fuck have I done?", and that was why he took those sleeping pills. He was trying to settle his nerves, his anxiety, whatever the hell else. But it was too late for Életke Kerekes by then. Way too late. The evidence of that was lying about ten feet from where the kid was crying his eyes out.'

'That was where Kerekes was – ten feet away?'

'Yeah.'

'She was on the bathroom floor – is that correct?'

Callson starts shaking his head. 'No, that's not correct.'

'Oh. I thought I read that she was lying –'

'Her legs were on the floor.'

There's silence in the room.

'Just her legs?'

Callson nods again. 'Just her legs. The rest of her was in the tub. He'd started trying to cut her up the night before.'

'She was being dismembered.'

It isn't a question this time, and Callson doesn't take it as such. He just looks into the camera. His expression could be mistaken for blank, except there's a prickle of anger high up on his cheeks that seems to leak colour into his eyes.

'We found a knife in the tub with her. The bathroom was . . .' He fades out and shakes his head again. 'There was blood everywhere.'

'The knife was the murder weapon?'

'One of them. She'd been stabbed in the throat. That's what killed her. But she'd also been beaten before she was killed. There were bruises over her face, her chest, her arms. She was beaten and then she was hit across the back of the head with a bronze paperweight. That's what actually put her down. Once she was down, he put the knife through the centre of her throat.' Callson pauses for a moment, jabbing the first two fingers of his right hand in towards his larynx. 'It went in so deep, the point of the blade came out of the back of her neck.'

Callson just stares into the camera, saying nothing for a long time. But then, finally, his eyes stray to the right of the lens. 'You remember what I said earlier?'

His voice is smaller, quieter, but hard.

'You remember how I said something got all screwed up? I said it wasn't what he'd done to her that had got to me, but who Életke Kerekes was to him. You remember I said that?'

'Yes, I do.'

'Well, now you understand why.'

There's silence from behind the camera.

'He'd only just turned sixteen,' Callson says, shaking his head. He reaches for his water again but doesn't drink from it. 'Sixteen years old and capable of that.'

He stares down into the glass. The mood has changed.

'Martin Nemeth,' Callson mutters.

'That was the name of her killer?'

'Yeah.' A single nod of the head. 'He was Életke Kerekes's son.'

54

I ordered another coffee and tried to process everything I'd just read. I watched cars pass the café, their brake lights blinking in the darkness, the noise of traffic like the perpetual growl of an animal, and thought about the Venice Angel. She'd been butchered at the Pingrove Hotel on 2 October 1953 by her own son. When police had entered the eighth-floor suite, they'd found him sitting on the edge of the bed, crying. Életke Kerekes's body was in the bathroom, partially dismembered.

At the time of the murder, her son, Martin Nemeth – who had retained his father's surname – was drunk and quite possibly high. Sleeping pills were found in his mother's handbag, which police believed he'd taken, presumably in an effort to try to counteract the effects of the speed.

He told police officers he had no memory of killing her.

His biography painted a picture of a troubled kid. He'd dropped out of high school at fifteen and, a month later, was arrested but not charged after getting into a fight outside a bar. Employees at Mulligans, the diner at which he'd been working, said that Nemeth was a heavy drinker, even at sixteen, and often talked about his mother in disparaging terms. Other times, he'd be quiet, or quick to anger, which seemed to tally with amphetamine use. Seven weeks prior to the murder, he was arrested by police again after pushing someone through a glass door. This time, he was charged with assault. His mother posted his bail.

In April 1954, Martin Nemeth was tried as an adult, found guilty of both assault and first-degree murder, and given the death penalty for the killing of his mother. He never went to the gas chamber, but he never saw the outside of a prison wall either. He spent twenty-three years on death row at San Quentin, until he died of a heart attack in 1977. He was only thirty-nine at the time.

I saw how that fitted with the true-crime book now: it was his death that was being referred to in the final lines of the missing chapter.

From the various websites, and using a Google image search, I'd found and saved three separate photographs of Életke Kerekes. There was the shot I'd seen on Wikipedia, taken at some point during 1949 on the American Kingdom studio lot. There was one of her at the Pingrove, surrounded by golden age Hollywood stars. She was perched on the arm of a leather chair, in a black silk lacc dress.

It was the third photograph that I couldn't rip my eyes away from, though. It was a shot of Robert Hosterlitz, waving to some crowds at the premiere of *The Eyes of the Night*. Behind him was a cinema somewhere in LA, a red carpet running like a strip of ribbon towards its doors. Flanking him were Saul Zeller and Glen Cramer, Zeller tanned and handsome, Cramer immaculate in a black suit. At the edge of the shot, next to Cramer, was Életke Kerekes. The men were laughing riotously about something – but while there was the hint of a smile at the corners of Kerekes's mouth, as if she was being polite, it didn't reach her eyes. Was it just unfortunate timing, or was there more to it than that?

I looked at my watch. It was almost 10.30 p.m.

Cramer would be leaving the *Royalty Park* party about now. I sank the rest of my coffee and then my eyes dropped again to the picture of Kerekes at the premiere. I looked at that tiny hint of a smile, at the stark contrast – in black and white – between the dark of her hair and the paleness of her skin – and then a memory formed.

Axe Maniac.

The terrible Hosterlitz horror film I'd watched in a hotel room three nights before. It was something to do with that. There was something in it. Something I'd seen but not really taken in. But what?

Switching to the browser, I went to one of the best European horror movie sites I'd found when I'd been trying to gather background on Hosterlitz's career in the 1970s and 1980s. Its awful design hid a comprehensive database of French, Spanish and Italian horror films, with screenshots of many of the most famous ones. Because *Axe Maniac* had been available in English, and to buy on DVD, the people who ran the site had been able to capture its cast in action, the gory deaths, and what they termed 'key moments'.

The screenshots were spread across three pages. On the first page, Korin was standing at a wardrobe naked, picking out a dress. I remembered watching it, but it wasn't the scene itself that interested me this time, it was the fact that she'd dyed her blonde hair black for this film and had cut it short; and it was the dress she'd removed from the wardrobe. Dark grey, with a sequined pattern.

Just like the one Kerekes wore to the premiere.

My pulse quickened. I went to the next page. Korin was putting on the dress, and zipping it up at the back, and then standing in front of a mirror, looking at herself. In the next sequence of shots, the camera began to track around her in a graceful arc, again showcasing the way Hosterlitz made his wife's scenes distinct.

Then I clicked through to the third page.

She finished styling her hair. She turned towards the camera. She was looking beyond it, beautiful in the sequined dress, her face as pale as snow. And the very corners of her mouth were turned up in the hint of a smile.

I felt my whole body compress.

He's turned her into Életke Kerekes.

In terms of their shape, they were completely different. Korin was fuller, curvier, bustier. She was taller too. Kerekes was more straight up and down – not boyish exactly, but smaller, slight, petite. Yet they shared something more than just the same dress, the same hair and the same smile.

It's their eyes.

Except, maybe for Hosterlitz, it went even deeper than some minor physical similarity. Maybe he saw something in Korin, and was drawn to her, not because of the way she looked but because of the way she *was* – her demeanour, her nature. Maybe that was the reason he became so obsessed with her, why he treated her scenes with such reverence, why he might fill an entire album full of photographs of her. Which made the scene in *Axe Maniac* what exactly? A tribute to Kerekes? A love letter? Or some sort of confession?

I desperately tried to dismiss it, coming at it from the other direction. I rewound to what Rafael Walker had told me, about the *National People* story being a plant. Now Glen Cramer had called me to confess to a secret he couldn't keep any more. Could it have been Cramer who'd phoned the *National People*? Why would he have done that? It was hard to see straight, impossible to see the lines connecting one part of this to another.

I looked at my watch again, knowing it was time to go – but still I couldn't move. Because now all I could think about was whether Lynda Korin had finally found out some terrible truth about her husband, years after she'd buried him.

I hope you can forgive me, Lynda.

Maybe the discovery had set this whole thing in motion. Maybe it was the reason she'd disappeared.

55

Glen Cramer arrived late, but not by much.

The taxi pulled up outside Limehouse station and an interior light came on. I could see Cramer reaching forward, paying the taxi driver. The driver clearly recognized his passenger: he was talking to Cramer animatedly, laughing, and made the effort to get out and open his door for him. Cramer shuffled across the back seat, hauled himself out, and flipped up the hood on a thin raincoat he was wearing. The night was still enough for me to hear the driver asking him if he definitely wanted to be dropped off here, and then the taxi was gone and Cramer was alone, half covered by darkness, face hidden inside the hood.

I was standing in the shadows of a doorway further down the street, but continued to watch him, looking for signs of a tail. He was on edge, anxious, but the more time that passed, the more certain I was that it was safe, so – after seven minutes of waiting around – I called him. He fumbled around in the pocket of his raincoat, a dinner jacket visible underneath, and answered his phone.

'David?' There was already mild panic in his voice.

'I need you to listen, okay? Head south, turn right at the end on to Ratcliffe Lane, and then left on to Butcher Row. Two minutes further down, on the other side of the railway bridges, you'll find a red-brick building. It says "Public Baths" on it. Are you getting this?' I watched him nod, and then he told me he was. 'The building's empty, but there's an arched entrance next to it that takes you around to the back, into a kind of courtyard. I'll meet you in there.'

I hung up, pocketed my phone and watched him. I knew caution was necessary, but it was hard not to feel a pang of guilt at the sluggishness of his movements: I was making a 91-year-old man walk half a mile in the dark.

I followed him at a distance all the way there, and when Cramer finally reached the building, he paused, placing a hand on the wall, the arched entrance that led to the baths' courtyard beside him. With a final look up at the front of the building – its windows boarded, its render chipped and gouged – he stepped through the arch and the night swallowed him up. I headed in after him.

Under foot was a floor of concrete, cracked and uneven, plants crawling out of the rifts and fissures, vines climbing the walls. Cramer was standing right at the back, at the edge of the shadows, his hands in his pockets. He looked frail and grey, the mix of darkness and light emphasizing the folds and creases of his face. I saw a shimmer in his eyes as I approached, a moment of fear. The closer I got to him, the more he seemed to shrink, as if losing weight in front of me.

Next to him was a set of doors. A rusting chain had been looped around the handles, and a padlock attached, giving the impression there was no way in.

It was all a lie.

Just like everything else in this case.

There was no mechanism inside the padlock, so while the shackle looked like it was secured into the body of the lock, it was all show. I pulled the shackle out, removed the padlock from the chains and began unravelling them from the door handles. Twenty seconds later, they were in a pile on the floor at my feet.

'I need to check your phone,' I said.

He seemed reluctant, but he did as I asked. I checked his Recent Calls, texts, emails – and found nothing – then checked for any sign of a trace; any apps that set off alarm bells, any additions to the phone itself. When I was done, I removed the SIM card and battery and left them on a window ledge. Maybe I was being paranoid. Maybe I hadn't thought any of this through properly.

My head started thumping again.

'Follow me,' I said.

Using a penlight I'd found in Egan's car, I led us deeper into the bowels of the building. It smelled damp, stagnant. Cramer followed close behind me as I wove a path through the decayed corridors, into the male changing rooms, past a shower block that smelled brackish and stale, and out into the main pool area.

The empty pool ran at a slant from one end to the other and, above us, there were chunky glass panels built into the curve of the ceiling. A lot were cracked or missing altogether, moss and vines twisted around the vacant frames.

I stopped about halfway along the pool, where a weak shaft of moonlight broke through the gaps in the roof and erupted against an alcove between two pillars. There was a slab of stone inside, a natural bench, and I gestured for Cramer to sit. As he shuffled in, a moment of unease struck me. I scanned the room, looking hard at the shadows that painted so much of it. The space was large, maybe three hundred and fifty feet from one end to the other, and most of it was dark, or barely lit. *I should have gone somewhere smaller.*

Somewhere more manageable. I looked down at the pool, at the place where people had once swum. It was a bed of bronzed mulch; the evidence of a thousand fallen leaves.

Cramer collapsed on to the bench with a heavy breath, joints popping, his entire body seeming to sigh. He looked pale under the moonlight, old and tired, every day of his ninety-one years. Mostly, though, he just looked scared.

'You said you had something to tell me, Mr Cramer?'

'Glen,' he said softly, eyes on the floor. He was at the edge of the bench, his legs perfectly adjacent to one another, a veined hand on either knee.

'Glen. What is it you want to say?'

He swallowed. 'I did something.'

Életke Kerekes. It had to be her.

'What did you do?'

He looked up at me, his eyes flashing in the half-light. 'When you came to the house on Saturday, asking about Bobby, you asked questions that made me think you might know more than you were letting on. As soon as you left, I started to panic. I started to think, "He knows . . ." That was why I ended up calling you on Sunday, and when I couldn't get through, why I called again this afternoon. I did it both times from a phone booth because I didn't want them to find out.'

'Who? Zeller and Egan?'

He nodded and took a long, crackling breath. 'I've got to tell someone before it's too late. I can't go to the grave with this on my conscience.'

'Why haven't you gone to the police?'

He shook his head. 'There's no time for that. Filling them in on who's who, on the background to everything, on years and dates and all that bullshit – it'll take weeks. That's time I don't have any more.'

I eyed him. 'Time you don't have?'

'My life is measured in days now, David.'

'Do you mean you're sick?'

He just shook his head. 'None of that matters. All that matters is what we did. All that matters is that we did something terrible.'

56

I looked at him, a pale sliver of a man set inside two stone pillars, and thought of the picture of Hosterlitz, Zeller and Cramer at *The Eyes of the Night* premiere, Kerekes off to the side.

'Are you saying you killed Életke Kerekes?'

Cramer's eyes were on the empty swimming pool, the cracks in its base. Softly, he said, 'We all had different parts to play.'

'What does that mean?'

'We didn't all brandish the knife, but we all did our part. Bobby, Saul, me – we all played a role.' His hands had been on his knees, but finally he moved them, lacing his thin, pale fingers together on his lap. 'American Kingdom – it's a lie. Every picture Saul green-lit in the time since that woman died is a lie, because he should never have been there to do it. Every film I did for them is the same. We should have been in prison. We should have been going to the gas chamber, not walking around doing *this*.' He gestured to the space above our heads, but I got his meaning. *This freedom. This success. This career. This money.*

'Tell me what happened,' I said.

Somewhere above us, a bird took flight, flapping its wings in the shadows. Cramer tried looking for it, his wet eyes searching, and when he didn't find it, he started nodding, as if he'd been waiting a long time for the question to land.

'Elaine,' he said quietly. 'We never knew her as Életke. I

never even knew that was her actual name until the papers ran stories about her. But I guessed she wasn't American, because she had this beautiful accent, like Sophia Loren.'

'When did you first meet her?'

'We used to go to this club on Sunset Strip called the Blue Orchid, before the Pingrove became the place to be seen. This must have been 1951, because I'd just done *Connor O'Hare* and I was starting to get a bit of attention.' He paused; a flicker of a smile. 'As hard as it is to believe now, I used to get quite a lot of female attention. Most nights at the Orchid, I went home with someone.'

'Did you go home with Kerekes?'

'Oh no. No, she was engaged to John Winslow by then. Elaine wasn't some floozy. She had class. She was intelligent. She took her commitments seriously.'

'So you just got talking to her?'

'Saul introduced us.'

'This was before she was employed as a screenwriter?'

'Yeah. The year before. Officially, she was still working for old man Zeller *and* Saul, running around doing their bidding. But they were starting to use her for more than just typing up letters. She had this . . .' He paused, his eyes squeezing shut as if he couldn't think of the word. 'This gift, I guess. She wrote these stories for kids, but it was more than that. These days, studios pay a fortune for someone like her, someone with that kind of intuition, who understands the audience. And Elaine, she understood kids' films. She got how kids were wired, and back then – when Disney were making millions from animated pictures – Elaine gave the Zellers an edge none of Disney's other competitors had. Did you know that most of the cartoons that AKI made in the fifties were based on her ideas? Saul was still mining her stories even after she was murdered. It was disgraceful.' His head dropped.

'So did she come with Zeller to the Blue Orchid that night?'

'She came with a bunch of guys from AKI. I was there with a date. Bobby was there too. He didn't bring anyone. He never did. I said to you when you came to my house that Bobby was a lonely soul. That part wasn't a lie. I loved him like a brother, but he had no interest in . . .' He waved a hand through the air, back and forth, to signify sex, or maybe love, or maybe both. 'Zeller used to call him a fag all the time – only half joking, I think – but at least if Bobby had been gay, he would have felt something. It was more like he was . . . I don't know . . .'

'Asexual.'

'Exactly, yeah.' He stopped again, rubbing at one of his eyes. 'Anyway, Saul brought Elaine over and – *wow*. I thought she was incredible. I couldn't keep my eyes off her. I had to pretend I was interested in my date, but it was really Elaine I was interested in. A little way into the evening, I watched as she went off to the bathroom, and saw my chance. I made an excuse and waited for her outside the restrooms, and when she came out, I stopped her and said, "Would you let me buy you a drink?" She smiled at me – this killer smile – and replied, "Thank you, Mr Cramer, I'd love a drink with you and your date. It'll fill the hour before my fiancé picks me up."' Cramer stopped, the hint of a smile. 'Like I said, she took her commitments seriously. Her work. Her family. Relationships. It all mattered.'

'But after her second husband died?'

Cramer shrugged. 'Saul and I, we both had a thing for her. I'd like to believe my feelings were more profound than his, because Saul's were simply lust. He just wanted to sleep with her, no more, no less. I think she spent most of her working day fending off advances from him, and I'm sure he tried to use that against her – "Put out, or you're finished at AKI", that sort of thing. But it was all bullshit and both of them knew it. Saul loved two things more than he loved women: money and power. Talent like Elaine had, like Bobby had – like I had, I guess – gave him those things. Saul surrounded himself with talent. It was smart and pragmatic.'

'So did you ask her out?'

He nodded. 'I waited, obviously. She was grieving for John Winslow and she was a mother. Kids should always be the priority. I never had any myself, but I know that. I think Winslow died in October 1952, so I called her and offered to help in any way I could, and then bought her lunch a couple of times a little while later, and gradually, over the course of five or six months, I got to know her better and it felt like we grew close.' He swallowed, rubbing his fingers at a dry spot on his face. 'I'm not going to pretend I wasn't physically attracted to her, because I was. I'm not going to pretend I didn't think about what it would be like to sleep with her, because I did. But I never tried anything with her – not for a long, long time. I just enjoyed her company, enjoyed getting to know her, enjoyed trying to make her laugh. In that time, I never went to her place, never met her son – she never invited me, and I never pushed it. I thought she was probably embarrassed about where she lived and that she wasn't ready to introduce a new man into her home life, and I understood that. So we'd just meet up somewhere and share a coffee, or go to a diner for lunch, or take a walk in Griffith Park. That was what it was, *all* it was, until, I don't know, May or June.'

'That was when you asked her out officially?'

'Yeah.'

'And what did she say?'

'She said no.' Cramer halted, clearing his throat. It was a soft, gluey sound, a mix of phlegm and emotion. 'I was shocked. I'd read the situation, gone over it in my head. I'd spent months waiting for the right moment. I thought it was what she wanted, just the same as me – and then she said no. But do you know what was worse? It wasn't because she didn't feel ready to date someone. It was me.'

'What do you mean?'

'It was me – or, at least, what I did for a living. She didn't want to date a movie star. She didn't want to be snapped every time she went out for dinner, or down to the grocery store. She didn't want the pond life from the *National People* slithering all over the steps of her house, where a kid might be playing one day in the future, or trying to catch her with her blouse off through the bedroom window. Basically, she didn't want to be known as some woman in the background of Glen Cramer's life. She had bigger plans than that. She had her own life, her own ambitions.' He swallowed again, but this time it seemed harder for him. 'In hindsight, I can see all of that. I admire it. Why *would* she settle for being Glen Cramer's new squeeze when she could be Elaine Kinflower, screenwriter? I understand that now, I do.'

'But you didn't back then?'

'No,' he said. 'No, I didn't understand it at all. In fact, I got angry with her. I swore at her, spoke to her in a terrible way, and accused her of leading me on. She told me she never believed she'd done that, and if she had she never intended to, and that we should have some time apart from one another, so that I could calm down. She said, "I hope we can still be friends," and I told her, "Fuck you."' Cramer looked crushed by the memory, his eyes watery and red. He let out a long breath. 'If I could take it all back, I would. I would do it in a heartbeat.'

'What happened then?'

'I spent a month screwing half the women in LA, trying to get Elaine out of my system. I got drunk most nights. But, whatever I did, I couldn't stop thinking about her – and, in my head, it was the same question, over and over: "If not me, then who?"' He glanced at me; wiped at an eye. 'I was infatuated with her. If I couldn't have her, I didn't want anyone else to. I'd lie there at night, with some woman next to me whose name I didn't even know, and all I'd be thinking about was Elaine. I hated the idea of her with another man. It was eating me up.' His words fell away, laced with embarrassment. 'Then I saw her with Bobby Hosterlitz.'

I looked at Cramer. 'But you said he was never –'

'Interested in women. Right. He wasn't. But then suddenly he was. He was interested in *her*.' He shrugged. 'You ever heard of the picture *My Life is a Gun*?'

I'd read about it. It was the follow-up to *The Eyes of the Night*, the film that Hosterlitz had been prepping for AKI before he was forced to flee the country.

'I'd been talking to Bobby about taking the lead in it,' Cramer continued. 'I'd basically agreed to it. I'd read the treatment. It was dynamite. Absolute dynamite. It was better than *The Eyes of the Night*. Anyway, I was at his office on the lot – I guess this must have been September 1953 – and we were talking, then he says he has to go, he's got to meet someone. So I said to him, "Let me drop you." I had this new Buick Dynaflow and I wanted to show it off. But he gets all sheepish about it and tells me not to worry. I tell him it's no hassle and he says to forget it – almost gets uppity about it. So I let him go. Except I didn't. I followed him.'

'He was going to meet Kerekes.'

'Yeah,' Cramer said. 'Yeah, that's right. I didn't know it at the time, I was just taken aback by how he'd been with me. He seemed different, agitated. I'd known him a while by then – four years or so – and I'd never seen him react like that. I swear to you, I didn't follow him because I even *remotely* suspected he was meeting Elaine. Hell, I didn't think he'd be meeting a woman of *any* description. That just wasn't Bob. I went after him because I thought, "If he's losing his grip, if something's wrong, if he's sick in the head, or an alcoholic, or suddenly addicted to drugs, I don't want to sign up to doing a picture with him and ruin my career." *That* was my thinking. It was purely selfish.' Cramer looked up at me. 'But then we ended up in Venice.'

His eyes had dropped to the floor and his hands were back on his knees. 'I parked a block away and let Bobby go in,' he continued, 'and then I got out and walked to the house. By the time I got there, Bobby was outside with Elaine, sitting on the front steps of that place she had. They were having lemonade, just sitting, chatting. They weren't doing anything – holding hands or kissing. None of that. In fact, Bobby was sitting apart from her. All they were doing was talking.'

'Because he wasn't trying to date her,' I said.

Cramer nodded. 'Right.'

'They'd become friends.'

'Yeah. Bobby shunned the spotlight, that's the thing. That's why it worked. He hated celebrity. If he had to do promotion, he would, but even after *The Eyes of the Night* went big, he kept a low profile. He directed a picture that won seven Oscars, and a lot of people – even internally at AKI – still didn't know what he looked like. That was the way he preferred it. That was the way Elaine preferred it.'

'That was why she let him in.'

'She let him come to her house. I spent six months paying for coffees and lunches and organizing picnics in the park, and she never once asked me back to her place. Not once. And yet I stood there that day and watched Bobby hitting balls to her boy in the yard, like he was his fucking dad or something. She'd spent six months with me and never as much as told me the kid's name.'

'Martin.'

'Yeah,' he said, almost a whisper. 'Martin.' There was a heaviness to his naming of Életke Kerekes's son, as if his guilt and shame were moored to it. 'Thing is, I think Elaine loved Bobby. Not in the traditional way, maybe. I'm not sure she loved anyone in that way at that time. Maybe she wouldn't have again. But I kept following him back there, day after day, watching them together, and I could see they had something. There was no lust, nothing physical. It was pure.' Cramer flattened his lips together, the tiny blood vessels in his cheeks colouring. 'Bobby was a part of it.'

'A part of their family.'

'A part of their family,' he repeated.

As Cramer fell silent, something else clicked into place. The photograph of Kerekes on the steps of her house, the one inserted into *Kill!* – I'd wondered where Hosterlitz had got it, years after her death. He must have taken it himself.

'I did something terrible after that,' Cramer said.

I looked at him.

It was obvious where we were headed now.

'You killed her,' I said.

He started at the sound of my voice, as if he'd forgotten he wasn't alone in this place, and then his eyes moved back to the broken curves of the empty swimming pool.

'Glen,' I said, 'is that when you killed her?'

'No,' he replied. 'No, I think I did something even worse.'

57

The baths were quiet and still, except for leaves fluttering downwards from the glass panels, like the broken rotors of a helicopter.

'I temporarily lost my mind,' Cramer said softly. His eyes were haunted. 'I became this person I didn't recognize. I was insanely jealous of what they had together – the innocence of it, the simplicity, the integrity. It was untainted. He knew I wanted to be with Elaine, because I'd told him. He pretty much knew I was infatuated with her at that point, which is why I think he didn't want to admit to what they had. It was an act of kindness on his part, but I never saw it like that. I saw it as a betrayal.' A shrug. 'So I told him a lie.'

'What lie?'

'I told him she'd started making fun of him in front of me. I told Bobby she said he was weak and pathetic, that she found him creepy and isolated, and she didn't like him hanging around her family. It just . . .' He faded out, glancing at me. 'It just poured out of me. I made it sound like I was doing him a favour, made him promise that he wouldn't tell her because *she'd* made me promise not to tell *him* – but I could see he was devastated. He had tears in his eyes. I took what they had and I ruined it. I took the purity of their relationship and I ripped it to bits.

'After that, I drove him to the Pingrove. Saul was having this huge house built at the eastern end of Mulholland, and while it was going up, he was staying in an apartment on the top floor of the hotel. During that time, he conducted a lot of meetings in one of the penthouse suites there, mostly because he was lazy and didn't want to have to drive back and forth to the lot in Burbank. Anyway, I knew that, on a Tuesday, they had a regular 5 p.m. meeting with the animation people in there. That included Elaine.' He looked at me, but not for long. It was hard for him to maintain eye contact. 'She was always last out. She had to write up all the notes from the meeting because she was still playing part-time secretary for the men there, even then. Bobby went up there, angry and hurt, embarrassed. He'd been belittled by her. Or, at least, I'd made him think he had. So he checked to make sure she was definitely alone, and then he confronted her.'

'Where were you?'

'I was downstairs in the bar. But, the day after, Bobby told me everything that happened up there.'

The heaviness of his words seemed to hang there in the darkness.

'Did Hosterlitz kill her?'

'No,' Cramer said. 'But he knocked her out.'

As he paused again, sections of what I'd read about the case online came back to me; how detectives had found bruising on Kerekes's face, chest, arms. It had been Hosterlitz who had put them there. Or maybe not just him.

'He lost his head,' Cramer continued. 'He said they had this huge fight. He accused her of belittling him, of calling him weird, and she was screaming, telling him none of it was true. And then ... and then he pushed her face-first into an oak dresser and knocked her out. He tried to wake her up, and when he couldn't, he went into a tailspin. He thought he'd killed her. A few minutes later, he finds me in the bar. He has to put on this act in front of everybody as if everything's fine, and he asks if he can talk to me. I thought he was going to tell me that he'd found out the truth – that she'd told him it was all a lie. But I follow him into the elevator and the operator takes us up, and as soon as we're out, Bobby bursts into tears.'

'And then?'

'And then I went into the suite. Elaine was starting to come around, so I told him to go back down to the bar and wait for me.'

A breeze picked up, the old building groaning.

'It was shameful,' Cramer moaned. 'I didn't see a woman lying there on the floor with bruises on her face, I saw an opportunity to replace Bobby. I know this sounds insane, but I saw a chance to be what Bobby had been to her. I saw a chance to sit with her on the front steps of her house and play baseball with her boy. So I picked her up off the floor, not because she was injured, but because I was insecure and lonely. I see that now. I didn't spend a single second thinking about her, really – it was all about what *she* could give *me*. But it all went wrong.'

'How?'

'When she'd gathered herself, she started telling me it was all my fault. She said, "I know it was *you* who put those ideas in his head." She saw right through everything. She'd figured it all out before I'd even arrived.'

As he breathed out, his chest wheezed like a tyre losing pressure. 'I'd never seen her so angry. She was in the bathroom, washing a cut on her face, telling me exactly what she thought of me. She didn't seem to blame Bobby at all – that was the thing. He'd put her on the floor, lights out, and everything was about me. I'd hoped to destroy everything they had, to step into the space left behind, but I started to realize

I'd done the opposite. She just kept shouting at me, telling me what an asshole I was, and the fuzz in my head' – he lifted a hand to his face, to the dome of his skull – 'it just got louder and louder, until I found myself grabbing her. She shook me off, so I grabbed her again, but harder, and she pushed me against the wall. And that was when I just . . . flipped.'

Cramer paused and squeezed his eyes shut.

'I slapped her. She said, "I'm calling the cops! You're going to pay for this. No one lays a hand on me!" I slapped her again, harder, but she just kept screaming at me, and when she went for the door, I panicked and . . . and I punched her. I went for her face, but I caught her in the throat instead. I winded her. She doubled over, was struggling to breathe, and the whole time it was just a haze behind my eyes. I was seething. Everything had gone wrong. Even then, she was still trying to speak, and though I could barely hear her, I could hear enough: she was telling me she'd ruin me, my reputation. I'd be arrested. I'd be destroyed in the press. So I picked up the paperweight – it was the nearest thing to me; I did it without thinking – and, while she was still bent over, telling me what she thought of me, I hit her on the back of the head with it.'

His eyes opened again, finding me instantly. 'I still remember the sound,' he said. 'It was like an egg cracking. She went down, just completely folded, but it was weird: she didn't black out this time. She just sort of lay there, bleeding into her hair, her eyes all misty, and then began trying to crawl in the direction of the bed – *under* it. She was moving in slow motion. It was as if she was trying to get away from me but she couldn't remember how to coordinate her arms and her legs. It was awful. She kept making these sounds in her throat, like she was gagging. I'll never forget it.'

I took a breath. 'But you're saying you didn't kill her?'

He shook his head.

'So who finished her off?'

Very quietly: 'Saul Zeller did.'

'How?'

'He runs into Bobby downstairs. Bobby's on his way home. Saul asks him for a drink and Bobby says no, and Saul can tell something is up. "What's going on?" he says. And Bobby tells him, "Why don't you go and ask Cramer?" So Saul gets the elevator up. He knocks on the door, tells me it's him, and I open up and say, "Go away, Saul. This isn't anything to do with you." But he doesn't go away. He looks over my shoulder and he sees Elaine on the floor, and he says to me, "What the fuck have you done, Glen?" And then a second later, it was like his brain switched, like he was a different person. He was suddenly seeing what damage it could do to us. I'm not saying he felt nothing for her, but ... but he ...' Cramer shifted slightly on the bench, his joints clicking. He looked at me, a pained expression on his face. I wasn't sure if it was his bones or his conscience. 'He had all he needed from her.'

I felt myself tense. 'Meaning what?'

'She'd handed him her stories already.' Cramer swallowed. 'She'd written hundreds of them and she'd handed them all over. At that time, AKI were putting out one animated film a year. Saul had enough material to last decades. It was the ideas. What he needed was her ideas. He already had writers to do the scripts.'

It was so unbelievably callous, it felt like I'd misheard him.

'I'm just telling you how Zeller saw it,' he said, seeing my reaction.

'But you were indispensable?'

He could hear the contempt in my voice but all he did in

return was shrug. 'I'd won one Oscar and was tipped to win another, and I wasn't even thirty. My picture was on magazine covers and in newspapers. I was on film posters all over the city, all over the country, all over the *world*. I had screaming women hunting me in packs when I went out to get smokes. I'd just signed a five-picture deal with AKI. And they needed me – they *really* needed me – because AKI back then, it was some pissant studio that Warner Brothers and Paramount and MGM used to snigger at. What had started to turn it all around was the Oscar win for *Connor O'Hare*. In a way, Bobby and I, we were the bedrock on which everything has been built since. *Connor, The Eyes of the Night* – they were what kick-started the good times for Saul Zeller. So if you want to know what Zeller saw that day when he looked at her and he looked at me, that was it. That was what he saw. A man on the verge of becoming the biggest movie star in the world – and then a woman no one knew, whose best ideas he already had.'

The temperature in the room seemed to drop.

'How can you have just gone along with it?'

He shook his head, as if I didn't get it. 'You've got to understand something. Saul needed Bobby and me, because we were making him money and winning him awards and turning AKI into serious players. Bobby needed Saul because Saul indulged him. He let him concentrate on making one film a year, which was unheard of back then. And Bobby and I needed *each other* because his scripts, his movies, they were the best – there was no one better. Bobby hated having to explain decisions he'd made in the script, or justify direction he was giving. He hated having to deal with actors who didn't share his vision. He never had to do that with me. I understood him, he understood me. We just . . .'

Cramer's words fell away, and he leaned forward, eyes flashing in the light coming through the roof. 'I guess what I'm saying is, if one of us went down, we *all* went down.'

Beads of sweat had formed on his lip, glistening like dew.

'So Saul stepped into the suite,' he said, 'and I expected him to look at her in horror, to flip out. But he didn't. He just watched her crawling towards the bed and said, "We need to fix this." She kept turning her head and trying to look at me, kept trying to say my name, but whatever damage I'd done to the back of her head, it was bad. Her words were just choking sounds.' He wiped an eye. 'There was a knife in the room. It had come up with some food they'd ordered for the meeting. Saul flipped her over on to her back and he . . . he just . . . just pushed it through her throat.'

His words stalled.

'He just kept going and going. Every time he hit resistance he would push it even harder. It was horrible. He ended her life like it meant nothing, and then – before she could bleed out – he grabbed her and dragged her to the bathroom. I stood there, frozen to the spot, and he turned to me and said, "Clean any blood off the carpet." It was like looking at an alien, a form of life that felt absolutely nothing for anyone. I don't think he even broke a sweat.'

I watched him for a moment, his eyes wet, facing the floor. There was a fine layer of dust on the toes of his brogues, and I found myself turning my attention to that, then to the cracks in the floor, then to the grimy, discoloured pillars and the vines laying claim to everything. I turned everywhere but to Cramer because, in that moment, I couldn't stomach looking at him.

'You don't understand what Saul was like in there, David,' he said, seeing my reaction. 'It was like he was taking care of a chore. He took over. He never seemed remotely scared. I said to him, "How can you do this? Why aren't you shitting yourself?" and he said, "I shot one hundred and twenty-seven Krauts in the war. I think I can deal with one dead woman." I mean, when I turned eighteen in 1942, I went to Europe too, but I was in the combat engineers and spent most of my time building bridges. I didn't see a lot of death, and not *this* sort of death. Not someone I knew and actually cared about.' He glanced at me. 'But Saul was different. He was almost subhuman.'

'Why did you leave her like you did?'

'The cops,' he said.

'The cops?'

'An hour after it happened, they suddenly pulled up outside the hotel. We thought they'd come for us. So we left her like that, part of her in the tub, part of her on the floor, and went to Saul's room. We showered and changed, we cut our clothes up into tiny pieces and flushed them down the can – but by the time we got downstairs to the bar, the cops were leaving again. They weren't there for us at all.' He shook his head, a humourless smile stretching his face. 'We'd panicked about nothing. They'd arrived to break up a fight in the lobby.'

'So why not go back up to the room and finish what you started?'

'Martin,' Cramer said. He seemed to fold in on himself, as if the mention of the boy's name was like a poison taking hold of him. 'Martin turned up in the lobby.'

58

'Martin turned up at the Pingrove?'

Cramer nodded. 'And Saul recognized him straight away.'

'How did Zeller know him?'

'Elaine hardly told me anything about Martin. I didn't know his name. I wasn't even sure how old he was, although I had a rough idea. One time we were out for lunch and she mentioned that he wasn't in high school any more and that he was working at a restaurant. I could see that hurt her. She tried to disguise it, but I could tell they'd fought about it. I picked up on other things. Not much, but enough. Martin never saw eye to eye with Winslow, her second husband – in fact, I think they plain hated each other – so I don't imagine the kid spent much time grieving when Winslow got hit by that car. That probably hurt Elaine a lot too. I think Martin was rebelling as well – more than a regular teenager, I mean – although Elaine never talked about it. I really only put it together when I spoke to Saul a few months after I'd tried asking Elaine out. I enquired how she was doing and – indiscreetly, as Saul could sometimes be – he told me she'd asked him to advance her four weeks' wages. When he'd asked her why, she told him it was a personal matter. Saul being Saul, he couldn't let that go – so he started digging around. That was just who he was. He always had to know.'

'She needed it for Martin's bail money.'

'Right. For his assault charge. It was a tricky time in the kid's life, I guess. No father. A mom whose focus wasn't entirely on him any more. He got in with the wrong crowd, started drinking, got into drugs . . .' Cramer trailed off. He had no business talking about any of this, and he knew it. Martin would have got six months for assault. Instead, thanks to Cramer and Zeller, he got sent to death row.

'So Zeller recognized Martin from the snooping around he did on Kerekes. Martin turned up at Pingrove. Then what happened?'

Cramer's Adam's apple shifted beneath the skin of his throat. 'Saul was at the bar, waiting for the last of the cops to leave before we headed back up to the room. Bobby had already left for the night, and I was in the restroom with my head in the can. I felt like I wanted to puke for ever. I could still smell her on me . . .'

His voice hitched like an old record.

'Martin came looking for his mom. It turned out she'd promised him a ride back to Venice after his shift ended. She'd told him she'd wait outside the diner, but she never turned up, and she always turned up when she said she would. As soon as the kid entered the hotel, we were in the shit. He'd be asking around about his mom inside two seconds, trying to find out where she was. Saul had Room 805 on a permanent booking, so no one was going to come and check on it. There was no maid service, at least until the morning. But it was an AKI room. The people at the hotel knew who was using it, so if Martin asked about AKI, about a meeting his mom was in, the staff would direct him upstairs. It was Saul's meeting room.'

'So he intercepted Martin?'

'Yeah. He went and got him and brought him back to the bar. I was coming out of the bathroom by then, so Saul waved me over and introduced the two of us. He was stalling for time at this point, trying to come up with something. Maybe he thought the kid would be impressed by being introduced to Glen Cramer. But he wasn't. There were other actors and producers in there, renowned Hollywood people, and this kid didn't give a shit about any of them. I don't know what the opposite of star-struck is, but he was that. He just looked at Saul and said, "Where's my mom?" It was like he knew we were trying to divert his attention somehow.' Cramer flattened his lips, pressing them together so hard they blanched. 'He had her eyes. I looked at him and saw his mother staring back at me. I saw the way she used to study me sometimes, like she was crawling inside my head. He'd already been on the booze that night, we could smell it on him – but he was smart. He was like her.'

He ran a tongue along the top of his gums, as if his mouth had gone sour. 'I'm starting to panic at that stage but trying not to show it. Saul, though, he's like the Sphinx. There's nothing. He doesn't seem fazed at all. He just turns to the kid, and he says, "Your mom's upstairs, finishing something off. Why don't we go up?" I know what he's going to do. I'm looking at him over the kid's shoulder and I'm *begging* him not to do it.' Cramer halted. 'I'm begging him,' he repeated softly.

'But you let him do it anyway.'

'Yes,' he said, and his voice tremored. 'Yes, I did. We took him up, making conversation with him like we were all the best of pals, and then Saul led him past the room and down to his own suite. He opened the door and she was obviously not in there, but he made a big show of it, like, "*Oh*, where has Elaine got to?" We went into Saul's suite and sat down and he handed out some tumblers of whisky, and then he told the kid he'd go and find Elaine, and left the two of us alone. I felt sick, looking at him. I had no idea what to say to him. I could act all day, every day, in front of the cameras, but there, in that room, I couldn't put on a show. He knew something was up and I couldn't think what to do, what lie to tell him, to persuade him otherwise – so he got up, sank the rest of his whisky, and started to say, "Where the hell's my mom? Why isn't she here?" That was the moment.'

'The moment?'

'The moment when I saw the truth. I saw how much he cared about her. All the bullshit, all the trouble he got into, everything fell away in that second. He was a complicated kid, messed up, but he loved her. He wanted to know where she was, why Saul and I were acting the way we were. That was when I could see it coming apart at the seams in front of me. But, in the end, none of it mattered.'

'Why not?'

'About thirty seconds later, he dropped flat on his face like he'd been shot in the back. He went from standing to unconscious in about a second.'

The sleeping pills. 'Zeller drugged his whisky.'

'Yes.' Cramer nodded. 'The kid was lights out. Gone. Saul returns and – between us – we carry Martin back to Room 805, and we close the door and I just stand there and watch Saul work. It was terrifying. So methodical and thought-out. He had a whole *box* of pills, which he put into Elaine's handbag, like it was hers and the kid had stolen some from her, and then he removed a bottle of whisky from his suite and poured some down the kid's throat. The rest he emptied into the sink. He took off the kid's shirt, soaked it in her blood and put it back on him again, then dragged the kid over and used her damn *fingernails* to make marks on his wrists. He wanted it to look like Martin attacked her and she tried to defend herself. But the worst thing was the hair.' Cramer looked up at me, eyes glistening. 'He ripped her hair out, big chunks of it. He laced them between Martin's fingers. I said to Saul, "What are you *doing*?" and he looked at me, stone-cold sober, and said, "He attacked her. She fought back. He grabbed her hair and ripped it out."'

Neither of us spoke for a while.

'We went back down to the bar,' he said eventually, 'like nothing had ever happened, and we made sure a whole bunch of people at the Pingrove saw us. Saul casually mentioned how we'd left Martin up there with his mother, how the kid was a bad egg, how he didn't seem to respect her, but he didn't overplay it. In the early hours of the morning, when everyone started drifting away, Saul made a big show of getting us a cab out to a nightclub on Sunset, chatting to the driver the whole way over so he'd remember us. Once the cab was gone, though, he told me to call Bobby at home so that the three of us could meet up.'

'To get your stories straight.'

'Right. We met at a spot near the duck pond in Franklin Canyon. It's up in the hills, north of the Pingrove. Bobby was still a mess. I went to comfort him, to say something, but before I even opened my mouth, Zeller had started talking. He told Bobby that Elaine was dead before I ever got up to the room. He said, "You killed her when you threw her against that dresser, Bobby. You damaged her head." I remember shooting a look at Zeller, this "What the hell . . . ?" expression, but he just stared me down, and I could feel myself shrink away from him. There was something so callous about him. He put a hand on Bobby's shoulder, and said, "If anyone finds out what you've done, you're going to the gas chamber. But they won't. We took care of it for you." It was such a confident lie. So convincing.

'Bobby was doubled over, hands on his knees, crying his eyes out, and Zeller had a hand on his back, talking softly to him. But you know something? Saul never took his eyes off me the whole time. Not once. It was a threat – almost a challenge. Just *try* and defy me. Just *try* and go against me. He was saying, *This is how it is, so you'd better be on board with it.* After that, I stood there in silence. I just watched as he said to Bobby, "What you need to do now is unfuck your head. It's done. It's over. It was a mistake and we've cleared it up for you. Someone else is going to take the heat for this." And then he said, "Is there anything in your house that links you to Elaine?" Bobby had a think about it and then he said that she'd given him this ornament one time.'

I looked at him. *An ornament.* I took out my phone, found a photo of the wooden angel and held it up to him. 'This ornament?'

Cramer stared at it. 'Yeah. Yeah, that's it.'

'Kerekes gave *this* to Hosterlitz?'

'Yeah, she made it for him out of a block of wood. She was clever like that. You showed me this picture at the house – where did you get it?'

I thought of Hosterlitz's message to Korin on the back of the angel photo that Egan had taken from the album. *I hope you can forgive me, Lynda.* If Korin had found out the truth about Kerekes before she disappeared, if that had been one of the catalysts for her vanishing, then the message made absolute sense – it meant she'd surely found out about her husband's part in the murder too.

'David, where did you get that picture?'

'I took it at Lynda Korin's house,' I said. 'So did Hosterlitz hand the ornament over to Zeller?'

'Yeah. He gave it to Saul, and Saul told me to get rid of it.'

'But clearly you didn't.'

'I thought I did,' he said.

'Glen,' I said, watching him closely, 'what's going on?'

Cramer looked out at the shadows of the baths.

Suddenly, there was a sharp breath of wind. It whistled through the holes in the walls closest to us, and then slowly began to fade again – and, as it did, something of it was left behind. The hint of a voice.

I backed up a step and looked along the edge of the pool, down towards the changing rooms. The building was silent now. When Cramer started talking again, my eyes were still on the doors into this place – the walls, its rifts and cavities.

'At Franklin Canyon, Saul started saying to Bobby, "You go back to work so everything looks normal. You get back on the horse, you go back to making *My Life is a Gun* – and you shoot the best damn film you've ever made."' I finally turned back to Cramer and found him grimacing, his head slightly bowed. 'It was just business to Saul. Nothing else. Bobby gave him credibility, and he made him money, and that was all that mattered. That was all Zeller saw.'

Physically, Cramer had long ceased to be that man in the hotel room, age laying claim to his features, to the square jaw and dark hair. He'd become frail, his spine curving like a bow. He was old and grey and blanched. And yet a part of him remained there, caught for ever in a maze of terrible choices, six decades old.

'So what happened after that was you sold Hosterlitz down the river with the *National People* story,' I said, pressing him. 'Is that it? You killed Kerekes in October 1953, and then you and Zeller planted the story the following May.'

It took him a second, but then he nodded.

'Why?'

'Bobby was starting to lose it. When he found out about Martin, how we framed him, he started drinking. He'd be drunk all the time. He was on pills and weed and who knows what else. He missed a deadline for delivering a first draft of the *My Life is a Gun* script, and then another, and then another, and then another. People started to notice. He'd already cast Lana Turner, and Lana and I would go to meetings at the lot and he'd never turn up, and Lana would ask me, "Where's Bobby? What's happening with Bobby?" Saul was starting to get pissed off too. He'd got Lana on a three-picture deal. She'd left MGM in 1954 to come to AKI, on a promise from Saul that her first movie would be a Hosterlitz film. But, after three months, there wasn't even a finished script, so Saul had to release her from her contract. She went to Warner, and that was when he got *really* angry.'

He paused, but only briefly, his words coming fast now: 'I tried to get Bobby to see sense, I swear. I'd go up to his place in Laurel Canyon, and when he wasn't ripped on bourbon or weed I thought I was getting through to him. But then I'd go up there again and he wouldn't answer, so I'd jump the gate and get into his yard, and I'd look through the windows at the back of his place and he'd be lying unconscious, surrounded by empty bottles.'

'Did you blame him?'

'No,' he said. 'I didn't blame him at all.'

'But you ruined his life, anyway.'

'It was Saul,' Cramer replied instantly. 'It was all Saul.'

That didn't even deserve a response and he knew it.

He smiled, almost apologetically, and then began again, even quieter than before. 'Seven months after Elaine was killed, Saul said we had to do something. Bobby got drunk at the Pingrove one night when we were all there, and someone overheard him talking about the woman who got killed on the eighth floor. At the time, Martin had already gone down for the murder, he was on death row up at San Quentin, and the cop who ran the case – Ray Callson, his name was – he'd interviewed Saul and me and given us the all-clear. But Bobby talking like that – it would get Callson interested again. It would be a one-way ticket for all of us.' Cramer made a long, painful noise, halfway between a sigh and a cry for help. 'The *National People* thing was Saul's idea. You couldn't just kill Robert Hosterlitz and hope no one noticed. He was a name people knew. But outing him as a secret communist – well, once you were tarred as a Red, you were finished. No one believed anything you said any more. Saul knew that Bobby wouldn't stick around long enough to be dragged through committee hearings, whether he was drunk or not. He'd hate the exposure, the vitriol, the media assassination.'

'So Zeller called the paper.'

'Yes. When the story came out in May '54, Saul said to Bobby, "Get on a plane, go to the UK, reinvent yourself – we'll always have a space for you back at AKI when it blows over." I don't know if he really meant it or not, but even then he was pretending to Bobby that we were on his side. But we weren't on his side. We were stabbing him in the back. We'd ruined a man's career in order to save our own.' Cramer looked at me, opening out his hands like he was waiting to be arrested. 'But then, when he came back to the States in '62, when he eventually shot *The Ghost of the Plains* and I saw him on the Paramount lot, it was like I told you at the house on Saturday. He was there with his script, making notes all over it, and he turned to me and smiled and said,

"I was hoping I might run into you." He was so genuine, it felt like the guilt might crush me. I invited him back to mine, that much was true, but what I didn't tell you before was that, in the end, the guilt got too much for me to bear. I sat there and watched him recount everything that had happened to him in the time since Elaine had died, and it just became too much.'

'So what did you do?'

'I told him Saul had lied to him.'

'You mean, you told Hosterlitz that he *hadn't* killed Kerekes?'

'No, not that. I didn't get as far as that.'

'So what did you tell him?'

'I said, "Saul lied to you." Bobby just sat there in silence. When he didn't react, when he didn't leap out of his chair and grab me by the throat and start screaming "What are you talking about? What lie did he tell me?", I started to panic. I had this sudden moment of clarity. I thought, "You've made a big mistake. You shouldn't have said anything." So I pretended it was a joke, an awful joke. I told him to forget it, that no one told anyone a lie, and – after that – I went straight to Saul and explained what I'd done, grovelling like a child. Saul went crazy, but what could he do? He couldn't kill me. I was one of the world's biggest movie stars. But the weird thing was, in the end nothing happened.'

'Hosterlitz didn't follow up on it?'

'No. Nothing. He didn't seem to process it when I told him at the time, and he did nothing about it afterwards either. He still believed he'd killed Elaine.'

But Cramer wasn't finished.

'There was something else too,' he said. 'Something I told Bobby but never admitted to Zeller.'

I took a step closer. 'What?'

He looked at the phone, still in my hands.

'The wooden angel,' he said.

'What about it?'

'I told Bobby what I *really* did with it.'

'What do you mean?'

'I mean, I *did* get rid of it after we killed Elaine, just as Saul asked me to – but not in the *way* I told him I did. He thought I'd dumped it in the ocean, or chopped it up, or thrown it into a fire. But I didn't do that.'

'So what did you do with it?'

'I took it to a building in Van Nuys.'

Van Nuys was a neighbourhood twenty miles north of Venice.

'What? Why did you take it up there?'

'I took it to this building on Pierre Street, just off Van Nuys Boulevard. It's closed now, but back then it was still open. It was on this long street full of three-storey houses that they knocked down at the end of the seventies.'

Three-storey houses.

Instantly, I thought of the footage that had played on the TV in Hosterlitz's horror movies, the camera tilted to show the upper windows.

Was Pierre Street the road in the footage?

'Why did you take it to that building?' I asked.

'It belonged there.'

'Why?'

Cramer was just staring at the floor.

'*Glen*. What was the building?'

Finally, haltingly, he looked up at me. 'Ring of Roses,' he said. 'The building was called Ring of Roses.'

I stared at him. 'Ring of Roses is the name of a *building*?'

'Yes. *Was* the name of a building.'

'Why take the angel there?'

Cramer went to reply – and then stopped.

From the silence of the shadows came another noise. It started quietly, but the longer it went on, the louder it got, like someone turning up the volume on a radio. When I looked at Cramer, it was obvious he had no idea what was going on. As he cowered in the shadows of the pillars, I stepped towards the changing rooms, the only way in and out of this place, and there was another sound: tiles crunching underfoot.

'Perfect timing.'

A voice from the darkness.

It was Saul Zeller.

59

Zeller emerged from the gloom, sliding out of it like a croco-
dile from a river. He was in his late eighties and walked with
surprising ease for a man of his age. He was straight, almost
rigid, no hint of an arch to his posture like Cramer, no sense
of fragility in his bones. He was dressed younger too, in a
black designer suit, the lapels a dark grey silk, his white shirt
unbuttoned, no tie. And yet his face was the opposite, his
creased skin colourless, the dome of his hairless head mottled with liver spots and old scabs. It was odd, unsettling, as
if the cold-blooded, devious young man that Cramer had
described was now hiding inside this layer of decay.

Two people followed him in.

Alex Cavarno came first. She was dressed in a long black
pencil skirt and a white ruffled blouse, her lipstick shining in
the light escaping through the roof.

She couldn't look at me.

The other was Billy Egan. He hadn't attended the party,
so he was dressed in jeans and a hooded top; the hood was
up, in an attempt to disguise a face that carried the reminders of our last meeting. His nose was broken, one of his eyes
had filled with blood, and his face was so bruised he looked
like a grotesque oil painting. He was pointing a gun at me.

Over my shoulder, I heard Cramer start to sob.

'Oh, Glen,' Zeller said. 'What have you done, old friend?'

His accent was soft and indistinct – American, but without a region.

'I'm not sure what Glen has told you, Mr Raker, but I doubt it was anything good.' He was talking to me, but his eyes hadn't left Cramer. 'You may have figured this out already, but the reason Glen isn't doing another season of *Royalty Park* is because, this time next month, he'll be six feet under the ground in Hollywood Forever.'

I just stared at Zeller.

'Hollywood Forever is a cemetery,' he said, as if he were talking to a child. I knew that part. It was next to Paramount in LA, and was the last resting place of actors like Valentino and Mansfield, and directors like DeMille and Huston.

What I didn't know for sure was that Cramer was dying.

I've got to tell someone before it's too late, he'd said to me as we'd arrived here. It would have taken him too long to confess to the police. He needed to unburden himself, but he didn't have enough time left to explain all the background. All the dates and names and locations and history and motivations – it would take days, maybe weeks, to define it all from scratch. What he wanted to do was confess – which is where I came in. Unlike the police, I knew enough already.

'Liver cancer,' Zeller said. There was a curl to his lips, but it was difficult to say whether the news pleased Zeller or made him sad. He had a starched, rigid aspect to his face, difficult to read, that reminded me of Cramer's descriptions of him – the way he'd coldly, quietly dealt with Kerekes; the way he'd told Hosterlitz it was all his fault and had stared down Cramer, inviting him to challenge the lie.

I glanced at Cramer again. He was bloodless, his eyes wet with tears.

'Anyway,' Zeller said, 'ever since I found out, I kept saying to my son, "Glen's conscience is going to get the better of him." All these years he saw the sense in keeping his mouth shut. He wouldn't have built a career as the world's biggest movie star without my help, without the things I did for him sixty years ago. He saw the logic in keeping our little secret. But gaining a sense of your own mortality, that can clear the head. All of a sudden, you start to worry about what comes next. So when Glen told me he was ill, I thought, "He's got a lot to get off his chest. He's got a whole shitload of guilt. He won't want to carry that to his grave. He'll want to get it out in the open and then go back to LA and die." I suppose, in a lot of ways, he isn't all that different from Bobby, God rest his soul.'

He looked between us. It was obvious that he was referencing the fact that cancer had accounted for Hosterlitz as well, and that the hidden messages in his horror films had been his own form of confession – the black frame, the photo of Kerekes, the delicacy of the scenes with his wife. At the scrapyard, I'd got the impression that, unlike Cramer, Egan had watched Hosterlitz's horror films. In turn, that meant that, even if Zeller hadn't seen them himself, he knew enough.

'We've been watching Glen for a while,' Zeller said, glancing towards Egan. 'We've been waiting for this moment. You're a smart guy, Mr Raker. We found a battery and a SIM card on a window ledge on our way in, so even if we'd gone to the trouble of bugging Glen's phone, we would have had a real hard time tracking you both to this place. But you never factored in a guilty conscience and old age. At the launch party tonight, Glen went to the restroom and left his phone on the table. He'd made a note on his cell of your meeting place at Limehouse Tube station, so we knew you had to be around here some place.'

Zeller shrugged. 'We all do what we have to do to

survive, it's just some of us are better survivors than others. I tried to help Bobby, I tried to help Glen, I try to help my daughter in her weaker moments – but you can only do so much.'

There was no reaction from Alex to that.

'The world didn't stop spinning when Elaine Kinflower died. It didn't stop spinning when your wife died either.' He paused, letting that last part settle. He was telling me he knew about my background, my life. He was trying to shake the sanctity of my marriage, to make my memories of it unclean. At his shoulder, Egan smirked, plainly amused by all of this. Alex hadn't said a word yet but, in her acquiescence to Zeller, I could see that he frightened her.

'I've run AKI for a long time,' he said. 'When I started, most of the industry looked at us like we were dog shit on the bottom of their sneakers. Everyone saw the same company that my father had started in a nickelodeon theatre back in New York. In order to change that, in order to get us to where we are now, I've done a lot of things. I've hurt people. Things have happened that no one can trace back to me, but which I've sanctioned nevertheless.'

He shrugged again, staring me down. Zeller had flown over for the launch party because, the minute I'd turned up at the Comet, Alex and Egan had let him know I was looking into Korin and Hosterlitz. He'd come over to deal with me, and once that was done, he'd return to the business he'd built on lies and blood. The actors who worked for him, the directors, producers, the public, no one knew anything of the real AKI, and they never would. Zeller had constructed the whole thing like a set, a façade, hiding the reality behind a Hollywood veneer.

'You know how many of the things I've done I actually

regret, Mr Raker?' He carried on studying me for a moment, as if trying to see into my head. 'Zero. None of them. When they write my obituary, it won't say, "He hurt some people." It'll say, "Saul Joshua Zeller was a fucking giant. He turned AKI from a joke into a multi-billion-dollar company." Full stop. The end.'

'Glen told me everything.'

I said it flatly, trying to suppress any fear that might have been building in me. There was one exit out of this place – and it was beyond the gun Egan was aiming at my head – but I kept my eyes fixed on Zeller.

The immediate comeback, the indifference of my response to him, seemed to unbalance the old man, and – on cue – Egan came around to his side. Alex had finally looked up at me as well.

'No,' Egan said. 'No, he's still chasing shadows.'

I looked at him. 'Not as many as before.'

There had been a faint smile on his face, but now it was gone. He looked at Cramer, blaming him for helping to build a better picture of everything that had happened. 'You should have kept your mouth shut, Glen,' he said frostily.

Cramer said nothing.

I looked back at him. He was sitting on the stone bench, staring at me. He knew I was lying – the question was whether he would play along. They'd come here to kill me, but they wouldn't kill him, whatever they said and however much they threatened him. They faced the same problem as Zeller had faced with Hosterlitz in 1954: if you wiped someone like Cramer from existence, even if you buried him deep, the media and public would ask questions. He was one of the biggest names on the planet. Plus, he would be dead inside a month, anyway.

I said, 'I know about Ring of Roses.'

Zeller flinched, shifting uncomfortably from one foot to another, his right hand opening and closing, like a shell snapping shut over and over again.

'Bullshit,' Egan said.

'It was a place on Pierre Street in Van Nuys. It doesn't exist any more, but it did back in 1953. Ring of Roses was a building.'

My words reverberated across the room.

Egan tried to shrug it off. 'So?'

But I could tell he was worried.

'I've emailed an account of everything Glen told me to a journalist friend of mine. He's going to meet me at 7 a.m. If I don't turn up, he publishes.'

Egan was shaking his head. 'No.'

'Yes.'

'No.' He looked across at Zeller, Zeller at him. 'No,' he repeated. It was said with more vehemence this time, but the ripple effect was palpable. The two of them were panicking. Egan took a couple of steps forward, anger in his face, the gun still raised. Behind the two men, in the same position as she'd been the entire time, Alex stared at me, an expression on her face that took me a moment to work out. *It's relief.* She *wanted* this secret to get out. She was tired of keeping it – the violence, the deceit, she hated all of it.

I ripped my eyes away from her and focused on Zeller again. 'All the pain you've caused, the people you've hurt, all the lives you've cost running your little empire, it'll be all over the front pages in two days if Egan pulls that trigger.' I looked between the two of them. 'You'll be ruined. People will be selling AKI stock faster than you can blink. Everything will burn to the ground around you.'

'And if Billy *doesn't* kill you?'

Zeller again. There was a tremor in his voice.

I've got them. I've got them exactly where I want them.

'If he doesn't, then we can talk about –'

'He's lying.' Cramer's voice hit as hard as a bullet. 'He's lying, Saul.'

I glanced at him.

He was looking at Zeller.

'I never told him what Ring of Roses was. I never told him anything, except that it was a building. He never emailed anyone at a newspaper. He's lying to you.'

60

Cramer's words were still echoing around the room as he slowly got to his feet. He looked at me, his eyes full of tears, and then across at Zeller and Egan.

'I'm sorry, David,' he said. 'I'm so sorry.'

He shuffled past me, disturbing the air between us – dust swirling like a sandstorm in his wake – and made his way over to the others. Egan was smiling again, clearly delighted that my gamble had failed. Zeller seemed less ready to let Cramer back into the fold, maybe because he didn't trust him, maybe because he thought this was some ploy the two of us had worked out together. Alex just looked broken.

Cramer fell in line behind her at the back of the group, his head bowed, the shadows binding him like ropes, and stared at the floor, a scolded boy. Egan came forward, in front of them all, the gun directed at my face.

I was alone.

'You're a dead man,' Egan said.

I stared at him, trying to remain unmoved, but fear gripped every muscle in my body, and my heart was punching against the inside of my chest.

'We need to talk,' I heard Zeller say to Cramer.

He'd couched it vaguely like a threat. Cramer nodded solemnly as Zeller turned back towards the changing rooms. I glanced around me, searching for possible escape routes, places to make a run for it – but when I looked back at Egan, he was even closer, maybe only six feet away, and could see what I was thinking. I backed up an inch, hands raised, feet crunching on a bed of broken tiles.

'Do it,' Zeller said to his son.

My whole body stiffened as Egan took another step closer. I swallowed. Shut my eyes. Waited for the shot.

But the shot never came.

Instead, I heard movement. As I opened my eyes again, I saw Cramer take two steps towards Alex and reach out to her with something. A split second later, she folded. She fell to the floor in a heap, hand at her throat where Cramer had made contact with her. Cramer bent – slower this time, his bones creaking – and touched her again with his closed fist. He was holding something.

A stun gun.

She jolted on the floor as another huge electrical charge travelled through her body. Zeller tried to make a grab for her, to stop the attack on his daughter, the fingers of his hand brushing the hem of Cramer's coat.

'*Get off her!*' he screamed.

Egan had swivelled by this time and taken two steps closer, automatically going to the aid of his sister. He switched the gun so the butt was facing up and brought it smashing down on to Cramer's head. There was a horrible *pop*, like a hollow piece of fruit splitting, and Cramer dropped like a dead weight.

I turned and ran.

I had no idea what the hell I was doing, or where I was going. The room was so large that great swathes of it remained in shadow. I just made a break for it and hoped.

A gunshot sounded. A second pinged off a piece of stone-work about two inches to my right, dust and chips of masonry spitting out at me. I could hear footsteps behind me, voices beyond that, but I just kept going.

All of a sudden, a raised square – about eight foot in diameter – came out of nowhere. It took me a split second to realize what it was: a plunge pool. It was full of dust and glass and fallen leaves. I had to sidestep to stop myself clattering into it, and as I reached for its edge, to try and grip on to something, my foot disappeared beneath me, into an open drain just next to it. Lurching awkwardly to my right, my leg dropped out of sight.

Straight away, I yanked it out again, looking for Egan, and then across the room to where Zeller, Alex and Cramer were, each of them positioned at the edge of the light. Alex was on her feet again, woozy, unsteady. Cramer was moaning and had rolled on to his back.

I looked down into the drain.

It was about three feet across, dirty and fetid, plants crawling out of it like the tendrils of some vast, hidden creature.

But there was a hint of light too.

I glanced from the drain to the back wall of the building – the light must have been coming in from outside, bleeding into the drain through a crack or a gap in the exterior wall, somewhere below me.

It could be a way out.

Or it could be a dead end.

I teetered on the edge of the drain, unsure, my head filled with thoughts of getting trapped down there, cornered, killed. But then I heard Egan somewhere in the darkness on the other side of the plunge pool and knew I didn't have a choice.

It was this or nothing.

I stepped forward and dropped inside.

'He told me he never killed her. Right from the first moment I arrived in that room. He said, "I never killed her. I swear to you, I never killed her." I remember it clear as day. I took him down to the precinct to book him, and he said to me, "Why would I kill my mom? Why would I do this to her?", and I said to him, "I don't know, son. You tell me." And he just kept saying the same thing, over and over again: "I didn't do it." '

Ray Callson pauses, pressing his lips together, as if he's trying to hold a part of himself in. He looks like he's about to speak, but doesn't. Instead, he starts rubbing his fingers together again; another echo of his former life as a smoker.

'The evidence was all against him,' Callson says finally. 'I let him sweat for an hour before I even as much as asked him a question, thinking that might clear his head. You know, give him some time to mull things over and face up to what he'd done. But I got back inside that interview room and it went completely the other way. Not only was he telling me he didn't do it, but he starts weaving this story about how these two guys, Saul Zeller and Glen Cramer, are somehow involved. I'm like, "Glen Cramer, as in the actor Glen Cramer? The guy who won an Oscar?", and the kid says, "Yeah, that's him. Him and Zeller. They're involved in this somehow." '

Even before he finishes the sentence, Callson is shaking his head. 'I thought it was pure fantasy land, like some fever dream, but all the same, I went to speak to Cramer at his house up in the Hills, then I went to talk to Zeller. He's the guy that runs American Kingdom. They were both real nice, real cooperative, gave me the run of their places — told me they were so horrified by the suggestion that they could be involved with Kerekes's death that I was welcome to turn their homes upside down if I genuinely believed they were hiding some deep, dark secret. Open house, basically. It was a waste of time. I mean, Cramer was a good friend of Kerekes. They saw each other all the time. There was absolutely nothing to back up what the kid was saying. So I went back and talked to Martin again, and I said to him, "This is the situation, son. You've got an assault beef hanging over you. You're a damn drunk at sixteen years of age. Forensics found speed and sleeping pills in your system, so the state's gonna paint you as a drug addict too. You got her blood all over you and her hair on your hands, and scratch marks down the inside of your arms, and you can't remember anything about last night — except that it's someone else's fault."'

'What did he say?'

Callson shrugs. 'Not much he could say.'

'Did he ever mention Cramer and Zeller again?'

'Oh, sure. He never forgot those two.'

'What do you mean?'

'I mean, he started off telling me that Cramer and Zeller were involved in his mother's death, whatever the hell reason they had for wanting to kill her, and then after he was done with me, he told anyone else who would listen to him at the station, and then, finally, he told his lawyer, and that was the point at which his lawyer probably said, "Whoa, whoa, shut your hole. You sound absolutely nuts. No one believes Cramer was involved with your mom's murder. He's a movie star and you're a waste of space, and you were found in that room with all the evidence in the world pointing at you, like a neon fucking sign." Words to that effect, I imagine. The best they were gonna get out of the jury was the kid being sent to the big house for the rest of his life. Him not going to the gas chamber once he turned eighteen — that would have been like a lottery win. But one thing was for sure: if Martin went into that trial shooting his mouth off about Cramer and Zeller and whoever else, the jury would turn against him like that.' Callson clicks his fingers. 'No one wanted to hear wild conspiracy theories from some delinquent kid. That would have been a disaster.' Callson stops again, this time for longer, and in the silence he scratches away at some dry skin on the knuckles of his hand. 'The irony, of course, was that Martin did exactly as his lawyer asked him to and never mentioned Cramer and Zeller at the trial – and it still got him a one-way ticket.'

'He was sent to a juvenile facility?'

Callson shakes his head. 'He was tried as an adult, remember.'

'So he got sent straight to San Quentin?'

'Correct.'

'But he was never actually executed?'

'No.' Callson thumps the centre of his chest. 'Heart problems. He blacked out in the prison yard about eighteen months after he got there. Congenital something or other. Anyway, even back in the fifties they weren't about to send some sick kid to the gas chamber, so he made his home on death row instead. Twenty-some years later – 1977 – his heart finally popped while he was working in the prison library.'

But there's a flicker of something in Callson's face.

'Mr Callson?'

'Did you know that kid wrote me once a month, every month, for the entire time he was at San Quentin? Twelve letters a year for twenty-three years.'

'No. I didn't know that.'

An unmistakable sadness blows like a cloud across Callson's face, and then lingers there. 'Every month, always the same. "I'm innocent of this. Please help me." I used to throw them in the trash to start with – just write them off as another asshole trying to clear his conscience. I'd had those letters before, these guys getting in touch with me, telling me I had it all wrong, giving me random names of the people who really did it — "The jury were paid off!" — all that bullshit. Those letters, they were an office joke. We all used to laugh about them, because we all used to get them. But, I don't know, Martin's letters . . .' He fades out.

He starts to speak and then stops again, and the words hang there for a moment. 'I guess it's just that it got me thinking,' he says eventually. 'After a while, I stopped dumping the kid's letters in the trash and I started to read them and I started to consider something: how much did you have to believe in something in order to write the same letter to the same person, claiming the same thing, over and over and over again? I mean, in those circumstances, you've got to be one of two things, right? You're either a total fruitcake — or you're not.'

'And which one was Martin Nemeth?'

Callson looks into the camera. 'I don't think he was a fruitcake.'

61

It had been a month since there was any hint of rain, but there was rain tonight: a faint mist drifted across the still of the night, swirling beneath the street lights like a swarm of insects. It dotted against my skin, cool and fine, as I opened the gates to my driveway. The hinges moaned gently. A few loose stones crunched beneath my feet. I paused, looking at the space where my BMW should have been, and then across to the darkness of my house. The windows and entrances seemed to be untouched. Everything appeared exactly like I'd left it.

I stood there, unmoving, all the same. It was just after 3 a.m. and the street was absolutely silent except for the muted hum of traffic further out. Curtains were shut. Cars were dormant and empty. Next door, I thought I could see a hint of a silhouette, one of my neighbours passing behind a set of blinds that hadn't been twisted all the way shut. I watched them disappear, and then returned my gaze to my own house. It was a rarity in this part of London because it was a bungalow. Usually, that was what I liked about it. But now, in the shadows, with everything that had happened to me, it seemed peculiar and unnatural; unwelcoming, cold.

Somewhere, I heard police sirens.

I grabbed everything I needed from the house and then left again, heading out the back, across the garden, and along an alley running adjacent to my home. Hailing a cab, I headed west and, thirty minutes later, was checking into a motel just off the M4. It was scruffy and faded, but it would be fine to lay low in. I paid in cash and kept my phone off – the battery out, the SIM too – and once I was in the room, spread everything out on the bed while the news played soundlessly on the TV.

Just after 4 a.m., a photograph of Glen Cramer in *Royalty Park* appeared above the left-hand shoulder of the newsreader for the first time. I felt my throat start to close. Reaching for the remote control, I turned the volume up.

' . . . tropolitan Police have confirmed that the body of Hollywood actor Glen Cramer, best known in recent years for his role in the drama series *Royalty Park*, has been found tonight at a disused public baths in east London. While a spokesperson declined to offer any further details, a source close to the investigation has told us that Mr Cramer suffered "severe head injuries". Clearly, this is a developing story, and details are coming in to us all the time, but we also understand that a man in his forties is being sought in connection with the death.'

Shit.

I suddenly felt nauseous, overwhelmed. Cramer had died at the scene and Zeller had just left him there – and now the police had zeroed in on me.

As I'd exited the baths through a broken wall at the rear of the building, I'd heard the approach of sirens, which meant neighbours must have reported hearing the gunshots. It meant there could have been a witness to my escape. It probably meant the police had got hold of Cramer's mobile and discovered the call I'd made to him at 11.14 p.m. They'd see the note he'd written on it to remind himself of our meeting place. They'd ping my phone and see that I called from outside Limehouse station when I gave him directions to the public baths. I was the last person to speak to him.

They probably thought I was the last person to see him alive.

Briefly, I considered handing myself in, and then let the idea go again. I had nothing to play with. I couldn't pin anything on Zeller. There were no direct lines to him. All I had was circumstantial evidence and a bunch of theories. The best thing I'd gathered in all this time was the testimony of a man now lying dead on a mortuary slab. Zeller wouldn't have wanted it to end for Cramer in the way it had, I still believed that, not because he had any affection for Cramer any more, but because the death of Glen Cramer brought questions and media headlines. But it was a complication. Zeller and Egan were both still in the clear.

Even if it was on their radar at all, which it wasn't, the Venice Angel case wouldn't interest the Met. It was so old and so far out of their jurisdiction that they wouldn't waste resources looking into it. There was no CCTV at Barneslow Scrapyard, so they couldn't put Egan or Alex there at the weekend. There were no cameras in and around the baths either, which was one of the reasons I'd chosen it. As for Zeller, even if I went direct to the US, no agency there would go to the expense of reopening a case, let alone digging up a sixty-year-old corpse, without substantial proof that the original conviction was wrong. Martin went to San Quentin for his mother's murder and he died there twenty-three years later. Hosterlitz was long dead, Cramer was gone now. There had been five people who could have shed light on what happened that night, and the only one of them left alive was Saul Zeller. I couldn't get justice for Kerekes with what I had.

Not without Lynda Korin.

She hadn't been found yet, not by me and not by Zeller and Egan either, but the fact they were still looking for her, still trying to silence her, seemed to prove something: she had information they didn't want out in the open. She had some sort of proof. Maybe she had the evidence that could bring Zeller down.

I had to find her before they did.

62

I didn't have much left in the way of casework.

My notes from before the scrapyard, my files, the physical photos of the angel, the security footage from Stoke Point – it had all been burned. All I could rely on was whatever notes I'd gathered from talking to Rafael Walker, what I'd seen in Hosterlitz's films, and what I could remember from talking to Cramer.

I flipped open the spare laptop I'd grabbed from my house, connected to the motel's Wi-Fi, and searched the web for 'Ring of Roses'. It felt like I'd done the same thing a million times over and, sure enough, I got the same mix of nursery rhymes and crèches as I had the first time around. Even when I entered the words 'Pierre Street' and 'Van Nuys' I hit a dead end. I searched business directories for Van Nuys, tried to locate maps for the area, and then spent half an hour trawling historical data.

Nothing.

I kept going, returning to accounts of the Venice Angel killing I'd already been through on the web. I went over everything Walker had told me, line by line, word by word – everything we'd discussed, all the tiny details I'd seen in the films. The hidden frame. The photograph of Kerekes. The footage of Pierre Street.

Still nothing.

What about Hosterlitz's voice-over?

I'd never asked Cramer about that because he'd never

even watched any of Hosterlitz's horror films. But what could 'You don't know who you are' mean? Was he talking to Korin in those moments? Someone else? Himself? The more I thought about it, the more it felt like an admission of guilt on Hosterlitz's behalf, a way to tell her the truth, as if he was saying, 'You don't know who you are *to me*.' I remembered what he'd written on the back of the photograph – *I hope you can forgive me, Lynda* – and it seemed even clearer: she'd been in a marriage with a man who loved her because she reminded him of someone else.

I felt a pang of sadness for Lynda Korin then. She'd never really known the man she'd lived with, loved, shared a bed with, shared a life with, until twenty-six years after he'd died; until, in 2014, she somehow figured it out – or, at least, figured *something* out. But *what* did she figure out? *How* did she figure it out?

How could she still be missing?

I thought of Wendy Fisher, of how she'd described Hosterlitz and Korin's trip out to Minneapolis in 1984. I'd talked to her about it already, her recollection of Hosterlitz's 'scouting trip', her opinion of him – but I hadn't really pressed her on how Korin had been during that week without Hosterlitz. Could she have discussed anything with Wendy that seemed insignificant then, but might be huge now? Suspicions? Concerns? Cracks in their marriage? I doubted it, but I was running out of moves to make. I needed a breakthrough.

I didn't have to switch on my phone to get her number – I'd made a note of it before I left the house – and I could just use the hotel landline to call her. It would cost me, but it would keep me off the radar for now. What complicated things was her job as a nurse, and the irregular hours she worked. If she was out on the ward, I might have to wait for a response, and I needed answers right now.

If she even had any.

I tried not to let the thought derail me, tried not to get bogged down in the idea that this was another dead end, and went to the hotel phone. Punching in her mobile number, I listened to six drawn-out rings. It hit voicemail.

'This is Wendy Fisher,' she said. 'Leave me a message and I'll get back to you as soon as I can.'

I hung up – and, as I did, something gave me pause, an idea I couldn't get at, buried far back inside my head. I looked down at my notes, but had no idea what it was. Ignoring it for now, and already trying to think about my next move, I grabbed my laptop, went to an online directory and started searching for her home number. I'd try her landline, and if I got no joy there, I'd go back to her mobile and keep phoning. If I kept calling, I'd get hold of her eventually.

Her home was in Lakeville, south of Minneapolis, and when I went to the White Pages online, I got sixteen hits for Fisher. The White Pages listed all people under that name, and which other Fishers they were associated with, so I found Wendy and then I found the name of her husband too. He was called Carl. Even if I got hold of him and he got hold of her for me, that would be better than nothing.

But then I stopped.

The Post-it note. I'd forgotten all about it. With Walker's help, I'd followed the trail to the *Kill!* timecode, but there were still the two lines of random letters above that. I flipped back in my notes. I'd written them down during my interview with Walker, trying to make something out of them, *see* something.

XCADAAH. EOECGEY.

I tried to find patterns in them, relationships the letters might have to the films that Hosterlitz had made, or to Korin's life before she disappeared. I broke them down and rearranged them to see whether they might be anagrams, added full stops to see if I recognized them as acronyms, did a web search for the letters as a group, in pairs, in threes. Every road I went down ended in the same result.

Even so, I kept going but, fifteen minutes later, I glanced at the clock and saw it was after five in the morning, and the energy seemed to leak out of me. I flopped back, bone-tired. Through the rear window of the motel room, beyond the rooftops opposite, I glimpsed a haze of orange, the accumulated light from the motorway. My eyes began to feel heavy as I watched it, shimmering like the margins of a marooned spacecraft, and then they closed completely.

Call Wendy. I jolted awake again, my inner voice like an echo, pushing me back to the surface. *Call Wendy.*

I never asked her about the Post-it note. I never asked about the two lines of letters, or what they might mean. *Maybe she knows.* Going to the hotel phone, I found the number for her landline again and dialled it. It was 11 p.m. there, but Wendy would understand. I waited, briefly energized.

'Hello?'

Someone had picked up. It was a man.

'Mr Fisher?'

'No, he's not here.'

'Is Wendy around?'

'No, neither of them are here.'

I tried to imagine who this guy might be.

'I can take a message,' he said.

'Can I ask who I'm speaking to?'

'Greg Fisher.'

He must have been one of their kids.

'Greg, my name's David Raker. I'm an investigator in the UK. I'm doing some work for your mum over here, looking into her sister's disappearance. I need to get hold of Wendy really urgently. Is she at work at the moment?'

'No, she's away.'

'Do you know what time she'll be back?'

'No, I mean, she's *away*. Mom and Dad are on vacation. They're up in Alaska somewhere.'

His words stopped me dead.

'Uh . . .' I tried to think. 'What do you mean, they're on vacation?'

'I mean, they're on a cruise.'

'For how long?'

'A month.'

'When did they leave?'

'About ten days ago, I guess.'

Before I'd even started the case. Before Wendy had ever got in touch with me. I thought back to the voicemail message I'd just heard from Wendy Fisher, and remembered how something about it had given me pause afterwards.

'Does your mum have a Facebook page, Greg?'

'What?' He sounded confused. 'Yeah, sure.'

I went to Facebook, searching for a Wendy Fisher in Lakeville, Minnesota. It didn't take me long to find her. Her profile picture was a photograph of her and Lynda Korin, sitting next to one another in a garden somewhere.

I'd never seen Wendy before in my entire life.

She wasn't the woman I'd spoken to on video call. This Wendy was much heavier, her hair was darker, she had a distinctive mole on the cleft of her chin and she wasn't wearing glasses in any of the pictures I could find of her. The Wendy

I'd spoken to had looked like a weightier version of Lynda Korin – the same cheekbones, the same eyes, the same mouth.

As my heart thumped in my ears, I started to realize why the recorded message on Wendy's mobile didn't match the voice of the woman I'd spoken to over the phone. I realized why the woman who'd hired me looked nothing like the Wendy I'd just found on Facebook.

Because Wendy Fisher hadn't hired me.

Lynda Korin had.

63

I sat there stunned for a moment, trying to deny it. But I couldn't. It was why she didn't want me to call her out of the blue, why she preferred to be emailed first. It was why her voice in our calls and the voice on Wendy Fisher's answerphone were different. It was why Wendy didn't look anything like Lynda Korin, and yet the woman I'd talked to over video had borne a striking resemblance to her. It had been Korin on the video call – except she'd dyed her hair and put on weight.

Or disguised herself – a costume, a wig.

I thought of something Marc Collinsky had told me about the garden room at Korin's place: *There were still a few old movie props in there – a clapperboard, some bags of old junk with guff like vampire teeth, and blood, and make-up in them.* Make-up. Could there have been prosthetics too? Moulds? Silicone? Korin had looked big on the video call, but she'd looked big *under* her clothes. She'd covered herself up. All she'd had to do was tweak her physical appearance just enough, fill herself out and use whatever had been left behind by Hosterlitz, because she knew the quality of the Skype call would disguise the rest of it. The call was poor – pixelated, jumpy – because her connection was poor.

Did that mean she was somewhere remote?

I put a hand on my notes, trying to think straight, trying to imagine all the reasons Lynda Korin would set this into motion in the first place. So I could find out the truth about what her husband had done? What Cramer and Zeller had done? If she already knew, why not just announce it to the world? Why go to the trouble of involving me? I drew the pad towards me, almost instinctively, and my eyes fell on to the lines of letters again, the ones on the Post-it note, and all the ideas I'd had as I'd attempted to figure them out. In my head, I spooled all the way back to that video call, trying to work out if there had been anything in the background to give away her location. There had been a mantelpiece, photo frames, but both had been bleached by sunlight from a nearby window. I wasn't going to get anywhere with that.

I went back to her Internet connection, to it being slow, to the idea that she could be somewhere remote. That made sense – but where?

I looked at the two lines of letters again.

XCADAAH.

EOECGEY.

Somewhere remote.

Somewhere remote, somewhere remote, somewh—

I felt an internal shift. My eyes zeroed in on the beginning and end of each of the lines. The top one began with X, the other finished with Y.

Bloody hell, that's it.

It was so clever. I could see it so clearly now, I was unsure how I'd ever *not* seen it. These weren't words. They weren't even really letters.

They were grid references.

I tore off a fresh sheet of paper.

The X axis was C, A, D, A, A, H. If each letter corresponded to a number, C would be 3 because it was the third letter in the alphabet, A would be 1, and so on. I worked through it until I had the Easting, the X reference. It was 314118.

I now had half a location on a map.

I quickly applied the same rules to the Northing, the Y axis, but I came out with seven numbers instead of six, because the second letter – O – corresponded to the fifteenth letter of the alphabet. Unless the O wasn't an O at all.

Unless it's a zero.

I pulled my laptop towards me and put the X axis in, then put the Y in as 505375 and hit Return.

The page loaded instantly.

It was an empty field.

I moved the map with the trackpad and a farm came into view, about three hundred feet north. Otherwise, there was nothing.

I zoomed out.

The farm was on a road, a thin country lane. It sat on its northern side, but the place where the pin had dropped, the grid reference, was in a field to the immediate south. The field must have belonged to the farm, but there was nothing on satellite that indicated anything in the field itself. Just grass, trees and drystone walls. Maybe a few animals. Was the grid reference an allusion to the farm, and not to the field?

Or had I just called this whole thing wrong?

I zoomed out again.

A lake came into view, about half a mile south-east of the grid reference and the farm. There was a hint of elevation to the north of the farm too. There looked to be a slope and the slope appeared to be blanketed in scree. I zoomed out again.

A name popped in over the lake.

Wast Water.

It was the Lake District.

*

I managed to get a few hours' sleep – and, at 8 a.m., I found the number for the farmhouse and called it.

'Hello?'

It was an older-sounding man, halfway through eating something.

'Oh, hi,' I said.

Now what?

'I'm not entirely sure if I've got the right number – or if you can help me – but I'm looking for Lynda.'

'Lynda?'

That was all he said.

'Yeah, Lynda.'

'There's no one called Lynda here, son.'

It was hard to tell, but there seemed no hint of collusion, no sense he was holding something back from me. I looked down at my notes, and my eyes came to settle on a line right in the middle. It said: Életke Kerekes = Elaine Kinflower.

A pseudonym.

'Sorry, my mistake,' I said, and then wheeled back to when I'd first found the box at Korin's house, and the business card inside for Tony Everett at Roman Film. Korin had told him her name was Ursula Keegan. 'Sorry, I meant Ursula.'

'Ursula?'

I heard movement, the line crackled a little, and then there was the ping of metallic blinds being parted.

'Nah,' he said.

'Ursula's not there?'

'Nah, it's not that she ain't here,' the man said. 'It's just it looks like the blinds are down on the caravan. I don't think she's even up yet.'

PART FIVE

64

Sun briefly peeked through the clouds, rinsing the slopes of Wasdale gold. The valley was a breathtaking sweep of summits and hollows, its vast peaks forming a rugged amphitheatre around Wast Water, a three-mile stretch of lake that sat like a sheet of grey glass at the bottom of scree-covered slopes. When the wind roused itself, ripples scattered across the surface of the water like a delicate and deliberate work of art; and yet there remained something bleak about the lake, a strange, indefinable darkness. In the winter, when the tourists had gone home and the routes into here had become impassable, I imagined the valley might feel like the loneliest place on earth.

The farm sat on the slopes of Buckbarrow, part of the southern ridge of Seatallan, a mountain to the north of the lake. It was a large cream building, enclosed within moss-covered drystone walls, and had two huge corrugated-iron barns at the back of it. I'd driven past and seen tractors and the rusting bones of old machinery in one, and on the way back, I saw pigs in the other, feeding at a trough. There were cows too, but they were out in the fields to the left of the farm, wandering the grassland with their heads down. Immediately behind the barns, the contours of the valley began to change, sloping gradually into a wall of scattered scree and burnt orange fern.

The grid reference was for a location in a field on the opposite side of the road to the farm itself. On the web, the satellite photography hadn't shown anything but more grass and more walls, but that imagery was four years old – and things had changed since.

There was a caravan there now.

It sat alone in the field, like a ship drifting out on an emerald sea, blinds dropped at its windows.

It had been that way since my arrival.

I'd hired a car in Ealing and had left London at just after 9 a.m. It had been a six-and-a-half-hour drive, slow around the cities and slower once I'd left the A road and started the climb into the National Park. On the radio, I'd been listening to my name repeated all the way up. It had escaped into the wild, my photograph too. It wouldn't be long before the Met discovered that I'd hired a car. Shortly after that, they'd find me on surveillance cameras, and be able to track me all the way north. I might have five or six hours. The fact that they'd have to coordinate with Cumbria might give me until the morning.

But, one way or another, they were coming.

That was why I was playing it cautiously for the moment – because maybe Lynda Korin knew they were coming too. Maybe the farmer had told her about my call. Maybe she'd heard about me on the radio or seen me on TV, and knew I was on my way. Or maybe this was all a trap. I didn't know what Korin's motivation might be for trying to trap me – and I wasn't sure I really believed that was the case – but she'd been gone ten months, hiding out here while Zeller and Egan had tried to track her down and kill her.

I wasn't about to underestimate her.

Sixty minutes later, I reassembled my phone and powered it on for the first time in eighteen hours. Messages and missed calls poured in. I swiped through them.

There were only two I was looking for.

Annabel had texted from her holiday in Spain, clearly up to date with the news back home. I told her everything was okay, and that it would get sorted out in a few days. I wasn't sure if that was true or not, but that was what she needed to hear. The other was a text from Melanie Craw, sent yesterday evening.

> We keep missing each other.
> CALL ME.

Part of me wanted to speak to Craw, to find comfort in a voice I knew, to tell her the same things I'd told Annabel: everything was all right, I'd get out of this because I'd done nothing wrong. But another part of me saw the reality – that calling her would only lead to an argument. She wouldn't understand. She was built like a cop, thought like one, acted like one, even as our relationship had become more serious.

I fixed my eyes on the caravan, its door, its blinds. It looked lonelier than ever in this place, with just the farmhouse for company and the scree and the ridges of the slopes. The next property was a mile and a half back. There were more vehicles than buildings here – and, as evening drew in, even the vehicles were drifting away. Pretty soon, I'd be the only one left.

I'd be alone again.

That thought lingered and grew louder, and the more time I allowed to pass, the more disturbed I became by it, the more I hated the idea. So I pushed Dial.

Craw answered after four rings.

'What the hell have you done, Raker?'

I thought about hanging up straight away – but I stopped myself. Instead, I kept my voice even and said, 'The media don't know what happened.'

'So what happened?'

I watched a Camper van chug past.

'I didn't kill Cramer. You know I didn't.'

'Then why are you acting *exactly* like someone who has?' She sighed. 'Why are you doing this again? We had this same conversation ten months ago. You remember that? You called me up to tell me you hadn't done it back then too. How many bloody times is this going to happen?'

This was a mistake. Hang up.

'It's a two-way street,' she said. 'You get that, right? It's not you and you. It's you and me. They'll go through your phone and see conversations between us. They'll see *this* one, Raker. They're going to crawl up my arse and –'

'I get it.'

'*Do* you? Because what you do affects *me*.'

'It affects your career.'

'What's that supposed to mean?'

'You know exactly what it means. Everything I do, every decision I make, you're not measuring it against what impact it will have on you as a person, or even us as a couple, you're measuring it against how much impact it will have on your promotion prospects – and what everyone else at the Met will think.'

'So what if I'm ambitious?'

'It's got nothing to do with ambition, Craw. You haven't even told anyone there that we're going out – *that's* why it's a problem for you.' I let her chew on that. 'No one you work with has a clue we're actually seeing each other, do they?'

She didn't respond.

'*Do* they?'

'No,' she said quietly.

We both took a moment.

416

'I didn't do this,' I said calmly. She didn't respond. 'I know you think I'm reckless, and maybe you're right – but I didn't do this. The thing that can't keep happening, though, is you pretending that I don't exist during the day, then expecting me to forget all about it once your shift is over. You were right earlier: it's you and me. But when I'm in a hole like this, I need you to stand up for me. I need your help.'

'I can't go giving you details about –'

'I'm not talking about procedural support, Craw. If I need something from the police database, I can get it. I'm talking about us actually acting like we're a couple, not some part-time sideshow.'

Rain spotted against the windscreen.

'This is why I wanted to talk to you at the weekend,' she said to me, her anger starting to dissipate. 'This is why I've been trying to get hold of you for three days. I needed to make a decision by yesterday morning.'

'A decision about what?'

She paused. 'At the end of last week, the chief super pulled me into his office. He said an opportunity had come up for me.'

'A promotion?'

'Yeah, to a superintendent role.'

'Okay. Well, that's a good thing.'

'*Is* it?'

'It's what you wanted, isn't it?'

'Yeah,' she said, sincerely. 'Yeah, it is. The thing is, though, to start with, it's for two years – but with a view to extending the contract if things go well.'

'What's wrong with that?'

'It's a secondment.'

I frowned. 'A secondment? A secondment to where?'

'To Glasgow.'

Both of us paused on the line, as if waiting for the other one to speak first, and then the rain started getting harder, popping against the body of the car like a shower of pebbles. I looked across the fields towards the caravan.

'I accepted the position,' Craw said, and then didn't say anything for a long time. 'Me and the kids are moving up to Scotland next month.'

But I was only half listening now.

Lights had come on inside the caravan. The door was open too – fanning open and closed as a breeze massaged and swirled the rain. A woman stood in the doorway in a red anorak, the hood up, blonde-grey hair matted to her face by the rain. A knife was in her right hand, pressed against the flat of her thigh, her fingers readjusting at the grip as if she was about to attack something.

She was staring right at me.

It was Lynda Korin.

65

As soon as I got to the gate at the top of the field, she disappeared back inside the caravan and the lights went out. Rain was lashing in hard now, drumming against the field, the parched soil so compact, puddles instantly formed in among the grass.

I opened the gate, its steel pins moaning, and paused there, water running off my face, my coat, my clothes. The door to the caravan remained open, shifting gently back and forth in the wind, but the only thing I could see inside it now was darkness. Without me even noticing, the whole valley seemed to have gone that way: shadows and flickers of light, everything oppressive and ominous, as if the mountains were falling in on me.

I crossed the field quickly, following the gentle slant as it dropped in the direction of the lake. There was so much rain, and it was coming down so hard, the surface had become slick underfoot, streams of crumbling, uprooted earth snaking through the grass like strands of hair. In front of me, wind erupted from the direction of the shoreline, savage and cold, ripping in as if it were a warning signal. The flanks of the caravan popped and bent against the force of it.

The door slammed shut.

I stopped short of it and reached out for the handle, looking along the side of the caravan. The blinds were still pulled. They hadn't moved an inch. There was no movement from inside either: no creaks, no subtle shift as she moved around.

Did I knock? Did I burst in?

I thought of the knife she'd been holding and then decided to play it safe. I opened the door and swung it all the way back until it locked into place on its clasp. The rain drummed a beat on my jacket, against the side of the caravan, on its windows, on the ground. Distantly, there was what sounded like the low rumble of a lorry, and then I realized it wasn't that at all. It was thunder.

'Lynda?' I said.

My voice got lost in the rain. I stepped closer.

'Lynda? It's David Raker.'

Lightning flashed across the sky.

'I followed your grid reference.'

For the first time, I felt a delicate shift in the caravan's axis; the slightest movement from back to front as if she'd gently changed position. I waited, seeing if she came to the door. When she didn't, I inched on to the steps and placed a foot inside the caravan. It creaked beneath my weight, tilting fractionally in my direction.

And then I was inside.

The caravan was about twenty feet long. There was a toilet immediately opposite me and a bunk bed to the right of the door where Korin had obviously been sleeping. Sheets lay crumpled, a blanket, a pillow. To my left, there were cupboards and drawers. Dishes were in a sink. Alongside that, a heater pumped out warm air.

At the other end of the caravan, everything was different.

The seating ran in a U-shape, with windows on all sides. Not that I could see them. Looking at the caravan from my car, and on the approach across the field, I'd thought it had been blinds at the windows. But it wasn't blinds at all.

It was sheets of grey cardboard.

All across the cardboard, things had been pinned and taped: photographs, itemized phone bills, email printouts, newspaper cuttings, colour reproductions of satellite maps. They spilled from the sheets of cardboard on to the walls, all over them, like a river breaking its banks. She'd even duct-taped printouts and cuttings to the ceiling, some of them peeling away and flickering where the air from the heater circulated. As I continued to look, I saw two clocks next to one another, one set to GMT, one to Minnesotan time, and then pages from a book in another corner – twelve of them, lined up next to each other. They'd been torn out of the true-crime book.

It wasn't Egan who'd removed them.

It was Korin.

There was so much to take in it was almost impossible to process it all. Things were untouched, or they'd been covered in pen; they were new and clean, or they were old and yellowed and damaged. Documents ran in patterns, in clear lines and spirals, or they ran in no pattern at all, entirely divorced from what was around them.

My eyes dropped to the seats.

Korin was sitting right in the middle of the U-shaped sofa, leaning forward so that her elbows were against her knees. She had a kitchen knife. She'd tilted her wrist so that the tip of the blade was directly pointing at me, and she was still wearing the red anorak I'd seen her in outside. Beads of rain clung to the coat, but most had already fallen away, gathering on the seat around her, soaking through the material so that dark patches formed on either side of her legs.

Her hood was still up, and it was hard to see her clearly, shadows at the corners of her eyes and mouth making it look like her face was being pulled at. Yet I could see her blue eyes, the lines of her jaw, the last ten months leaning heavily on her but not heavily enough to erase her extraordinary beauty.

She glanced at the knife she was holding, and then up at me.

'You found me,' she said.

66

'You finally found me.'

Her voice was quiet and it sounded old, and for a minute it broke the spell. She was a 62-year-old woman who had been on the run for almost a year. She'd spent that time in a caravan in the middle of nowhere sticking pieces of old paper to the walls of a home twenty feet long. She looked exhausted and scared.

I glanced at the knife.

She hadn't lowered it yet, as if she wasn't prepared to believe it was me even as I stood in front of her. 'It's okay, Lynda,' I said gently, showing her the palm of my hand. 'You asked me to find you, and I have.'

She nodded once, and then a second time, hesitating – but then, finally, she put the knife down. As she did, her body seemed to sag: drained, overcome.

'I'm sorry,' she muttered. 'I'm so sorry I had to lie to you.'

I wasn't sure what to say to that. Her lie had almost got me killed, and yet I felt no antipathy towards her. Standing here now, none of it seemed to matter.

'You figured it out,' she said.

I looked around the caravan. 'Most of it.'

She nodded; a half-smile. 'It's the small stuff that takes the most thought. Like how to make it look as if I was calling from Minnesota.' She shrugged. 'I found this app that lets you disguise your number and replace it with another. If you'd dug deeper, you'd have seen something wasn't right – but why would you?'

She was right. Why would I? I thought of the calls we'd had, her number prefixed with 001 and followed by 952 – the area code for Lakeville, Minnesota.

'I knew the video call would be where it either began or ended,' she continued. 'The farmhouse here has the Internet but it's slow as hell. Joe, the guy who owns the farm, he lets me use it – so I chose a day when he was out, because I thought, "David will want to Skype as soon as possible. He'll want to get me on video to get a read on me." I knew the poor connection would help me. In truth, I hoped it would bomb out altogether and we could just do what we had to do on the phone. But I knew if I could get through the Skype call, if you still believed I was Wendy by the end of it . . . I knew you would help me.'

'But why? Why get me to find you?'

'Like I said, I needed your help.'

'With what?'

She eyed me. 'The angel.'

'The *wooden* angel?'

'Yes.'

'Then it's been a wasted journey,' I said to her, 'because I thought you had it. I don't know where it is. All I've found are photographs of it.'

She shook her head. 'No,' she said. 'No, you don't understand.'

She got to her feet and opened up a cupboard above her head. A moment later, she brought something out, cupped in her hand.

It was the angel.

I frowned. 'You've got it already.'

'Yes,' she said, handing it to me. 'I took it when I left.'

It was about eight inches high and beautifully carved, the craft obvious up close, even six decades on. The wood was discoloured in places and there were chips in it, especially along its edges, hairline cracks all over it too. But it was the angel in the photographs. The damage I saw now matched up with the damage I'd seen in the pictures – and it had the crucifix, marked on its neck in faded black pen.

'I don't understand,' I said, holding it up to her. 'How can I help you when you already have it?'

'There's something about it.'

I looked at the ornament. 'What do you mean?'

'It's the answer to something.'

'An answer?'

She glanced to her right, to where a railing had been used to hang pictures. I saw photos of Zeller and Cramer from the fifties, of Hosterlitz during that period; and then I saw the same picture of Életke Kerekes, sitting on the front steps of her house, that Hosterlitz had embedded in his films. I saw other photos too, including one that I thought must be John Winslow, Kerekes's second husband, and then another of the same man holding a baby. It made me realize it wasn't Winslow at all, but in fact Kerekes's first husband – the man who had dumped his wife and son just two years after they'd landed in America.

The baby was Martin.

'I never knew he'd collected all of this stuff,' she said. Her eyes flicked to the photograph of Kerekes. 'I never knew about the things he'd hidden in his films. I never knew about any of it. I've added things to these walls over the past ten months, but most of this is his. Most of this is his,' she said again, and this time there was so much sadness in her voice, such an obvious feeling of betrayal, it seemed to tremor through her muscles. 'After I did that second interview with *Cine* in early July, talking about Robert, remembering him, it made me miss him desperately. It made me want to go back through the things I still kept from our marriage, the things I cherished – to be close to him again. It was why I decided to clear out the garden room – I wanted to see if there was anything I'd missed. There was so much junk in there, but I wanted to go through it all, just in case.'

'Are you saying you found all of this stuff in the garden room?'

'No. But what I found in there led me to the boxes.'

I frowned. 'Boxes?'

'He left all of this in boxes,' she replied, meaning the things on the walls. 'But there were so *many* boxes, and they were all unsorted. Every single one was a mess. When I first came across them in July, after the interviews, they meant nothing to me. But, by August, I was starting to get an idea of what I might have on my hands.'

I looked around me. *The history of a cover-up.*

'The truth is, though, if I'd taken all of this to the police in August, I still wouldn't have known enough. I was still playing catch-up, still trying to sort it into some kind of order, *understand* it. The police here would have said to me, "It's a sixty-year-old murder that happened on the other side of the world – what are we supposed to do with this?", and the cops in LA would have said, "What actual hard evidence do you have against Saul Zeller?"' She stopped and looked across at me. 'And my answer would have been, "I don't know. I just . . . don't know."'

I watched her, rooted to the spot.

'But that didn't mean I couldn't see where it was going,'

she went on. 'I looked at what Robert had left behind for me and I thought, "This is going to take me somewhere dark. Sooner or later, this stuff is going to force me to run for cover." I didn't necessarily think about disappearing, not back then, but the more I read of what he'd left me, the more weeks that passed, the more the idea started to form. I'd go down to Stoke Point, keep turning up there and watching the same people, and I'd think about what I would do if I disappeared, how I would do it. Wendy called me one day and said she was having issues with her emails, and I offered to help her, and I knew, deep down, the reason why: so I could gain access to her inbox. She would report me missing, because she was all I had left – so if I could get into her email after I was gone, I could see what the police were telling her. It was all so calculated.' She stopped and a worn smile cracked across her face. 'In that sense, I suppose I wasn't that different from Robert.'

As her last sentence echoed against the walls of paper, I said, 'Why not just go to the police in September or October instead?'

'Because I ran out of time. I was finally starting to get on top of it all by October. I still didn't have enough on Zeller, not enough to fight him with, but I could feel that I was close. I thought, "It's just a question of biding my time. I'll keep on going through the boxes until I find exactly what I need." But then it happened how I feared it might: I was forced to run for cover.'

'Because of Marc Collinsky's web article.'

'Yes. I talked to Marc about Ring of Roses in the first interview without having a clue about what it was – it was just something I'd heard Robert mention before he died. I thought it was innocent – some script, some idea, that kept him going through his last years of sickness. But by the time that article went out on the Internet on 27 October, I'd spent almost four months going through Robert's boxes, and while I didn't know everything, I knew enough. I knew that, when Marc put my name in that article, next to "Ring of Roses", he was signing my death warrant, so I had no choice but to disappear. And I knew that the ornament you're holding was the only way to protect myself, because the angel's what Robert called "the answer".'

I looked at the angel. 'But the answer to what?'

'To everything.' She studied me. 'I heard on the radio today that the police are looking for you. They think you killed Glen Cramer. *Did* you kill him, David?'

'No. Zeller's son did.'

She nodded. 'I think the angel will clear your name. It'll stop Saul Zeller. I think it'll bring Zeller down and make him pay for what he's done. I just don't know how. *That's* why I employed you to find me: because I've hit a dead end. In Robert's notes, he calls the angel the answer, but I don't know what the hell he means. I've spent ten months with these things he left' – she gestured to the walls of paper – 'and I've worked out most things, but I *still* don't know what he means by that.'

'Why do you even need the angel?'

She frowned. 'What do you mean?'

'You've got walls full of evidence here.'

'This isn't evidence. This is a case history. This is one man's point of view. Robert left all of this so I could under-stand what had gone on. But it's not proof.'

I looked at the angel again.

'But how can an ornament possibly help us?' I asked.

'I don't know,' she said, 'but you can help me find out. I

428

know you can. I needed you to understand the case, to wade through the horror of it, to see the terrible things that had been done to that woman and that boy – not just by Zeller, but by Glen Cramer and . . .' She paused for a long time. 'And by Robert.'

Her hands clenched into balls.

'Zeller needs to pay for what he's done,' she said, 'otherwise all of these things on the walls, all the risks you took to get here, all the risks *I* took running and hiding and lying awake every night thinking Zeller would find me and kill me before I could finish – all of it has been for nothing.'

67

We were both sitting. I'd made us some tea, giving her time to recover her poise, and she'd lowered the hood on her coat, pulling her hair into a ponytail. More of her hair had greyed in the time she'd been missing, and some of the colour had drained from her cheeks. She'd lost weight too. Not much, but enough to start tugging at her. Even so, hers was a beauty that was difficult to subdue. As we started trying to work things out together, as she began talking again, I found myself looking into her eyes, unable to turn away.

'I was twenty-four when I met Robert,' she said. 'He was fifty-one, so the age gap was huge. He'd only been left with a slight stiffness in his arm after the stroke in 1974, but he'd spent the five years before that ruining his liver with drink and painkillers. He was an alcoholic, basically. That was where you could see his age. So many people said to me, "He's nearly thirty years older than you – what are you doing?" I understood why they would say that. He wasn't unattractive, but he was tired and sad.' She paused as she dug out those memories of him. 'I never cared. I'd dated plenty of men my own age, and plenty of older men too, but none of them were like Robert. He had this subtlety to him. This mystery. You'd dig down to one layer, thinking it was as deep as you could go, then he'd reveal some other part of himself. He'd talk about film and literature and music, even stuff like politics and religion, things that academically clever people bore you with at parties, and he would just bring them alive. It was like I was discovering the world with him.'

She took a sip from her tea, her knees pressed against her chest.

'I know I told you lies to get you here, but I told you a lot of true things too. I don't have that many friends. I've never given much of myself away. I love my sister dearly, but she's a conformist – she's fitted in everywhere – and I was always jealous of her. She made it through high school, college, got a good job, had a family, everything, and she never had a single problem at any point. I had nothing *but* problems – at least, until I met Robert. When I met him, it was like looking in a mirror: he'd been hurt like me, he'd done things he'd regretted like me, he was introspective and flawed and never wanted to talk about it. He had secrets.'

Immediately, I recalled her line about that in the *Cine* article.

'About a year after we got married, his secrets came out. Well . . . I *thought* they came out. I *still* thought that, even by the time I was doing those *Cine* interviews in June and July.' For the first time, there was a flash of anger in her face, but then it quickly became something else: upset, disappointment. 'We were at home one night and I looked up and he was just watching me. We'd been shooting *Hell Trip*, so this would have been 1979. I looked up at him and . . . and he was in pieces.'

'He was crying?'

'Yeah. I'd never seen him cry before. I went to him and asked him what the matter was, and he just said, "You're an angel." He just kept saying that, over and over.' She paused, her eyes meeting mine, the rest left unspoken: *He was crying because, when he looked at her, he saw Életke Kerekes.* 'In some ways, I think he saw me as a literal angel, a reincarnation, a chance to put right what he'd done wrong. I know that now – but I didn't back then.' She cleared her throat. 'In that moment, it felt like the most beautiful thing anyone had ever said to me.'

She idled on the words he'd used, clearly still hurt by their subtext, by his refusal to tell her the truth. 'It poured out of him after that. All these old secrets he'd bottled up. He admitted to using prostitutes before he met me. After he was chased out of the US by the HUAC, he said he was just so lonely. He didn't want a partner at the time because he didn't want to have to share his past with anyone. So he used call girls for years – right up until he had his stroke.'

Korin stopped again, eyeing me.

'He liked to watch,' she said a moment later.

I already knew exactly where this was going: to the conversation I'd had with Veronica Mae about how Hosterlitz had behaved on-set, how he'd watched his wife from the corners of the room.

'From about two years into our marriage, he started having . . .' She halted, as if guilty at having to give voice to the words. 'He started having problems. He couldn't function in the bedroom. He said I should leave him, but it never crossed my mind.' She stopped again, this time for longer. 'I didn't think about it at the time, but it seems so obvious now. The reasons he liked to watch, I mean.'

'He looked at you and he saw Életke Kerekes.'

'Yes,' she said flatly. 'Yes, that's exactly what it was.'

She turned away from me slightly, the grey in her hair like silver thread.

'Like I said, it just poured out of him,' she went on. 'He said he'd taken too many painkillers, too many other drugs. He said he knew he was an alcoholic too, although he never touched a drop during our entire marriage.'

'So you figured those were his big secrets?'

She nodded. 'And I still thought that. Until last year.'

But then my thoughts snagged on something she'd just said. *He never touched a drop during our entire marriage.*

'He definitely never drank again while you were married?'

'Never,' she replied, adamant. 'Why?'

'Zeller's daughter told me he was drunk all the time in retirement.'

'That's a lie.'

'Glen Cramer said that Robert flew out to LA in 1984, just after Christmas, and turned up on his doorstep, drunk.'

'Oh,' she said. 'The "scouting" trip.'

'That's right, yeah. Did Robert tell you he was going to LA?'

'No.' She looked at me, her expression neutral. It was hard to tell how she felt about it now. 'He took his Super 8 camera with him and said he was going to drive to the state forests to do some location-scouting. That trip happened two weeks after he got told he had cancer. I'd spent the entire time crying my eyes out, but he'd barely reacted. He was numb. I figured he needed to be alone.'

'So why'd he go to LA instead?'

'To confront the ghosts from his past.'

'Cramer and Zeller?'

'When you get the sort of news Robert got a fortnight before we flew out to see Wendy, your priorities shift. The doctor said he might have two years, but he lived for almost four. He didn't know he'd have an extra two years at the time. He wanted to face down Zeller and Cramer, and do it before he died.'

'So Cramer was lying?'

'About Robert being drunk?'

'Yes.'

'They told all sorts of lies to him, and about him. That was just another one. Robert never took another drink after 1976.'

I looked at the walls of the caravan.

'All this stuff you found in the boxes – where did Robert leave them?'

This time she moved. She got to her feet, her joints stiff from sitting for so long. She walked to the end of the caravan, opened a flip-up drawer, and began to riffle through some clothes. After a couple of seconds, she took something out, pushed the drawer shut again and returned to her seat. She held it out to me.

It was a wedding-ring box.

'What's this?'

'He didn't give me the box. Just what's inside.'

I took it from her and snapped it open.

Inside was a silver key.

'At some point, he'd bought a garage from the council on a housing estate outside Bath,' she said. There was so much pain and bitterness in that sentence, it seemed to draw all the energy out of the room. 'I never knew a thing about it. The key is for the garage. When I opened it up, I found twelve boxes full of this stuff, and each of the boxes was this high.' She held a hand about four feet off the floor. 'There was no order to it. Like I said, it was a mess. None of it made sense.'

'He'd left the key to the garage in the garden room?'

'Yes.'

That was when I finally understood. In the garden room, I'd found minor indentations in the corners of the freshly painted grey panel, where a piece of plasterboard had once been attached. The board had been used to hang tools.

'The key was hidden under the plasterboard,' I said.

I recalled what she'd told me earlier: how doing the interview with *Cine* had made her miss Hosterlitz. She'd started sorting out the garden room, sorting through the shelves and junk for things of his she may have forgotten about.

'I dumped most of what I found in there, because it was useless,' Korin said. She looked on the verge of tears for the first time, vulnerable and misled. 'I never had a clue about the council garage. There was never anything on our bank statements. He was sick for most of those four years we were in Somerset. Some days were good, some were bad, but I don't ever remember us being apart. We must have been, though. He must have disappeared for afternoons. He must have done things while I was out of the house.' She paused, swallowed hard, looked at me and then away again. 'Because, when I decided to rip that plasterboard down, the key had been taped to the panel with duct tape, and pinned up next to that was a letter.'

'A letter saying what?'

She pointed at the wedding-ring box. 'Lift up the padding.'

I did as she asked. Underneath the felt padding for the ring was a folded piece of paper, reduced to a square about an inch and a half across.

I took it out.

It was thin, delicate, and smelled old and faintly perfumed.

'Do you know what Ring of Roses is?' she asked.

I looked at her. 'It was a building in LA.'

'Not just a building.'

'So what else was it?'

Korin glanced at the letter. 'The answer's in there.'

68

The moment seemed to hang in the air.

I unfolded the letter. When I glanced up at Korin, she wasn't looking at me, she was looking at the letter, her gaze fixed on it. It was an extremely thin sheet of A4, not far off the consistency of tracing paper. Hosterlitz had filled both sides of it, his hand spidery and hard to read. The ink had faded to a watery blue, and there were spots where the fountain pen had leaked. In the very corner was a date: *March 1988.*

The month he'd died.

My dear Lynda,

There seemed to be so much time to write this, and yet no time. When the doctor gave me two years, I thought, 'Well, at least I have two years.' When the two years was up, and I still felt the same, and the doctor said, 'You're still alive, Robert — make the most of it', I think a part of me started to wonder if there had been a mistake. Maybe they were wrong about me. Maybe I wasn't dying! I knew, deep down, that wasn't the case, of course, but I think it lured me into a certain laziness. I let things drift. I kept telling myself that there would be time to tell you everything and I kept not telling you. And now this. I hope I find the courage to tell you the truth to your face. But I know, equally, I can't stand the thought of the last days of my life being an argument with you. I couldn't stand to see you look at me as nothing but a betrayer, and die with that image of you burned into my mind. So I'm writing this letter as a back-up. A coward's

*way out, I suppose, but a letter that will bring to light some things
that I should have told you a long, long time ago. At my check-up
last week, Dr Rodgers said I may have a month. So, by the time you
finally bury me, this letter will be finished and left for you to read.*

I stopped. 'That's why you only found it last year,' I said
aloud, although it was more to myself than to Korin. Hosterlitz thought he had more time – three weeks, a month – but,
in the end, he'd only had days. He'd hidden the letter behind
the plasterboard, working on it when he could, in the belief
he had the time to finish it and then leave it somewhere she
would be able to find it.

Instead, it had remained hidden for over a quarter of a
century.

*The key I will leave for you is for a council garage in Bath. The
address will be on a tag I'll leave with the key. In the garage, you will
find twelve boxes. I haven't had time to sort them out, and I don't
think I will now. I'm so sorry. I wanted to make it as easy as
possible for you, but I'm afraid the thought of having to look at some
of that stuff was too painful for me.*

    *However, the boxes will tell the story of who I really am. They
will tell you that I did a terrible thing in 1953. They will tell you that
I had a part in taking a woman's life, but not the part – until I
found out the truth – that I thought I had. I thought I killed her. I
thought she died at my hands. But she didn't and, I suppose, if there
is a Heaven or a Hell, that will allow me some degree of absolution.
Her name was Életke Kerekes, but most people knew her as Elaine.*

Hosterlitz began telling the story of what he believed had
happened in the Pingrove that day, the aftermath, how the
media had hounded him out of the US, and how his career

had fallen apart. He wasn't aware that he hadn't killed Kerekes himself until Cramer said something in passing to him in 1966, while Hosterlitz was in America making *The Ghost of the Plains*. I remembered Cramer saying the same thing – that he almost told Hosterlitz the truth, but then panicked.

Glen told me that Zeller had lied to me, and that he, Glen, had taken an ornament of mine – an angel that Elaine had carved for me and given to me as a present – to a building called Ring of Roses on Pierre Street in Van Nuys. At the time, I sat there and didn't say anything to him. I wasn't in a good state of mind back then. Away from the film set, I was drunk pretty much constantly, I used speed to keep me awake and alert when I was shooting 'The Ghost of the Plains', and the comedown was awful. I was a mess. But when he started to tell me it was all a joke, something awoke in me. I looked at him and I saw through the haze, and I thought, 'He's not joking. He's just pretending he is.' So I started looking into this Ring of Roses building, and I found out that it belonged to the CCS.

I looked up at Korin. 'What does CCS stand for?'

'It stands for California Children's Services.'

Something began to congeal in my stomach.

'Ring of Roses was an orphanage?'

'Yes. They had this water fountain at the front of the building, made from marble and granite, and it sat in the middle of a flowerbed surrounded by roses. That's how the name came about.'

'So why did Cramer take the angel there?'

'Because he felt guilty,' she said.

And then the truth crashed against me like a wave.

I looked up at the photograph I'd seen earlier, of Kerekes's first husband holding Martin as a baby, and then I thought of something that Cramer had said that had never really registered at the time: *Elaine didn't want the pond life from the* National People *slithering all over the steps of her house, where a kid might be playing one day in the future.* I thought he'd been talking in general terms about Kerekes having another child with someone, at some point, in the years to come.

But he hadn't been talking about that at all.

My eyes remained glued to the picture of Martin as a baby, cradled in the arms of Kerekes's first husband – except, what I realized for certain now, was that it wasn't her first husband, and the baby wasn't Martin.

The man was John Winslow.

The baby was his and Kerekes's.

'*You don't know who you are*,' I said quietly.

I tore my eyes away from the photograph and looked up at Korin.

She was nodding.

'My real name is Viktoria Winslow,' she said, her eyes slowly filling up with tears. 'Életke Kerekes was my mother.'

69

Everything started falling into place.

It was why Cramer seemed so confused when I showed him the photograph of the angel at the baths. In the days after I first asked him about the ornament at his house, he must have gone back over everything, tracing the angel's path from the orphanage all the way to Lynda Korin, and finally made the connection: Korin was Viktoria Winslow. That made me think that Zeller and Egan would have a pretty good idea about who Korin really was too.

The minute they discovered the angel photos in Korin's attic, they would have known that Cramer had lied about destroying it in 1953. From there, they'd have connected the same dots as Cramer, seeing the age gap between Korin and Hosterlitz, the similarities between Korin and her mother, the fact that Korin had ended up with the angel in her possession, and that Hosterlitz – a man who'd never dated, who'd never held any interest in relationships before – married her inside six months. Egan had found the one photo in the album with something on it too – a handwritten message from Hosterlitz to Korin, asking for forgiveness. Maybe it was written years ago and never discovered by Korin, or maybe it was written in his last few days, but it confirmed their worst fears: Korin was Viktoria Winslow, Hosterlitz had told her everything, and now she knew what the three men had done.

It explained why Hosterlitz had photographed Korin over

and over until her pictures spilled from the pages of an album, why he treated her film scenes with such reverence. It explained the end sequence too. Korin covered in blood was the violence that took a family from her. His voice-over was the truth he had never been able to say to her face. The footage on the TV was the road that led to the orphanage, to a life she never remembered. All ripples on the same pond, caused by the same men.

'Cramer wanted you to have the angel,' I said.

She nodded. 'Guilt makes you do stupid things. My birth mother made that angel for Robert, Robert was forced to give it to Cramer to get rid of, and Cramer found out where I'd been taken and returned it to me because the guilt was too much for him to bear. I was only one at the time, so I remember nothing. I guess maybe he left it somewhere outside, with a note next to it, or put it in a shoebox. I mean, it wasn't like Glen Cramer could walk into a building at that time without being noticed. However he got it to me, that angel has been with me my entire life. I just never realized my true connection to it until I read Robert's letter.'

As I chewed on that, something else gnawed at me. How did Hosterlitz end up married to the daughter of Életke Kerekes? The odds of them happening to meet were impossibly huge, almost incalculable. But before I got a chance to ask, Korin looked up at me and said quietly, 'Robert wasn't really impotent.'

It was the truth that she never knew herself until she read it in his letter: he wasn't impotent, he just came to hate the idea of sex with her. To him, she was – and always would be – the daughter of the first, perhaps only, woman he'd ever loved. The daughter of a woman he'd hit so hard she'd blacked out. But watching Korin from the corners of the set, that would have been different for him. He wasn't the one touching her any more, and watching her was a natural extension of what he'd always done with a camera. Her beauty, her nature, the ways in which she mirrored her mother and made him feel like he'd been given a second chance – *those* were what he loved. Sex with Korin crossed a line that he came to loathe.

'You knew nothing about your background?' I asked.

She shook her head. 'My father – my adoptive father – worked at the GM plant in Van Nuys. They adopted me when I was eighteen months. Then my dad got offered a job in Minnesota. I remember moving to our house in Lakeville when I was about three. That's my first, clearest memory. And I remember snow. *Lots* of snow.' A smile traced the corners of her mouth, and was gone again soon after. 'I never knew I was adopted because they never told me. I don't know if they were *scared* to tell me, or if they ended up leaving it so long that, after a while, they couldn't break the news, but I guess they didn't think they could have kids naturally until Wendy was born. I know it's easy to say now, but I always felt different. I loved them all, I really did, but I never quite felt like I belonged.'

She fell silent and I returned to the letter. Hosterlitz was explaining how he finally worked out what Cramer meant when he'd 'joked' about Zeller lying.

After Glen made his 'joke', it didn't take me long to find out what Ring of Roses was – it was an orphanage out in Van Nuys. Back in 1953, when Elaine died, all I could think about was Martin and you. I knew you must have gone into the system somewhere. I just kept thinking, "Where are you now? Are you okay? Are you in a happy home?" but I couldn't ask around at the time because it would have

*raised too many questions. It would have incriminated me. But, by
1966, I don't say I didn't care any more about whether I incriminated
myself, because I did. I didn't want to go to prison. But I needed to
know the truth. I needed to know what happened to you after your
mother died, and I needed to know how Martin was too. In my sober
moments, of which I'm ashamed to say there were very few, you two
became everything to me. So I did two things.*

*Firstly, I drove all the way up to San Quentin to see Martin. I
wasn't there that night in the bar at the Pingrove, so he didn't suspect
my involvement. He just suspected Saul and Glen. I went all the way
up there to tell Martin the truth . . . but, in the end, I couldn't. He
was so different from the boy I knew back in 1953, so big and hard
and cold, so embittered. I always understood why: he'd been in prison
for 12 years by that time. He was innocent. He'd been on death row
wondering if this month, this week, was going to be when he got sent
to the gas chamber. Of <u>course</u> that would grind the life out of you. Of
<u>course</u> you would change. I can see that now. But I'd gone up there to
talk to the boy I knew . . . and that boy didn't exist any more. And,
when it came down to it, I'm sorry to say I just couldn't see enough of
the Martin I once knew to tell him the truth.*

*The second thing I did was start looking for you. It wasn't like it
is now. Adoptions weren't dealt with in the same way, with the same
level of care, so the paper trail wasn't as complete, but information –
when it was there – was easier to get at. I paid hundreds of dollars in
bribes. Any money I earned, I ploughed into finding you.*

'He followed a trail of breadcrumbs,' Korin said, 'but it
took him years.'

I looked up at her.

She grimaced, some colour forming in her cheeks as she
did, her eyes speaking eloquently of how she felt. '*The Ghost
of the Plains* bombed at the box office in 1967, and that sent

him into a spiral. Then his mom got worse, and he had to go back to TV – which he *hated* – and then, in 1969, his mom finally passed on. He was addicted and he was depressed, and he was a mess. But through it all, little by little, like he says in the letter, he wanted to find out what had happened to me. He did so much wrong. He did a terrible thing, and sometimes I'm not sure I can forgive him for it. But he was, I think, a good man.'

'He had a hand in killing your mother.'

'A mother I never knew.'

'An innocent woman, then.'

'I know.'

'He kept quiet, knowing your brother was innocent.'

She shrugged. 'I know what he did. That's why I said I'm not sure if I can forgive him. But that doesn't change who he was to me for ten years. I loved him. He was the kindest, gentlest, most interesting person I'd ever met in my life.'

I gave her a moment and then pushed on.

'So when did Robert finally track you down?'

Her eyes jumped to the walls, zeroing in on a piece of paper high above me on the right. I turned and stared up at it. It looked to be some sort of timeline, typed on a sheet of yellow paper. The typewriter had a broken *E*, so every time Hosterlitz had incorporated a word containing the letter, it was missing.

'He says on there that it was just before he had his stroke in 1974,' Korin said. 'He was back here in the UK by then – had been for four years. In between all the horror movies he was making, the booze, the pills, whatever else, he kept coming back to his research. That's what he called all of this – his research. All this stuff he collected over the years. On the timeline up there, he says he connected me to the

Ring of Roses orphanage sometime after 1966, and then went on to film the whole of Pierre Street on his old Super 8 before the TV work dried up and he was forced to leave the States in 1970. He made those videos so he could remind himself of what the building and the streets looked like. He said he often played the footage when he got to the UK, trying to keep himself motivated. That footage was only supposed to be for reference, but of course, in the end, he used the video of the road and some of the building itself in his films.'

'So he figured everything out in 1974 – then what?'

'Two years later, after he recovered from his stroke, he found me. I was doing some modelling in Paris. I got a phone call in 1976 from Isaac Murray, the producer on the *Ursula* films, asking me if I wanted the lead in a movie. It took me completely by surprise. I had very little acting experience. I told him that and he said it didn't matter because I had "natural charisma". That was a polite way of saying he liked how I looked.' She smiled. 'I always thought I owed my acting career – if you could call it that – to Isaac Murray. But it turned out that Robert was the one who had put my name forward when he agreed to the *Ursula* gig.'

'He wanted a chance to meet you.'

'Just once, yes.'

'And what was he going to do after he met you?'

'He was finally going to turn himself in.'

'To who?'

'To a cop called Ray Callson.'

'*You started to believe Martin Nemeth was innocent?*'

Ray Callson sucks in a breath. '*Put it this way, him writing me every month, it got me thinking. It got me wondering if I'd missed something. Problem was, if I'd gone to my captain and said, "I think there's something screwy going on here," I'd have been placed in a holding pattern for the next ten years. Every juicy case that comes up after that, you get shoved aside for, because you're the guy who reopened a case that had already been solved and prosecuted, and everyone was happy with. Reopening a case like that – it makes the cops look bad, the DA, the court system, whatever else you want to throw in. But yeah, when one of the kid's letters arrived, I'd sometimes dig the case file out and take a look at it, and after I put it away again the same things would stay with me: Zeller and Cramer, and why the kid was so adamant they were involved – and then the booze and the drugs.*'

'*The booze and the drugs?*'

'*I'm teetotal, see? Always have been. Went to World War Two as a kid and got good and plenty drunk out there a bunch of times, but when I came back I stopped and I just kind of stayed that way. Point being, at the time I didn't know a whole lot about booze. Still don't, really, but you learn as you get older. Anyway, the empty whisky bottle on the floor of Room 805, it was Carcraig's. Ever heard of it?*'

'*No.*'

'*It's Scottish, single malt – and it's expensive. A hundred bucks a*

447

pop these days, the equivalent back then too. You can probably see where I'm going. How the hell does a kid working in the kitchen of an ass-crack diner afford whisky like that?'

'Maybe he stole it.'

'Yeah, maybe he did.'

But it's clear Callson doesn't believe that.

'As for the sleeping pills, back in the day, not a lot of people were combo-ing drugs like Martin Nemeth did that night. Or, at least, not in the full knowledge of what they were doing. What I mean to say is, unless you were in the medical profession, most ordinary joes weren't aware that one counteracted the effects of the other. We just didn't see shit like that when we were dealing with narcotics cases.' He shrugs. 'So maybe the kid was just ahead of his time, right? Maybe that's the explanation. We tried to trace Életke Kerekes's prescription history, to confirm they were hers, but 'scrips at that time were a mess. There were no computers, so everything was done on paper, and the problem with paper is that it can disappear pretty quickly if a business isn't inclined to be organized. Plus, doctors back then, they were handing out pills left, right and centre, to anyone who wanted them. One prescription for one woman — that would be like looking for a needle in a barn full of haystacks.'

'Are you saying you don't think the pills belonged to Kerekes?'

Callson sniffs and glances out of the window. 'At the time, I totally bought it,' he says softly. His voice is laced with regret. 'All the evidence pointed to the kid. The pills were hers, because we found nothing that said they weren't. Her nail marks were all down his arms, her blood was all over him, her hair was in his fingers, it was so compelling, it was hard to argue with it. In fact, if you'd argued against it, you'd have looked like a nut. These days, you'd throw it all over to forensics and they'd crank it through the computers they've got, and the technician would come back and say, "This is all bullshit." But, in the fifties, that sort of stuff, it was a science-fiction film.'

'What about the speed?'

'The kid was adamant he didn't take any.'

'But it was found in his system.'

'Could have been pep pills. We sometimes used to call them "bennies". We were given them during the war to keep us awake. At the time, amphetamines were in drugs for sinus inflammation, obesity, a whole bunch of stuff. And it was all available over the counter. I'm not saying he didn't take a ton of them, fully aware he could get high on them – but, equally, there's a chance he took them because he had sinus problems or whatever. I mean, you'd open a magazine or a newspaper and – boom – there's your benzedrine sulfate or something else phosphate. Everyone was on them. So, if he bought them, he wasn't doing anything illegal.' Callson runs a hand through his thinning hair, his scalp shining in the light of the room. 'Like I said, first few years, all his letters would go in the trash. But then, maybe seven, eight years later, something just made me decide to read one of them. After that, I started reading them all.'

'So what happened then?'

'In 1976, I get a call. Now I haven't forgotten about Martin or his case – not least because his letters keep coming – but it's been a long time.' Callson swallows and rubs his fingers together. They make a coarse sound, like sandpaper. 'I kind of think about it less often, I suppose. Something about it still eats at me, but only when one of his letters turns up, or I open that file again, which isn't happening as much.'

'Who called you?'

'Someone patches the call through and says the guy won't give his name but that he's requested me specifically. So I pick up and the guy says, "Is that Detective Callson?" and I say, "Sure." And he says, "I'd like to talk to you about the murder of Életke Kerekes and the wrongful conviction of Martin Nemeth."'

There's a pause.

'I was in my fifties by then. I'd been a cop for over twenty-five years. I was thinking of getting out. The seventies, they were a pretty shitty

449

time at the *LAPD*. *Racism and corruption and whatnot. I guess what I'm saying is, I was pretty down on the job when the call came through – I didn't give much of a damn – but when I picked up, it was like my blood started pumping again.'*

'You were excited?'

'For about thirty seconds, yeah.'

'Only thirty seconds?'

'This guy,' he says, and then stops.

'Did he tell you who he was?'

'No. Not to start with.'

'Did you meet him?'

'No. He said he was "overseas" somewhere. It was a long-distance call, so the line was terrible. But this guy, he sounded . . .' Callson looks away. He seems uncomfortable. 'I thought he was some sort of kook.'

'Crazy?'

'Yeah. I mean, he was talking so fast I could hardly even hear him, and when I told him to slow down, I realized the guy was loaded.'

'He was drunk?'

'Yeah, absolutely stinko. I said to him, "Hold on a second, hold on a second. Let's start with the basics here. What's your name?" He said to me, "It doesn't matter what my name is, just listen to what I'm trying to tell you," and he started telling me how Glen Cramer and Saul Zeller were responsible for the death of Életke Kerekes, and that another man who he didn't ID was involved too, and that they – all three of the men – framed the kid to cover up what they'd done.'

Callson pauses for a moment. 'I said to him, "I'm extremely interested in what you've got to say" – and I meant every word of it – "but I need your name before we can go any further," and he said, "Just look into it! Just look into it!" I mean, he's screaming down the phone like a fucking lunatic at this point. I said, "Calm down and give me your name, sir. I want to hear what you have to say. I genuinely mean that."

450

But he was already talking over me again, saying, "Zeller will try to tell you someone else did it, but it was him, it was him. I know it was him. He killed Életke Kerekes, so did Cramer, so did . . ." He stops short of telling me the name of the third guy. Then he said, "Look, if you don't do anything about it, I'm going to go to the newspapers." At that point, I knew he was bluffing. He wasn't going to go to the newspapers, or anyone else for that matter, because he'd already given himself away. He'd given himself away when he'd stopped short of telling me who the third guy was. So I waited there, let him chew on the silence for a while, and I said to him, "Were you the third guy that night, sir?" '

'What did he say to that?'

'He said he wasn't.'

'Did you believe him?'

'I'm not sure what I believed at the time. You've got to remember, this guy sounded like a crank. We had junkies and freaks and fanatics calling us all day every day confessing to things, trying to get people they hated arrested for crimes they'd never committed. Half my time used to be spent filtering out pricks like that. But this case was so old by that time – why would someone call up over twenty years later just to feed me a bunch of bullshit?' Callson looks over at the windows, huge and black now that night has fallen. 'It didn't make any kind of sense to me.'

'So what did he say next?'

'Nothing. He hung up. He got cold feet.'

'Cold feet?'

'I think the reason he called was to confess. I could hear it in his voice. But he didn't have the stomach for it. He couldn't bring himself to do it.'

'Did you go and see Zeller and Cramer again?'

'Yep.'

'And what happened?'

'Same as before. I didn't tell them about the phone call I got, because I couldn't corroborate it. I just told them I was looking through some old *files and came across the Kerekes murder. They were just as helpful in '76 as they had been in '53, but two decades after the crime, what the hell was I likely to find tying them to a murder?'*

'Nothing.'

'Exactly. Zero.'

'But, eventually, you found out it had been Robert Hosterlitz who had called you that day – is that correct? And you found out that he was telling you the truth?'

'That's right.'

'How did you find out it was Hosterlitz?'

Callson, who has been looking directly into the lens, shifts his eyes left, just to the side of where the camera is set up on its tripod.

He is looking at the person asking the questions.

'Because, two days ago, he turned up on my doorstep.'

70

The rain had finally stopped.

I dropped my eyes to the letter again, to the last few paragraphs. The handwriting had become less legible, the letters slanted, everything more hurried.

All I'd wanted was to meet you once, to see you again as a grown woman, to see with my own eyes that you were flourishing, and then I'd hand myself in and take the punishment that I deserved. But, halfway through that conversation with Callson, I just had this epiphany. I was drunk when I called him – that was the last drink I ever took – but not drunk enough to misunderstand the opportunity I had. As I talked to Callson, I thought, 'It doesn't have to be the end. I can make things up to Viktoria' – or Lynda as you were then. 'If I go on and do this movie with her instead of handing myself in, I can work with her every day.'

Again, basically, I was – I am – a weak man. I suppose, in a way, this cancer is my punishment. To die like this is my punishment. I never dreamed you might be attracted to me. All I wanted was the chance to meet you and spend some time with you – to listen to you talk. I would have been happy just to look at you and watch you. But I got more than that, much more, and it was wonderful. And yet, the whole time, the secret I was keeping from you, the fact that I still hadn't confessed, was playing on my mind. A part of me needed to confess, even then, because I knew it was the right thing to do, the moral thing; but another part couldn't because I didn't want to hurt you, and I didn't want what we had to be over. Our life, our marriage. So that was why I hid those messages in my films. I was confused, caught between the devil and the deep blue sea. Maybe I thought the truth would pass to you by osmosis — the more you watched the films, the more questions you'd ask, the more you'd understand what I was saying. But the better I hid things, the less likely I realized that would be, and that made me happy too. I tried to tell you and I tried not to tell you; I wanted to and I didn't want to — and that was the battle that raged inside me for ten years.

Didn't you ever wonder why I always used to film your eyes in close-up? Why I'd use them as windows to the rest of the scene? You would reflect silhouettes and shadows, as if they were the memories of the life you never knew, playing out inside your head. Didn't you ever wonder why I repeated the same sequence of events, over and over? Maybe you did, but you never asked. I think a part of me was _waiting_ for you to bring it up. Once, when I asked you for that paperback for my birthday, that true-crime book, I actually handed it to you and said, 'I think this one case is particularly fascinating,' and I pointed to the chapter on the Venice Angel. I did it blatantly, almost willing myself to be caught, for you to finally ask, 'Why do you find that case so fascinating?' But when you didn't read it, I was so relieved. My whole existence with you was both utterly wonderful and quietly torturous.

I thought a lot about Zeller and Cramer too. I needed them to know that I hadn't forgotten. I wanted them to see the footage of Pierre Street in my films. They never would have known you were Viktoria at the time — it took _me_ so long to realize it myself — but they would have seen your likeness to Életke. They would have understood the message I was sending them both. But the sad truth was, no one watched those films. I was sending a message into the void.

The letter ended, unfinished, soon after that.

454

I don't have the original negatives for any of the films we made together in Spain. Maybe they're lost for ever. But everything I have is in the garage. Do you remember that old Super 8 I had? That's there too. There's something else as well. I bought it after I went to see Zeller and Cramer in LA. Once you get into the garage, you won't be able to miss it. I've taped instructions to it. You'll need your wooden angel as well. Look in my notes and you'll see why. It's the answer to everything. I'd hoped to have enough time to do everything myself, but, alas, I'm not sure I have.

That was the last thing he'd written. He didn't sign off properly because he thought he was going to come back to it.

Instead, he'd died days later.

I looked at Korin. 'What's this thing he talks about – this thing he bought and stuck instructions to?'

Korin studied me for a moment. 'Did you ever wonder why I carved that illustration into the tree at Stoke Point before I disappeared? Why I left a key in the back of the photo, and that box next to the electric meter? What about the security footage? The Post-it? Did you ever wonder why I left those?'

'Because you wanted me to find you.'

'Yes,' she said. 'But it's not as simple as that.'

'What are you talking about?'

'I spent *months* reading about you. I saw what kind of man you were. I saw the cases you've solved and the people you've helped. I knew you wouldn't give up once you caught a glimpse of what was going on here, because that's who you are. You care. You know what's right. But I could only have you begin to look for me when I was *ready* for you to start looking. It took me ten months to get to that stage, because Robert left instructions. But they were so hard. It's so hard.'

'What the hell are you talking about?'

'That's why the clues I left were so difficult,' she said. 'I didn't want Zeller using them to find me before you did. I'd taken my work as far as it could go up here, and I needed you to help me figure out the rest. I needed you to help me with the final piece of the jigsaw – the angel.'

'Stop talking in riddles, Lynda. What's going on?'

'I can't find any reference to it in his notes. I don't know why he calls it "the answer".'

'*Lynda.*'

But this time she didn't reply.

Instead, she looked down towards the door of the caravan. In the silence, I became aware of the rain again, driving against the windows on which Korin had built the hidden history of her husband.

'Lynda?'

'Do you hear that?' she said.

'Hear what?'

'That.'

'The *rain*?'

But then there was something else: a dog barking.

I glanced at the door. 'A dog – so what?'

'It's coming from the farm,' she said, and there was a flicker of fear in her face now. 'Joe, the owner, the guy who rents me this place, he's away now. He's not home again until tomorrow. That dog – she's so soppy, so quiet. She never barks unless . . .'

'Unless what?'

Her eyes flicked to me. 'Unless she's barking at someone.'

71

The valley was dark.

I told Korin to stay where she was and lock the door, and then I headed towards the farm. The rain was hammering down hard, only vague shapes visible beyond the cone of the torch Korin had given me. I could make out the farmhouse in front of me, its angles like the pale lines on a blueprint, and – behind that – the ominous blackness of mountain slopes that climbed, and dissolved, into the night. When I looked back down the field to the caravan, it had been reduced to squares of dull light. The glow from the interior, subdued by the cardboard at the windows, made it look like a boat drifting to oblivion.

I climbed the gate and crossed the road, then slowed my pace. There was a potholed concrete track at the side of the farmhouse. I swung the torch from side to side, as the smells of the place hit me: mud, wet grass, ferns, manure, silage, straw. A tractor sat under a corrugated-iron roof to my left, and then the track split in two: one half wound its way to the house, where an alarm box blinked above a blue door; the other half ploughed further onwards, in the direction of the two barns. The dog was inside the house, barking so hard she was almost hoarse. She was scratching at the door too, her paws sliding on lino, the sound so distinct and desperate I could hear it even above the rain.

Something had definitely set her off.

Up close, the barns seemed vast, like the hull of some

huge supertanker. In one I saw a quad bike and a furrow plough, and in the other I could see the vague, swollen shapes of the pigs. They were largely silent and most seemed to be still, but when I passed the torch across them, a few shifted and one made a deep snort. The dog started barking more vociferously.

I passed along the side of the barn with the pigs and found an annex built on the back, about the size of a garage. It looked like it might once have been a workshop, the only window – a panel of tall near-opaque glass – flecked with sawdust. The odour of old wood clung to it, even with the weather as it was, and there was the smell of oil, spirits and paint as well. The annex's slanted roof had a tile loose, hanging at an angle like a puzzle piece that hadn't clicked into place, and with no guttering, water fell from the roof in a sheet, machine-gunning against the ground and turning anything that wasn't paved into an instant sloppy bog.

A noise.

I paused, listening. As if on cue, the rain eased off slightly. I directed the torch along the edge of the annex, down towards the back of the other barn. The only things there were old equipment, half submerged in mud, grass and old bricks. I turned my attention to the annex again. The door was a faded red that had peeled like burnt skin, and there were slide bolts top and bottom, both secured.

Then I heard the noise again.

I looked back the way I'd come, using my torch to illuminate the path. Rain drifted across the light like silver strands. In the barn, I could hear the pigs moving. In the house, the dog was barking even more frantically than before.

'Hello?'

My voice disappeared into the night. I remained there, in

front of the annex, my eyes on the path. Everything was still.

'Hello?' I said again.

When I got no response a second time, I headed back, swinging the torch from side to side. The beam cut through the dark, shadows forming in the ridges of the barns, in the brickwork of the farmhouse – but anything further out, beyond the lines of the light, was invisible.

Except that wasn't quite true.

As the rain stopped, I noticed a very slight colour change on one side of the farmhouse, as if the building was being backlit by a security light. I hadn't taken note of it on the way in.

I moved more quickly, tracing the circumference of the barn. The pigs reacted to the fall of my footsteps, snorting, scattering, and as they did, the dog became even more desperate than before. I checked the farmhouse windows and then moved along a flagstone path to the front door. The dog was going crazy on the other side now, the door jerking against its frame.

I tried the door, but it was definitely locked.

Backing up, I continued in the direction of the caravan, along the path pitted with holes, between mountains I couldn't see and trees I could only hear.

The caravan hadn't even come back into view when something suddenly registered with me, giving me pause for a moment: the colour change I'd noticed on the house was an orange, not a white.

It wasn't a security light, it was the caravan.

It was on fire.

72

Something ignited inside the caravan. A dull, guttural *whump* ripped across the darkness, and then smoke and fire erupted out of a window on the side, close to where the kitchen had been. For a split second, the entire valley lit up.

I broke into a run, crossing the silent road and springing over the gate. As I landed in the field – soil sodden beneath my feet – thick balls of smoke began to chug from a hole in the kitchen window. The faster I ran, the less control I had, my feet sliding on the grass. One hundred feet short of the caravan, the heat hit me, like running head first into a solid wall – and then I could smell the petrol. I pushed on, watching holes forming, a section of the roof seeming to drain away like liquid running into a plughole.

'Lynda!'

Flames crawled and twisted, tendrils of fire wrapping themselves around the carcass of the vehicle – with no rain, there was nothing to stop it any more. One of the windows splintered and began to fall away, the grey of the cardboard that had been stuck to it long since gone. Minute pieces of paper – the remnants of the documents and photos that Korin had so meticulously mounted to the interior – were disappearing towards the sky in a trail of ash. Pretty soon, all that she'd found in the boxes would be gone for ever.

'Lynda!'

I stopped twenty feet short of the caravan. The flames were so intense, I couldn't get close enough to the windows to put my face to them and look inside for Korin – but as I glanced around, trying to see if she'd made it clear, I noticed something smeared up the exterior of the caravan, right next to the open door.

Blood.

I felt a twinge of alarm.

The light from the fire cast a circle around the caravan, an ethereal glow, and then a breeze rolled up from the lake, the smoke whirling and changing course, and my eyes shifted from the door, back to the windows.

This time, I could see something.

It looked like a human shape, slumped over. I tried to get closer, the heat still holding me back, but I managed to inch near enough to make out a shoulder, visible at the bottom of the window. And then I realized what else I could see: a red anorak.

My heart sank.

It was Korin.

I moved to the door of the caravan, trying to see if there was any way I could gain access, any way I could get to her and pull her out. But it was impossible. The vehicle was an inferno, crackling and popping, all of it going up in smoke. Korin was inside, and so was the story of her and Hosterlitz's life; the letter he'd written her; the photos of her mother.

Movement.

I swung around instantly, directing the torch down towards the drystone wall at the front of the caravan, the light skittering across its ridges. There was no one there. Uncertain of what I'd seen, I turned and faced back up the slope, re-establishing my grip on the light. My head was throbbing, the cool of the night and the heat from the fire prickling against my skin. I felt goosebumps scatter along my spine, sweat at my lip, at my brow, on the palms of my hands.

Egan.

I spun on my heel and looked down the slope for a second time, to where the wall separated this field from the next. The mix of smoke and flames, the way the shadows tilted and altered, made it difficult to judge what was moving and what was a trick of the light. I lifted the torch to shoulder height, trying to use elevation as a way to spread its impact.

'Egan,' I shouted, 'I know it's you!'

I moved to the front of the caravan, shining the torch through the gap between its tow bracket and the wall. The field seemed to go on for ever on the other side, falling away into black. But the torch had a range of about sixty feet, plus there was the light from the fire, so if he was heading out that way, making a break for it across the field, I'd have been able to see him. But what if he hadn't come to this end of the caravan in order to make a break for it?

What if he's just done a loop of the van?

As I turned to face back up the field, he smashed into me so hard my feet left the floor. I had enough time to see the glint of what may have been a knife and then, a split second later, I'd careened against the top of the drystone wall, spiralled over it, and hit the wet bank of grass on the other side. I landed even harder than I'd left it.

Dazed, stunned, I rolled on to my back, old injuries reawakening – my arm, my chest, my face. I winced, my head swimming, and managed to haul myself up on to all fours. The torch was out of reach next to the wall. Some-where, I thought I could hear the lake. Somewhere else, I heard a part of the caravan collapsing, the sound of metal and plastic folding like paper. Another *whump* and then fire erupted like a fountain, painting my side of the wall a brief, brilliant yellow.

That was when I saw him.

Egan.

He stood there, slightly hunched and breathing hard, about six feet from me. I scrambled to my feet. He didn't come for me this time. His skin was flushed, and there was blood running from a deep laceration in his gut. It was a knife wound, jagged and coarse. Korin must have got a hit in before he killed her.

He sliced his own knife across the air in front of him – the same knife he'd threatened me with at the Portakabin. I scrambled to my feet, able to see the caravan being reduced to ashes on the other side of the wall. He followed my gaze and then turned back to me, a faint smile on his face. But it quickly became something else: a wince; a grimace of pain.

Without warning, he rushed me.

I backed up automatically, and the ground seemed to give way. Sliding, I lurched to my left and fell, rolling through a tangle of ferns. As I tried to get to my feet again, I heard Egan's footsteps thump against the wet grass directly to my right, and then he started slashing at the plants, slicing through them as he tried to get at me. I rolled again, in an attempt to get away, and then again, and again, feeling the ground angle away, my clothes soaked through with mud and rain – and then, with a crunch, I hit another wall.

I looked up the slope.

Egan was coming, backlit by the fire, a shape ripped from the fabric of the night. The knife swung at his side like a pendulum, glinting orange, and then he raised it, slashing the blade from left to right, as if he thought I was closer than I was. He lost his balance and staggered to his left. I tried to imagine why he hadn't just stuck me with the knife when he'd had the chance at the caravan – but then, as he swiped it across the front of him again, I realized his perception was shot. It was all fading for him. He'd had every intention of stabbing me earlier, of putting me down for good, but he'd missed. That was why I'd seen the flash of the blade come so close to my head. He'd gone for my face or my neck, and misjudged it.

I hauled myself up.

'Billy,' I said.

He stopped, his feet sliding a little on the grass.

'You're dying, Billy.'

He didn't say anything, either because he couldn't hear me or he didn't have the strength to respond. There was blood all over his shirt. There was blood on his lips now too. He tried to make himself big again, to shake off the damage that Korin had inflicted upon him, and then he came at me a third time.

He had the knife out in front of him like a spear, his eyes like blobs of oil, his face contorted. But halfway between us, he lost his footing, sliding on a streak of mud, and then stumbled forwards and to the side, past me, into the wall. This one was smaller, and he smashed into it hard at thigh height, his momentum carrying his upper half forward and over the top. He hit the other side and rolled the rest of the way, out into the middle of another, smaller field, where the heavy rain had failed to drain away and formed a shallow pond in a cleft.

I sprang over the wall.

He'd dropped the knife as he'd fallen into the field, so I left it where it was and approached him. He hoisted himself up on to an elbow, searching for his weapon, and when he

464

didn't find it, he tried to clamber to his feet again. He got about halfway and then staggered back. His legs seemed to roll out from under him and he collapsed on to his knees, half in the pond, half out. It was a slow movement, almost in stages and, when it was over, he stared down into the water gathering at his legs – his clothes soaked through with rain and mud, blood leaking out of his guts.

'That fucking bitch,' he said, looking at his stab wound.

If I'd felt any pity for him, it disappeared as I thought of what he'd done to Korin. And then something else hit me even harder, like an anchor dragging me down into the darkness of the lake itself: *Egan had tailed me all the way here.*

I'd just cost Lynda Korin her life.

I dropped to my haunches, suddenly woozy, nauseous, my head pounding. Egan noted the movement and looked at me, eyes narrowing, as if trying to read my mind. He broke into a smile, blood smeared across his teeth.

'You got nothing,' he said softly.

He glanced up at the slope, past the walls, to the caravan. It was hardly visible any more – just flames and smoke. Ten months of a life reduced to dust.

'*You got nothing!*'

Egan screamed it this time.

His voice carried off into the darkness, and then there was only silence between us, filled with the soft patter of rain on the pond.

'You got nothing,' he said again, descending into a coughing fit.

'The police know who you are, Billy.'

He smiled. 'So?'

'Zeller will take the fall for what you've done.'

He shifted position in the water. In the dull light carrying down from the fire, I could see more blood ooze from his stomach. He only had minutes left.

'They can't connect me to him,' he wheezed.

'You're his son.'

'A son he couldn't control.'

He meant Zeller would deny he ever knew what his son was involved in, or capable of. Then it became the police's job to try and find a connection. I thought of Egan's phone, which I'd found at the Portakabin, empty of numbers, calls, any Internet history, any activity at all. I saw the shape of a new phone in his pocket too. It would be the same. But there would still be a record of calls, texts and Internet history at the phone company.

'The police will go to your phone comp–'

'They're burners. I brought them with me from the States.' He stopped, coughing again. 'They're not even UK phones.' Another pause. 'You think the police will go to the effort of chasing down US phone companies for phones we're dumping at the end of every week?' He laughed, but then it turned into a series of hacks. 'They won't. And even if they did . . .' He coughed again, raw and painful, and when it was over, he gestured up the slope to the fire. 'I did this. That's all the cops'll need to know.'

One of Egan's hands was planted in the water for support. He lifted it out and wiped at his eyes. Water trails ran down his cheeks, mixing with the blood.

'You got nothing,' he said again. 'Anything you might have had . . .' He stopped, his chest wheezing. 'Anything you had, it's lying dead up there or it's . . .' He coughed. 'Or it's burning to a crisp. You're going down for Cramer's death. And if the cops don't nail you, the old man will see to it. Whatever it takes.' He smiled, struggling to breathe.

'Whatever justice Saul doesn't get for me, whatever evidence he doesn't have . . . he'll find it. That's what he does.'

He coughed again, a thick, distressed sound.

'You got no proof . . . about anything.'

One last fading smile.

His eyes lingered on me for a moment more, and then they started rolling back into his head. He toppled sideways into the pond, like a collapsing building.

'They're . . . gonna . . . come for you.'

He meant the police. Or maybe he meant Zeller.

Either way, I knew he was right.

I had nothing.

73

I headed back up the slope, my legs feeling weak, my mouth tasting of blood. The heat from the caravan had faded, but flames still licked at its blackened skeleton.

I stood there, watching it burn.

I didn't have any moves left to make. Korin was dead, and with her went my last hope of trying to prove anything. Even if what she'd pinned to the walls of the caravan was gone for ever, her testimony, her intimate knowledge of the case and her connection to the victims would have been infinitely more than I had now. Instead, as smoke belched into the night sky, and the smell of burnt plastic carried off on the wind, I had to face reality: the man who'd killed her mother, who'd coldly set up her half-brother, and who'd changed the entire course of her life, was going to get away with what he'd done. There was no one left to dispute Zeller's account of what happened in 1953. He was protected not only by money, influence, power – but also by history, and by time. Six decades on, anyone who had ever cared for any of the victims was dead.

I got out my phone and looked at the display. In everything that had gone on since I'd arrived at Wast Water, I'd forgotten to turn it off, to take the battery and the SIM card out. It had been like that for a couple of hours, maybe longer. If the police were looking to pick up my location, I'd made it even easier for them.

As another part of the caravan collapsed in on itself, I

thought about how detectives might come after me. I tried to think clearly about how to connect dots, how to avoid falling into their traps, whether there was anything I could defend myself with. And then my mind began to wander, back to the phone call I'd had with Craw. *She was leaving.* It had barely registered with me at the time, because I'd been so focused on Korin, but it hit hard now: she was leaving me, the case had escaped me, the police were on their way.

I was alone. I'd failed.

I was done.

Then something moved.

Through the melted, twisted remains of the caravan, on the opposite side of the vehicle, I could see it. At first, it was difficult to make out, a swirling sheet of rain creating a gossamer curtain on that side of the caravan. For a second, I thought it was an animal, crawling through the grass.

But it wasn't an animal.

It was Lynda Korin.

I immediately broke into a sprint, tearing around the burning wreckage of the caravan, to where Korin was lying, belly down, in the grass. As she heard my footsteps, she started to moan – a terrible, glutinous gurgling in her throat – and then her fingers tried to gain purchase in the mud. I dropped to my knees next to her, speaking to her softly, and saw blood all over her top, all over her trousers, all over her face.

'Lynda,' I said. 'It's David.'

She stopped trying to crawl away but couldn't angle her body in order to see me, so I slid an arm around her waist and another around her neck and rolled her over. She made a great sigh, like a breath of wind, and then tried to find me.

Her eyes rolled in her head.

It was hard to look at her, to see her like this. She had burns down one side of her body, her clothes reduced to cinders, her skin melted like candle wax. In the light from the fire, I could just about trace her path back to the caravan, a trail marked out with flattened grass and the blood from a knife wound Egan had put high in her chest. Hers must have been the blood at the door. She'd shrugged off her red anorak inside and managed to make it out.

Resting her head on my knee, I grabbed my phone and dialled 999, even though I knew it was futile. It would take them too long to get here, whether they came by road or by air.

Korin was dying.

Egan had killed her – and I was the one who had led him here.

Suddenly, an overwhelming sense of remorse shrouded me. I wasn't sure if it was for Korin, for the role I'd played in the death that was surely coming for her, or whether it was the certainty that some aspect of me – an innocence that had always been a part of my DNA – had escaped and wasn't coming back. Out of nowhere, I thought of my doctor, Jhadav, and what he'd said to me – *If you're not careful, this job of yours might cost you your life* – and I started to wonder if he had been talking about moments like this. Not my life coming to an end, not being buried in some cemetery where all that would be left of me was dirt and a headstone, but instead being altered in some way. Maybe this would be the illness that would eat me up from the inside – not black-outs and headaches and disease. Maybe it would be the weight of these moments. The regret I felt for them. The idea that I could never take them back.

On my lap, Korin shifted, her breathing shallow and

painful. She opened her good eye. It was filmy and unfocused, like a cloudy marble.

I ran a hand across her face, through hair that had become matted with dirt and blood, and thought of all that she'd told me in the hours before, the strength she'd shown, the suffering she'd had to endure, and wished I'd had the chance to know her better in life.

Again, she shifted against my leg.

But this time, haltingly, she moved her hand to mine, dug her nails in and directed my hand to her pockets.

She tried to speak, but all that came out was a low moan, like a whimper. When my hand reached her left side, she pressed my fingers hard to her trouser pocket and then her own hand slipped away, and mine stayed there, on her hip. There was something inside. I reached in and took it out.

It was two matching keys on a ring.

I looked down at Korin's face, but her eyes were shut, and there was water leaking out from under the lids.

'Lynda, what are these for?'

She didn't respond.

'Lynda?'

She moaned slightly. 'An . . . gel . . .'

Angel. Automatically, I looked back at the caravan and, as I did, I saw something lying in the grass about ten feet to the right of me. It was covered in her blood, in mud and rain – but it was there.

The angel.

She'd grabbed it before crawling her way out.

Laying her down as gently as I could, I went to pick it up and then brought it back to her – but her eyes remained closed, her breathing shallow and laboured.

'Lynda?'

Nothing.

'Lynda, I don't know what I'm supposed to do with this. I don't know how it can help.'

When she didn't respond, I looked into my hands.

The wooden angel. A set of keys.

I glanced from her to the caravan, and then from the caravan to the farm, and a memory came back to me. I remembered heading past the farmhouse and skirting the barns. At the back, there had been an annex, close to the pigs, old and faded, smelling of wood and paint. The annex had a faded red door.

The door had two slide bolts.

And on the bolts were two padlocks.

74

I carried Lynda Korin to my car and placed her on the back seat, and as I headed towards the farm again, I could hear police sirens for the first time. They were a way off yet, but they'd be here before long.

I quickened my pace.

The dog was still barking as I passed the farmhouse, but not as loudly, and her noise merged with the rain as I circumvented the barns and arrived at the annex. Wedging the torch between my arm and body, I used both keys to spring the padlocks, and then inched back the slide bolts. The red door bumped away from its frame, like a pressure valve releasing, carrying with it the smell of old wood.

I looked for a light switch, but couldn't find one, so swept the torch from side to side. There were two tables, placed length-wise next to one another. One was full of junk – rust-speckled equipment I struggled to recognize even under the glare of the torch – but when I got closer, I realized they were parts: obscure chunks of metal that looked like they'd been ripped from an old car engine.

The other table was covered in a sheet.

I placed the angel on the floor and whipped the sheet away. It turned out it wasn't a table at all, but a refrigerator and a bookcase.

I went to the refrigerator first.

It was full of 35mm film cans.

A plastic temperature gauge hung from a hook inside and

read $3°C$, and on the bottom of it, a label read: *Acetate film =* $0–5°C$. On top of the film cans there was a series of ziplock bags. I counted twenty. One contained a videotape with a VHS-C logo on it. The other nineteen all held the same thing: reels of Super 8 film. The 8mm stock must have been what Hosterlitz had shot in his spare time. Korin had talked about him owning a Super 8 camera, and he'd told her in the letter that he'd left it in the garage for her along with the boxes.

I moved on to the bookcase.

It was full of archaic hardbacks, browned and worn. I took one out at random and found it was coverless. The title page read: *Film Noir 1940–1959*. It had been bookmarked with different colour Post-it notes and, when I opened it to see which pages the Post-its were marking, I saw that they were all passages or chapters dealing with Hosterlitz's films. They talked about his techniques, his trademark use of close-up, his long takes, his dialogue. Korin had underlined sections and added notes to the margins in red pen, but it was hard to read anything she'd written. I'd seen her hand before and it had never been as opaque as this – so had she deliberately made it difficult to decipher?

If she had, it had to have been an insurance policy against people finding the books, a way to conceal her thoughts. But why did it matter? When I removed another book called *Film Styles*, and a third, *Narrative: A Beginner's Guide*, I saw there were Post-its inside those too, and similar, handwritten notes. I checked the rest of the shelves and found books on the history of cinema, technical manuals, film encyclopedias. Korin had marked various sections in all of them, paying particular attention to passages that dealt with the techniques that Hosterlitz had employed during his most successful years as a director.

Outside, the sirens had begun to get louder.

I put the books back, got to my feet and shone the torch out across the rest of the room. Hidden in the shadows, at a diagonal from me in the corner, was what looked like another table. It was disguised with a blanket but, underneath the cover, the surface of the table appeared to be littered with objects. I couldn't see what they were, but the blanket had formed a series of peaks and troughs as it fell around whatever Korin had left there.

Grabbing the blanket, I pulled it off.

But this wasn't a table either – or, at least, not in the traditional sense.

It was a flatbed editor.

A movie editing table.

Instantly, I remembered the end of Hosterlitz's letter to Korin, where he'd talked about leaving something else in the garage unit, as well as all the boxes.

I bought it after I went to see Zeller and Cramer in LA. Once you get into the garage, you won't be able to miss it.

He must have been talking about this.

There was a picture viewer in the middle – about the size of a small, portable television – and then countless plates and rollers. The film reel was placed on to one of the plates, it was fed through the rollers, and then a prism projected the image of the film on to the viewer. Before digital, this was how all movies had been cut together: yards and yards of negative being fed through from one side to the other, the film's editor using the viewer to help make precise cuts – marking it with a chinagraph, chopping it, reassembling it into an edit.

I glanced at the fridge full of film, and then at the shelves on the bookcase, full of technical manuals and 'How To' guides. She'd made notes all over them. She'd underlined things. She'd studied her husband's work and other directors'.

Because she was teaching herself.

She was teaching herself to edit film.

What Korin said to me in the caravan flooded back. *But I could only have you begin to look for me when I was ready for you to start looking. It took me ten months to get to that stage, because Robert left instructions. But they were so hard. It's so hard.*

My eyes dropped to the floor.

Beneath the editing table was a cardboard box. I bent down and pulled it out. Inside was an old typewriter. The E was broken on it, and I remembered the typewritten time-line I'd seen on the wall of the caravan that Hosterlitz had compiled for Korin, which had been missing all its E's. The typewriter had been his.

Next to that was a portable DVD player, scratched and dusty, and DVDs of all the Hosterlitz films that Korin had removed from their cases and taken from her house. As I pulled the DVD player out of the box, I saw that it had a lead and plug attached. I opened it up. The screen had fin-gerprints on it, small scratches too, and when I popped the disc drive, I found a DVD on the spindle.

It was marked *Version 12*.

There was one other thing in the box. A dark blue plastic folder containing a stack of white paper. As I quickly started going through the paper, I heard the wail of sirens again, clearer for a second above the beat of the rain on the roof.

The paper stack consisted of invoices and receipts, letters that Korin had written on the typewriter – clearly keen to avoid using the Internet or email – the missing *E*'s filled in by hand. They were all correspondence with the same company, and the same person – a place called CineLab UK in Manchester, and a technician called Greg Plumstead. Under their corporate logo, at the top of one letterhead, it said they were specialists in transferring 8mm, 16mm and 35mm film to digital formats like DVD and Blu-ray. I glanced at the fridge on the other side of the room, home to 35mm film cans and nineteen ziplock bags of 8mm.

But then the receipts and invoices stopped.

Halfway in, the stack of paper became something different. It became a single, ninety-page document, bound together with two brass fasteners on the side. I swallowed hard as I realized what it was.

Alex, Egan, Zeller – they thought Hosterlitz was finished. They thought, in retirement, he was too sick, too washed up, to do anything that might harm them. 'Ring of Roses' was just the name of a building, long buried in a past they'd managed to suppress.

But they were wrong.

It had never just been a building.

I looked down at the film script, at its title page, the corners curled, the paper browning. There were six words typed on it.

Six words that Saul Zeller never thought he'd see.

Ring of Roses by Robert Hosterlitz.

75

My heart was racing. I found a power point next to the flat-bed editor and plugged in the portable DVD player. Setting it atop the table under which the cardboard box had been stored, I turned the volume all the way up and pushed Power. As the disc began to whir noisily and I waited for it to load, I started turning the pages of the script. They were old, yellowed, and curled at the corners. But they were intact.

```
AGAINST BLACK:
NARRATOR
(V. O.)
If I make my bed in hell, behold, thou art
there.
CAPTION: Psalm 139:8

FADE IN:
INT. CAR. DAY
We are passing a nondescript street watch-
ing homes, apartments and stores blur
past. The footage is being shot on a Super
8 camera. It gives the whole thing a
home-movie feel. But then the car starts to
slow down.
```

From the portable DVD player, sound began to play softly. I looked up. It was tinny through the speakers and there was no imagery at all – just the hum of a car engine, and then traffic noise, and then the sounds of a city, fading in one after the other. Against a black screen, the titles appeared in plain, stark white – RING OF ROSES – and then faded out again, to be replaced by more words, in the same typeface: A FILM BY ROBERT HOSTERLITZ. Seeing his name sent a charge of electricity through me. The sound had settled into the gentle rhythm of a car travelling. I shuffled closer to the seven-inch screen, the script open on my lap.

'If I make my bed in hell, behold, thou art there.'

His voice came through the speakers, almost in a whisper. It was him. It was Hosterlitz. *He's the narrator.* On screen, the Bible quote appeared, just as it was written in the script, just as he'd spoken it, and then it all faded to black.

After a beat, the movie started.

I felt myself tense. It was Super 8 footage, just as the script described – but not only that. It was the footage Hosterlitz had shot of Pierre Street in Van Nuys; in fact, *exactly* the same footage he'd run on the TV in his horror movies. Except this footage didn't end after ten seconds. It carried on – the street, buildings, people, other cars, continuing to blur past. After a minute, the car finally started to slow down and – in the glass of the window – there was a brief but absolutely clear reflection of a taxi meter.

He filmed it from the back of a cab.

As soon as that was gone, there was the squeal of brakes and the taxi came to a halt. The camera tilted to its right and directly outside the window was a fountain. Circling the fountain was a beautiful bed of pink, yellow and red roses.

The Ring of Roses orphanage.

The film snapped to black.

A brief pause, and then another male voice: 'My name's Raymond J. Callson. I was an officer with the Los Angeles Police Department for thirty-two years.'

Callson.

The detective on Kerekes's murder.

The action returned. Callson looked like he was in his early sixties. He had grey hair, perfectly parted, and was well turned out in a collared shirt and jacket. He was in some kind of office. Behind him, through the windows, I could see the LA skyline. After introducing himself, a date came up at the bottom of the screen.

29 DECEMBER 1984.

Hosterlitz's trip to LA.

He didn't just go there to confront Zeller and Cramer. He'd gone there to interview Callson too. But this footage hadn't been taken on his Super 8. From the hint of scanlines at the top and bottom and the way the colours bent and warped slightly, he must have hired what he thought would be newer, better equipment. In 1984, he would have had access to early camcorders, running off VHS or Betamax tapes. I glanced at the fridge again, recalling the VHS-C inside it.

That must have been the Callson interview.

Callson talked for a minute or two about his experiences of being a cop in LA, until Hosterlitz asked him, 'Are there any cases that have stuck with you?' and Callson started to nod.

'Yeah,' he said. 'Yeah, I can think of one case right off the top of my head.'

It snapped to black again.

Before the next scene started up, I looked down at the

script, trying to see how closely the action onscreen was mirroring the directions written down. It was an exact replica. Everything that was happening in the film was in the script.

The tinkling sound of a music box.

I looked up again.

The camera was close in on something in the foreground, the object completely out of focus, while in the background a music box – *in* focus – was playing quietly. Then everything switched, back to front, the music box disappearing into a blur in the background of the shot, while the object – close in – pinged into sharp focus.

The object was the wooden angel.

'Életke Kerekes was born on 22 December 1918 . . .'

Hosterlitz. He'd started to narrate again, his voice low and crackly, like a television reception that needed tuning. He filled in the background on Kerekes, her marriages, kids, her job at American Kingdom, while different shots of the angel were intercut with stock footage – immigrants arriving in the US, the mass migration of people from the Midwest to LA in the first half of the twentieth century. This must have been what was in the 35mm film cans.

I'd always believed he'd taken so many photographs of the angel because the angel had been given to him by Kerekes. And maybe that *was* a part of it – but it wasn't the only reason. It had also been to help him find angles he liked, to see what lighting worked, to visualize how it would look through the Super 8 lens.

The movie switched again, this time to some historical footage of Venice, where Kerekes and her children had lived during the fifties. Hosterlitz's narration contrasted it with the opulence of the places that the Hollywood elite frequented. His last shot was a photograph of the Pingrove Hotel. 'Her house in the slum by the sea was modest,' his commentary continued, 'but she made the best of it. She gave her children a home. And, at work, she'd seen an opportunity – and had taken it.'

A film poster for *Tiger Goes to Town* appeared.

It was the first movie AKI adapted from one of Kerekes's stories. Then more posters appeared, one after the other, showing all the films which had been inspired by her stories. Over the top of it all, Hosterlitz was talking softly about her, referencing her abilities, the way she was a woman ahead of her time, and how she rose to prominence in a world dominated by men. 'Her talent, beauty and single-mindedness, brought her to the attention of the Hollywood elite.'

Snap to black.

'I met her at the Blue Orchid, the same night Glen Cramer did.'

And, for the first time, Hosterlitz appeared onscreen.

He was poorly lit. I thought maybe he was in the council garage he'd bought, but wherever he was, it was hard to look at him. He was desperately ill. He'd thinned right down to the bone, his colour gone, his clothes hanging off him. He was staring into the camera. It looked like he'd been crying.

'She was beautiful,' he said, and the hint of a smile ghosted across his face. 'Her beauty wasn't a thing she used as a crutch or a weapon, to stand out or to get on. I wouldn't have blamed her for using it that way, because Hollywood was – is – a monster waiting to eat you up, and you have to use any advantage you can. But it was more than that. She was more than that. Her beauty was just there. It was in everything she did – as a storyteller, as a mother, as a friend.'

He stopped and then began to cough, softly at first, and then harder, his face creasing up in pain. When it was over, silence rang out and he sat there, looking into the camera, shoulders rising and falling. 'I think I loved her from the first moment I saw her.'

It cut to a photograph of the Blue Orchid nightclub, as it was back in the early 1950s. He was doing the lead-up to her death. I reached forward and pushed the Fast-Forward button, conscious of the sirens closing in now. For a while, Hosterlitz mostly used a mix of still photography and stock footage, until the night Kerekes died, when the film returned to the interview with Ray Callson.

I reached forward and pressed Play.

They were talking about the scene in the hotel room. I wanted to watch more of Callson – he was compelling, heartfelt – but I didn't have the time. After a couple of minutes, I hit Fast-Forward again.

The action sped through more of Callson, and then – like a punch to the throat – there was a series of photographs from the crime scene, which he must have kept, even after retiring from the LAPD. Pictures of Martin followed too – front on, his shirt, his fingers, the scratch marks on his arms. The empty whisky bottle. The sleeping pills. It moved to his mugshot. He looked younger than sixteen, his fingers small around the placard that listed his name, age, date of birth and booking ID.

Then they were gone.

There was more Super 8 footage – which Hosterlitz must have shot during the same 1984 trip – of the duck pond at Franklin Canyon, where the three men had met afterwards, and then Hosterlitz appeared onscreen again. I hit Play. He must have recorded these to-camera sections late on, because there was a stark difference between his voice here and his voice in the interview with Callson.

'Zeller made me believe I'd killed her,' Hosterlitz said, almost wheezing the words into existence. You could hear the sickness in his voice, vibrating in the timbre of his words. 'And I believed him. I didn't doubt him for even a second. I think, perhaps, a part of me even felt I wanted to carry that burden. I wanted to feel the full impact of what I'd done. I'd hit her. I'd knocked her out. I'd laid hands on a woman who had allowed me into her home, who had trusted me with her kids.' He raised his head, eyes on the camera. 'Cramer made me believe she found me weird and creepy, but I should have known. I should have known.' He shook his head, and the tears came again, and then it became hard to watch. He was a frail old man crying for what he'd done and what he'd lost. 'She wouldn't have said those things,' he whimpered. 'That wasn't Elaine. I should have known.'

For the first time, through the open doorway of the annex behind me, I saw a faint hint of blue light in my peripheral vision. *Shit.* The police. They were in the valley now. I could see them coming as well as hear them.

I pushed Fast-Forward again.

More of Callson, who must have been talking about the investigation, the way it was solved, then a shot of the *National People* front page: SEX-OBSESSED HOSTERLITZ OUTED AS A RED. Photographs of Zeller and Cramer followed, which didn't need explaining – they'd planted the story. From there, the action showed the slow descent of Hosterlitz's life. There was a mix of stills and archive footage of him in London, in Germany, and then back in the US in 1966. More photos of Cramer from the mid 1960s – which I guessed must have been a reference to the conversation he'd had with Hosterlitz, the 'joke' Cramer had made. Finally, there was a fade to black and a slow fade in again: we were back in Van Nuys, watching the same Super 8 footage of Hosterlitz travelling in the direction of the orphanage.

But then something went wrong.

76

The movie came to an abrupt halt and, onscreen, a picture of the wooden angel appeared – one from the album at Korin's place. Over the top of the image, there were four words: PLACEHOLDER – FOOTAGE TO COME.

'No,' I said. 'No, don't do this.'

I rewound it to the last moments of the Pierre Street footage and pressed Play. Hosterlitz was on voice-over: 'I've been so weak all these years. I should have confessed to my part in this and taken my punishment, not waited until I was dying. I know I've wronged. I know I deserve everything that's coming to me. But I have, at least, acknowledged it.' He paused as, onscreen, the car slowed to a halt outside the orphanage. 'Zeller will never admit to what he did.'

The Ring of Roses building came fully into shot.

'So I have to try and make him.'

The film cut to the picture of the angel and the place-holder text, and as the seconds ticked by on the DVD player, it dawned on me: Korin only got this far.

I could only have you begin to look for me when I was ready for you to start looking. She meant once she'd edited this much of the film. *It took me ten months to get to that stage, because Robert left instructions. But they were so hard. It's so hard.* He wasn't only asking her to read through his confession and to sort out the detritus of his life, his secrets. He was asking her to piece it together for him.

He was asking her to make *Ring of Roses*.

She'd had to learn how to edit, how to follow his instructions, his wishes, his script. If sorting through the boxes had taken months, this had taken longer. It was why Korin had disappeared and never come up for air. Alex Cavarno had wondered why Korin, knowing what 'Ring of Roses' meant, never took what she knew to the police or the media. This was why. She was seeing out her husband's dying wish. She'd been trying to finish the film because she knew that if she finished it, presenting the authorities with a movie – detailing the whole story, the evidence, in a format that would grip them – would be the most powerful testimony of all.

Even so, a sinking feeling grabbed hold of me. All of this, all of Korin's efforts, and how did it help? Hosterlitz was dead. Korin was dying. There was still nothing here that could bring down Zeller.

Inside the silence of the annex, I heard more sirens – louder, closer, their blue lights painting the edges of the farm. I could see blue on the walls to my right and left, as if they were actually in the room. As I stared at the placeholder text, at the picture of the angel, I thought of how Hosterlitz had called the angel 'the answer', and how Korin had never been able to work out why. She'd hired me to find out what he meant. But I had no idea.

I *still* had no idea, even now.

But then suddenly, unnervingly, as if a ghost were talking from the corner of the room, Hosterlitz's voice started up again, speaking over the placeholder image. 'Instructions for loading film on to the flatbed editor are as follows . . .'

He started going through the process.

I was completely thrown by it – confused, off balance. What the hell was this?

Instinctively, I glanced back at the door to the annex, wondering when the police would find me, when the net would close in on me completely – but instead my eyes came to rest on the angel. It was sitting where I'd left it. I looked at the placeholder image of it on the DVD screen, and then back to the real thing. Hurrying to my feet, I scooped it up off the floor – and, for the first time, something struck me about it.

Something that had never seemed important before.

It was hollow.

And not only that: the chips on it, the hairline cracks across it, what I'd thought had been evidence of its age – it wasn't that at all.

It was where it had been glued back together.

In the background, Hosterlitz's audio instructions continued – step five, step six, step seven.

I looked down at the ornament cradled in my hand.

The answer.

Gripping it, I brought the bottom half of the angel down hard against the solid oak of the bookcase. The impact levered open the crack, splintering it.

The bottom of the ornament fell away.

Inside was a roll of 8mm film.

77

As I took it out, some of the sirens outside stopped altogether, engines were switched off and there were shouts in the distance.

But I hardly heard them.

Hosterlitz had called the angel 'the answer' – but not just because of its history and what it meant to him and Korin.

Because he'd used it as a hiding place.

He knew, whatever happened, Korin would take the angel with her – she'd had it her whole life. When he deliberately broke it, inserted the film, and glued it back together, he must have spun some story for her, apologized for damaging it, acted like it was an accident. But it wasn't an accident, it was an insurance policy.

He needed to ensure the safety of the film.

And whatever was on it.

Rewinding Hosterlitz's instructions on the DVD, I started loading the film on to the flatbed editor. I had no idea what I was doing, but Hosterlitz's audio instructions helped – their softness, their composure. He was precise and detailed, and as I looked closer at the flatbed, I saw that Korin herself had stuck masking tape to individual rollers and plates, adding arrows and explanations and warnings of what not to do. At one stage, she'd followed these same instructions herself.

I didn't know much about looking after film like this, but I knew enough: damage it, and it stayed damaged. Because of that, I went more slowly, more carefully, than I might have done otherwise, even as I heard the voices in the distance grow nearer. A way into the film, I saw evidence of splice tape on it. This suggested that it had been cut and reassembled at some point – edited in some way.

Finally, I had loaded it in.

I paused there, terrified it would unravel straight away, or break up, or tear. But I knew I didn't have a choice. It was now or never.

I started up the editor.

With relief, I saw the film image appear on the viewer. From speakers set into the top of the editor, there was a series of pops and then a soft, steady hiss.

It took me a second to work out what was I seeing.

The camera had been placed in between what looked like two plants. *It's in a flowerbed.* I could make out a driveway, a closed gate, and then a figure on the floor, slumped under a tree next to a gatepost. I leaned in closer.

The figure was Hosterlitz.

The footage jumped a little, cracks and specks visible on the film, and then – from out of shot – a car pulled into the driveway. It was a Ferrari 288.

That was when I understood.

The car was a mid 1980s model. The house was in Los Angeles. Both of them belonged to Glen Cramer.

This was the night Hosterlitz had doorstepped him, drunk.

This was December 1984.

Hosterlitz had recorded it all.

78

The headlights from the Ferrari washed over Hosterlitz's slumped frame. I leaned in closer to the picture viewer. Cramer got out, leaving his door open. 'Bobby?' he said, his voice crystal clear. *'Bobby?'*

There were spots and scratches on the film, the condition of the negative having deteriorated over time, but it was good enough to see what was going on. It was the sound that remained more impressive, though: even from this distance away, it was easy to hear Cramer. Hosterlitz must have used an external microphone.

He'd thought it all through.

'What the hell are you doing here, Bobby?'

Cramer dropped to his haunches next to Hosterlitz, who moaned. When he got no response, Cramer used a hand to rouse Hosterlitz, to try and stir him. When he still got no reaction, he said, 'Bobby, how much have you had to drink?'

As he asked that, I suddenly thought of something that Korin had said to me. I'd asked her about Hosterlitz being drunk when he'd turned up at Cramer's house that night. *They told all sorts of lies to him, and about him,* she said. *That was just another one. I told you already, Robert never took another drink after 1976.*

Hosterlitz had turned the lie around.

He wasn't drunk that night – he was just pretending to be.

On the film, Cramer helped Hosterlitz to his feet. Hosterlitz stumbled a little, and then reached out to the wall for support, one hand planted against it, the other rubbing his face. For that night only, he must have drunk enough for the smell to stick to him, or maybe he'd sunk a non-alcoholic beer. Either way, it wasn't enough for him to lose any control. He knew exactly what he was doing.

'I'm dying,' he said quietly.

Cramer stepped closer. 'What?'

'I've got cancer, Glen.'

'Shit.'

Hosterlitz stood there, saying nothing.

'Shit, I'm so sorry, Bobby,' Cramer said, staring at the back of Hosterlitz's head. You could hear the authenticity in his voice, the shock. 'I can't believe it.'

'I've maybe got a year,' Hosterlitz said. 'No more than two.'

I watched Cramer, the colours on the film twitching as he moved closer to Hosterlitz. He'd been as culpable as Zeller, as culpable as Hosterlitz, in covering up the truth about what had happened to Életke Kerekes, and had destroyed his friend's life in order to save his own. Yet, despite everything, it was hard not to feel something for him. Not sympathy exactly, but a sense that – like Hosterlitz – he'd never been able to bury his shame. He'd never been able to forget.

He knew he was guilty.

'I'm so sorry, Bobby.'

Hosterlitz turned to face Cramer, unsteady on his feet. 'I need you to tell me your part in what happened,' he said, his words slurred. He took another step closer to Cramer. 'I need you to tell me what Zeller did that night.'

A sudden cut to another driveway.

The shift disorientated me for a moment. The camera had been left in the same sort of place, next to a tree midway across a garden. A yellow Lamborghini Countach was parked in front of a pale cream Spanish-style house. Beyond the roof, the lights of the city twinkled in the dark. This was Mulholland Drive.

The engine of the Lamborghini was still running and, for the first time, I could see two people inside. Zeller was one of them. He switched off the engine and got out. He was in his late fifties, lean and fit, dressed in jeans and a short-sleeve button-up shirt. He was carrying a pile of papers – scripts maybe, or forms.

Billy Egan was the passenger. He was seventeen or eighteen. He opened his door, looking similar to the person I'd known, except for a covering of brown hair. He was thickset, muscly, intimidating. As he climbed out, in a shirt and a pair of jeans, he didn't say anything.

'Hello, Saul.'

Both of them jolted, Zeller almost dropping the papers, Egan spinning on his heel to face the shadows at the double garage adjacent to the house. Zeller pushed the door of the Countach shut, looking around for the source of the voice, when Hosterlitz stepped out of the blackness. He was acting again: he stumbled slightly, came around the rear of the car and placed a hand on it for support.

'*Bobby?*'

'I need to talk to you,' Hosterlitz said, looking from Zeller to Egan. He seemed thrown by Egan being there. 'I thought you would be alone.'

Egan's appraisal of Hosterlitz was odd. He seemed to know exactly who he was, without the need for an introduction. He wasn't shocked by him being there or the fact that he was drunk. He came around the Countach at the front, on the opposite side to Hosterlitz, and then perched himself on the bonnet, watching the two men, as if he was waiting for something to play out. *Because Zeller had already told him everything.* Zeller handed his son the pile of papers, which he took.

'What the hell are you doing here, Bobby?'

'I'm dying, Saul.'

Zeller's first reaction couldn't have been more different from Cramer's. He glanced out into the road, looking for passers-by, for neighbours, for anyone who may have been able to place Hosterlitz at the house, and then came around the back of his car. 'What the fuck are you doing in LA?' he spat.

'I've got cancer.'

'So?'

Hosterlitz looked at Zeller; blinked. He glanced at Egan too, who gave no reaction to the news either. Hosterlitz seemed genuinely thrown by their lack of pity.

'*So?*' Zeller said again. 'So what? Lots of people get cancer, Bobby. What I want to know is why you're back in LA. Because I'm praying you're not here as part of some final attempt to confess your sins.' He looked out again at the road, as if expecting to see a police car there, as if expecting to be under surveillance. 'Is that what this is, Bobby? Have you come back to talk to the LAPD? Have you come back to get a few things off your chest before they put you in a box?'

Egan pushed himself off the bonnet and walked up the driveway. He looked up and down the road – once, twice, a third time – and then turned back to Zeller and shook his head. He was saying, *There's no one around.*

'Saul,' Hosterlitz said, using the Lamborghini for support. 'I need you to admit to what you did.'

'Get your hands off my fucking car.'

Hosterlitz didn't move.

Zeller ripped his fingers away and pushed Hosterlitz back against one of the garage doors. It chimed against his weight. Shadows formed around them. Hosterlitz seemed to realize that he and Zeller weren't going to be visible, so he pushed back at Zeller and stumbled after him, the two of them hitting the car with a dull thud.

In a flash, Zeller had thrown him to the ground.

'Don't touch me, you fucking prick!'

'I want to hear you say it!' Hosterlitz shouted up at him.

Zeller, teeth gritted, muscles taut, grabbed Hosterlitz by his coat, checked with Egan that the coast was still clear, and then started dragging Hosterlitz across the driveway and on to the manicured lawn. They were ten feet away from the camera, but on the edge of the shot. Again, Hosterlitz seemed to be aware of it: he rolled left and Zeller went after him. Now they were perfectly framed.

Come on, Zeller. Admit to what you did.

Say something I can use.

Zeller glanced out into the road again and then leaned over Hosterlitz. 'What are you doing in LA, you drunken sack of shit?' He'd whispered the words, but his proximity to the camera, to the mic, made them sound noisy and vicious.

'I want you to admit to what you did, Saul.'

Zeller flicked a look out into the road again, then back to Egan, who was perched on the bonnet of the Countach, a half-smile on his face. 'Do everyone a favour,' Zeller said to Hosterlitz, 'crawl away and fucking die.'

'We killed Életke Kerekes.'

Zeller didn't reply.

'*You* killed her – and we framed her son.'

Zeller slapped Hosterlitz hard across the face, and then – just as Hosterlitz was recovering from that – he kicked him in the stomach. I glanced at Egan, still expecting a reaction from him, some response to what was happening, to the idea that his father had sent a kid his age to death row for a crime he hadn't committed. But there was nothing.

Egan just watched, impassive.

'The world needs to know the truth, Saul,' Hosterlitz wheezed, lying on the grass in a foetal position at Zeller's feet – small, pathetic, subdued.

The film cut again – back to Cramer.

It picked up at some unspecified time after Cramer had found Hosterlitz at his house. They were still at the gates, a brief silence passing between them.

'I'm so sorry, Bobby,' Cramer said quietly.

There was a tremor in his voice. This was nothing like the angry, drunken confrontation that he'd described to me. It had never played out like that. That account had all been a lie; a construct invented by him – or, more likely, Zeller. It just became another script to Cramer; more lines he had to learn.

'I'm sorry for what we did to Elaine.'

Hosterlitz didn't say anything.

'For what we did to Martin.' Cramer swallowed, the name like chalk in his mouth. 'For what we did to you. If I could take it all back . . .'

'I believe you, Glen,' Hosterlitz said, no indistinctness to his words any more. He seemed to have forgotten he was supposed to be drunk – and Cramer, emotional, exhausted even then at having to keep such a secret, had stopped noticing.

'I need Saul to confess,' Hosterlitz said.

'Why?'

'I want to hear him admit to what he did.'

'You know he killed Elaine – what difference does it make?'

Hosterlitz glanced in the vague direction of the camera.

'It makes all the difference in the world.'

The movie cut back to Zeller's front lawn.

Hosterlitz had stumbled to his feet. He was unsteady, and not because he was putting it on. Zeller was at his right, watching him, eyes narrowed, as if trying to work out what was going on inside Hosterlitz's head.

'Everything you've built at AKI is based on a lie,' Hosterlitz said.

He sounded groggy – not drunk now, but ill.

'You don't know what you're talking about, Bobby,' Zeller said, prodding a finger into Hosterlitz's temple. 'It's the sickness – it's screwed with your brain.'

'You shouldn't have been around,' Hosterlitz mumbled. It was hard to tell whether he was acting or just dazed. 'You shouldn't have been around to build the company into what it is now. You shouldn't have had this house, this car, this *life*. We should have been in prison. We should have taken the fall for what we –'

'"We, we, we" – what's this "we", Bobby? Huh?' Zeller glanced at his son, who was looking faintly amused on the bonnet of the Lamborghini. Egan's silence seemed to massage Zeller's performance, his ego. He became even more aggressive. '*You* were the one who pushed that whore against –'

'Don't call her that.'

'You pushed that whore against the wardrobe. You knocked her out.'

'You made me believe I killed her.'

'You believed what you wanted to believe.'

'If people knew what you'd done –'

'But they don't, do they?'

'You killed her, Saul!'

Zeller didn't reply.

Come on. Admit it.

'We sent Martin to prison!'

Zeller looked out into the road, then grabbed hold of Hosterlitz's arm, just above the elbow. Hosterlitz flinched. There was an almost mesmeric moment when the two men stared at each other.

And then Zeller's expression changed and he suddenly started laughing. 'Oh, I get it,' he said, and then glanced back at Egan. 'I get it. You think you were – what? Some sort of surrogate *father* to that kid? Is that what this is all about? Is that why you can't forget him?'

'He was just a boy. We sent his one-year-old sister to the orphanage!'

Hosterlitz sounded tearful now.

'You thought you were some sort of father figure to them – is that it? You weren't any *father* figure, Bobby. You're a chickenshit. If you'd been any sort of man, you would have realized what I did for you. You would have sucked it down and gone back to work and made a hundred movies.' He shoved Hosterlitz away. 'You could have been the most successful director in history. You could have made millions if you'd had any balls. You could have had a house like this. Instead, look at the state of you. You're an old drunk making films no one gives a shit about. You're a fucking disgrace, Bobby. The world's better off without you.'

Hosterlitz was looking down at the floor, motionless except for his hands. At his side, his fingers were rolling into balls, opening and closing, forming fists.

Zeller noticed. 'What, you gonna hit me, Bobby?'

He's trying not to react.

He knows he's almost got it on tape.

'You gonna hit me, big man?'

Zeller pushed Hosterlitz hard. He stumbled out of shot and then returned again – not to attack Zeller or defend himself, but to put himself back in frame.

'You know something?' Zeller said, dizzy with adrenalin now, swaggering in front of the boy he'd go on to mould and shape.

It was a vile, angry display of machismo, but it was exactly what Hosterlitz wanted. At first, he may have been thrown by Egan being there that night – but he'd realized, by this point, that Egan was going to be Zeller's undoing.

'You know *something*?' Zeller said again. 'You got nothing on me, and you never will. Someone else got sent down for that murder. That fucking boy of hers . . .' Zeller shook his head and leaned right into Hosterlitz, his eyes checking the road again, checking Egan was watching. He dropped his bottom lip in a depiction of someone blubbing. '"I didn't do this. I didn't kill my mommy."'

His words silenced the entire scene, as if every noise in the city had died at once. Hosterlitz closed his eyes.

Beyond them both, Egan moved for the first time, sliding off the bonnet of the Countach on to his feet, as if realizing Zeller might be about to go too far.

'"I didn't kill my mommy, I didn't kill my mommy."'

'Dad,' Egan said.

'"Why would I kill my mommy, Detective Callson? Why would I drink all this whisky and take all these pills? Don't send me to the gas chamber, *please*."'

'Dad, stop.'

'"I didn't chop off her legs! I didn't!"'

'*Dad.*'

The scene was quiet for a moment, Zeller and Hosterlitz opposite each other, like boxers in their corners. Hosterlitz was still looking at the floor, fists squeezed shut. Zeller was opposite him, his breathing slowing, his gaze fixed on the man whose career he'd ruined and whose life he'd changed for ever.

'I did what I had to do,' he said finally.

'You set up Martin.'

'Yeah.'

Hosterlitz looked up. 'And you killed Elaine.'

'Yeah, I did.'

A long, funereal silence.

'It's been thirty years,' Zeller said, calmer, back in control of himself. 'It's time to forget her now. It's time for you to go home and die, Bobby.'

Everything went black.

The film was over.

79

'Mr Raker?'

Startled, I turned in my seat.

The annex was quickly filling with cops, each of them with a torch and a baton. I'd been so absorbed in the film, in the confession, I hadn't realized they'd actually found me. One of them, a huge bear of a man in his forties, grabbed my arm and lifted me out of the chair. The *Ring of Roses* script slid off my lap, thumping against the floor of the room.

'Are you deaf?' the cop said.

He meant they'd called my name and I hadn't responded. As he pulled me away, I glanced back at the picture viewer. There was nothing showing now. There were no credits, no music. It had just ceased.

Zeller's confession – and then nothing.

I tried to imagine why Hosterlitz hadn't taken the film of Zeller and Cramer to the police in the four years before he died; why he'd placed it inside the angel instead, sat on it, hidden it. But then I remembered his letter to Korin: *A part of me needed to confess, because I knew it was the right thing to do, but I didn't want what we had to be over . . . I was caught between the devil and the deep blue sea . . . I tried to tell you and I tried not to tell you; I wanted to and I didn't want to.*

That was the battle that raged inside me for ten years.

It was what the letter was supposed to have been: a map to the boxes, to the truth about what lay inside the angel, a trail that Korin could follow in the weeks and months after she buried him. After he was dead, he wouldn't have to face her as she realized who he was and what he'd done, but he would have confessed his sins.

Instead, he died before he got the chance to complete his work.

She eventually found her way to the boxes. She followed his map all the way to the truth about who she was. But he'd forgotten to direct her to the last piece of the jigsaw.

The roll of film inside the ornament.

Instinctively, I tried to reach down to the floor, to scoop up the script, to find out how *Ring of Roses* was supposed to end, but the cop yanked me towards him and proceeded to march me out.

'Wait a second,' I said.

But he wasn't listening.

We moved out into the cool of the night, the whole place swarming with police, with firemen, with paramedics. I remembered Korin in the back of my car.

'Lynda Korin,' I said. 'She's in –'

'We've found her.'

'Is she alive?'

But he didn't reply.

He kept his hand firmly gripped on my arm and then led me away, around the barn, back in the direction of the caravan. The fire was already out, hosed down, and all that was left were its smouldering remains; a charred, twisted skeleton.

The police interview room was small and plain. White walls, blue carpet, a table, black plastic chairs, a recording device. There was an air-conditioning unit as well, but it had been turned off: the room was hot and completely silent.

I rolled my neck and looked down at myself.

Blue cotton trousers. A plain T-shirt.

My clothes had been taken as evidence and my possessions bagged by the custody sergeant as soon as I'd arrived at the station. I gazed at my hands, along the ridges of my knuckles, and could still see the faint traces of blood, and then grazes from further back than that, when Billy Egan had hunted me through the canyons of the scrapyard. On the underside of my arms the scratch marks had scabbed over now. It made me think of Martin's arms after Zeller had finished with him.

I'd made my call to a solicitor, a guy I'd never met from Whitehaven, and had told him everything I knew. Then he'd sat next to me, taking notes, as two Cumbrian cops called Taylor and Annechy spent an hour asking me questions.

Taylor was in her early forties, attractive and quietly spoken, with short blonde hair. She had very bright, very grey eyes, like stones polished by the flow of a river, and she smiled a lot, which I imagined was effective in situations like this. A smile built trust and suggested understanding.

Annechy was olive-skinned and acne-scarred, a thick beard attempting to disguise the evidence. His hair was slicked back. He never said a thing.

'What a mess,' Taylor said.

There was silence for a moment. They both looked at me, plainly having a hard time processing everything I'd told them. I didn't blame them. It was a long, complex journey, from one side of the world to the other, involving a case that was six decades old. They hadn't expected this when they'd clocked in today.

'We just spoke to a guy called Greg Plumstead,' she went on.

Plumstead was the man that Korin had been talking to at CineLab UK in Manchester. His company had the technology to scan and transfer the footage on the 8mm and 35mm film stock – as well as the VHS-C tape – into a digital format.

It was how most of *Ring of Roses* had ended up on DVD.

'What did he say?' I asked.

'He said he'd been working with Korin for six months, although he didn't know her by that name. He knew her as Ursula Keegan. They only communicated by typewritten letter – which he found a bit weird – landline, or in person on the rare occasions when she'd go down and see him. She never did anything over the Internet or by mobile phone. He said he thought she was some kind of eccentric film hobbyist, or a collector. He asked her a couple of times what the film was about, and she told him it was a docudrama she was making for her own enjoyment, principally to teach herself how to edit and direct, and that she was reusing old movie footage she'd picked up at a car-boot sale years before.'

'And he believed her?'

'He said he could never make much sense of the film because she always delivered it in small chunks that she'd already cut herself, and that it was always delivered out of sync – as in, one week she'd give him ten minutes from the end, and a fortnight later, she'd give him five minutes from the start. After a while, he just scanned everything in without asking questions, and once the footage was scanned, she kept it all on an external hard drive. We found a laptop too, in a lock box at the back of the annex. The laptop was loaded with film-editing software and a DVD burner. That was how she got the different cuts of the film on to DVD. Any research she did online, she did via the farmer's Internet connection, and she wiped her history after every session, presumably so the farmer wouldn't see it.'

'How did she afford to pay CineLab?' I asked, thinking of the financials I'd been through. There had been no activity after her disappearance, and no sign of her siphoning off funds in the months before she went on the run.

'She worked on the farm, cash in hand.'

I nodded and then thought of something else. 'Have you been through all of the footage in that fridge? Do you have any idea what's on it?'

'*We* don't,' Taylor said.

I eyed her, slightly confused by the response, and then looked at Annechy, who had a frown on his face, his arms crossed.

'Wait a second, are you saying Lynda's still alive?'

The two of them looked at each other for a moment, then at my solicitor, and then – finally – back to me.

'Yes,' Taylor said. 'She's in a bad way, but she's still alive.'

80

Two detectives from the Los Angeles Police Department spent a month working with the Cumbrian and Metropolitan Police forces in Carlisle and London trying to piece together what had happened. I was released on conditional bail, pending further enquiries, and had to relinquish my passport in case I planned to skip the country. It seemed unnecessary but I didn't fight it, and after a while a part of me started to wonder if the idea hadn't come from the Met. As Craw had always told me, officers there were waiting for the chance to catch me in a lie. They'd see it as revenge for having crossed their paths, for refusing to back down, for solving cases they'd long committed to the vaults. It saddened me that I'd made so many enemies there. I'd never set out to do that and I'd never wanted it.

In my quieter moments, I began wondering if Craw might become one of those enemies herself. The full gravity of her decision to take up the secondment in Glasgow, and to move away, didn't really sink in until I was alone in the interview room, waiting for Taylor and Annechy. In the days after, I tried to speak to her on the phone, but she refused to pick up. A week after that, she finally sent me an email where she suggested in a few terse sentences that we should use the time away from one another to reassess what we had. I wasn't sure any amount of distance would help bridge the gap between her need to protect her career, and the life I'd chosen in finding missing people.

So, in the end, Craw drifted away from me, and then so did the suggestion of any charges being brought against me. Either Taylor, Cumbria Police, officers at the Met, or the CPS decided it would be a waste of time and money to take it any further.

I moved on, alone.

The murder of Glen Cramer gave the media a star around which they could orbit everything else. His crimes – his involvement in the killing of Életke Kerekes and his complicity in the framing of Martin Nemeth – weren't revealed in full until months later, so in the days after he died, any connection he had to anything that Zeller and he had done seemed to get forgotten relatively quickly.

The crimes were old, which didn't help – it made them less resonant to news crews looking for a modern Hollywood angle to sell – but his appearance in the fourth series of *Royalty Park* – which started two days after the events at the farm – was the most effective bleach of all, whitewashing his history as the public reconnected with his gentle portrayal of Stan Isserman, the elegant ambassador that he played on the show. It was a dismal illustration of the power of celebrity.

Even more sad to me, at least at the beginning, was that Robert Hosterlitz barely warranted a mention, his unfinished film still a piece of evidence in a police lock-up that the media hadn't seen yet. Without him, there would never have been enough to convict Zeller. His guilt, his pain – his decision to eventually face up to what he'd been a part of – was the glue that bound the case together.

And so the trajectory of the media coverage traced a predictable line for a couple of months. Stories came out from

AKI insiders about how staff had always known Saul Zeller was 'cruel', about the dark arts AKI had practised under his watch. Alex Cavarno was painted as a control freak and a fanatical egotist drunk on the power that Zeller had given her. In the first few weeks, AKI suffered badly, its share price nosediving, an assortment of Hollywood stars taking the chance to go public and put some distance between themselves, Saul Zeller and Alex.

Eventually, though, after Életke Kerekes was exhumed from a grave in a Venice cemetery and DNA trace evidence linked Zeller to the body, Zeller was charged, sacked, and a new president – Dan Chu of AKI Asia – began to steady the ship. Alex Cavarno was extradited back to LA, along with her father, and a few days later I watched them both, live over the Internet, take the stand during their arraignments. Zeller seemed unaffected by it all, by the court proceedings, by the death of Billy Egan, and I realized any hopes I'd had that he might actually show some contrition had just been a fantasy. Alex followed after he was done, and couldn't have been more different. She sobbed throughout, her face blanched, her beauty finally subdued. At the same time as that, a campaign had begun to clear Martin Nemeth's name.

About a week after the events at the farm, I got a call from Chu. He was softly spoken, surprisingly so, and had a heavily Americanized East Asian accent.

'I'm sorry you got caught up in our dirty laundry,' he said.

'No one saw this coming – least of all me.'

'We're going to try and push through the Comet reconstruction, despite everything. I think we need some good publicity.' He stopped. 'All we need to do now is find an architect who isn't a cold-blooded killer.'

It was a joke, and we both knew it, but there was a kind of sadness to the statement too.

We talked for a little while longer, and then – just as he was about to call off – he said, 'Have you been to see Lynda yet?'

'No. They said she wasn't ready for visitors.'

'Okay. When you do, give me a call. I've got something I'd like you to help me with.'

81

On a sub-zero morning in early December, just over three months after I first agreed to begin the search for Lynda Korin, I met her at an office near Spitalfields market.

Her hand was still wrapped in bandages, one side of her face too. She'd had a second skin graft a few weeks before, and – because of the knife wound she'd sustained in her chest – she was confined to a wheelchair as well. She looked uncomfortable and in pain, but she had a nurse with her – funded by AKI – who seemed to be well attuned to her needs. Every time Korin started to struggle, the nurse would try to put her at ease again by tenderly adjusting her position.

The truth was, though, the really hard work was probably yet to come for her. Rehabilitation would involve not just healing, not just gaining control over her physical injuries, but accepting the way she looked now. One side of her face remained as striking and timeless as it had ever been; the other was a memorial to the man who'd tried to kill her, and to the fire that had almost consumed her.

A couple of weeks after the events at the farm, I started visiting Korin in hospital. I'd sit at her bedside and we'd talk, as best she was able, and then, when she was well enough to leave the ward, I'd buy her lunch at the hospital café and we'd sit under its glass roof, discussing the idea Chu had come up with, while watching the autumn sun pour through the panels. After she was discharged, we met more frequently, throughout the rest of October and November, and every time we did, it was in the same conference room with the same people: Chu on satellite link, three technicians, and a documentary maker that Chu had flown over from New York, who'd begun on the project full-time. On a couple of occasions, Rafael Walker was invited along as well, generously loaning the production company the original negatives that he'd so lovingly kept at his flat.

Some days, I'd be at the back of a room while Korin and the director went through Hosterlitz's script – page by page, line by line – and, when Korin started to flag, I'd do my best to help out if I was asked. Most days, though, I'd just watch. I'd look on as they discussed individual scenes, I'd see rough cuts projected on to a conference-room wall, and I'd see the emotion in Korin's face as the director invited a composer to play her the music he was proposing for the soundtrack.

It took two months and twenty-two days but, on Monday 7 December, I finally got a call from Lynda, asking me to come over early in the morning the next day.

The first complete cut of *Ring of Roses* was ready.

Hosterlitz had collated as much footage as he could before his death, he'd written the script and recorded the narration, but it had been left to Lynda Korin to make sense of it all. She'd opened a garage door and found a world she never knew existed, the shadows of a man she'd barely glimpsed, and a history she never knew she had. It said a lot about her, a lot about how she felt for her husband – even after all that he'd told her in the letter – that she hadn't walked the other way.

She'd studied the basics of film editing, using technical manuals she'd found in second-hand bookshops, and YouTube videos she accessed via the farm's Internet connection. Editing was so complicated, such a specialized skill, that she could only ever learn the bare minimum, but the bare minimum had been just about enough. She learned how to use the editing table and she'd cut sections according to the instructions that Hosterlitz had left her. She'd then found an old VHS unit at a car-boot sale, had bought a VHS-C adapter using the farmer's eBay account, and had watched the day, in December 1984, when her husband had been to interview Ray Callson, the cop who had never forgotten the case.

I looked Callson up afterwards.

Until then, I'd always assumed that he'd agreed to do the interview with Hosterlitz in exchange for what Hosterlitz knew about the Kerekes murder, and the framing of Martin Nemeth. It made me wonder why he hadn't passed any of that information on to ex-colleagues of his at the LAPD as soon as it was over.

The reason turned out to be a sad one, not entirely out of place among the tragedy of the case. His wife had been dying in a nursing home near Hancock Park, and he hadn't wanted the last months of her life to be filled with interviews and court dates that would take him away from her bedside. In the information I could find on him, he once described his wife as his rock and his sanity.

The day she passed away in her sleep, he took an overdose of sleeping pills. Staff at the nursing home found them lying next to one another.

They were holding hands.

*

On Tuesday 8 December, at just before 10 a.m., I watched from the back of the screening room as the final minutes of *Ring of Roses* played out. The last words of Zeller's confession were over, and now a shot of the flowers at the Ring of Roses fountain had replaced it. They swayed in a slight breeze, a sea of colour perfectly moving in time – soundless, hypnotic, beautiful.

After a time, the movie cut to Korin.

She was on her knees at a flowerbed, the house in Somerset visible behind her, a trowel and a spade next to her. She was in her mid thirties and looked absolutely beautiful, her skin shining, her eyes flaring with the brightness of the sunlight. She said something into the camera but there were no words any more, no background noise – just a gentle melody on the soundtrack. This footage, and more like it, was what had been on the rolls of 8mm film in the fridge at the farm: just hours and hours of her.

I turned and looked at her, to the left of me in the screening room. She was leaning over in her wheelchair, her good arm taking her weight. The far side of her face was bandaged, covered over – but on this side I could see everything.

Every tremor. Every moment.

Every tear.

When I looked back at the screen, the camera had been placed on a wall and Korin was getting to her feet. From the side of the shot, Hosterlitz appeared, joining her. He was an old man – sick and thin and grey – but he was smiling. The smile filled so much of his face it seemed to transform him somehow. He was bigger and healthier all of a sudden; there was a new colour in him. He slid his arm around his wife's waist and brought her into him so they were side by side, and

513

then he whispered something into her ear. She burst out laughing, and they both looked into the lens of his Super 8 camera.

Slowly, the screen faded to black.

The credits started rolling.

And thirty years after he'd first begun making it, *Ring of Roses* – the last ever Robert Hosterlitz film – was finally complete.

Robert Hosterlitz Filmography

1949 – *My Evil Heart* (Monogram)
1951 – *Connor O'Hare* (American Kingdom Inc.)
1952 – *Only When You're Dead* (American Kingdom Inc.)
1953 – *The Eyes of the Night* (American Kingdom Inc.)
1954 – *My Life is a Gun* (American Kingdom Inc., unfinished)

1957 – *West End Knife* (Wick Films/ABPC)

1960 – *Das Geheimnis des Schwarzen Himmels* (Rialto)
1961 – *Die Leiche im Fluss* (Rialto)
1961 – *Der Teufel von London* (Rialto)

1963 – *Petticoat Junction*, 'Honeymoon Garden' (CBS, TV)
1964 – *Bonanza*, 'The Kid from New Orleans' (NBC, TV)
1964 – *Bonanza*, 'Exit, Stage Left' (NBC, TV)
1964 – *The Twilight Zone*, 'Don't Look Now' (CBS, TV)
1964 – *The Defenders*, 'Ashes to Ashes' (CBS, TV)
1964 – *Bonanza*, 'No Room at the Inn' (NBC, TV)
1965 – *Bonanza*, 'Cardinal Sin' (NBC, TV)
1965 – *The Defenders*, 'Court of Law' (CBS, TV)
1965 – *The Alfred Hitchcock Hour*, 'Eagle Snare' (NBC, TV)
1965 – *Bonanza*, 'The Hanging of Jessie Lee Jones' (NBC, TV)
1965 – *Bonanza*, 'A Man Walks into a Saloon . . .' (NBC, TV)
1966 – *Bonanza*, 'Chase' (NBC, TV)
1966 – *Bonanza*, 'When the Devil Comes Calling' (NBC, TV)

1967 – *The Ghost of the Plains* (Paramount)

1968 – *Bonanza*, 'Lonesome Heart' (NBC, TV)
1968 – *Judd, for the Defense*, 'Color of Money' (ABC, TV)
1968 – *N.Y.P.D.*, '44 Minutes' (ABC, TV)
1968 – *N.Y.P.D.*, 'The Dead Can't Speak' (ABC, TV)
1969 – *Judd, for the Defense*, 'Sampson and Delilah' (ABC, TV)

1971 – *House of Darkness* (Amicus)
1972 – *Blood of the Undead* (Obelisk)
1972 – *Werewolf! Werewolf!* (Obelisk)
1973 – *Princess of Monsters* (Obelisk)

Under the alias Bob Hozer

1977 – *Ursula of the SS* (Olympia Filmproduktions)
1978 – *Ursula: Queen Kommandant* (Olympia Filmproduktions)
1978 – *Ursula: Butcher of El Grande* (Olympia Filmproduktions)
1979 – *Cemetery House* (Mano Águila)
1979 – *Hell Trip* (Mano Águila)
1980 – *The Drill Murders* (Mano Águila)
1980 – *Axe Maniac* (Mano Águila)
1980 – *Beware of the Woods* (Mano Águila)
1981 – *Kill!* (Mano Águila)
1981 – *Cemetery House 2* (Mano Águila)
1981 – *Zombie Outbreak* (Mano Águila)
1982 – *Savages of the Amazon* (Mano Águila)
1982 – *Die Slowly* (Mano Águila)
1984 – *Death Island* (Mano Águila)

2015 – *Ring of Roses* (American Kingdom Inc.)

Author's Note

As I'm a huge fan of the movies, *Broken Heart* was an incredibly interesting book to research. I'd particularly like to thank Vic Pratt at the British Film Institute for his endless patience as yet another email about 35mm negatives dropped into his inbox.

As always, I've taken some small liberties in the interests of the story – both in terms of film history and film production, and in terms of the structures and processes of the UK police force – but I hope it's done subtly enough for it not to cause offence.

Acknowledgements

I feel blessed and very honoured to be published by the team at Michael Joseph, who are among the nicest, most talented and most brilliant people in the industry. Thank you to each and every person there (and across the whole of Penguin) who has had a hand in bringing *Broken Heart* to life. In particular, I'd like to give a shout-out to my incredible editor, Emad Akhtar (aka Ricky C), who waded into the swamps of *very* early versions of this book without even batting an eyelid, and my copy-editor, Caroline Pretty, who makes my life a thousand times easier by knowing David Raker back to front.

Huge thanks, as always, to Camilla Wray, the loveliest, funniest, smartest and bulldog-iest agent in London, who's also a black belt in dealing with my many and varied mid-manuscript meltdowns. I'd also like to thank the ladies of Darley Anderson too, particularly Sheila David in Film and TV, and Mary and Emma in foreign rights.

To Mum, Dad, Lucy and the rest of my amazing family: thank you so much for all your love and support. To my daughter, Erin, who makes me so proud, and my wife, Sharlé, who keeps me going when The Doubts kick in – which is every time I sit down in front of my computer – thank you both for keeping me sane.

And, finally, the biggest thanks of all go to you, my readers. Without your support, Raker would be nothing more than an idea on a scrap of paper.

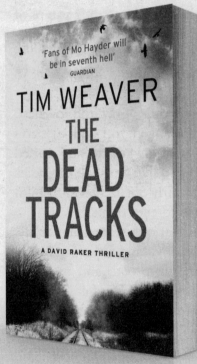
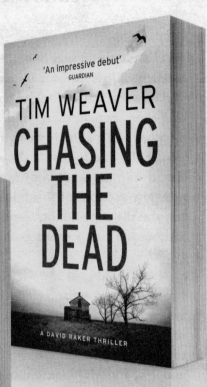

Also by Tim Weaver

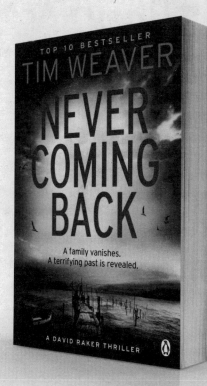

Out now

Also by Tim Weaver

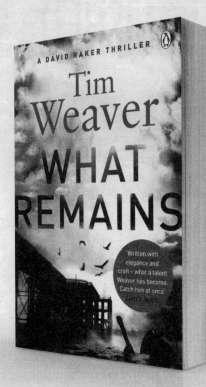

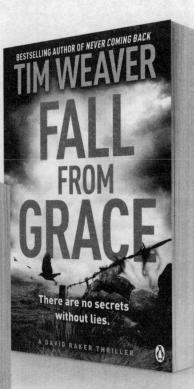

Out now